BEST SPORTS STORIES
————————1980

BEST SPORTS STORIES
1980

A Panorama of the 1979 Sports World
including the 1979 Champions of All Sports
with the Year's Top Photographs

Edited by Irving T. Marsh and Edward Ehre

E. P. DUTTON / NEW YORK

To the Memory of
Jesse Abramson,
A Great Reporter
and
Lou Little,
Teacher and Coach

For information contact:
Elsevier-Dutton Publishing Co., Inc.,
New York, N.Y. 10016

Library of Congress Catalog Card Number: 45-35124

ISBN: 0-525-06626-8

Published simultaneously in Canada by Clarke, Irwin & Company
Limited, Toronto and Vancouver

10 9 8 7 6 5 4 3 2 1

First Edition

Contents

Illustrations

Preface

Here is No. 36 in the *Best Sports Stories* anthologies that began in 1944.

The panel that selects the award-winners in our prize competition—John Chamberlain, syndicated columnist for King Features, who used to be a book reviewer; John Hutchens, a former book reviewer now with the judging panel of the Book-of-the-Month Club; and Jerry Nason, former sports editor of the *Boston Globe*—thought the current collection is one of the best in the series.

But Nason had one negative criticism.

"I was badly let down by this year's so-called news-coverage contributions," he wrote, "in which, mostly, news facts were buried and hard to find."

(That leads to an aside from Marsh: "That's the so-called New Journalism for you," he admonishes, "in which the writer really takes a long windup in his lead paragraph before he lets go with the pitch. 'New Journalism?' Bah!" Says Ehre: "You two are a pair of old flatii [sic]. You can't stop progress!")

Be that as it may: Most of the 1980 contributors have appeared in our series before. In fact, three of them have won prizes in the past—Bill Conlin, Maury Allen, and Roger Kahn having been so honored. This year Conlin captured the news-coverage award for his story on the second World Series game, Allen's feature on Mickey Lolich tied with newcomer Dave Newhouse's story on the old-time Yankees for the best feature-story prize, and Roger Kahn took the magazine award for his story on athletes past their prime.

Contributions came in in the largest number since the series started, and added to his criticism on the reportage entries Nason said, "But in the other categories I truly believe you have the best to yet appear in a BSS edition."

As has been the custom throughout this series, the stories were submitted to the judges blind, each identified by a one- or two-word "slug," newspaperese for an identifying label. Hence you will note that each story was so called by the judges in the box score and their comments, which follow:

THE BOX SCORE

News-Coverage	Chamber-lain	Hutchens	Nason	*Total Points
2d Series [Roberto Clemente's Ghost Prowls by Bill Conlin]	3	3	—	6
Wimbledon [The "Old Lady" Bows Out by Joe Gergen]	2	—	3	5
Belmont [Nothing Left but Heart by Edwin Pope]	1	—	2	3
Rutgers [Now They Know Where Rutgers Is by George Leonard]	—	2	—	2
Zoeller [A Place for a Smile and a Laugh by Maury White]	—	1	—	1
Open [Lucky or Good? by Gary Nuhn]	—	—	1	1

News-Feature Stories				
Lolich [One for the Books by Maury Allen]	3	2	—	5
Yankees [The Old Yankee by Dave Newhouse]	2	—	3	5
Gordie [Howe: History on Skates by Joe Resnick]	—	3	—	3
Homer [In Pursuit of Loftier Goals by Jim Smith]	—	—	2	2
Paterno [The Joe Paterno School of Football by Paul Hendrickson]	1	—	—	1
Redeemer [The Great Redeemer's Companions by Jim Bolus]	—	1	—	1
Super [Mood Over Miami by Ron Martz]	—	—	1	1

Magazine Stories				
Age [Past Their Prime by Roger Kahn]	3	—	2	5
Mike [Body and Soul by Tony Kornheiser]	2	—	1	3
Sugar [Boxing's His Business by Phil Berger]	—	3	—	3
Ping [The Aristocrat of Hustle by Dave Hirshey]	—	—	3	3
Memphis [The Memphis Red Sox by Kenneth Neill]	—	2	—	2
Giants [The Civil-Service Giants by Allan B. Jacobs]	—	1	—	1
Running [Craig Virgin: A Heartland Saga by William Barry Furlong]	1	—	—	1

*Based on 3 points for a first-place vote, 2 for a second, 1 for a third

JUDGES' COMMENTS

John Chamberlain

News-Coverage Stories

1. 2d Series [Roberto Clemente's Ghost Prowls by Bill Conlin]
2. Wimbledon [The "Old Lady" Bows Out by Joe Gergen]
3. Belmont [Nothing Left but Heart by Edwin Pope]

1. I like the blend of contemporary drama and historical perspective in the news-coverage story that brought Manny Sanguillen, the last Latin Pirate link with the famed Roberto Clemente, to bat against the Orioles at a critical moment. It was a bad-ball hitter against a bad-ball pitcher. The night was foul; the game was a mud-caked farce. Pittsburgh, going badly, needed a victory just to hang in. If the Pirate manager had used Lee Lacy or Rennie Stennett, each an obvious choice, as a pinch hitter, it would still have been a tingling situation. But Manny Sanguillen went to bat as Clemente's deputy from the long ago when they had co-starred in the 1971 World Series, a year or so before Clemente's death in an airplane that he had chartered to fly supplies to Nicaraguan earthquake victims. The writer lets history perch on his shoulder as he describes Sanguillen's winning hit. Sanguillen himself supplied the sentiment: "I hit the ball and I give it to . . . the great Roberto Clemente." A Latin flourish in a most observant story.

2. "All victories are alike; defeat alone wears an individual profile." So wrote James Gibbons Huneker, the literary critic. He might have been describing Billie Jean King's "last great scene on Center Court" at Wimbledon, when the "Old Lady" of tennis almost—repeat, almost—turned back the 16-year-old Tracy Austin.

3. Spectacular Bid was supposed to win the one hundred sixteenth Belmont Stakes, which would have meant the Triple Crown. But the horse that had finished first in 12 straight victories just wore out in the last furlong. I often wonder, when reading about the Derby or the Belmont, whether the horses really care. But the men who train them and ride them certainly do, and the author of the news-coverage story about Spectacular Bid's failure makes the most of the human drama connected with it.

News-Feature Stories

1. Lolich [One for the Books by Maury Allen]
2. Yankee [The Old Yankee by Dave Newhouse]
3. Paterno [The Joe Paterno School of Football by Paul Hendrickson]

1. Mickey Lolich's story of working with a mentally retarded fat black kid at a summer camp isn't strictly a sports story. But it is a heartwarming account of the rescue of an individual in a situation that would have been completely flubbed by a bureaucratic approach. A great feature that, incidentally, involves two sports figures, Lolich and his camp co-worker Al Kaline.

2. Is my own age showing? I was particularly touched by the account of an interview with Mark Koenig, the Yankee shortstop of the mid-twenties, conducted in the dust and clutter of an unkempt house in Glen Ellen, California, where the once spry contemporary of Babe Ruth and Lou Gehrig shuffles about on legs of lead. Koenig takes care of a wife who is in a wheelchair. He told his interviewer there was no use talking about present circumstances. But he had plenty to say about Gehrig, "a nice kid," and the Yankee manager Miller Huggins, the "best manager" Koenig ever played for. (He thought Bill Terry of the Giants was "a lousy manager").

3. Joe Paterno, the Brooklyn boy, hated State College, Pennsylvania, when he went there as a teacher and assistant football coach. But he remained in mid-Appalachia to recruit strong-armed and fleet-footed coal town boys for his Penn State teams, gradually shedding all of his Flatbush character save his accent for a new and lasting way of life he came to love. The "place" is "eastern" football; the "way of life" includes a love of Nathaniel Hawthorne, for Paterno is a teacher of literature as well as a man capable of matching wits with Alabama's Bear Bryant.

Magazine Stories

1. Age [Past Their Prime by Roger Kahn]
2. Mike [Body and Soul by Tony Kornheiser]
3. Running [Craig Virgin: A Heartland Saga by William Barry Furlong]

1. "The temptation to conclude too much persists." The author of "Age" has successfully resisted the temptation through a long and varied story of how different athletes have played "tactical games with time." Mickey Mantle, at 39, was an assistant batting coach; Carl Yastrzemski, at the same age, was still a star. The difference? "Yaz wanted it more." But that is not the whole story, as the author shows while making his investigations into "athletes aging into other men's prime time." The human body was not designed to play catcher from April to October or to fight for the heavyweight championship at the age of 36. The author tells us why in a most interesting anecdotal fashion . . . but Ali was still winning at 36.

2. The Phillies' Mike Schmidt, forced to contend with intangibles in the effort to live up to his self-adopted middle name of "potential," is a most interesting psychological puzzle. He also has a most interesting wife who recognizes that she may have a life job in solving puzzles. The author, a sensitive student of personality, makes the most of his opportunity to study Mr. and Mrs. Schmidt.

3. There's more to running than putting one little leg after another. The story of Craig Virgin's attempt to control his own training and career from an unlikely farm base in central Illinois reminded me, oddly, of Willa Cather's *One of Ours*, the story of another midwestern farm boy who had to fight it out with destiny in the effort to fulfill his potential, yet remain loyal to his own place. Willa Cather wouldn't necessarily have understood running, but she would have understood Craig Virgin.

John Hutchens

News-Coverage Stories

1. 2d Series [Roberto Clemente's Ghost Prowls by Bill Conlin]
2. Rutgers [Now They Know Where Rutgers Is by George Leonard]
3. Zoeller [A Place for a Smile and a Laugh by Maury White]

1. Baseball doesn't know many more exciting dramas than the one in which a possible pinch hit with two out in the ninth inning and the potential winning run on base, can mean a victory. This one, in the 1979 Pirates-Orioles World Series, was a classic of its kind, especially because the pinch hitter was sent in by a manager for whom he had once been traded. It was a drama the more gripping because in the background were the spirit and memory of the late, great Pirate superstar, Roberto Clemente, for whom the pinch hitter had once appeared.

2. A fine account of one of the astounding upset football triumphs within memory—greatly underfavored Rutgers over Tennessee—a story the more effective because of the clarity of its narration for readers lacking in knowledge of the sophisticated techniques of gridiron strategy.

3. Good-humored, easygoing conversationalists don't make off with the title in so grim an event as the Masters. But here is one, and a delightful piece about him this is.

News-Feature Stories

1. Gordie [Howe: History on Skates by Joe Resnick]
2. Lolich [One for the Books by Maury Allen]
3. Redeemer [The Great Redeemer's Companions by Jim Bolus]

1. A most impressive chronicle about one of the great athletes in American sports history, the most comprehensive study I have ever read of Gordie Howe and his incredible record of hockey longevity and sundry superlative performances.

2. As moving a sports story as you are likely to come across, this one about two first-class baseball players, who are seen here as that and something more—a pair of gentlemen who, with utmost compassion, give new life to a retarded boy. The most exciting thing that ever happened to him in twenty years of baseball, said pitcher Mickey Lolich. This story makes you believe it.

3. One of the most comical stories of the year, and in its cheerfully morbid way one of the most interesting, this one about the hopeless nags that have somehow been allowed to run in the Kentucky Derby. Which one is your choice? I'm inclined to favor the candidate selected for the 1930 Run for the Roses: he had "never won a race, never finished in the money, never earned a penny."

Magazine Stories

1. Sugar [Boxing's His Business by Phil Berger]
2. Memphis [The Memphis Red Sox by Kenneth Neill]
3. Giants [The Civil-Service Giants by Allan B. Jacobs]

1. Splendid, thorough portrait of Sugar Ray Leonard, boxing's new wonder, his talents and his character. His admirers will regard him even more highly after perusing this absorbing look at one who may well join the greatest champions of his craft.

2. Even baseball fans with a more than average acquaintanceship with the game will find a lot to fascinate them in this neglected return to the sport as it was played with major-league skills prior to the Jackie Robinson breakthrough in 1947.

3. A major-league baseball team as a civil-service crew employed by a city and county? It sounds unlikely, but it made for melodrama, and nearly a championship, last year in the case of the San Francisco Giants. One of the weird chapters in the national pastime's epic.

Jerry Nason

News-Coverage Stories

1. Wimbledon [The "Old Lady" Bows Out by Joe Gergen]
2. Belmont [Nothing Left but Heart by Edwin Pope]
3. Open [Lucky or Good? by Gary Nuhn]

Increasingly more difficult to encounter is an authentic example of sports "news" writing—vibrantly written, yet hard-nosed, the-facts-ma'am! reporting. Frankly, I felt that many of the entries in this classification, news-coverage, should have been submitted as news-features. Callously buried deep in their verbiage was such vital information as final scores, game or match details so basic to a news report, if not to a feature or a sports column. Many read suspiciously hours removed from deadline writing.

"Belmont" was the best example of a report done right on top of the action against a Sunday-paper deadline—fast, factual, exciting—but I picked "Wimbledon" for its unusual Older Gal versus Kid Prodigy story while fully aware that the writer from a base in England enjoyed five-hour grace before cabling a superb report.

News-Feature Stories

1. Yankees [The Old Yankee by Dave Newhouse]
2. Homer [In Pursuit of Loftier Goals by Jim Smith]
3. Super [Mood Over Miami by Ron Martz]

In my judgment, news-features provided the best, most evenly matched race for this year's Dutton awards—a mass quality run down the final stretch. In a blanket finish at the tape, so to speak, my pick was "Yankees." Admittedly, this may be a slightly prejudiced selection, since this well-conceived, touching, but not tear-sodden piece was about Mark Koenig of the immortal 1927 Yankee baseball team, and those 1927 pinstripers had been all 7 feet tall in the imaginative young mind of a future writer of sports. Many of those old boyhood heroes are dead now. Mark Koenig lives, but time has treated him shabbily. He who reads this story without a shred of emotion has never in his boyhood known sports heroes 7 feet tall.

Intriguing subject material (from head football coach to divinity school and the money-grubbing backdrop to Super Bowl game) dictated my "place" and "show" selections. Half-a-dozen other fine stories were hot on their heels.

Magazine Stories

1. Ping [The Aristocrat of Hustle by Dave Hirshey]
2. Age [Past Their Prime by Roger Kahn]
3. Mike [Body and Soul by Tony Kornheiser]

The agony of decision was even more rampant in the magazine category, distinguished by an abundance of quality writing on or around subjects with strong readership appeal. I gave the decision, finally, to "Ping," the story about the ultimate hustler, Marty Reisman. Any man who can become a folk legend in his time by merely blending style, con, and a table-tennis racket clearly deserves story attention from a writer's writer. The Fat Kid who finally wrote the story obviously knows a great deal about Reisman, about table-tennis, con, and writing—not necessarily in that order. Beautiful job.

"Age" is top-drawer reading—and the best pure baseball writing in the book may be the sensitive study made of Mike Schmidt, the awesome if erratic hitter in Philadelphia.

Am I wrong in suspecting that much of the sharpest writing being done today is in the area of sports?

As for the photos: the editors think they're eye-catching and punchy.

So, here's our No. 36. Hope you're as happy with it as you've been with the previous 35.

IRVING T. MARSH
EDWARD EHRE

THE PRIZE-WINNING STORIES

Best News-Coverage Story
WORLD SERIES GAME II

ROBERTO CLEMENTE'S GHOST PROWLS

By Bill Conlin

From the Philadelphia Daily News
Copyright, ©, 1979, Philadelphia Daily News

Roberto Clemente would have been listed as a doubtful starter on this kind of night, a night of October cold laced with the heavy feel of coming rain.

His back would have ached, the bursitis in his right shoulder would have throbbed, legacies of too many off-balance throws from the warning track and a near-fatal fall at his home in Rio Piedras, Puerto Rico. "I don't see how I can play tonight," Clemente would have whined, his voice contradicting the tongue of flame in his eyes.

And on many such nights, Roberto Clemente would shrug off the aches and go 3 for 4 with a screaming homer down the right-field line, run down a ball in the gap, and gun a runner out at third with a pirouetting release and a throw that seared the air like a tracer bullet.

The ghost of Roberto Clemente prowled Memorial Stadium last night as game two in this mud-caked farce of a World Series slithered toward catharsis in a driving rain.

Clemente was there in the dugout when Pirates' Manager Chuck Tanner pondered who to pinch-hit for reliever Don Robinson with two outs in the top of the ninth, the Orioles locked in a 2–2 tie, and runners on first and second. While Don Stanhouse, a.k.a. Stan the Man Unusual, dawdled in an increasing rain which began in the seventh inning to mar an evening which began as merely uncomfortable, the field was rapidly becoming unplayable.

A high-skidding bouncer by Ed Ott which came off the infield glop and the chest of second-baseman Billy Smith gave Stanhouse the runner he seems to need to be effective. Then he issued an almost obligatory walk to Phil Garner and it was time for Tanner to choose between three excellent right-handed pinch-hitters.

He had Lee Lacy, the Dodgers' former clutch hero. But Lacy is a guy Tanner likes to use in more of a long-ball situation. What he needed here was contact and he could have filled the bill with Rennie Stennett, who stroked a pinch-single Wednesday night.

Stanhouse lives and dies by the 3–2 count. He doesn't like to throw a lot of strikes. His equivalent of a pitch down the middle is a ball at the knees and one sixteenth of an inch off a corner.

How better to counter a bad-ball pitcher than with a bad-ball hitter? And there have been a few better bad-ball hitters in the history of the game than Manuel de Jesus Sanguillen, a 35-year-old Panamanian who represents the last Latin Pirate link with Clemente.

Sanguillen is a journeyman now, but when the Bucs whipped the Orioles in the 1971 Series he was a star, a .300 hitter with outstanding speed. Manny hit .379 in that Series. He lashed 11 hits. But Clemente dominated it with his bat, his baserunning and his fielding brilliance. Less than 14 months later, Roberto would be dead, snuffed out when a rickety DC-3 he chartered to fly supplies to Nicaraguan earthquake victims went down in 1,000 fathoms of water near the San Juan Airport.

Stanhouse surprised Sanguillen and 53,739 witnesses by throwing his first pitch down the middle for a called strike.

Manny wasn't falling for that ploy. No way he was gonna pop-up a pitch down the middle. He fouled off a ball up around his eyes, took ball one, and fouled off another pitch that looked close enough to swing at.

He slung a 1–2 pitch into right field and Ott, who runs well for a catcher, beat the two throws the Orioles find necessary to disguise the weakness of Ken Singleton's arm.

"I try to make contact with two strike," Sanguillen singsonged after the Bucs squared the Series with a 3–2 victory. He could be the model of *Saturday Night Live*'s Chico Escuela. But he deserves the courtesy of consecutive translation.

"I didn't want to try to pull the ball, I just wanted to hit it back through the middle," he said. "That was a good pitch. I don't think it was a strike. He threw me two strikes and I fouled them off.

"I hit the ball and I give it to No. 21, the great Roberto Clemente.

"Everything we do in this World Series we will do for Clemente."

Only three players remain from the 1971 Pirates, Sanguillen, Willie Stargell, and Bruce Kison.

"We still sense his presence," Stargell said, presiding over a large pile of crab legs. "Roberto's spirit is with us. Only three of us go back to playing with him, but we've tried to keep what he meant to us alive."

Sanguillen became the first player in baseball history to win a game for a manager he was once traded for. When Tanner came to the Pirates from a season managing in Oakland after the 1976 season, Charles O. Finley demanded compensation. And what he settled for was Sanguillen and $100,000. The Pirates brought

Manny back home a year later in a deal which sent Miguel DiLone, Mike Edwards, and Elias Sosa to the A's.

He can't throw a lick anymore—one of the 1971 controversies involved his ability to keep the Orioles from stealing the Series—but he can still swing the bat. And his happy singsong fits well in the Tower of Babel that is the Pirates' clubhouse.

He resists the rap that he is a bad-ball hitter. Manny has his own interpretation of that. "People call me a bad-ball hitter," he said, "but that is not true because I can see the ball real good and get a good swing at many pitches that are not strikes. I think a bad-ball hitter is one who can only hit the bad ball. I can hit strikes, too, you know. I just don't like to take a lot of pitches."

The Orioles had an excellent chance to finally score a run off the Pirates' brilliant bullpen and take the lead in the sixth. They had the tying run home on an Eddie Murray double and one out when John Lowenstein lined sharply to Dave Parker in right.

There was only one way to go, challenge Parker's howitzer arm and send the runner. Make the Pirates execute.

Dave's scorching throw skidded to Ott on a long, true bounce.

Murray was close enough to the plate to contest the out, either by sliding or ramming into Ott, a burly former linebacker. Didn't he watch Parker elude a sure out Wednesday night by kicking the ball out of Mark Belanger's glove after Mike Flanagan picked him off first?

Murray took neither option. He pussyfooted into a stand-up tag and that's tea-dance baseball.

"Eddie Murray is a gentleman and I guess we're not," said Phil Garner. "Maybe he was a dead bird, but this is the World Series. If I had got an elbow to the chin [as Belanger did on Parker's savage slide], I'd sure know what it's all about."

Murray did not have the benefit of a game-winning homer to mask his blunders the way Doug DeCinces did in game one.

Maybe he did keep the Orioles out of a triple play on that weird eighth-inning sequence, when Earl Weaver tried to catch the Bucs in their bunting rotation by letting John Lowenstein swing away with runners on first and second and nobody out. But his judgment was questionable when he cut off Singleton's throw to the plate on Sanguillen's single. A baseball usually skids and accelerates off wet grass.

The Orioles played safety first baseball in their home yard last night and that is not the way to beat the Pirates. Not when Parker is going for the jugular and Chuck Tanner has the ninth-inning luxury of choosing between Lee Lacy, Rennie Stennett, and Manny Sanguillen in a 2-2 ball game.

Last night Sanguillen bounced out of the dugout into the rain and he walked to the plate with the ghost of Roberto Clemente at his side.

Best News-Feature Story (Co-Winner)

BASEBALL

ONE FOR THE BOOKS

By Maury Allen

From the New York Post
Copyright, ©, 1979, New York Post Corp.

He's always looked like a bartender, a fat guy with a beautiful beer belly, a warm smile, and a gregarious personality. It was his left arm that separated him from the other guys in the beer leagues.

Mickey Lolich won 207 games for the Detroit Tigers, pitched them to the 1968 World Championship with three victories against the Cardinals, and starred for a dozen seasons.

Then he came to the Mets when they wanted to dispose of Rusty Staub. Then he quit, sat out a year, and joined the San Diego Padres. He was in advertising sales the year he sat out, played first base on a beer-league softball team, and ran a summer camp with five other athletes, including longtime teammate Al Kaline.

"There was this one kid that I'll never forget," Lolich was saying earlier in the week at Shea. "Sit down if you are ready to cry and I'll tell you the story."

Camp Huron, outside of Detroit, was a sports camp where guest instructors worked with promising athletes. Lolich spent a lot of time there in the summer of 1977.

"I couldn't believe my eyes when I met this boy, Vincent Waters, for the first time," said Lolich. "He was 14 years old, a fat black kid, about 240 pounds, about 5-10, mentally retarded with difficulty in speaking, walking, and talking.

"He couldn't do anything right, he put on his T-shirt backwards. He couldn't put a key in the locker door. He couldn't hold a baseball or catch it. The other kids made fun of him, tortured him, treated him terribly."

It was impossible to watch. Kaline suggested the boy should be sent home for his and the other boys' good. One of the partners, Bob Fenton, was instructed to call Vincent's mother and have her take him home. The money would be completely refunded. Fenton made the call.

"I'm on welfare," the mother told Fenton, "I saved and scraped all I could to send Vincent to the camp. His father left us when he was born.

"All his life Vincent has only cared about the Tigers, that's the only thing. He idolized Mr. Kaline and Mr. Lolich. He would sit in front of the small television set with his bat and glove. Couldn't he just stay around, just to be near Mr. Lolich and Mr. Kaline?"

"When Fenton told us the story we decided to try again," said Lolich. "Al took him behind the field, away from the other boys, and threw baseballs with him. Soon he was able to make contact with the bat. The other kids began to understand. We asked them to help. They invited him to the pool. He said he couldn't swim and they said they would watch him. They began inviting him into all the kid games."

In the second week of camp Vince was given a uniform and allowed to sit on the bench. The score was tied in one game and Vince was sent up as a pinch hitter.

"I do all the pitching in these games so all the kids can say they hit against a big-leaguer," said Lolich. "I lob it in and they all have fun. Vince came up. I lobbed it in and he missed the first pitch. Then he missed the second. When he missed the third I called it a foul ball.

"Then I did the same thing on the fourth and fifth and sixth miss. On the seventh the ball hit the bat and dribbled out toward short-stop. The shortstop, a 12-year-old kid, understood. He picked up the ball, rolled it around his glove, took a couple of steps, and threw it to first. The umpire yelled safe and both teams leaped all over Vince to congratulate him.

"At the end of the week a banquet was held. Awards were given out to the kids—most valuable player, best hitter, best fielder, most improved player.

"When I announced Vince Waters as most improved player, the building rocked. Vince walked up to the microphone, stammered a little, and said, "Can I say something, please?"

"He didn't talk clearly, but we all heard him say, 'I want to thank my mother, my girl friend, and Mr. Kaline and Mr. Lolich for the greatest week in my life.' Then he turned around and gave me and Al a giant bear hug."

"When I saw how much they had done for my boy," Mrs. Waters says now, "I couldn't thank them enough. They saved Vincent's life. They made him somebody. That was just the kindest thing I ever heard of."

"I've been in baseball twenty years," said Lolich. "I think that was the most exciting thing that has ever happened to me."

The fat guy with the bartender beer belly walked into the trainer's room. He needed a towel. The tears were streaming down his face.

Best News-Feature Story (Co-Winner)

BASEBALL

THE OLD YANKEE

By Dave Newhouse

From the Oakland Tribune
Copyright, ©, 1979, Oakland Tribune

The old Yankee slouched in a chair. A spider web was fixed inside a light fixture near his head. A leftover meal, crusted by time, sat on a table behind him. Dust and clutter filled the room, loneliness permeated it.

"We're more or less hermits, my wife and I," said Mark Koenig, shortstop on the famous 1927 Yankees' Murderers Row. "We don't have many friends and very few visitors."

He looked around the unkempt house, otherwise shaded and cooled by the woodsy atmosphere of this tiny Sonoma County town where Jack London's life burned out at 40.

"This used to be a nice house, but now it's a mess. I can't do it anymore," said Koenig. "My wife has had two hip operations and is in a wheelchair. She has become . . . imbecilic. She wets the bed every night. I have to clean it up.

"I've had a cataract operation on my right eye. I've got back problems. I'm 75. My legs feel leaden all the time. Ah, it's no use talking."

It's easier to remember. Deep in the recesses of his mind, the sound of thousands cheering echoes faintly and long-ago World Series flags wave at Yankee stadium.

"Babe Ruth? He was a big, overgrown kid, that's all he was," said Koenig. "I don't think he read any books. He didn't know the difference between Robin Hood and Cock Robin. He was just interested in girls and drinking and eating.

"But what a beautiful swing he had, even when he struck out. And I never saw him drop a fly ball. He was a good fielder, pretty fast for his size, even with his pipestem legs.

"We never saw much of Ruth during the season. He had his private room on the road. But Ruth, [Bob] Meusel and I used to go to a place called Jimmy Donahue's in Passaic, N.J. There'd be long tables filled with food and waiters would run up the stairs from the bar below with steins of beer. We had some wonderful times."

It was the Roaring Twenties, and no figure, perhaps other than Lindbergh, is more remembered from that dapper, flapper period than Ruth. The Babe was a king in layman's garments.

"Babe stood up the queen of the Netherlands," Koenig recalled. "They were supposed to meet on the courthouse steps in Minneapolis, but Babe didn't show up. He didn't give a darn about anything.

"The Yankees had an infielder named Mike McNally. He heard Babe was going to be in the Follies after the season, so he asked him for a couple of Annie Oakleys. Babe said, 'Sure, I'll get you two of the swellest blondes in the show.'"

Lou Gehrig was the Pride of the Yankees, Ruth the Pulse of the Yankees. They posed often, Ruth's arms around the younger, socially correct Gehrig. Yet, they weren't friends, we are told.

"That's not true," Koenig declared. "Oh, they might have had their differences, but that's all.

"Gehrig was a nice kid. Never said much. Benny Bengough and I had an apartment, One hundred eighty-first and Broadway. Gehrig was there three or four times a week. Meusel and I used to go to his home. Gehrig's mother and father, what dinners they put on. Oh, boy.

"Meusel was one of my best friends, so was [Herb] Pennock. Meusel was very quiet . . . drank a lot."

Koenig and Tony Lazzeri were the Yankees' shortstop and second baseman during the 1926–27–28 pennant years. Poosh 'Em Up Tony once scared the daylights out of his double-play partner.

"Lazzeri had epileptic fits, but never on the ball field," Koenig recalled. "He'd be standing in front of the mirror, combing his hair. Suddenly, the comb would fly out of his hand and hit the wall.

"One morning in Chicago, he had a fit. He fell on the ground and started foaming. I didn't know what to do, so I ran out the door without a stitch of clothing on to get Waite Hoyt, who was a mortician in the off-season.

"Lazzeri recovered, but that's what killed him, you know. He had a fit, fell down the stairs, and broke his neck."

Ty Cobb was nearing the end of his unparalleled career when Koenig broke in with New York. Time hadn't blunted the Georgia Peach's bat or his abrasive personality.

"I didn't have no use for Cobb," said Koenig. "I remember facing Lil Stoner in Detroit, when Cobb was the manager. Stoner had a beautiful curve and he got two by me right away. For some reason, I turned and winked at Gehrig near the batting circle.

"Sure enough, Stoner throws me a fastball on the next pitch and I hit it into the right-field stands. As I'm running around the bases, I see Cobb in the outfield holding his nose and waving his arms up and down at Stoner. Cobb was a miserable man."

Trains and games. Life was fun when the Yankees first clickety-clacked down baseball's tracks toward becoming the game's greatest dynasty.

"The train cars were air-cooled," remembered Koenig. "Just as well, because St. Louis was 110 in the shade. There was a colored place downtown with great big racks of ribs. We knew where to get some home brew too. We'd go sit in the boxcar, drink beer, and gnaw on ribs. Then we'd fire the empty bottles at the telegraph poles.

"I was with Cincinnati [1934] when they became the first team to fly. Jim Bottomley and I wouldn't fly. We took the train. I never flew as a player."

The Yankees had incredible talent—Ruth, Gehrig, Earl Coombs, Lazzeri, Meusel, Pennock, Hoyt, Joe Dugan. Manager Miller Huggins scribbled out a lineup card, leaned back, and watched the fireworks. He expected and got results and didn't worry about such minutia as curfews and drinking.

"There were no rules on the Yankees about having to be in your room by midnight," said Koenig. "We used to come in at 3 or 4 in the morning and the elevator guy would say, 'Gee, I just took a load up.'

"We stayed at this beautiful hotel in Washington, where ambassadors walked around with ribbons on their chests. We came in one morning at 2, wanting to take a swim. The clerk said they were draining the pool. That did it. [Johnny] Grabowski took off his clothes and dove in. He came up with a big bump on his head."

The tiny man in charge looked the other way.

"Huggins was the best manager I ever played for," said Koenig. "He understood human nature. He never bawled anybody out. When sports writers were saying 'Koenig's got to go,' he called me in and said, 'Listen, as long as I want you to play, you're going to play.' He gave me confidence.

"When I joined the Giants [1935], Bill Terry had rules where you had to be in your room by 11 P.M., you had to get permission to go out to eat. Terry was a lousy manager. If you had a bad day at the plate, he wouldn't even talk to you."

Mark Koenig Anthony was born in San Francisco. Hardly a day of his youth passed that he wasn't playing at Big Rec in Golden Gate Park.

His first professional contract was with Moose Jaw, Saskatchewan. He was 17. Then came Jamestown, Des Moines, and St. Paul, where he homered off Lefty Grove in the Little World Series. The Yankees bought him up the following year, 1925.

"I was a small cog in a big machine," said Koenig of his parceled slice of fame. "The Yankees could have had a midget at shortstop. I was a lousy infielder, I made a lot of errors. I had small hands and we didn't have the butterfly nets that fielders wear today. I did have a powerful arm."

Koenig and Meusel were the goats of the 1926 World Series. Each made an error in the seventh game as the Cardinals scored three unearned runs in the fourth inning to win 3–2. Of course, the game is remembered more for Grover Cleaveland Alexander's staggering out of the bullpen to strike out Lazzeri.

"Alexander has whisky bottles hidden all over the hotel during the Series, like behind the potted palms," said Koenig. "He was a drunkard. He struck out Lazzeri on a bad pitch. The ball was outside."

Koenig hit .271, .285, .319, and .292 during his four full seasons in the Yankee pinstripes. His batting average in three Series was .125, .500 (tops in the 1927 Series), and .158. New York won four straight from both Pittsburgh and St. Louis the next two years after losing to the Cardinals in 1926.

The 1927 Yankees generally are considered the greatest team in baseball history. Koenig doesn't see it as all that cut-and-dried.

"There have been other great teams, but we did have a great aggregation," he said. "You'll never see another Ruth. He hit 60 home runs that year and Gehrig 47. And there were just a few good long-ball hitters then.

"I batted second in the lineup behind Combs. We didn't have to run, not with that kind of hitting. We could be six runs down in the eighth and still win. I was on third base with a triple when Ruth hit his sixtieth against Washington's Tom Zachary.

"Our pitching made us, though. We had Pennock, Hoyt, Dutch Ruether, Urban Shocker, and Wilcy Moore, who was the best relief pitcher you ever saw. He had one of the first good sinker balls. He'd go in with three men on, they'd never score."

Koenig's fielding problems finally made him expendable in 1930, when he was traded to Detroit. The Tigers thought he needed eyeglasses and tried to convert him to a pitcher.

By 1932, he was in the minors. His career appeared about over. Then a gun shot resurrected his career.

"Billy Jurges of the Cubs was shot by some girl in a hotel room," said Koenig. "So the Cubs bought me. When I joined the club, we were six games behind St. Louis. I had a heckuva month and a half, batting .353, and we won the pennant."

Despite his contribution, Koenig was voted a half-share by his Cub teammates as they prepared to meet the Yankees. Ruth was incensed by Chicago's treatment of his former teammate.

Both teams came through the same tunnel before the first game. Ruth was waiting when the Cubs emerged.

"He called them penny pinchers and misers," said Koenig.

Supposedly, Ruth's anger prompted that historic moment when he did or didn't point to the fence before clubbing a home run off Charlie Root.

"He pointed kind of like this," said Koenig, waving his arm quickly. "But you know darn well a guy with two strikes isn't going to say he'll hit a home run on the next pitch.

"But I wouldn't put it past him. He would come into the dugout some days and say 'I feel good. I think I'll hit one.' And, by God, he always did."

Koenig didn't actually clarify whether Ruth called his shot. It doesn't matter. Let us forever think that he did.

Koenig looks like he has worn the same soiled T-shirt for two weeks. His pants are baggy, and he needs a shave—the hair on his neck is so long, it has curled.

"It was a good life," he said of his baseball career. "I put in 17 years of professional ball [12 in the majors, .279 lifetime B.A.]. I got into five World Series, made some extra dough."

He retired in 1936 after two years with the Giants, bought two gas stations in San Francisco, and later worked for a brewery. He married a second time and eventually moved to Glen Ellen, located on Highway 12 between Sonoma and Santa Rosa.

"I have one daughter. She lives on an olive-almond ranch in Orland. She comes down once in a while to help out, but this place needs a thorough cleaning. I never see any of my grandchildren and I was good to them when they were young."

No one stays young forever, however. Nothing is eternal.

"There's only about five of us 1927 Yankees left . . . Hoyt, Bob Shawkey, Dugan, George Pipgras, Ray Morehart," he said. "I write to Hoyt and Dugan, but if you don't write to them, they never write to you. . . ."

Koenig looked at the floor, counting the ghosts.

"Meusel is dead, Combs is dead, Ruth is dead, Gehrig is dead, Lazzeri is dead, Pennock is dead. Oh, my God."

Then a voice from the other room. "Who you talking to out there?"

Koenig excused himself. A few minutes later, he wheeled in his wife, stopping her in front of the crusty food on the plate. She began eating.

The work he can't keep doing started all over again.

Best Magazine Story
GENERAL

PAST THEIR PRIME

By Roger Kahn

From Playboy
Copyright, ©, 1979, by Playboy

The pitcher telephoned me, which should inform you that he was a veteran athlete. Young baseball players do not waste change telephoning writers who are male.

He was coming to town, the pitcher said, and he was going to start a baseball game in Yankee Stadium. There weren't many games left in his arm and I knew that he had become afraid of the rest of his life. But mostly his fear was stoic, wreathed in resignation, like the fear of certain brave, old, dying men. Anyway, after the game, he wanted a woman. The pitcher felt a fulminating lust for a particular tennis star, and when I called her, she agreed to meet him with one proviso. I would have to date someone she called her "new best friend." That was the woman superintendent of the brownstone house where the tennis player cohabited with cats and fantasies.

The building super, I thought. A woman who spends days stacking garbage bags and reaming toilet drains. Dating her would be some enchanted evening. We would all turn into frogs, I thought. But I owed the pitcher certain favors.

"What should I know about the tennis player?" he asked me on the morning of the game. He didn't have to ask about opposing hitters anymore. He knew all their rhythms and weaknesses. "I mean, gimme a little scouting report on the lady, so I can plan my moves."

"Miss Center Court," I said, "loves to talk dirty, and if you don't press hard, she gets wild and delicious. But she has one peculiarity. She has to be the one to talk dirty first. If the man comes on raunchy, Miss Center Court turns off."

"Got ya," the pitcher said, with a confident nod. He then lost to the Yankees, 6–1, in punishing sunlight.

When the ball player marched into an East Side bar at 7:30 that night, he was swaggering bravado. Actually, of course, he was covering up. He had always despised losing and he hated losses even more now that so few afternoons of stadium sunlight were left.

Technically, he suffered from an irreversible chronic tendinitis in one shoulder. The condition would be annoying, but not much more than that, for an accountant or an internist or a bond salesman. But this man was a major-league pitcher, and chronic tendinitis meant something more extreme. His major-league arm was all but dead.

He looked at the tennis player and blinked and smiled. She was attractive, not merely for a lady jock. She was large-eyed and lissome and she wet her lips before she spoke. Abruptly, the ball player became desperately cheerful.

"Say," he said, dropping into a captain's chair, "you all know about the city boy and the country girl and the martinis? This here country girl had never heard of martinis and the city boy got her to drink a batch." The pitcher's tongue was brisker than his slider. "Finally, the country girl says, 'Them cherries in them maranas gimme heartburn.'

"The city boy, he says, 'You're wrong on all three counts. They're not cherries, they're olives. They're not maranas, they're martinis. And you don't have heartburn, your left breast is in the ashtray.' "

The pretty tennis player made a face like a dried apricot. Then she and my date, the woman superintendent, went to the washroom.

"Dead," I told the pitcher. "The German word is *tot*. I believe the French say *mort*. The Yankees knocked you out this afternoon and you just knocked yourself out now."

"It's a good joke," the pitcher said. "I used it at a supermarket opening in Largo, Florida, and they loved it, even the mothers with kids."

"We're north of Largo. Didn't you listen to me? Miss Center Court has to set the tone herself. If she lets guys start the rough talk, it might seem as though she's easy."

"Isn't she?"

"That isn't the question. The question is style."

The women dismissed us civilly after dinner and the pitcher said, the hell with them. He knew a Pan Am stewardess who could do unusual things with a shower nozzle. He called and an answering machine reported that its mistress was in Rome.

"Forget it," I told the big pitcher. "Everybody has nights like this. John Kennedy had nights like this. The dice are cold. Let's go to sleep."

"Stay with me," the pitcher said. We rode down to a Greenwich Village club that was cavernous and loud with bad disco and empty of talent except for a dark-haired teen-aged girl from Albany. The pitcher was quite drunk by now. He scribbled love notes and sexual suggestions on cocktail napkins, which a small Spanish waiter delivered. The girl from Albany paid her check and fled in fright.

A serious thought suddenly made the pitcher sober. "I can't pitch big-league ball no more," he said.

"You knew this was going to happen," I said.

His voice was naked. "But now it's happening."

One tear, and only one. rolled down the man's right cheek. "Shee-yit," he said, embarrassed. "Shee-yit."

"Like hell, shee-yit," I said. "You've got something to cry about."

He was 39, hardly old. He was well conditioned and black-haired and every movement he made suggested physical strength. Most would have called him a young man. But because he was an athlete, his time was closing down. He had won premature fame at 22 and now he was paying with a kind of senility at 39.

The adulatory press conferences were ending. He would not again travel as grandly as he had; he would never again earn as much money as he had been making. Already his manner with attractive women had regressed. He was finished, or he thought he was finished. The two often are the same. I thought of Caitlin Thomas's wrenching phrase, created after Dylan's final drink: leftover life to kill.

Santayana wrote:

Old Age, on tiptoe, lays her
jeweled hand
Lightly in mine.—
Come, tread a stately measure.

This may have been true for a philosopher, who sought out the stony tranquillity of cloisters, but time rings for athletes with a coarser cadence:

Old age, in nailed boots,
wrenches at my limbs,
And stomps my groin.

In the usual curve of ascendancy, the American male completes so-called formal education in his twenties and spends the next 15 years mounting a corporate trapeze. If he is good and fortunate and very agile, he will be soaring by 40. More than that, he will proceed in sure and certain hope that even more triumphant years are beckoning.

Athletes follow wholly different patterns. They soar almost with puberty. Life for a great young athlete is different from other children's lives, even as he turns 14. Already he is the best ball player of his age for blocks or miles around. He is the young emperor of the sandlot.

With enough toughness, size, nutrition, and motivation, the athlete will feel his life expanding into a diadem of delights. He does not have to ask universities to consider his merits and tolerate his college-board scores. A brawl of jock recruiters solicits him. If necessary, they offer him a free year at prep school, finally to master multiplication tables.

Assuming certain basic norms, the athlete has a glorious pick of women. Pretty wives are not an exception around ball clubs; they are characteristic.

It is all a kind of knightly beginning to life, isn't it? Doing high deeds, attended by squires moving from stately courts to demi-mondes? But most knightly tales conclude with the hero full of youth.

I remember a marvelous quarterback named Ben Larsen who dominated high school football in Brooklyn. His passing was splendid and he ran with a deceptive gliding style. Perhaps 30 colleges offered him scholarships. He chose one in the Big Ten, where the wisdom of football scouts proved finite. Ben was suddenly pressed harder than he had ever been, by athletes of comparable or higher skills. He wilted quickly and never finished college. He was the first of my acquaintances to become an alcoholic.

Larsen's life reached its peak while he was a schoolboy. For many, the climax comes in college or as a young professional. Others (Carl Yastrzemski and Fran Tarkenton) can play well and enthusiastically as they approach 40. Once an aeon, a Satchel Paige or a Gordie Howe makes it to 50. Technical literature doesn't yet tell us much. Studying human behavior is still a science of inexactitude. But broadly, and obviously, we're dealing with two elements.

The first is physical. An athlete must be granted a good body, a durable body, and—I hate to be the one to make this point—he'd better take care of it. I don't know whether or not all those careless nights cut short Mickey Mantle's career, but unwillingness to do proper pregame calisthenics and to perform therapeutic drills on all those hung-over mornings sure as hell cut off his legs.

Then there is emotion, world without end. How long can an athlete hold all his passion to be an athlete? How long can he retain all his enthusiasm for repetitive experiences?

One hot afternoon last spring, Johnny Bench, Tom Seaver, and I were riding together to make an appearance at a book fair in Atlanta. Bench at 26 was the best catcher baseball has known. Not perhaps; not one of; just the best. Last spring, at 30, he was in decline.

Bench's batting average lounged below his old standard. He was getting hurt frequently. His matchless play, his Johnny Bench-style play, seemed limited to spurts. "You get bored, John?" I asked in the car.

"With what?"

"Catching a baseball game every day."

"Do I?" Bench has a broad, expressive face and he lifted his eyebrows for emphasis. "You know why I envy him?" he said, elbowing Seaver.

"For my intellect," Seaver said. "My grooming and my skills at doing the *New York Times* crossword puzzle."

"Because he's a fucking pitcher," Bench said. "He doesn't have to work a ball game but one day in four. All that time off from playing ball games. That's why I envy Tommy."

Seaver grew serious and nodded. Both men are intelligent, curious, restless. As they grow older, and recognize that the universe is larger than a diamond, it becomes increasingly difficult to shut out everything else and play a game. It also hurts more. The human body was not designed to play catcher from April to October.

It was also not designed to fight for the heavyweight championship at the age of 36.

Last September, I flew to New Orleans to watch Muhammad Ali make a fight he really did not want to fight. He won easily over Leon Spinks, the St. Louis Cypher, but a new sourness invaded Ali's style. "It's murder, how hard he's got to work," said Angelo Dundee, the sagest of Ali's seconds.

The motivated athlete responds to the physical effects of age by conditioning himself more intensively. "That Spinks, he looks like Dracula, but he's only 25," Ali said, in a house he had rented near Lake Pontchartrain. "So I have to make myself 25. I have been up every morning, running real long, real early for five months. Five months. I've done the mostest exercises ever, maybe 350 different kinds, so's I could become the first man ever, in all history, to win back the heavyweight championship twice."

For the first two rounds in the New Orleans Superdome, Ali toyed with a dream of knocking out Spinks. But all the roadwork and the sparring could not bring back the snake-tongue quickness of the hands. Ali missed badly with two hard rights. Then, yielding to reality, he made a perfect analysis of Spink's style and how to overcome it.

Spinks had no style, really. Move in standing up, move in, move in, punch, lunge. Devoid of style, he still is strong and dangerous. From the third round, Ali simply moved around and about Spinks, flicking punches, holding, sliding, holding, always staying three moves ahead of the St. Louis Cypher. It was a boring and decisive victory and it must've hurt like hell.

Afterward, at a press conference in the Superdome, Ali spoke in the crabbed tones of age. First of all, this huge crowd—70,000, give or take a few thousand—had come to a black promotion. "Wasn't no blond hair or blue eyes doing no promoting," the champion said. That is accurate but only in a lawyerly way. The man who put together Ali-Spinks II (and the marvelous undercard) is Robert Arum, whose hair is black and whose eyes are brown. He is, however, white. Under the Arum umbrella, so to speak, two blacks and two whites, all from Louisiana, were subsidiary promoters. They are now suing each other.

Having stretched truth until it snapped, Ali offered a brief return to his old form. "Was that a 36-year-old man out there, fighting tonight? And not only fighting but dancing? Was that dancing man out there 36?"

"Thassright," chirped a parliament of votaries.

"That *Time* magazine," Ali said, "that great *Time* magazine, goes all over the world, they wrote Ali was through. Could *Time* magazine be wrong . . .?"

Crabby again, he was settling an account he had already closed in the ring, treating a buried story as though it were alive. It was a graceless effort from a man Dundee says now has to work too hard.

Why, then, does Ali drive on past his prime?

Supporting himself and his children and his wife and former wives and his retinue and his properties, Ali said not long ago, costs $60,000 a month, after taxes. His investment income is far short of that. He fights on because he believes he needs the money.

Over three recent months, I explored cash and credit, concentration and distraction, professional life and professional death—in short, how the jock grows older—with 31 remarkable athletes. They have worked their trades—baseball, boxing, basketball, football, hockey—from San Diego to New England. One (Fran Tarkenton) was sufficiently sophisticated to evoke Thomas Jefferson. "Doing a variety of things, like Jefferson did, keeps you fresh." Others (Lou Brock, Merlin Olsen, Brooks Robinson) showed positively Viennese instincts for self-analysis. One (Roger Staubach) declined to be quoted because of the nature of this magazine. (Debating morality with someone who makes a living out of the commercialized, televised, knee-shattering violence of the National Football League tempts me, but it will have to wait.)

"Did anyone say that money had nothing to do with why he kept on playing?" asked Fred Biletnikoff. He's been a wide receiver at Oakland for 14 seasons.

"Some said the money wasn't primary."

Bilentnikoff drew a breath to prepare his own comment. "You know," he said, "they're full of shit."

Generally, the athletes were honest and direct. Away from cameras, one-on-one, athletes speak more honestly than entertainers or politicians.

Most shared annoyance at America's blinding obsession with youth. They found subtle prejudice against age in certain executive suites. "In the front office I have to put up with," one 41-year-old baseball player said, "they're always looking for a reason to replace me. Maybe it's because a young guy would cost less, but I think it's not just that. They got a mind-set on the axiom that baseball is a young man's game."

Willie McCovey, the mighty first baseman who reached 41 in January, is discomfited by a particular fan in Chicago. "There's this dude who sits behind the on-deck circle in Wrigley Field," McCovey reported, "and when I get a hit, he doesn't make a sound. But every time I swing and miss, I hear the joker holler, 'You're washed up.' "

McCovey shook his head in annoyance. "That's shit," he said. "Doesn't the guy know I missed pitches years ago? Does he think I never made an out until I was 35?"

"He's just needling," I said.

"Well, I say needle with a little intelligence. Judge me by my performance. Forget my age. I try to forget my age myself. Too much thinking about your age can psych you. It can make you press and panic and retire before your time." McCovey believes that is what happened to his friend Willie Mays.

Every geriatric athlete that I talked to maintained an unabated passion for the game. It was a passion to win, to prove certain points, to keep on making money. To those men, sport was no small sliver of the consciousness; it dominated them.

Brooks Robinson, the fine third baseman who played until he was 40, said, "My whole life had been baseball. Passion? It sure was for me. In the eighth grade back in Arkansas, I wrote a whole booklet about how I wanted to be a ball player until my reflexes told me it was time to stop. By then I'd played almost as many big-league games as Ty Cobb."

"Didn't age hit you like a rabbit punch?" I asked.

"The first time something was written about my age, I was thirty. 'The aging Brooks Robinson,' the story said. I thought, What do they mean by aging? I'm a young man. And I went out to play harder. When they called me aging at 35, it didn't hit me either way. I knew they were accurate in sports terms. But then, when I was called aging at 39, the thing became a challenge all over again. It stayed a challenge until I accepted what time can do and go out."

A few old athletes remain absolutely juvenile in their enthusiasms. George Blanda, the quarterback and place kicker, was 48 when he played his last game in the National Football League. "Hell, I didn't retire even then," Blanda said. "They retired me, I enjoyed it. I always enjoyed it. Proving myself week after week. Ego-building week after week. Who wouldn't enjoy all that?

"If you have the right conditioning and you keep the right attitude, the air smells cleaner, the food tastes better, and your wife looks like Elke Sommer."

Across the past decade, big-time sport has become an explosive growth industry. That's fine for many investors and some of the athletes, but growth industry is no buzz phrase for fun. It suggests hard-knuckled grabs for every dollar anywhere in the country.

Newspaper reporters have concentrated on the new high salaries paid to athletes. It doesn't seem that important an issue to me. Ball players are entertainers, television performers. At last, Reggie Jackson and Bill Walton are being paid on the same sort of scale as Farrah Fawcett. That doesn't mean, as some journalists suggest, that the rich athletes will become complacent. (Was there ever a less complacent team than the rich and magnificent New York Yankees?) It does mean that the athletes work longer and harder and so may wear out sooner.

A generation ago, major-league baseball extended only from St. Louis to Boston. The professional hockey season was half the present schedule. Pro football was a secondary sport. The sporting life, the sporting pace was leisurely and more conducive to longevity than today's Sunday-afternoon and Monday-night fever.

I was fortunate enough to begin covering sports before the disappearance of the American train. Going from New York to St. Louis was a 24-hour hegira. You traveled in a private car and you ate in a private diner and a drink was never farther away than a porter's call button. Moving at double-digit speeds, trains gave your body a chance to adjust as you crossed time zones.

"But jet travel now is part of the package," said Lou Brock, a major-league outfielder since 1961 and the man who broke Ty Cobb's record for stolen bases. "Mentally, it doesn't make sense to eliminate or separate different aspects of a ball player's life. If you want the cheers and the fame and the money and the victories, you've got to accept the 2 A.M. jet rides. They go together."

I first traveled a sports circuit in high excitement. I had never seen the Golden Triangle in Pittsburgh or the Lake shore north of Milwaukee, or the drained malarial swamps around Houston, for that matter. Like the young men in the old stories, I ached for travel. Then, very quickly, sports travel—as distinct from a pleasure trip to Cozumel—became a minihell.

You had to be in St. Louis on four simmering July days because the team you covered was playing four games there. Often that was the week when a Chicago blonde called and said, "Please visit." You had to be in Philadelphia when the team was there, or Boston, or Cincinnati. Human nature being what it is, sports travel came down to a matter of always going to the wrong place at the wrong time with the wrong companions.

"I don't look at travel like that," said Brock, "not like that at all. To me, travel is still exciting. When I think of travel, I ask myself, How else can I get to my opponent? Get to where he is and whip him?"

Various athletes play tactical games with time. Phil Esposito, the hockey forward, keeps his weight 12 pounds lower than it was a decade ago. Tony Perez, the first baseman, says that at 36 he is far better at anticipating pitches than he was when younger. If you guess low slider and the pitcher throws a low slider, you stay in business. "You can sometimes beat the younger guys with your head," said Dave Bing, the basketball player, who decided to retire last August, when he was 35. "You figure their weaknesses and you play into them, But in the end . . ."

Merlin Olsen, the Mighty Mormon who played on the line for the Los Angeles Rams across 15 seasons, believes that athletes who endure are able to anticipate danger. "It's a kind of sense you have," Olsen said. "Don't push yourself harder this time. Don't extend with everything you've got just now. There's danger out there."

I remembered the kindly horses in all those terrible Western movies. The animals always knew that a bridge was out or that a landslide would be gathering its roaring strength or that 29 feet to the left, under a clump of gray-green sage, a sidewinder coiled.

"Good movie stuff, Merlin," I said. "Friends of mine have paid rent bills writing sixth-sense themes. But practically . . ."

"Practically," Olsen said. "I played in the pits on a pro-football line for a long time: Consider all that tonnage and the carnage. But I was never seriously hurt."

I have before me 27 pages of single-spaced comments from professional athletes, but curiously, or not so curiously, I keep turning back to Lou Brock. "When I think of travel, I ask myself, How else can I get to my opponent. Get to where he is and whip him?"

Major sport is American trauma. Crumpled knees drive halfbacks into early retirement; pitchers' arms go dead; hockey players slammed to the ice twist in convulsion. Before this onslaught, both the body and the psyche tremble.

The complete athlete measures pain against glory, risk against profit. He considers what is left of his body and then, I believe, he subconsciously decides whether or not he wants to go on. In the end, the difference between Carl Yastrzemski, a star at 39, and Mickey Mantle, an assistant batting coach at that age, is that Yaz wanted it more.

A temptation is to conclude with too much certitude on so-called qualitative distinctions among the experiences of various athletes aging into other men's prime time. Is Tony Perez, who grew up in the balmy poverty of Cuba, markedly afraid hard times will come now in the North? He says not. Is Gordie Howe, who still works hockey at the age of 50, clutching to the withered stump of his boyhood? Hell, no. Howe says his wrists hurt and his legs are gone, but he loves playing pro hockey on the same team as his sons.

This temptation to conclude too much persists. To me it is rather like the saucy little tennis player was to the veteran pitcher. The object looks so damned attainable; then, in a blink of too-bright eyes, it is gone.

My journalistic interviews are not excursions into therapy. You ask, the athlete answers. You press a little. He tries to be honest. You press harder. He thinks of his image. He also tries to be macho. He tries to keep his dignity. You ask some more. You think. And you move on.

So I fight temptations glibly to write about predictable crises, self-flagellation, or variable testosterone levels. If I can hear and share a little of the bar of music that is another man, I have my accomplishment.

The best and bravest and most competitive athlete I knew was Jackie Robinson. Breaking the major-league color line in 1947, he played with teammates who called him nigger. Rivals from at least four teams tried to spike him. The best I can say for the press is that it was belligerently neutral.

What Jack did—his genius and his glory—was to make obstacles work for him. Call him nigger and he'd get mad. Mad, he'd crush you. Misquote him out of laziness or malice and he'd take his disgust out on rival pitchers, as though they were the boozy press. Bar him from the dining room of your hotel in Cincinnati at lunch, he'd dominate your ball park in Cincinnati after dinner.

It was a cruel, demanding way to have to live. His career burned out in a decade and his life ended when he was 53. "This man," the Reverend Jesse Jackson intoned from the funeral pulpit, "turned a stumbling block into a stepping-stone."

That is the fundamental. Something of what Faulkner meant in his famous speech at Stockholm. It is not sufficient to endure, he said. Man must prevail.

Only a few extraordinary athletes—Stan Musial and Joe DiMaggio—are able to prevail in retirement. Their glory intact, they move from the ball park to other arenas, still special heroes. Some, like Jack Dempsey and Casey Stengel, even achieve Olympian old age. All these men learned how to transform obstacles into stepping-stones.

"Did Robinson know he was dying?" my friend Carl Erskine, once a Dodger pitching star, asked after the funeral.

"I think maybe he did."

"How did he bear up?"

"It was amazing. He was getting blinder and lamer every day, and working harder and harder for decent housing for blacks."

"He was a hero," Erskine said.

"Apart from baseball," I said.

"But don't you think," Erskine said, "that disciplining himself the way he had to, and mastering self-control and commanding a sense of purpose—don't you think the things he had to do to keep making it in baseball taught him how to behave in the last battle?"

Before that moment, I had a distaste for people who saw sports as a metaphor for life. Where I grew up, life was less trivial than a ball game.

"I never thought of that till now," I said, still learning.

Other Stories

TENNIS

THE "OLD LADY" BOWS OUT

By Joe Gergen

From Newsday
Copyright, ©, 1979, Newsday Inc.

If it was her last great scene on Center Court, something she will not concede, at least Billie Jean King played it to the hilt. She played it to 15,000 spectators and a real, live princess in the Royal Box. She played it before Olivier.

That's not a shabby way to close out a wondrous singles career in the most prestigious of tournaments. King vowed she'd be back next year, sharper and tougher than ever, after an enthralling two-hour, two-minute struggle with Tracy Austin. That is her way, a competitor to the end, no less so than Bill Russell or Bob Gibson or Pete Rose. But King will be 36 next year, and it boggles the mind how good Austin will be at 17. The world will not stand still for King.

The action was riveting yesterday as King set out to defeat the years and Austin set out to prove that she was ready, here and now, to reach for the top. Potential be damned. At 16, Austin has the game to win it all. It only added to the drama that there in the Royal Box at the south end of the court sat Princess Alexandra and Lord Laurence Olivier. Larry to his show-business friends.

Sarah Bernhardt or Lynn Fontanne couldn't have played the moment better than King, who calls herself the "Old Lady." It unfolded in the twelfth game of the second set, King trailing one set to love and 6–5 in games. At 30–15, King served, rushed to the net, and hit a cross-court forehand volley that flirted with the sideline. The linesman signaled out. Hands on hips, King fumed. Austin nodded her head and pointed that the shot had been out.

King stalked back to the service line, slammed in a serve and, with body English, willed Austin's return off the court. Then King pounded her racket on the grass, started back toward the south end, looked up, and yelled, "It's my game."

Center Court at Wimbledon, with its sloping roof and tight enclosures, has the acoustics of a theater. Her voice rang out with the authority an Olivier could appreciate. Listening, no one could doubt that she would win the game and the set.

She did just that, ripping a backhand volley on game point while Austin slipped undecorously on her yellow pants and then taking a 7–5 tie breaker through the sheer force of her personality. Yes, she was saying, the Old Lady wasn't dead yet. The moment was memorable and touching.

But the moment could not be sustained. King did survive three breakpoints to hold service in the first game of the third set and she did break Austin in the second game. Then it slipped away from her. She tried to keep it going in the third game by jumping up and cheering herself after a good point but, one point from victory, King was passed by Austin and the youngster ran out the game.

Austin easily held service in the fourth game. The fifth game was the pivotol one. They played 14 points, Billie Jean grabbing Tracy by her pigtails and Austin flailing away with her remarkable two-fisted backhand. Four times King held the advantage, four times Austin fought back with an amazing service return.

Even the sound was dramatic. King grunted with the exertion of her serve and Austin let loose a high-pitched squeal as she ran down the balls. Finally, King hit a wide backhand off a fine Austin lob and Tracy broke the six-time Wimbledon singles champion with a slashing return at King's ankles. For all intents, the match was over. Austin ran out the last three games, making it six in a row, for a 6–4, 6–7, 6–2 victory.

"She really pushed me," Austin said. "She made me work very hard. She made me pull out everything I had."

It was only fitting King had put everything into the match. She dusted off some shots she hadn't used in years. She hit more topspin than ever before. She hit flat sizzlers. She hit sliced backhands. She hit moon balls and lobs and a clutch of drop shots. She showed Austin the entire arsenal.

But it was not enough to overcome the lack of tournament toughness and the 19-year difference in age. "I don't think I sustained this," King said. "At two–love [in the third set], I let her back in. But she played great in the fifth game. If you had to isolate one game, that was it. She was great on the ad points."

King would not acknowledge that it was a great show. That was for others to judge, she said. "I'm ticked at losing," she said. "It may have been entertaining, but not for me. I'm not going to say [and here she raised her voice three octaves to matronly level], 'Oh, really nice. Jolly good show.' I was busting my gut out there."

She had first come to Wimbledon in 1961 as Billie Jean Moffitt, a brash 17-year-old schoolgirl from Long Beach, California, who, when cheered, would yell, "Don't just applaud, throw money!" She won the women's double with Karen Hantze that time and came back for 18 more titles. She's still alive this year in the women's doubles and the mixed doubles.

She still has a shot at a record-breaking twentieth Wimbledon championship, but she was disappointed at her loss yesterday, nonetheless. "I thought my chances in singles were as good as in doubles," she said. "In doubles my partners try so hard to help me get that twentieth they can't breathe. I have to give them tranquilizers before we play."

Austin was three years old when King won her first Wimbledon singles title. "Tracy knows not only who she [Billie Jean] is," said George Austin, Tracy's father, "but what she's done for women's tennis. She really was looking forward to this match. It was exciting, almost too exciting for me."

No longer the awed little girl who walked onto Center Court in a pinafore at 14, Tracy smiled brilliantly as she stepped into the spotlight yesterday. She appeared delighted to be there. "We all had dinner last night, her grandparents, her brother, her coach," George Austin said, "and she was superconfident. She was happy and laughing and as loose as she's ever been."

She played that way, slashing winners cross-court and down the line. "I just had to keep telling myself to forget that she had won 19 Wimbledons and everything else worth winning," Tracy, the youngest Wimbledon semifinalist of the century, said.

"I honestly thought it was going to be straight sets," said Robert Lansdorp, Austin's coach. "But I thought Billie Jean played very well. Tracy was intimidated for a while, I think, going for too big a shot when Billie Jean came to the net. But Tracy is capable of pulling her game up when she has to. Somewhere she has the reserve."

And now she has a meeting with defending champion Martina Navratilova, a nervous 2–6, 6–3, 6–0 winner over Dianne Fromholtz yesterday. "If Martina lets up a little bit," Lansdorp said, "Tracy's going to take her."

It wouldn't surprise anyone. Not any more. Tracy Austin has arrived. She crept into the corner of the interview room yesterday while King was concluding her thoughts and was there to greet the loser at the door. "I told 'em you were a creep," King said to Austin. And she laughed aloud and hugged her.

That, too, was a gracious exit.

HOCKEY

HOWE: HISTORY ON SKATES

By Joe Resnick

From The Kansas City Star
Copyright, ©, 1979, The Kansas City Star Company

Most National Hockey League players today would have to depend on history books for bits of the past that Gordie Howe could find by simply rummaging through his scrapbooks.

During Howe's first season in the NHL with the Detroit Red Wings (1946–47), Harry Truman was president, Bess Myerson was completing her reign as Miss America, and Assault captured horse racing's Triple Crown.

Now a 51-year-old grandfather, Howe is in his thirty-second season of major-league hockey. Naturally, he has earned a few well-chosen monikers along the way: "The Fossil . . . Mr. Hockey . . .Old Man Winter . . . Father-Time-and-a-Half."

All the records he has garnered for goals and points fall second to the longevity marks. The following facts illustrate the uniqueness of his career:

All but three of his Hartford Whalers teammates hadn't been born yet when Howe began his National Hockey League career, including his son Mark, a right wing.

He is 11 years older than the second-oldest player in the league, Bobby Hull of the Winnipeg Jets. Fred Shero of the New York Rangers, who is three years older, is the only coach older than Howe.

When Howe made it to the Whalers' January 2 game with the Edmonton Oilers, he became the first man in any major-league team sport whose career bridged five decades.

It has gotten past the point where people ask him when he will retire. If he wanted to quit he would have nine seasons ago when he "retired" the first time from the NHL.

But that was before the birth of the World Hockey Association, a new league that gave Howe a new lease on life. It represented a once-improbable opportunity for Gordie to play with Mark and his other son Marty, a defenseman. The senior Howe jumped at it and has been going strong ever since.

"It's not a job anymore. It really is a way of life," said Howe, whose 86-year-old-father is the only member of the family who has asked Gordie to retire lately.

"He worked for the city of Saskatoon for years as the city's superintendent. He says he retired too late [at 67] and he didn't want me to retire too late. All he said was that I should retire and enjoy life."

Gordie's last remaining goal in hockey is to play with both sons in an NHL game. That was postponed by Marty's demotion to the minor leagues before the season—the first in the NHL for the Whalers, Oilers, Jets, and Quebec Nordiques. The four remaining survivors of the WHA had joined the NHL this season in an expansion program.

Mark says his father wanted to play another season, whether it was in the NHL or the WHA. "He just loves that game so much that he keeps working and working. That's why he's still playing at 51," he said.

Inevitably, Gordie's age finds its way into every interview he consents to. But although Howe treats the subject with patience, it hasn't always been necessary to refer to it. "They don't have to remind me some days. When you're playing at 51, it's almost like playing hurt all the time," he said.

Few players if any survive five seasons in this often brutal sport, let alone 32 years, without suffering injuries. Howe's worst injury, on March 28, 1960, almost ended his life.

As Howe went to check Ted Kennedy of the Toronto Maple Leafs, Kennedy sidestepped him and Howe went into the sideboards headfirst. He received a concussion so serious that an operation was performed to relieve pressure on his brain. It didn't end there, as Howe lay near death for several days before recovering.

Through the years, the majority of Howe's confrontations have ended with much different results. It is interesting how many of Gordie's longtime opponents remember vividly their first "board meetings" with him.

"The second time I played against him, in 1960, I had my hand up and his elbow came back and hit my hand. He said, 'Watch out. That elbow always comes back quickly.' I remember that," said Dave Keon, Hartford teammate. "It was nice of him to warn me. I don't think he did that to too many people."

"I remember my first stitches in the NHL he gave me right here," the Rangers' Phil Esposito said, pointing to a spot between his nose and upper lip. "There were six of them. I think his elbow strayed."

Carol Vadnais, Esposito's teammate, was playing with the old California Seals when he went into the Detroit Olympia the night after receiving 16 stitches in his ear from blocking a shot by Montreal's Jacques Lemaire.

"I don't know for what reason, but they put me on left wing to check him and he gave me a two-hander right across that ear, so I took a run at him. He told me, 'Hey kid, if you don't want anything else, you just cool off.' "

Now, years later, Howe commands as much respect from teammates and opponents alike as he had when he was a young colt.

"His greatest asset is his strength. If he wasn't as strong as he is, I don't think he'd have been able to play as long as he has," said Keon.

"He doesn't look out of place, that's for sure," Esposito said. "I don't think he's right on top of the puck like he used to be, but he plays his position extremely well, and you don't fool with him. God bless him, that's all I can say. To me, he's the greatest athlete who ever lived."

Getting this far was no accident for Howe, whose health habits are close to impeccable. "He's never been a heavy drinker, he's never been one to stay out late, and he's taken very good care of himself since he was young, and that's what keeps him going right now," Mark Howe said.

"Some guys today, by the time they hit 30 they're all washed up because they never took care of themselves off the ice. He did a lot of hard work as a kid growing up, and I think it's paid off for him over his lifetime."

Gordie keeps in shape by cutting wood at his Glastonbury, Connecticut, home, which sits on 16 acres about eight miles east of Hartford. "We had a lot of dead wood after an ice storm went through here earlier this year and killed a lot of trees, which are still standing. So, whenever I want to stock up with some wood, I just knock one down and cut it up," he said.

Howe, who averaged 40 minutes on the ice every night during his heyday, conserves his energy now, limiting himself to three shifts a period plus a penalty-killing stint now and then. But by no means is he there as an ornament.

"I'm old enough and stubborn enough to realize if I can be of aid to the club at all, then I want to be on the ice when I'm at my best," he said. "But if I get really bad, and if it comes tomorrow, then that's fine because I've far exceeded any longevity rules that I ever had for myself."

Playing at age 51 was the furthest thing from Howe's mind 36 years ago when he left his home in Floral, Saskatchewan, to play junior hockey. But when he reached his destination, the 15-year-old hockey player was told he couldn't play.

"I had to sit around for a whole year," he said. "They wouldn't let kids under a certain age transfer from one province to the next and I was underage."

It was the only time in Gordie Howe's life that his age was an obstacle.

BASEBALL

BODY AND SOUL

By Tony Kornheiser

From Inside Sports
Copyright, ©, 1979, Newsweek Inc. All rights reserved

> He took it out on the ball, pounding it to a pulp as if the best way to get even with the fans, the pitchers who mocked him, and the statisticians who had recorded (forever) the kind and quantity of his failures, was to smash every conceivable record. He was like a hunter stalking a bear, a whale, or maybe the sight of a single fleeing star the way he went after that ball. He gave it no rest and was not satisfied unless he lifted it over the roof and spinning toward the horizon.
>
> —Bernard Malamud, *The Natural*

Springing from the couch, feeling so pumped up, so very pumped up now, Mike Schmidt went into his hitting stance, grabbing an imaginary bat, sliding his hands down low on the handle, turning sideways and flexing his arms until the veins in his biceps threatened to burst through his skin onto the carpet. He stood there, his hips swaying slightly, waiting on the ball, so entranced that he could not hear the sounds from the kitchen, where his baby daughter cried and his wife trying to calm her, sang a feathery lullaby. As the sweat stains under his arms spread like syrup, Schmidt gritted his teeth and, borrowing a voice he had heard Kirk Douglas use so many times on so many late shows, said he was going to kill it; he vowed he was going to kill it. It would, of course, come in high and hard, as big as the moon, so he could not only see the stitching but read Chub Feeney's signature.

There—moving to the outside, flirting with the black.

As he swung, the tension in his muscles tracked across his body from right to left, causing his shirt to ripple like a flag in the wind, and the force from the swing made the iced tea in the glass on the table shimmy. His eyes followed the flight of the ball, through the picture window, past the backyard pool, over the trees. Only when he was certain the ball had escaped New Jersey and traveled all the way to Delaware did he drop the bat and exhale.

That would show them.

That would shut them up.

The effort had reddened his face the color of baked brick—the same color as his hair, so it was difficult to judge where the hair ended and the face began. He flopped down on the couch, slapping the insides of his thighs. There was a clown's grin on his face as he said the word *potential*, a word he has heard so many times it ought to be part of his name.

Last name: Schmidt.

First name: Michael.

Middle name: Potential.

"I have the problem, you know, with my potential," he said mocking the word. "I'm a natural. I know everybody says it, but it's true. I've always had great coordination. Name the sport; I can pick it up in a second. Bowling. Tennis. Golf. It doesn't matter. I played all three sports in high school—basketball, football, baseball. Hell, this one college, Marietta, offered me a scholarship in all three. I ended up with baseball because I thought I was best suited to it, and after two years I was starting in the majors.

"People were always talking about my potential. The media picked it up and started telling the world. 'Hey, this guy should maybe be the best ever.' I really dug it. In 1973 and 1974 I was really eaten up by it when Ozark would say, 'This guy will make more money in the game than any guy ever.' I was really on an ego trip when people talked about my ability, 'cause I knew I had it. There was no way you could ever tell me that the guy on the mound or the guys hitting in front of me or behind me had any more ability than I had—I knew they didn't. It was just a matter of me putting a couple of years together with monster statistics to prove I had it."

By now the grin was gone. The hands had moved from inside the thighs to the top of the knees, and Schmidt was leaning forward, as if some inner force were pushing hard on the small of his back. He had gone from Emmett Kelly to Hamlet. To be or not to be—the only question.

"Well, I got the home runs. Nobody in baseball has more than me in the last five years. But I never hit for average. What am I lifetime? Around .225? I've looked in the mirror and said, 'Damn, when are you going to find yourself? What is it going to take?' I assume there are guys who look in the mirror and say, 'You're the best.' Like Muhammad Ali. He tells people, 'I'm the greatest. You don't think so? C'mon up here, Chump, and prove it. You're a loser, 'cause I'm the best ever.' But I looked in the mirror and said, 'What do I have to do to bring the ability out?' Maybe inside I know Parker and Foster and Rice don't have any more ability than I have. Possibly I haven't reached my potential because I want to so bad. Let's put it this way: If I didn't know what my potential was—if nobody ever told me about it—I might have the stats."

That was early in the season, when summer was coming and the pitchers were still ahead of the hitters. Later, in mid-August, Schmidt's finger was squeezing the trigger on a bat that was so hot it glowed. He was leading the majors in home runs, leading the National League in runs scored, runs batted in, and walks. For the first time in his career he was approaching the standard he had set for himself, and numbers like 55 and 130 did not seem unreachable—especially coming off a July when he had 13 and 31, when the only way to keep him off the scoreboard was to lock him in the trainer's room. Four, maybe five times in July they had cheered him so unceasingly that Schmidt had had to climb out from the dugout and tip his cap. Had he bared his head like that in 1978 someone in the Vet might have tried to lob a beer. But if you had been there this summer you might almost think they loved him. And they almost did.

"You never put it all together for six or seven months," he said "but I'm approaching this level of consistency . . ." He smiled briefly at the sum of his July. "I was doing so well it was scary to me. I was wondering at times if it was possible for a player to be this good, this aweing as a hitter."

"Aweing."

He was so good he had to make up a word for it.

Although he was hitting only about .280 not getting to .300 didn't torture him the way it once did. He talked about "covering a lot of ground as an individual," about "learning a lot about hitting a baseball," about "having a great experience." If hens were so contented they would lay omelets.

But his bat alone could not make up for an overload of incompetent arms, and the Phillies sank under the weight, losing three out of four in a crucial home series against Pittsburgh. In the final game, which the Pirates would win big, 9–2, on national television, all fans got was a tease, a screamingly loud Schmidt answer to a Jim Bibby fastball. As 25 million people watched, umpire Eric Greg, kneeling on the third baseline, waved it foul. Two pitches after, he struck out. The moment stolen from them, the fans could not control their disappointment. What started out as cheers turned to dry and dusty boos.

The more things change, the more they stay the same.

The nameplate on the office door says, simply, D. Ozark. Danny Ozark has been the manager of the Philadelphia Phillies for seven years, yet there is nothing in his office to suggest permanence—or even tenure. No photos. No plaques, no mementos. It seems as if Ozark is a squatter—as soon as someone else with the rent money comes along Ozark will be on the street.

He is 55 years old, a man with basset-hound ears and 5,257 lifetime at-bats—none of them in the majors. He once said, when asked if his managerial job were in jeopardy, "I will not be co-horsed," and then, to prove it was not just a single brush with genius, said, some months later, "I've always had a wonderful repertoire with my players." Ozark is the only major-league manager Mike Schmidt has ever had.

When Schmidt came to the Phillies, in 1973, Ozark saw something special in him—some perfect flash of marble. And, with Ozark's sculpting, there would someday emerge a full-blown David, ensuring the manager's place in baseball history as his Michelangelo.

Ozark's voice is soft, almost tired, working on mysteries without any clues. "I thought this guy would be the player of players." He still swears by Schmidt, still says there isn't a better player in baseball—not even Dave Parker. But when he is asked why it is that certain players never get past the "po" in potential, he says, "Maybe they put too much pressure on themselves." He points to his head. "Up here's the thing that plays games with you, and that's the thing playing games with him. Why? That's the $64,000 question. I'd like a psychologist to tell me. I've always said that the next manager of this team should be a psychologist."

Ozark's face squinches, like it has been drenched by a tidal wave of lemon juice. "If he was dumb, it'd be better." His eyes shine, having seen the clear light of truth. "There've been a lot of great dumb ball players, you know—so dumb they couldn't even remember yesterday."

It's not that Schmidt isn't a very good player, maybe even a great player—171 home runs, 497 runs batted in, 520 runs scored, three Gold Gloves in the last five years—it's that he isn't the Best Player. He gets paid $565,000 a year. The only other athletes in town making that kind of money are Pete Rose and Julius Erving. Rose is the best salesman since Willy Loman, and Erving is a doctor. Hey, this is South Philly. We're talking Fabian, Frankie Avalon, hey, yo, Rocky. For 565 big ones a year if the guy is only gonna hit .255, he better be able to sing "Dede Dinah" and go the full 15 with Apollo Creed.

Last year he couldn't. .251/21 HR/78 RBI. Boo.

"Let's just say it was bad," Schmidt says.

"It was awful," says Tug McGraw. "They made Schmidt the scapegoat for the team. He was the first enormous contract to be publicized. The fans here are blue-collar and they gauge performance by money. They just weren't ready for him not to have a great year."

"I couldn't even go to the games," Donna Schmidt says.

It is an afternoon in midseason. The Phillies will play St. Louis, at a 7:35 start, and at 12:30 the only player in the Phillies clubhouse is Schmidt. He is there to star in a local commercial for Canada Dry. The Canada Dry people love him. If they said, "He's a super guy" once, they said it 93 times. The commercial requires some acting, some phrasing, and some intelligence. The last requirement eliminates 50 percent of the major-league players. From the beginning Schmidt knows exactly how to do his part. He takes the ginger-ale can in his hand, looks into the camera, grins, and says, " . . . best-looking can I've ever seen. It's got me, Mike Schmidt, on it." It's a 30-second spot, with maybe 28 seconds of dialogue. It goes eight, nine, 10 takes.

Eleven, 12, 13.

"I don't like getting into double figures," Schmidt says.

Fourteen, 15, 16.

"Let's take a break," the director says. "Anybody got a soda? Can I get a Coke here?"

"You caught me at a good time," Schmidt says during the break. "Hell, I'm in hog heaven now. Base hits. Home runs. No boos. But I know just how quickly it can change—I know how badly those fans want us to win. We get 30,000 people coming out every game, and 25,000 of them are from South Philly and their whole lives are coming out to the ball park, then going to their local taverns and talking about the Phillies. Damn, it's their lives. I said it in the playoffs. We get so uptight trying to win for these fans that it's like they're affecting us more than the other team. They think we owe them one. Hey, I don't owe them anything. I gave 100 percent every time I walked onto that field, and I'm a winner no matter what it says on that scoreboard."

It is not said so much in anger as disdain, not so much in disdain as diffidence, not so much in diffidence as cool.

Captain Cool.

"Yeah, some of the writers have called him that," says Bus Saidt, who has covered the Phillies for the Trenton *Times* for more than 20 years. "The cool is completely misinterpreted by the fans. The fans see him strike out and not break his bat in the dugout and they think he doesn't care. It's like they blame him personally."

Schmidt does not like to talk on the record about the Scapegoat Theory. He does not like to step on other people's toes, and any elaboration on the Scapegoat Theory would cause some spike wounds. Maybe on No. 10. Maybe on No. 19. Maybe on No. 3. So, for public consumption, Schmidt says things like, "I can take my share of blame, just as long as it's not too big a share."

Privately he listens to the Scapegoat Theory, which goes like this:

Who else could they blame? They're not gonna blame the pitchers—the pitchers are mediocre. They're not gonna blame McBride or Maddox, because they're black and Philadelphia fans consider a black player or two a necessity but not worth wasting praise or blame on. Forget Trillo—he's Latin. Boone? A nice catcher, that's all. That leaves you, Rose, Bowa, and Luzinski. Rose is a legend. He already has the rings. If you guys don't win, it's because you all dragged Rose down to your level. They love Bowa—he's a dirt eater, a little Rocky. The Bull? Are you kidding? He's a one-dimensional player—a slugger. He's an outside linebacker who got dropped into the wrong clubhouse. Plus, he spent all those bucks on free tickets for those kids in the Bull Ring. That leaves you, Schmidt. The Natural. The best white man in the game. You're the only one they can blame. You're the one who can put this team on his back and put this city on the map. You read the Bible all the time, don't you? Five hundred and sixty-five big ones, 30 pieces of silver—it's the same old jazz. You let these people down and it's betrayal. See you at supper, Babe.

In the basement of Schmidt's house, on a table across the room from his Magnavision screen, is an elaborate model-train set. It cost $1,200, and when he saw it he had to have it. He'd loved model trains as a kid in Dayton, loved to watch them go around and around and up and down, always stopping exactly where he wanted.

Last winter, with the boos ringing in his ears, he would play with his trains for hours, as if to say—I'm not 29, I'm not in Philadelphia, I'm a kid again and nobody can hurt me because I don't even hear them. He would put on his engineer's cap, stick the chaw of Red Man in his cheek, and become Choo-Choo Charlie. And, because he aspires to perfection and admires authenticity, especially in detail, he scribbled some grafitti—"M.S. + D.S."; "Viola [his grandmother] loves Pete [Rose]," you know—on the miniature table.

A more confident man might have scribbled something really cutting on the depot. After all, Graig Nettles, who is supremely confident, writes E-5 on the back of his glove.

Mike Schmidt might have scribbled "Schmidt Chokes."

But he did not.

But not to get carried away with dark and brooding images. Schmidt isn't quite Hamlet. He is far from tortured. He loves his wife and daughter, considers no household task beneath him—not taking out the garbage, not washing the dishes, not changing the baby's diapers or wiping her vomit from his shirt. He is hardly ever angry, almost never raises his voice, and he's very proud that, as he told his best friend, Garry Maddox, earlier this season, "I don't think anyone on this team dislikes me." Ask him if he's happy and he answers, unequivocally, "Yes," Not "yeah," but "yes."

He has been known to smile easily and often, and he can get off a wisecrack with anyone. On a promotional tour for the Phillies last spring he told a group of fans that while James Caan would surely play the title role in *The Mike Schmidt Story*, who else could play Pete Rose but Buddy Hackett? And when you talk to him about his physique—the 6-2, 203 pounds often called "the best white body in baseball"—he says, "Tell me about it. First of all, I've got a bubble butt and second of all I've got hemorrhoids." Should any party get oppressively dull, Schmidt can get everyone laughing by doing his Danny Ozark-walking-to-the-mound-to-take-the-pitcher-out routine, in which Schmidt does a pantomime that resembles Goofy the Dog behind 24 Quaaludes.

But before we get St. Peter calling a cab for the man, remember the overriding characteristic of Michael Jack Schmidt—that he is a Natural. And Naturals are different.

Most of us are afraid of failure. Naturals are often afraid of success. Because it comes so easily, they see it as a private road. Most of us have to overcome hardships to succeed athletically—no speed, no range, no agility. Naturals have to overcome not having to overcome anything.

"Let me tell you something Davy Johnson said to me when he played here. He said, 'There's nothing worse than great ability and a complex mind.' "

Mike Schmidt, who likes to think of himself as living proof of that theory—that kind of Gibranian sponge cake you might find on a placemat at Burger King—rests his case.

It shouldn't come as a surprise that Schmidt likes James Bond and Clint Eastwood movies. He enjoys watching Bond and Eastwood brought to the brink of death and ultimately, and repeatedly, rescued by their own strength and cunning. Millions of men do. The difference with Schmidt is that he empathizes.

Schmidt grew up in Dayton, Ohio, upper middle class. His father owned and operated a self-service restaurant that was attached to a private swimming club owned and operated by his mother's family. It was just Schmidt and his younger sister and he had everything he ever wanted—a park 50 feet from his house, a good job every summer, a car, a pool, understanding parents. "I've been a spoiled child." He ran a B-minus average at classwork without ever being interested in a single course except drafting, where he ran As. Maybe the easiness of the life helps explain the historical pattern in his life of flirtation with failure.

The act of God came early, when he was seven and, to break his fall from a tree branch, he grabbed a live wire—4,000 volts. Rubber soles saved his life, but he still has a shiny patch, about the size of a silver dollar, on his shin where the electricity escaped. It was a death dance, and Schmidt walked away with the music in him. Years later, after a religious conversion, he looks back and thinks that God was looking after him.

His parents were very strict, German, authoritarian, and not forthcoming with explanations, and he "had to sneak around a lot more than the other kids." In high school he was briefly suspended from the baseball team after the note he had passed in class, arranging a time and place for a drinking party—You bring the beer, I'll bring the cherry vodka, and we'll go get bombed (or something like that)—was discovered. At Ohio U., during the Kent State backlash, he joined in a campus demonstration and threw some rocks. Schmidt wasn't there for the politics—"If someone asked me about Vietnam, I'd either say, 'We shouldn't be there,' or, 'We have to stop communism.' I'd go either way"—he was there for the fun. Every once in a while he just liked to "raise a little hell." He "never got floored enough by any one experience to stop me from driving around with a can of beer in my hand to screwing around over the grounds of the seminary with a girl friend in the back seat."

Part of this was natural rebellion, perfectly normal for a good boy, but part may also have been an unconscious search for some obstacle dangerous enough to jar him.

Certainly a dose of failure came to him in 1973, his rookie season in Philadelphia, when he batted .196 in 367 at-bats. Ozark tried to befriend—even father—Schmidt, and Schmidt reacted with hostility and confusion. To make things worse, Schmidt had the training-table habits of Hunter S. Thompson. "I was eaten up with the major-league single player's life. I was under the influence of some sort of drug every night after the game until I passed out," he says. "I knew I could sleep all day and go to the park fresh, right?"

Schmidt made two moves to get back on track. He played winter ball in Puerto Rico for Bobby Wine, a Phillies coach, and he got married. Three weeks after meeting Donna Wightman, a Philly girl who sang in a soft-rock group that had once toured as an opening act for the Byrds, he asked to marry her.

She was a couple of years younger, but having grown up working class and gone on the road, she was more worldly and mature than Schmidt. Donna Wightman Schmidt is a lively and chatty "My life is an open book; I'm a soap opera" woman who can make you feel like one of the family as soon as you enter her house, but she is not, she insists, Cheryl Tiegs. "It didn't seem to make sense," she said. "He was dating beautiful stewardesses and Playboy bunnies. He could've had any woman he wanted." She had her doubts about Schmidt's eagerness, and she insisted that before marrying Michael—she always calls him Michael—they live together. After a few months, she knew.

In his next four seasons Schmidt averaged just under 38 home runs, 105 runs batted in, and 107 runs scored, making him the most productive slugger in baseball. He gives his wife much of the credit, and surely she was what he needed, being part lover and part mother. Still, in Schmidt's mind there was something missing. He still hadn't even approached .300. Even in 1977, after signing that six-year contract and hitting 38 home runs, driving in 101 runs, and scoring 114 runs, he felt unfulfilled.

It was then, after the splendid 1977 season—and not, as most people believe, after the terrible 1978 season—that he underwent a spiritual conversion and welcomed Christ into his life. "I did it when things were good for the kid," he said.

What the born-agains have in common is a litany of "used to be." The born-again invariably talks about how it was then and how it was now, dividing his life neatly into eras as easily as the daily standings divide performance into Ws and Ls.

It's not that he proselytizes; he really has a sense of humor about it. At a recent shooting of a fashion commercial in the Phillies clubhouse the photographer wanted one of the posing Phillies—Schmidt, Dick Ruthven, Bake B. McBride, Greg Luzinski, Pete Rose, Tug McGraw, Bob Boone, and Garry Maddox—to wear only a towel. Before Schmidt (who has the body Rose once said he would "trade mine, my wife's, and throw in some cash" for) volunteered, he turned to Maddox and asked, "You think this is a Christian thing to do?"

Schmidt says he has never been happier, never more content. He says his priorities have changed; he is a husband and father first, a ballplayer second. No longer does he feel the need to hit .350, 50 home runs, 150 RBI. He pleads *nolo contendere* to the charge of pressure—"It's up to the Man upstairs." Schmidt talks about "this guy, Christ, sitting on my shoulder," and he pulls out the modern-day Book of James and reads from it: "Be happy, for when the way is rough your patience has a chance to grow . . . don't try to squirm out of your problems." Schmidt says his faith is absolute.

Converts are always so sure.

Donna Schmidt hopes so. She thinks her husband's conversion is the best thing that ever happened to him. But forever? She is alone in the house now; Schmidt and his agent have left for the game. The baby is sleeping, and Donna Schmidt, who loves her husband dearly and thinks he is the nicest, kindest man she has ever known, is considering a question that's making her slightly uncomfortable. "I hope so," she says, "but it's tough to answer. Michael is so easily led. In the past, he always did what was in, always wore what was in. Dick Allen, Dave Cash, they led him around. He talks about how much he admired Dick Allen. Poor Michael is always so strongly for the underdog. He doesn't always see what is happening to him."

Her smile is so sympathetic, her care so genuine.

"He's a midwestern kid who lived at home all his life until he went to college, and now that he's a professional athlete he gets everything done for him. He's young, and so trusting. When we have arguments they're always about the same thing—I'm just waiting for him to catch up to me. I can't say yes or no about his faith because I'm not sure about his attention span. He's not a reader. He'll read one page, that's it. He can't sit down and watch TV without jumping up after a minute. I love him so much, but when you talk about forever . . ."

The first-choice words from the Phillies on Schmidt are *great, tremendous,* and *awesome.* Pete Rose uses all three in 15 seconds, like it was a vocabulary test. Larry Bowa talks about some of Schmidt's streaks: "If he did it every day he'd be unbelievable." Tim McCarver concentrates on his fielding: "Brooks was fantastic for two or three yards on either side, but he had neither the arm nor the range of Schmitty. That's the only company Schmitty deserves to be with."

But.

He thinks too much.

Bobby Wine, who managed him in Puerto Rico: "He gets too deep"; Bowa, who subscribes to the KISS (Keep It Simple, Stupid) Theory: "If he's going real good he'll say, 'Well, this can't last.' He'll talk himself into a slump"; Ozark: "He's too concerned"; McGraw, known throughout baseball as a thinker: "He overcomplicates"; McCarver, Schmidt's personal public relations machine: "He's so very pensive"; Maddox: "He does have a tendency to think too much"; even Ken Boyer, manager of the Cardinals: "The word on him is that he can't throw off an O for 4 easily as most guys. People say he's always thinking about it."

Well, Stan Hochman, the columnist for the Philadelphia *Daily News,* describes Schmidt's method: "He'll be up at bat, and he'll think, 'Let's see, he got me out on an inside fastball last time [strike one], but he knows he can't come back with that because I remember, so if he goes low and away he's smart [strike two], but when I'm going good I can drive that pitch to right, and now I'm going good, so what if he comes high and [strike three] outside?' So he's left standing there with the bat on his shoulder."

He's too cool.

There are two aspects of this theory. Schmidt's lack of demonstrable emotion has been so pronounced during his career Ozark once told him, "I wish just once after striking out you'd get mad and tear up the clubhouse." This is the Dirt-Eater Thesis, which holds that Philly fans will never warm up to Schmidt because he neither dives enough nor breaks enough bats, batting helmets, or light bulbs in the clubhouse to show his desire. The players have stopped caring about this. "He's just not a flamboyant character," McCarver says. "When Pete Rose gets a double, it appears he's gotten three hits the way he moves around; when Mike gets a double, he hits it real hard and runs to second base and stands there. The same double, right?"

The Dirt-Eater Thesis is best expressed by Bowa, who takes care to explain first that he is a fan of Schmidt's and thinks that each day Schmidt is getting closer to his potential. Then he says, "I've got nothing natural. I've had to work at it. I've seen him get two hits his first two times up and then maybe he relaxes—maybe he says, 'I've got my two'—maybe he says, 'I'm Mike Schmidt and I'm such a Natural that I only have to give 70 or 80 percent,' but, maybe if I was in his shoes I'd be the same way.''

The other aspect of this thesis is never spoken about publicly. It has to do with race. Some Phillies think Schmidt tries to be cool because black players are cool, and maybe he'd rather be black.

It's a thesis, no more. But it stems from a few tangible things. The man does have a "black" body—wiry muscles, bubble butt, and all. The athletes he admired growing up were all black: Jim Brown, Frank Robinson, Oscar Robertson, Walt Frazier. Of Frazier he once said, "He looked pressure right in the face and remained an Ice Man." Schmidt loves black music. "Look at our albums," Donna Schmidt says. "We don't have more than two or three albums by white people [his favorite group is Earth, Wind, and Fire]." Schmidt's best friends in the club were always black: Dave Cash, Dick Allen, Garry Maddox. Schmidt says that he and Maddox, a Christian also, are inseparable on the road. Now, add the memory of the Broom Closet Incident. In 1976, in Montreal, on the day the Phillies clinched their first division title, there was a general team party in the clubhouse. But a few black Phillies, including Cash, Allen, and Maddox—and Schmidt—gathered in a broom closet at Allen's request and gave a prayer of thanks. Then they skipped the team party. Schmidt says, "I haven't thought about that in years." But Maddox remembers. He said, "I don't think it's ever really forgotten. It wasn't a good scene. It almost caused a racial split on the team." And Donna Schmidt hasn't forgotten either. She said, "Michael may not think so, but definitely some white guys on the team dislike him for it. I know. I've heard it from the wives."

Thinks too much.

Too cool.

Schmidt has a very un-Christian word for those theories. But if you want to get into it, OK, he'll get into it. So you listen close. Mike Schmidt is back on his living-room couch. Dave Landfield, his agent, is on a chair next to him. Donna and the baby are in the kitchen, but she will, from time to time, come in. We are listening to Michael Jack Schmidt, who could be the best player in baseball, talk. There is a tape recorder on the table in front of him, and he is saying some things, once and for all, that he wants said.

"Do you know how many times I've heard that I think too much? Do you know how many times it's said after I strike out a few times in a game? OK, I strike out in bunches. I'm intimidated by striking out. As much as I know why I might strike out—there's millions of reasons—I have a tough time accepting that the guy made a great pitch on me. I went the first two weeks of this season only striking out twice in 30 at-bats. I just know that in the next 30 I might go out 15 times. But I've watched Greg Luzinski strike out nine times in a row and nobody says anything. Only with me, because I'm supposed to be the superathlete. You think that's fair?

"Nobody expects Greg to do what he does. Nobody expects Pete Rose to do what he does, and when he does it people say he's the greatest player on earth because he doesn't have the ability to do it, right? People think Graig Nettles is great. He is. I rate him over me defensively. I'm in awe of him. But nobody ever said to him, 'I can't believe you only hit 30 homers and drove in 90 runs.' Hey, if ever there was a 150-RBI and 50-homer man, it's me. I just go out there and rattle off 10 in nine games anytime I want. That's what people think. What scares me is how easy it is for me a month at a time, and then how tough it is the next two weeks. In 1974, 1975, and 1976 I had 38 homers and 100 RBI and I did it all in three months. If I only need three months to have my great years, imagine if I ever put six months together. It's a matter of staying within myself and relaxing. I've always known that, but I've never been able to do it.

"That 'he thinks too much' stuff stinks. Who says it? I know Ozark says it. I don't want to say anything against Danny Ozark. He's the only big-league manager I've ever had and I have a great deal of affection for him. As a human being he's one of the finest, most likable men I've ever met. As a baseball manager Danny Ozark lacks very much in many areas. He has no quality for motivation whatsoever. He has no tact. I could manage the Phillies and be a better motivator. . . . Sure, there have been times when I've overthought. I can see where people say it about me, but they only say it when I'm going bad, when I have that look on my face. I'll be sitting in the dugout with that perplexed look on my face, where it looks like I'm trying to find the perfect batting stance. But you can bet that if I hit .350 they'll say it's because I stopped thinking, and if anyone believes that they're crazy.

" . . . Okay, now let's talk about being cool. All my life I've heard that—Schmidt thinks he's cool. They say it about anyone who doesn't show emotion. My father never showed emotion. Ask Donna. She'll tell you I'm the spitting image of my father. All you gotta do is have a mediocre year when you're making big money and you don't care, or strike out 150 times and not break a batting helmet and you don't care—you can't care. People in South Philadelphia have an image of dirt-eating major-leaguers. If they don't have dirty uniforms at the end of the game from diving or breaking stuff in the dugout, they're not trying.

"I don't know how to answer what Bowa said. None of us puts out 100 percent all the time—you can't. But nobody on that team tries harder or cares more or is in the ball game more than I am. OK, sometimes I have a problem in that if I'm going bad I dwell on what's going wrong with me and how to correct it. Maybe it hurts the team, but what about when I go 4 for 4? Nobody says I was too cool then, do they?

"Let me tell you about getting dirty. I dove for six balls already, but I couldn't get my uniform dirty because it was on Astroturf. But I jammed my thumb. I don't dive for a reason. I've got a bad left shoulder. If I land on it the wrong way, my career could be over. A lot of times I get in position without diving and I can still throw the runner out. If I dive for balls I can't, so diving for balls and getting your uniform dirty as a defensive player is a lot of crap. A lot of balls Nettles dives for—as great as he is—he could get to without diving.

" . . .What they said, I'll be the first to admit, has gotten me to dive for balls this year. I'll probably dive for 50 before the year's out. I just hope I don't dive myself out of a good year. In a sense they got to me. But don't think I'm always cool. Don't you think I've thrown my helmet? Sure I have. But my thing about that now is to be a Christian, to try to be Christ-like. Now don't take that out of context, but I tell kids, 'If Jesus Christ struck out, do you think he'd slam down his bat or break his helmet?' That's my reaction to the being-cool question. And, look, don't you think the pitcher knows he's completely gotten to me if I go, bam, throw my helmet down? I'll be an easy out the next time. But if I just stand there calmly and give the pitcher a look, like—'You know I'll get you next time.' Isn't that better? Ain't none of them I haven't caught up with yet.

"That's part of my psych. He knows it. There's 15 to 20 players in the game playing a psych game. Anyway, I'm no good at breaking things. Bowa's good at it. He comes in, throws a helmet, smashes all the light bulbs in the dugout. That's him. Then there's Willie Stargell—Gentleman Willie Stargell. He's still laying that bat down after strikeouts, and he's the all-time career leader. He'll be doing it till the day he dies—laying that bat down calmly and jerking one out the next time.

" . . .As for trying to be black, that's ridiculous. I can't even dance. It's an interesting question—why my friends are black, why most of the athletes I admired are black? I don't know. Maybe being an athlete I knew I'd have to get along with the brothers. I get along real well, you know, a lot better than most white players. I guess maybe black guys pick out white guys they think they can dig. But who the hell wants to be known as a white guy who wants to be black? I'm white. I know that. And let me tell you something that I've learned from Garry. I've had a lot of deep discussion about race with Garry. He's very sensitive. All white people have prejudice—all of them. But I've got as little as possible. If people say I try to be black, I can't take that as a compliment, but if they mean that I'm trusting like black people, that I'm honest like the black people I've know, that's fine. Sure, I remember what happened in Montreal now that you mention it. We singled ourselves out and that was wrong. Tug McGraw brought it up. 'Why did the blacks . . . blah-blah-blah?' But it's dead now. You know I grew up in this all-white neighborhood. My high school was all white and mostly Jewish. I was scared to death of blacks. Maybe that has something to do with it.

"Maybe we're getting too heavy with all this. If we talk too much, it'll get more than one paragraph, and that's all I want to have. Just say that I get along well with black players and I'm proud of it."

The monologue took up almost an hour. By the end, when Donna said the chicken was ready and everyone should come in and eat, Schmidt's shirt was soaked with sweat.

The talk at the table was refreshingly small. Schmidt explained some of his fidgety habits on the field, scooping up dirt to keep his hands dry because he gets sweaty palms—"And how cool is that?"—picking up pebbles near third so often that it seems his father was a Hoover and his mother an Electrolux. Then he got on the subject of Pete Rose's obsession with statistics. Schmidt is an unabashed admirer of Rose, a man whose ego is approximately the size of the Arctic Circle. "I never met a guy who would wear a T-shirt with his own picture on it and the word *Superstar* underneath the picture and pull it off," Schmidt said. "But the guy is just super. You know how he knows all his own numbers? Like how many right-handed doubles he needs for another record, or how many left-handed walks in the bottom of the fifth—all those crazy numbers? Well, he says them so much he's got me memorizing his numbers. But the amazing thing is, he knows my numbers. I'll hit a homer and he'll say, 'Six more for 200.' He's unbelievable."

He was actually starstruck.

Donna noticed it too. She leaned forward.

"Sure, Pete'll have an effect on me, a positive effect. He'll take a lot of pressure off me. But people don't print it when I say that Dave Cash had the same effect on me in 1974. Dave, Pete, Dick Allen, these are guys you know are successful, and when you know they hold you up there with themselves—when they sit on the bench next to you and confide in you—there's no reason to doubt yourself. If they think that much of you, you must be a pretty good dude."

Donna cannot believe this. She opened for the Byrds. Stars, she knows. Her smile says—Gimme a break already. Catch up to me.

There is little time left before Schmidt must go to the park. How can you let him go without asking about the World Series?

"The World Series?" Schmidt asks. "The World Series? Oh, yeah. I'd love to let it all out and get flowin' in the World Series. Let the world see how good I could be."

Even as he spoke, the sweat was once again beginning to seep onto his shirt. And as he instinctively went into his hitting stance it was clear that he was already pumped up, so very pumped up.

HORSE RACING

NOTHING LEFT BUT HEART

By Edwin Pope

From the Miami Herald
Copyright, ©, 1979, Miami Herald

Suddenly the coronation was a funeral.

Desperately 220 yards from horse racing's twelfth Triple Crown Saturday, the almost mythological colt named Spectacular Bid began bucking his rear and staggering like a pack mule pushed too far up the mountain.

A yellow-silked streak named Coastal shot inside him to win the eleventh Belmont Stakes.

Bid's merely losing was trauma redoubled.

But the three-and-a-quarter-length victory by Coastal, who had won only $80,669 to Spectacular Bid's $1,123,587, was not just over the Kentucky Derby and Preakness champion.

It was the margin between Coastal ($10.80, $4.80, $2.10) and Golden Act.

Bid finished a shamed third, a neck behind Golden Act. Worse, he finished as though the farther the race would have gone, the farther back he would be.

Did Bid's jockey, 19-year-old Ronnie Franklin, blow it?

You could not severely fault Franklin for what became Spectacular Bid's first poor race after an unprecedented 12 straight stakes victories coming in here.

"He ought to go right for the lead," Lucien Laurin, trainer of 1973 Triple Crown king Secretariat, had said Saturday morning.

Franklin did. It was part of his undoing. He had been instructed to die, if he must, in front, to avoid possible trouble.

"Ronnie rode a perfect ride," said trainer Bud Delp, eating crow as graciously as any man ever did. "He rode the race I would have ridden had I been the jockey. A rider can't carry a horse. A lot of exceptional horses can't go a mile and a half. I now have to assume Spectacular Bid is one of them."

Probably. But I have to wonder what a more experienced rider—
say, an Angel Cordero—might have done with a horse dying under
him in the stretch.

Cordero has his detractors but he can hold a horse together better
than any jock alive. I remember watching Cordero do just that three
years ago in this same race in the same Belmont Park stretch.

It's academic anyway. Ronnie was doing what the trainer told him
to do.

But when Franklin pumped Bid into the lead past Gallant Best
entering the backstretch, he was going against the colt's nature. Bid
rebels at being forced to run hard early.

And when Coastal came barreling withers to the rail down the
highway of loam that all America had expected Spectacular Bid to
have to himself, Bid had nothing left to offer but heart.

"Spectacular Bid just wore down the last furlong," Franklin said.
"He was rank [wouldn't relax] before the race and also during it.
Then he 'gargled,' sort of coughed and rattled, about the three-
eighths pole, and he couldn't make it the last eighth of a mile."

The Belmont at its draining mile and a half is American racing's
prototype marathon. The human original, like Spectacular Bid's
horsey equivalent, was born in tragedy.

Legend has it that Greek warrior Phidippides ran home from
Marathon bearing news of beating the Persians. He dropped dead at
the end of 26 miles 385 yards.

At 5:39 P.M. Saturday, Belmont Park track announcer Marshall
Cassidy bellowed, "The flag is up!"

Colts were in the gate for The Race of No Excuses.

Just past 5:41 P.M., at that part of the race where eight other colts
had fumbled the third jewel of the Triple Crown, Ronnie Franklin
must have been asking himself what Olympic gold medal mara-
thoner Frank Shorter since has asked of Phidippides: "Why couldn't
he have dropped at 20 miles?"

Spectacular Bid under Franklin had hit the dreaded "wall."

And William Haggin Perry's Coastal, the Majestic Prince-Alluvial
colt ridden by 28-year-old Panamanian Ruben Hernandez, rammed
the wall as though it were tissue.

Hernandez had moved to send his colt outside Spectacular Bid a
furlong from the wire.

"But then I see him drifting out, and I go inside," Hernandez said.
"I could tell Bid was weakening gradually. I knew I still had a big
handful of horse."

Too big for Bid.

I had trembled in 1973 when Secretariat creamed Gallant Man's
16-year-old Belmont record of 2:26 3/5 by 2 3/5 seconds in that
historic 31-length runaway.

Saturday simply left me numb—with thousands of other "bridge-jumpers" who sent in $699,999 to win on Spectacular Bid at 1–5 odds.

Even Coastal's 34-year-old trainer David Whiteley sounded shocked.

"Five eighths of a mile from home [when Coastal was fourth behind Bid, General Assembly and Gold Act], I thought we were dead," Whiteley said. "I turned to Mr. Perry and said, 'Let's hope he's just waiting.' "

Coastal was.

He cut down Spectacular Bid as clinically as Bid had annihilated everything he had run against since last August.

"It was a terribly slow last mile," Whiteley said. "A minute and 41 seconds."

That was 4 1/5 seconds slower than Affirmed's record-closing mile last year.

"Coastal was shortening stride the last one-sixteenth mile," Whiteley said "Obviously he was getting tired, but still he was drawing away from the others. They were all tired. The others must have been tireder than mine."

Bid was supposed to get tired.

Two days ago Whiteley was told that an expert handicapper felt that Coastal, raced only three times this year, was coming to the Belmont the sharpest of any dark horse since Stage Door Johnny upset Forward Pass in 1968.

"That guy is more confident than I am," Whiteley said.

Coastal's $10.80 payoff was the same as Stage Door Johnny's.

Conspicuously absent was any competitive confrontation between Franklin and General Assembly's rider Cordero. They have been playing Russian roulette with horses for bullets through the Preakness and here this last week.

General Assembly dropped as though pole-axed in the stretch turn. He finished sixth, reinforcing wonder as to why owner Bert Firestone wanted to enter him after his Derby and Preakness shortfalls.

Cordero seemed more pleased by Franklin's defeat than chastened by General Assembly's late listlessness.

"Ruben, we win this for all the spics," Cordero, the Puerto Rican, screamed to Hernandez. The reference was to Franklin's ethnic slur of "those spics" in accusing Cordero and Panamanian Jorge Velasquez of unsuccessfully trying to gang him in the Florida Derby.

Then Cordero addressed a band of reporters.

"Look at your super horse now. You write and write for weeks that this Spectacular Bid is a super horse. Super horse, super bleep."

Cordero paused, savoring revenge. "Every turkey has his Thanksgiving."

Yet even in the dreary collapse of the "super horse," there was a Faulknerian exhilaration at Coastal's emergence practically from nowhere.

"It is not just betting," William Faulkner wrote years ago, "that draws people to horse races. It is much deeper than that. It is a sublimation, transference: Man, with his admiration for speed and strength, physical power far beyond what he himself is capable of, projects his own desire for physical supremacy onto the agent . . ."

Saturday's agent was supremely Coastal, oceanically swallowing the horse we all thought was the greatest mouthful extant.

FOOTBALL

IN PURSUIT OF LOFTIER GOALS

By Jim Smith

From Newsday
Copyright, © 1979, Newsday Inc.

There was a steady drizzle at dusk, and Homer Smith clutched the collar of his beige raincoat as he trotted up the steps of ancient Andover Hall at the Harvard Divinity School. The cornerstone had two dates, 1807 and 1910. "There's a feeling of permanence here," Smith said. "That's what I like about it."

He walked briskly down a marble-floored corridor. It was lined on one side with stained-glass windows, on the other with crammed bulletin boards. "This is where I have my Islam class," Smith said, motioning to a dark room littered with one-arm desks. "Today's class was about the mystical elements in Islamic religious history. About famous mystics—saints, martyrs. It was beautiful. Almost sexy. Just a delicious 50 minutes."

The drone of intense conversation wafted into the classroom from a cocktail party next door. "I usually go to these things," Smith said, peering inside. "This is the first one I've missed. They want you to take part in school life." He stopped in for a minute to chat with a friend, Fernando Viesca, 30, from San Antonio. The two had been assigned to make a joint class presentation.

"Fernando's going to carry our discussion Monday," Smith said, tongue firmly in cheek. "I'm going to ride on his coattails."

Viesca laughed, sipping wine from a plastic cup. "He's kidding," Viesca said. "From his participation in class, I know he's very assertive. He has knowledge and he's not afraid to express it. And he's logical. He strips things to the bone and works from solid ground. I thought he might be from a seminary or something. Somebody clipped an article from the paper that he was coming over. To me, he's just another student."

Until last December 2, Homer Smith, 47, was the West Point football coach.

Kathryn Smith said her husband had talked of becoming a minister during high school back in Omaha, Nebraska. It's just that three decades of football intervened. Smith says he is not sure whether he would like to don a religious collar now. But he is enrolled at the 350-student nonsectarian divinity school as a special student in a two-year program, and his wife's family are helping him pay the $3,300 tuition.

"I've studied every day for 32 days," Smith said, "like a starved man going after food—and I was starved. I'm taking my first early steps toward something I think is the most important of all work, resolving conflicts among nations. I'm going to apply for jobs in about a year and a half—to foundations, schools, and maybe foreign governments. I'm not sure exactly what I'll do. But I have faith that if you keep your health and work steadily, good things happen."

Smith and his wife rent a second-floor, two-bedroom condominium apartment in a big, old, restored (circa 1860) house on Harvard Street. The furnishings are early American, with a wood-burning stove, framed parchments on the walls, and a female golden retriever—Bambi—curled up cozily on the living-room rug.

The apartment is within walking distance of the muddy Charles River, bustling Harvard Square, and the school. Smith walks home for lunch every day, sometimes works out at the Harvard gym, and spends nights in his study studying. "We've had only one guest here in 32 days," he said, "the administrator I called about coming here."

Mementos of Smith's football past are carefully boxed in the cellar. There are no team pictures on the walls, no trophies on the mantelpiece. The only evidence of his connection with the Military Academy is a brass nameplate on a black captain's chair in the study. It is a gift from the 1975 Army football team.

"Football was all I thought about from seventh grade until last December," he said. "There was never a time—even when I was in the Army—that it wasn't foremost in my mind. There were only two falls in all that time that I wasn't on the gridiron. This is a wrenching experience that I've not completely gone through yet."

Smith had known all season that he would be fired if Army lost to Navy last fall. He says he got virtually no support the entire year from Army athletic director Raymond P. Murphy, superintendent Lt. Gen. Andrew J. Goodpaster, and deputy superintendent Brig. Gen. Charles W. Bagnal. The previous season's success—7–4 and a 17–14 victory over Navy—merely postponed Smith's firing.

Kathryn Smith said she sat alone in an end zone seat at West Point's Michie Stadium for home games last season. "It bothered me to hear people saying such ugly, hateful things about kids who were trying so hard," she said. "Coaching is a very stressful occupation. Not only the games. Your lives become intermingled with the lives of so many people. It's hard sitting up there hearing people criticize the players and the coaches for dropping passes."

When Navy beat Army, 28–0, on December 2 in Philadelphia, the Smiths knew that their days in the rent-free "Coach's House" across Lusk Reservoir from the stadium were over. His contract, for $28,000, expired January 31. Smith's five-year record at Army was 21–33–1; he was 1–4 against Navy. His last team went 4–6–1.

"Coaching is terminal," Smith said. "How many of 'em go to 65? I entered the profession in 1958. How many of the people I entered with are still around? Maybe one fourth?

"Why do we do it? I think it's an addiction to all the feelings—the locker room after the victory, the sweat, and the intimate communication with players and their problems. The people in coaching want it very, very much. I wanted it very much. I thought I did pretty good. But I'm not sure I had the opportunity to build an impressive record during my years at Army."

The day after the Navy game the Smiths followed in a car behind the Army team bus on the way back from Philadelphia. When they stopped for lunch along the way, Smith said he addressed the team, telling the players he was resigning.

"There was stone-silence," Smith said. "I told them. 'Men, I had to win. I'm history.' It's up to you to build and sustain the program. I hope you get a great football coach—and I hope he keeps the staff.' Then I just turned and walked out. Twenty-four hours earlier I had been their leader. Most of them I recruited and knew intimately."

The Smiths then continued the drive to West Point. Near their house a close woman friend saw them drive up. She turned her back and scurried into her house. "My wife was shattered," Smith said. "She cried. I told her, 'Let's make a move; let's drive to Cambridge.' " (Smith said he had called the divinity school in advance, anticipating a move.) He telephoned assistant coaches Mike Mikolayunas and Ed Wilson to tell them where he was going and that he had resigned.

"The next morning I called the office [from Cambridge] at 7:50 and Wilson told me to call my brother's number in Omaha."

Smith's youngest brother, Dean, had been killed when his car slid on ice and struck a train. The Smiths drove back to West Point, "I said to the deputy superintendent, 'I give you the easiest problem you've ever had.' And he [deputy superintendent Bagnal] came over to my house with a typed statement, held it in front of my face, and asked me if I wanted to sign it. I told him, 'My brother's dead.' "

The statement was Army's announcement that Smith's contract was not being renewed. It spoke of a need for "revitalization" of the program. Smith said he refused to sign it. "I really wanted to leave in an orderly way," he said. "I really did." He didn't.

The headlines across the nation read: "ARMY COACH HOMER SMITH FIRED."

Two weeks later, on December 17, Smith released an eight-page statement to the Associated Press detailing what he described as the "organizational hell" he lived with during five years at West Point. He charged Army officials with numerous NCAA recruiting violations. The allegations received national attention and sparked an NCAA investigation. This week, Dave Berst, NCAA director of enforcement, said he could not comment on the status of the investigation.

"I had asked them for an apology," Smith said, "I wanted to resign—to exit gracefully. I thought I had, to the team. No coach should have had to put up with that. I had people standing around at the funeral home asking me questions about football. It was just the most awful thing in the world. I went to pieces when my brother died. And they put out that statement. If I wanted to stay in athletics or in coaching, 75 percent of my opportunities were canceled. I can't believe it was not malicious."

Smith responded by charging Army officials with:

• Transporting prep-school prospects to and from West Point and not counting their visits among the NCAA's allowed number.

• Using more assistant coaches (14) than the NCAA permits.

• Telling B-squad coaches to recruit—a violation.

• Feeding extra meals to prospects who came to West Point for physicals.

Academy officials characterized Smith's allegations as "sour grapes," claiming that the violations were "old stuff" and had been corrected by 1978. "The biggest violation was that they covered it up," Smith said. "God, the pressure they put on those cadets to tell the truth. I heard all this talk about honor and I was worried, because we were into things that were clearly illegal."

Smith said that his program also was disrupted by a scandal involving illegal telephone calls by two players in 1975 which split the team and coaches; four players' involvement in the academy-wide honor-code involvement of 1976; and a written ultimatum to Smith that mandated seven victories in 1977, including one over Navy.

West Point officials secretly revamped Army's football scouting system midway through the 1977 season, Smith said, taking away all recruiting responsibilities from his six civilian assistant coaches. They also removed a black assistant coach, Larry Lock, from his job as a recruiter in Texas in a move that Smith interpreted as racially motivated. "It was an earthquake," Smith said.

After that season, Smith said, he was ordered to fire two civilian assistants—Dick Bowman and the late Bruce Tarbox. He refused. The men were fired, anyway.

Smith got only a one-year contract for 1978—even after achieving the goals spelled out in the ultimatum of January 21, 1977.

"As soon as that happened," Smith said, "I was an object of curiosity, something to be observed. Much as I wanted everything to hum again, I just couldn't get it going. We had some injuries. We lost some games we shouldn't have." Homer Smith went out a loser. It was quite unlike his entrance.

Smith had started for three years as a fullback at Princeton. He was captain, all-East and all-Ivy League in 1952 and 1953. He was class president and the winner of Princeton's outstanding athlete award. He served two years as an Army artillery officer, then earned a master's degree in business administration at Stanford.

Smith remained at Stanford as freshman football coach and director of recruiting through 1960, then spent four years as offensive backfield coach at the Air Force Academy. In 1965 he accepted his first head coaching job, at Davidson College, and by 1969 he took Davidson to the Tangerine Bowl. Smith was head coach at the University of the Pacific the next two years, before joining Pepper Rodger's staff at UCLA. The Bruins were 17–4 his two years there.

"My jobs were all difficult jobs," said Smith. "Except at UCLA—which was my only chance to coach highly recruited athletes.

"A coach knows his job is terminal and when he gets fired for losing he should not complain. Every young coach should have to sign a statement that he understands that before he goes into it. I know that sounds like I'm talking out of both sides of my mouth [because he blasted Army], but the game is played in front of people who demand to have hope, demand to win.

"A football coach has to produce a winner. It's a law of life. I never minded the ultimatum—never. I got up from that round-table meeting that year, one of my coaches called me and we said, 'At least we know what we have to do. Let's go to work.' No one ever tried harder to get the job done.

"Why did I become so bitter? Well, it's obvious that I have. My bitterness is as hard as granite rocks. I never was given a chance to resign. When I got back from my brother's funeral I stood in the kitchen and read the papers on the counter. It just blew my mind. The athletic director had made comments about my management, use of time, and leadership. I had been through hell. It was a tough time. I didn't need that. They broke me. They just broke me."

His spirit sagged, but Smith kept his sanity. He seems very much in control now, sure that he is on the right path, relieved to be out of coaching. While his wife figured out their 1978 income tax in the bedroom the other night, Smith philosophized in his study. He would not indict the system, only the Army officials whom he thought had wronged him.

"Coaching keeps you so busy you hardly have the time to read a newspaper during the season. It's all-consuming." Smith said.

"That's the way it should be. It should consume you. I think coaches are remarkable men who put up with enormous pressure.

"I took trips to watch people coach. At times I was very competent technically. I went everywhere all over the country where good wishbones [offenses] were played. I wrote a book on installing the wishbone. I like to remember that I coached the team which scored the most points in one quarter [49] at Davidson.

"I didn't think I was the greatest football coach in the land. I think probably my greatest shortcoming was that my mind wandered too much into the drama of it. Like, I played [running back] Jim Meriken more than I should have against Navy this year. I was a softy, yes. I had seen the effort he'd made to get well [from an injury], his urgency about getting ready to try to play. His playing contributed to the defeat. To coach properly you have to be pure—make a purposeful effort to win.

"Woody Hayes to me is one of the greatest ever to put a whistle on a shoestring, because he's a real purist. He focused on winning, and in doing so his players had great experiences along the way. I think Woody, Bear [Bryant] are better football coaches because of their aloofness. As a head coach I think I lacked something there."

It was suggested by an Army insider at the press conference at which Smith's successor, Lou Saban, was presented on January 5 that "the easiest hour the players had each day was the one Homer had them." Smith disputed that. "At UCLA," he said, "they told me I couldn't be that tough. I was as tough as anybody on the field. We had an hour and 53 minutes to practice at Army—10 minutes less than the year before. The most limited amount of time of any major-college team in the nation. Something like that is insulting to me and my staff.

"I don't blame them for regarding me as persona non grata up there now. I knew it would happen. I thought long and hard about that. I thought about my daughter marrying a West Pointer [former Army quarterback Leamon Hall]. About going to reunions. But I couldn't accept what happened to me. I've got the feeling they're not going to bring me back for anything. Cahill, Hall, Paul Dietzel [other losing Army coaches]—they haven't been back, either.

"I wouldn't say there's no chance [of returning to coaching]. But I did not succeed in coaching. It ended with the score 28–0 and I accepted that as stoically as anyone ever did, I recognize a feeling of anonymity now. When you're in coaching you are anything but anonymous. I can browse in a bookstore now."

In Smith's last theology class there was a discussion of Langdon Gilkey's "Naming the Whirlwind." "It was about where secularism leaves you," Smith said. "At the abyss—represented by questions like 'What? Where? When? Why?' God-questions. They are as inevitable as the sunrise. Ultimate questions." Smith will ponder them.

"It's a fast-moving life-style I have now," he said. "One dictated by academic requirements. I study about nine hours a day. I'm not sure what job I will seek. If I could organize a course on the subject of world conflict—with the idea of resolving it, and teaching it to good students—that would be an exciting trip for me.

"I want to have in my 16 courses [over two years] some sense of completeness. Next semester I want to take Hinduism and Catholicism. I very much want to take an ethics course in the business school, and something on international legal questions. I want to feel I had a good tune-up job when I finish. Right now I'm batting 4 for 4. Four excellent courses. Confucius would say, 'Homer, don't get too excited about this.' But I am."

Is Smith worried about starting a new career so late in life? "The most important things you need to prepare for an abrupt change in life," said Smith, who describes himself as a Christian, "are health and faith. I think I have faith. People have put up with a lot while holding onto their faith. Solzhenitsyn wouldn't take [exchange] anything for his first prison cell—where he started to feel his strength growing.

"I've had a traumatic experience, but my excitement over the teachers and the course content here has eclipsed whatever else is down inside me. How many men would like to be studying, would like a sabbatical? That's what Leamon Hall told me when I told him I had a chance to go to UCLA as an assistant this year. He said, "I think you should take a sabbatical."

BOXING

BOXING'S HIS BUSINESS

By Phil Berger

From The New York Times Magazine
Copyright, ©, 1979, Phil Berger

The moon is dimming in the early-morning sky over Landover, Maryland, as two men appear at the top of a hilly street called Belle Haven.

One wears a rust-colored knit mask that covers his face except for slits where the eyes and mouth are supposed to be. The other has on a blue watch cap that is pulled back on his head, revealing a high-cheekboned dolorous face.

At the bottom of the hill is George Palmer Highway. On the corner is a shoe store designated as the place where they are to meet a pair of strangers—one with a note pad, the other with a camera—whom they find sitting on the hood of a rented car.

"Who you waiting for?" the one in the knit mask asks.

Told it's Sugar Ray they want, he rolls the mask up his face and smiles, an agreeable 100-kilowatt smile that has become as much Ray Leonard's trademark as the deft footwork and blurring combinations of punches that constitute his wage-earning skills.

At 5:52 A.M. on this cool spring day, there is good reason to be cheered at the thought of being Ray Charles Leonard. For as he and the other man, his fighter-brother Roger, cross George Palmer Highway on the start of a three-mile jaunt through Prince Georges County, Leonard is professional boxing's newest hero, an undefeated welterweight (147 pound limit), with high standing in the boxing rankings and in television's Nielsen ratings as well. The 23-year-old Leonard has fought on all three major networks and Home Box Office, and has become a unique commodity, a contender whose box-office appeal exceeds that of most of the current champions. Already, the former gold medalist at the 1976 Montreal Olympics is being groomed as the man to fill the void created by the apparent retirement of Muhammad Ali. As the fight game's newest hero, Leonard has rapidly progressed through the pro ranks—maneuvered by sharp boxing and business minds. With a 22–0 record, he is on the verge of a title shot, an opportunity he puts on the line this afternoon when he fights Tony Chiaverini, a rugged southpaw, on ABC-TV.

Leonard's appeal is based, in part, on a boxing style evocative of past crowd pleasers like Kid Gavilan and Ray Robinson (a.k.a. Sugar Ray) and Ali himself—fighters so smooth, so photogenic as to bring an element of art to a brutal sport. But there is more to the success of Leonard than his flash in the prizefight ring and the skein of victories—several over ranking fighters—that it has produced. Quite simply, Leonard, by the variable magic of personality, has become a hero, the reasons for which go beyond the euphonious name, the smile, and the style.

"What everybody gets with Ray," says Eddie Hrica, a matchmaker from the Baltimore-Washington, D.C., area, "is the all-American boy. He loves Mom, apple pie, the American flag. His kind has been gone for a while. But Ray is bringing it back."

Warming to his subject, Hrica says, "There's a boy named Bobby Haburchak—maybe 12, 13 years old—who's a great fan of Ray's and comes to his fights in a wheelchair because he suffers from cerebral palsy. Well, Ray always makes it a point to spend time with him at each fight. One night, Ray gave the boy the set of gloves he fought with and autographed them. Bobby's mother wrote me. I've got the letter, I think. Yes. Here. 'Dear Mr. Hrica. Thank you doesn't seem sufficient. If you could have seen how happy all of you made my boy. He is still riding high.'

"And the thing with Ray is he doesn't do things like this for show. One time Ray made money for a TV commercial and ended up donating it to the Palmer Park [Maryland] Recreation Center, where he learned boxing. Donated it so they could buy equipment. And it never got in the newspapers or anything.

"That's typical. With the money Ray's earned in boxing [in excess of $2 million to date], he's become the provider for his whole family. He could have said this is all mine. But instead he's taken over the role as the head of the family. I've never met anyone who did not like him or feel he was genuine."

In a business where the working stiffs utter slanders about one another as routinely as hello/good-bye, boxing men tend to sound out of character when speaking of Ray Leonard, resorting to the kind of nice-Nelly idioms more familiar to a church supper than the manly art. And yet such is Leonard's reputation that the truth compels these ready encomiums. In an era of athletes spoiled rotten by inflated salaries and given to outrageous egotism, Leonard is an anachronism: He is nice. A Joe Palooka. A straight shooter.

The he looks the part does not hurt either. Leonard is clean-cut and smooth-featured. And though he is by nature a private person, not covetous of the spotlight, he takes on a glow when he is before the public. The smile, the soft speech—reasoned and mostly grammatical—convey an essential decency.

Heroic in deed, Leonard is cut from ordinary dimensions. At 5-9½, 147 pounds, he is not constructed with the brute-force V torso of many fighters but along sleeker, merely mortal lines. After an epoch of the larger-than-life Ali, this is a swing back the other way.

The gym is in Capitol Heights, Maryland, a white-frame building set atop a sloping lawn. The sign says Oakcrest Community Center. Sugar Ray Leonard trains here. The place is a disappointment to those seeking the colorful seediness associated with the fight game. Oakcrest is a long, low-ceilinged room, clean and well-lighted. No debris clutters the floor. A sign reads: "Our gym is your gym. While you are using it, keep it C-L-E-A-N [signed] Jake."

"Jake" is David Jacobs, a balding sunny man whose portly figure belies the fact that he fought professionally as a featherweight nearly 30 years ago. Jacobs trained Leonard as an amateur in Palmer Park and has stayed on in that role since Leonard turned pro.

Moving through Oakcrest—he is boxing director there—Jacobs has the clear-eyed serene manner of a man at peace with the world. Something of his role as a deacon in the Pentecostal Holiness Church in Washington, D.C., is reflected in the signs that proliferate among the fight posters at Oakcrest: "Any man that believes in God is a winner," and, "Do unto others as you would have them do unto you."

On the afternoon of Leonard's early-hour roadwork, Jacobs is on his knees in the gym's green canvas ring, sparring with five-year-old Ray Charles Leonard Jr., who is frequently referred to as "The Little Sugar Man." A few weeks earlier, Sugar Ray's son had put on boxing mitts and tried them out by belaboring the ring posts, an experience he found so satisfying that he has insisted on regular workouts ever since.

On this day, Sugar Ray Sr. is seated outside the ring in street clothes as Jacobs circles on his knees, encouraging the boy ("There you go. Yessssirrr. Good shot.") to assault a padded red glove that the trainer wears. "Miss the glove and hit Jake one time," a ringsider jokes.

As Ray Jr. rests between rounds, an observer tries to trick him, shouting, "Tiiiime," the gym equivalent of a bell. The boy looks straight ahead, not budging. When Jacob cries "Tiiime," he moves out smartly from his corner, his sharp-witted response provoking laughter.

Later, Leonard himself works out. He shadowboxes, hits heavy and speed bags, all in five-minute timed rounds. The session is conducted in a not overly martial atmosphere. Family and friends stop by and kibitz; laughter is not considered out of place. Even Roger Leonard, a prelim fighter who must box in his brother's considerable shadow, is able to joke about his lack of fame.

JACOBS: Roger, where's your black robe at?

ROGER: I don't know. One of my many fans stole it.

Jacobs and others stagger around the gym in amusement. The laughter subsides; soon the workout is over. Jacobs peels the gauze wrapping from Ray's hands, telling him: "Gotta take care of them million-dollar hands."

"Two million, Jake," says Leonard, smiling. "Inflation."

In August 1976, when Ray Leonard returned to Palmer Park from the Olympics, his visions did not include the lofty finances of big-time boxing. After he won the gold medal, he told the press: "This is my last fight. My decision is final. My journey is ended. My dream fulfilled."

Back home, he planned to enroll in college and to enjoy the spoils of Olympic glory: his picture on the Wheaties box, subsidiary income rolling in. The reality fell short of that. Way short.

Days after his return to Palmer Park, the *Washington Star* ran a story under a bold-faced headline that read: "SUGAR RAY'S PATERNITY SUIT." The "suit" came about after Juanita Wilkinson, the mother of Ray Jr., applied for public assistance. At the time, Leonard (who never denied paternity) was in Montreal. As the *Star*'s ombudsman, George Beveridge, later wrote: "First impressions are important. And standing alone, [that headline] could well have suggested to readers that the question of Leonard's paternity might itself be at issue. It wasn't—the 'suit' to affirm legal paternity was, as the story said, a part of the mechanism required in Maryland to determine an applicant's eligibility for public assistance."

Things were to grow worse. Leonard's sudden celebrity brought out the schemers and scam men, with offers and ideas supposedly to enhance Ray's fiscal position. But when it got down to the gritty particulars, Leonard's end of things somehow was always on hold.

The irony was that Ray was running himself ragged, driving long distances to speak to school-age audiences for free. At the same time, he was finding that his Olympic celebrity was yesterday's news. Accompanying his insurance salesman friend Janks Morton, 39, on his daily rounds, Leonard was often met by blank stares when he was introduced to prospective policyholders.

Though he had declared he was through fighting, people tried to change Leonard's mind. He and Morton went to New York in late September 1976 as guests of fight promoter Don King at the Ali-Ken Norton championship fight and came back with an offer to turn pro. Other offers followed. By now, Morton, a college football player who had himself tried but failed to make it professionally with the Cleveland Browns, moved to get Leonard's life in order. He brought Ray to Michael G. Trainer, a Silver Spring, Maryland, attorney, to sort out the complications that had arisen after Leonard's success at Montreal.

Working for several months without a fee, Trainer hired a publicist to sift through requests for personal appearances. And he himself screened offers involving commercial possibilities, circumspectly asking all callers to put their proposals in writing, a request that killed off most of the deadbeats.

Leonard's life simplified, but he now was having second thoughts about boxing. Before the Olympics, his mother had suffered a minor heart affliction. And now his father required hospitalization for a lingering serious illness. "I saw," says Leonard, "that the family was not moving." He also saw the obvious. Ray Charles Leonard was about to be Sugar Ray again.

There was one hitch, though. As an amateur, Leonard had chafed when professional fight managers referred to their charges as "my fighter" or "my boy"—the possessive pronoun had a demeaning sound to him. So while he wanted to turn pro, he did not want to be owned.

That obstacle was overcome after Trainer remembered that he had borrowed money from a bank to launch himself as a lawyer. He decided to put together a group of backers that would lend Sugar Ray the capital to get started and would receive in turn 8 percent interest on the loan.

As word of his idea got out, Trainer was so besieged with calls from interested parties he convened a public meeting. "What happened," he says, "was, I guess, predictable. A traveling salesman—he sold jewelry—said he'd put money up if Ray would go on the road and help him sell twice a week. A retail store owner wanted Ray to work the floor once a week. I told them to get out, adjourned the meeting, and decided to ask only friends and clients for the money."

Trainer got 24 people to kick in $21,000, and then incorporated the fighter as Sugar Ray Leonard Inc. "I issued all the stock to Ray," he says, "and signed him to a personal services contract with the corporation."

The wheels were in motion. Jacobs signed as Leonard's trainer. Morton became assistant trainer and adviser. Trainer agreed to continue handling business matters. Only one thing was lacking: expertise in the pro boxing business. "The only way I could see Ray being sidetracked," says Trainer, "was if we got snookered. We needed someone who knew the business inside out. We wanted every edge we could have."

Enter Angelo Dundee.

Angelo Dundee is a small wiry 56-year-old, most noted for being the trainer of Muhammad Ali.

In Ali's first fight against Sonny Liston—back when Muhammad was Cassius Clay—it was Dundee who pushed his fighter off the stool at the start of the fifth round when Ali, semiblinded from liniment in his eyes, wanted to quit. Ali ended up as heavyweight champion that night.

Angelo is an old-school boxing man. In 1948, he quit his job as an inspector of naval aircraft in Philadelphia and moved to New York, living and sleeping in the Capitol Hotel office of his brother Chris, then a fight manager. The hotel was catty-corner from the old Madison Square Garden on Eighth Avenue (between Forty-ninth and Fiftieth streets) and was a few blocks from Stillman's Gym.

At Stillman's—and in boxing arenas—Dundee was educated by a now vanishing breed of wily trainers. Angelo got an eyeful. "Like one night, I saw Ray Arcel do something. His fighter knocked the other guy down. And as the referee counted, Arcel climbed the steps to the ring and made like he was throwing the robe over his fighter's shoulders. What this did was divert the referee. He got confused with the count, and counted the guy out even though the guy had gotten up in time. Well, a few years later, I'm managing a featherweight named Bill Bossio. Same thing happens. The knockdown, the robe, and the messed-up count. I cut Bossio's gloves off real quick while the other guy's corner is screaming bloody murder about the fast count."

A fighter of Angelo's is not apt to be snookered. Nor is he likely to be overmatched. Dundee has a wide-ranging knowledge of opponents. and what he doesn't know he can find out. Angelo is an easygoing man, who tells you, "Costs nothing to be nice." As a result of that congenial outlook, Dundee's friends in boxing are legion. In a pinch, he can phone anywhere in the country or to Latin America (Dundee speaks fluent Spanish, learned while handling fighters in pre-Castro Cuba) and get the lowdown on a prospective opponent.

The sentiment among boxing people is that Dundee has done his job well, that Leonard has grown as a fighter in a series of measured tests. Slow-teach, Dundee calls it. Others refer to it as the Thumbscrew principle. By either label, it refers to the small and calculated risk an astute manager exposes his fighter to in each opponent, hoping his man has the "reach"—the ability to stretch his skills to meet the increasing challenges.

Though Dundee is Leonard's manager of record, he hasn't the proprietary hold most fight managers have over their boxers, a clout beginning with a 30 percent or better cut of the athlete's purses and usually including contractual renewal clauses that can lock a pugilist in with a manager far longer than he might desire. Dundee's share of Leonard's earnings is reportedly 15 percent and his role is not as domineering as the average enfranchised-manager.

In fact, Dundee does not turn up in the Leonard camp until several days before a bout. He checks out the arrangements for the fight, watches the final workouts that Jacobs conducts (offering an occasional insight), and helps promote the fight by being a quotable source for the news media. During a fight, though, it is Dundee who addresses the boxer between rounds.

Dundee's approach has brought Leonard to world-class status—he is ranked No. 3 by the World Boxing Council and No. 2 by the World Boxing Association. Frequently, though, Leonard has outrun Angelo's slow-teach pace. In March 1978, for instance, Dundee matched Leonard against Javier Muniz. Muniz had gone the distance in a 10-round bout against Roberto Duran, the hard-punching former lightweight champion, a certifiable indication, Dundee felt, of the staying power he wanted Leonard's next foe to have. Sugar Ray knocked Muniz out in 2 minutes and 45 seconds of the first round.

Against most foes, Leonard has been simply too quick and too clever. "Ray's success," says Dundee, "is based on doing what he has to do to be champ. He never flubs on his roadwork or rest. He don't burn the candle. He's clean-living. Family-oriented. And he's a little like Muhammad—he's a student of boxing. You should see him studying boxing films. I think he's the happiest when he's sitting in front of the TV with the Betamax and a bunch of cassettes of different fights."

For his pro debut in February 1977 against Luis (The Bull) Vega, CBS-TV paid Leonard $10,000. Sugar Ray added $30,000 more from his share of the $72,329 gate. By March he was in the enviable position of owning himself.

Trainer's approach with his incorporated fighter has been to maintain nearly complete control of Leonard's commercial potential, rather than relying on fight promoters to stimulate his revenues (and take the lion's share of the profits).

"OK," says Trainer. "Let's say you want to promote a Leonard fight. Forget TV. We get all the TV money, though we'll black out your market. As promoter, you'll work off the gate. But before we walk in, we get a guarantee [in a letter of credit]—and we'll also end up with a percentage of the gate—usually at least half the net profits.

"I'll ask you to figure what it will take for you to make a buck. I might say, 'How much do you want to make?' If it's consistent with our own ideas, I'll say, 'go ahead and make the fight.' "

The margin of profits—Trainer claims promoters average $10,000 to $15,000 profits per bout—is considered too small for boxing's two major promoters, Bob Arum and Don King. And this suits Trainer fine. Part of his scenario is to keep Leonard free of the entanglements that Arum and King weave when they secure options to the services of both boxers signed to a title bout. Trainer insists that any deal for a future championship bout will exclude options on his fighter's service. "They may turn around," Trainer concedes, "and say, 'Well, you won't get the fight.' But I don't think so. Money has a way of taking care of things. And whoever promotes a Ray Leonard title fight would make a lot of money."

Leonard's drawing power appears to support Trainer's theory. In his very first pro fight, against Vega, Sugar Ray attracted 10,170 people to the Baltimore Civic Center, a boxing record for that arena. This past January he broke his own Capital Centre (Landover, Maryland) record when he TKO'd Johnny Gant before 19,743 fans. Six of Leonard's first 10 bouts were in the Baltimore-D.C. area. Since then, he has fought regularly outside his home base—mostly for unknown promoters, some of whom are curious additions to boxing.

Dan Doyle is the 30-year-old head coach of the basketball team at Trinity College in Hartford, Connecticut. While working on his doctoral thesis on sports administration, he began promoting athletic events in Hartford, Springfield, Massachusetts, and Providence, Rhode Island. Eventually he approached Trainer and asked to promote a Leonard fight in Hartford: "I think Trainer was interested intellectually in what I was trying to do. But he was also pleased with the $12,000 guarantee I offered, back when not every boxing guy thought Sugar Ray was worth that kind of up-front money."

Doyle's Hartford event on June 10, 1977—it was Leonard's third pro fight—grossed $40,000, according to the promoter. Since then Doyle has staged Leonard bouts in Providence, Springfield, New Haven, and Portland, Maine. The Portland bout—Sugar Ray won a 10-round decision from Bernardo Prada there on November 3, 1978—had a reported gate of nearly $54,000 and a state-record crowd of 6,000 fans, more paid admissions than even Ali and Sonny Liston managed in their return title match in Lewiston, Maine, in 1965.

"Places like Portland," says Trainer, "are necessary. People in Detroit, Cleveland, other big cities look at what Ray draws in Portland, and think: 'If he does that kind of business there, imagine what he can do for us.' It makes it an easier sell."

Trainer can afford to experiment with his markets because Leonard's purses are usually sweetened by television revenues. Television has been the key to Sugar Ray's growth as a fight attraction. At the outset of his career, he signed a six-bout nonexclusive agreement with ABC-TV for a reported $320,000. (A new five-bout nonexclusive agreement for an undisclosed amount was signed early this year.) Leonard's appearances on NBC-TV, CBS-TV, and Home Box Office are also part of Trainer's idea of leaving his options open.

At present, the welterweight division has two championships—the WBA's Jose (Pipino) Cuevas and the WBC's Wilfredo Benitez. Cuevas is a brutally effective puncher whose blows have hospitalized foes. As former Madison Square Garden assistant matchmaker Bruce Trampler says: "Fight Cuevas? God bless you. This guy throws rocks." Leonard's title shot is more likely to be against Benitez.

Benitez who is 20 years old, has grown beyond welterweight proportions. For his last title defense this past March against Harold Weston, Benitez was forced to lose 14 pounds in five days to make the 147-pound limit. By next year he is expected to be fighting among the middleweights (160-pound limit). A bout against Leonard makes sense for Benitez's last hurrah as a welterweight. Sugar Ray is the only foe who can carry him to prime-time money.

Leonard now draws a six-figure annual salary as the sole employee of Sugar Ray Leonard Inc. In addition, a pension fund, maximally funded, has been set up. Other monies have been invested in real estate, such as apartment houses, and tax-free bonds. "I'm a conservative individual," says Trainer. "I wear dark blue or gray suits. I don't own stock. Neither does Ray. I'm more careful with his money than mine. His pension plan is in bank certificates of deposit and government securities. The money's going to be there."

Ray Charles Leonard was born May 17, 1956, in Wilmington, North Carolina, one of seven children. His father, Cicero, moved the family to Washington, D.C., when Ray was four. The Leonards struggled. As the fighter's mother, Getha, a warm, effusive woman, recalls: "I worked at night as a nursing assistant at a convalescent center, and my husband worked in a produce market from 2 A.M. to 10 A.M. loading trucks. The children took care of themselves.

"I wanted Ray to be a singer. I named him after [rhythm-and-blues singer] Ray Charles. As a boy, he was a little shy guy. I never had to go to school because of problems with him. Ray was good. He sang with two of my daughters in church, and people said he sounded like [rock 'n' roll singer] Sam Cooke. He sang till he was 14½. Then his older brother Roger turned him over to boxing. And like Ray used to tell me, 'Mamma, I put the singing into swinging.' "

By the time Ray turned to boxing, the family had moved to Palmer Park, a small beltway community. Even then, he was, as trainer Jacobs discovered, still a shy individual: "Very bashful. Like you'd explain something to him, he couldn't look at you. He'd look to the side or drop his head."

The shyness stemmed from a boyhood of poverty. "A feeling of inferiority," says Leonard, "from not having anything. There were never clothes to wear. Or money for things as simple as school field trips—like $1.25 to go to the Smithsonian. On days there were field trips, I wouldn't go to school. Even lunch money was a problem. In our family, there were always bills, always bills."

As a boxing beginner, Leonard took his lumps for a while. Getha Leonard recalls her son's coming home from the gym with black eyes and swollen lips: "I'd say, 'Hey, you wanna stop?' He'd say, 'No, Mama, I'm going on.' Each night that he'd come home like that, I'd go in the room and cry."

In time, Leonard was the one handing out the lickings as an amateur boxer. By 1974, he'd caught promoter Hrica's eye. "Even at that date," says Hrica, "I though he could beat the best pros we had around the area. Like Johnny Gant, who fought for the WBA welterweight title. That's how good Ray was. I proposed his turning pro. But Dave Jacobs had other ideas. He told me, 'No, Eddie. This kid's going to win the Olympics.' "

The flash of Sugar Ray in the prizefight ring—right down to the prefight kisses he throws the crowd—is part of his boxing persona, a creation that, but for Leonard's graciousness, would verge on being secondhand Ali. Out of the ring, though, the strut disappears and the image changes. He becomes the classic case of the sports star as a good guy.

He is conscious of the image and says that it is based on respect: "If you give respect, you receive it." What worried him most about the *Washington Star* brouhaha was how it would affect his standing with young people. For many athletes, helping small fry is obligatory PR. But Leonard's concern seems real enough. Without coaxing, boxing people cite the unpublicized visits to amateur gyms that Leonard makes to affirm the hopes of others.

The evidence is that though he is a pleasing presence in public he is not an eager one. "I consider myself," he says, "a loner. I have a couple of friends. But in my mind, I'm a loner."

Hrica: "Ray would like to be left alone. But he realizes that the limelight is part of the business. He indicated to me once that he used to like to go to dances. But now he can't go as Ray Leonard. Now he's Sugar Ray. Everyone wants to talk with him."

Dundee: "Ray enjoys little things. Sitting down, rapping with the guys he grew up with. Meeting the amateur fighters. Being with his family." (Leonard lives with his high school sweetheart, Juanita Wilkinson—she wears his engagement ring; no wedding date has been set—and Ray Jr., in a two-bedroom apartment in Greenbelt, not far from the home he bought his parents in Landover.)

Trainer: "When we interviewed people for the job Angelo Dundee has, some of them wanted Ray to relocate in places like New

York and Philadelphia. That was out of the question. Ray Leonard wants to stay here."

Jacobs: "He's a home boy. Four, five days away and he wants to come home."

Though others characterize Leonard with words like *decent, level-headed, mature, sincere*, he is not a caricature of the type, a Goody Two-shoes. He has what Steve Eisner, a fight promoter from Arizona, calls composture. "Composture," says Eisner, "is a word I used to hear in Detroit among fight people. They mistakenly combined composure and posture, as in, 'He lost his composture.' Or, 'That cat got real composture.' Somehow, though, I like the word better than the one it was trying to be, that is—'presence.'"

Leonard has presence—and more. "Let me tell you a story," says Eisner. "I wear a pair of diamond-studded boxing gloves around my neck. They're worth a fortune. Fighters are impressed by diamonds. And a lot of them have asked me to get them a pair. But I never would break out the mold until Ray asked. He came on straight-up, said, 'I'd really like to own a pair of these gloves.' I felt comfortable saying I own a pair and he has the other. So sometime later, I had the designer make another pair. When I told Ray, he seemed really touched. And because I had remembered, he was almost in tears. His eyes were definitely watery."

Tucson, Arizona. It is Sugar Ray versus Daniel Gonzalez, a world-ranking boxer from Argentina. The afternoon of the bout, last March 24, mariachi musicians are serenading the patrons in the expensive seats of the Tucson Community Center. In the ring, a peewee bout finishes, followed by a local tradition—the tossing of coins and crumpled bills to the grade-school gladiators.

Away from the tumult, off a narrow corridor of the arena, Sugar Ray sits in room 135-1.

Meanwhile, promoter Eisner is wondering about Angelo Dundee. "Before he showed up in Tucson," says Eisner, "he sent me three pairs of Everlast gloves, one of which Ray Leonard was to use. Now he tells me he wants a different brand—Reyes, a Mexican glove. Everlast gloves have more padding around the knuckles. Reyes are more uniformly padded, which means they make more impact when they strike. I tell him, 'Hey, Angelo, Reyes are a puncher's gloves. Your guy's not a puncher.' Angelo says to me, 'You may be surprised, my friend.'"

"See what happened," says Dundee, "is I walk into 134-1, Gonzalez's room. I notice there are a lot of guys in there. Lotta guys. Too many. Because of that, I notice Gonzalez hasn't been able to warm up properly. He's not sweating. And, my friend, that's a no-no."

Dundee returns to room 135-1, tells Leonard: "This guy is cold as ice, nail him."

Sugar Ray nails him in round one with a quick left-right combination that knocks Gonzalez down. He rises glassy-eyed and spits out his mouthpiece. He is in orbit. Leonard finishes him with a right-left-right combination two minutes and three seconds into the fight.

At ringside, some news photographers (who did not see the blows causing the first knockdown through their viewers) are suspicious about the results. In 135-1, though, there are no complaints, except from Getha Leonard. "They gave me 5 milligrams of tranquilizer," she says, "and it hasn't even taken hold." A few minutes later, her son, Ray Charles Leonard, wearing a training suit and richer by more than $200,000, walks out of the arena. He does not need a shower.

In April in Las Vegas, Leonard decisions Adolfo Viruet. A month later in Baton Rouge, Louisiana, he wins his twenty-second straight victory with another decision—this one over Marcos Geraldo.

By early summer, negotiations had begun for a year-end Benitez-Leonard title fight. For Sugar Ray, everything is still no sweat.

FOOTBALL

NOW THEY KNOW WHERE RUTGERS IS

By George Leonard

From the Nashville Banner
Copyright, ©, 1979, Nashville Banner

"A lot of people in Tennessee don't seem to know where Rutgers is," said Frank Burns, coach of the Scarlet Knights, at his postgame press talk.

Well, that still may be true.

But they know now—the 84,265 at Neyland Stadium in Knoxville Saturday do—that Rutgers has an excellent football team. And that—big surprise—those eastern players can hit just as hard as they do in the Southeastern Conference.

And they'll be talking about this game that underestimated, unrespected Rutgers wasn't supposed to win—or even come close to winning—a lot longer than if things had gone as everyone in the Volunteer State thought they would and Tennessee had won in a breeze.

Fans of the Vols sat in disbelief at homecoming on the campus and watched these supposed pushovers from what has been called the weakest section in college football destroy their heroes 13–7 in an unforgettable game.

Rutgers alumni of a long time ago were proud that this institution played in the first intercollegiate football game on November 6, 1869. And won, defeating Princeton. What happened Saturday may be equally celebrated.

As Dino Mangiero, 255-pound left tackle and ebulient spokesman for the 1979 team, Rutgers one hundred tenth, said, "I don't know much about our ancient history, but they've got to put this at the top. Our rallying cry was, 'Let's take this one back to Jersey [New Brunswick, New Jersey, by the way].' Sure, Tennessee lacked emotion, playing us between their games with Alabama and Notre Dame. Fine. So we came in and stuck it to them."

"They whipped us every way possible," said Tennessee Coach

Johnny Majors whose repeated attempts to warn the Volunteers last week that Rutgers was no team of cream puffs and shouldn't be regarded lightly were unavailing. "It was probably the most convincing whipping I have ever experienced in coaching. We were fortunate not to be beaten worse."

Majors said players, coaches, and fans alike showed no respect for the eastern team, which has won six of eight games. Intensity was missing. Too late, the Vols tried to win. The spectators never did seem to get aroused.

It was as if Coach Frank Burns—coincidentally, both Burns at Rutgers and Majors, then at Pittsburgh directing a national champion, had 11–0 season records in 1976—told his people before the game:

"We can beat them right here in their own backyard if each of you makes a personal commitment to play better than the Tennessee man at your position."

Essentially, that's what happened and it's a large part of the explanation for the amazing events on a windy, chilly but sunny afternoon.

Ed McMichael, Rutgers' junior quarterback, outplayed Jimmy Streater, Tennessee's all-time total offense leader, by a wide margin. Passing, McMichael was almost perfect. He completed 11 of 12 throws, one for his team's only touchdown and several at critical moments. He led the Scarlet Knights inside the UT 20-yard line seven times. Two opportunities were wasted because of fumbles, one at the seven-yard line. That's what Majors meant when he said the scoreboard beating could have been worse.

Rutgers receivers never dropped the ball no matter how hard they were tackled. Flanker David Dorn caught only two passes but both were needed for Rutgers to win. One was a 37-yard toss five seconds before the first half ended for the tying touchdown. Late in the game, with Rutgers backed up in its own territory, third down and 11 yards to go, McMichael daringly threw long. Dorn came down with it for a 39-yard gain.

"For some reason, nobody covered me on the touchdown pass," said Dorn. "The cornerback [Danny Martin] lined up opposite the tight end. Then he couldn't recover when he saw the ball was coming to me."

But the most extraordinary catch was by split end Tim Odell who refused to give up the ball after being violently tackled in midair by Roland James and Wilbert Jones simultaneously. Play was suspended 10 minutes to determine the extent of his injuries. It was reported long afterward that no bones were broken or vertebrae crushed.

"He's some guy," said McMichael. "We've been playing three years and I've never known him to drop a pass."

Rutgers attacked the Vols constantly with reverses. The game plan was cleverly devised by Burns and his staff because, as he explained, "Tennessee is very fast and they pursue well. We felt we had to come back against the grain."

The Scarlet Knights, with Bryant Moore the top gainer (103 yards), netted 214 yards rushing—to 95 by Tennessee—and 388 yards overall to 257. The team from New Brunswick dominated the action following Tennessee's 84-yard drive for the game's first touchdown in the early going. Rutgers ran 77 plays, the Vols only 58, and maintained ball possession 63 percent of the time.

When James Berry crashed over the goal line from one yard away, the crowd cheered perfunctorily and waited for an expected parade of touchdowns. But Tennessee never threatened seriously to score again until the final moments.

Dorn's touchdown—Rutgers scored on the second of two straight passes of 23 and 37 yards in 15 seconds following the second of Streater's three interceptions—made it a 7–7 tie at half time. Kennan Startzell kicked 43- and 32-yard field goals in the third period.

The Scarlet Knights were trying for the clincher with 29 seconds left. But Tennessee end Brian Ingram blocked Startzell's attempt at a field goal from the 13-yard line. Johnny Watts almost got away, being tackled at the UT 49.

"I started to say a few prayers," said Burns. He needed them because Streater's second long pass to swift Anthony Hancock (offensive pass interference was called on the first one) appeared on target for a touchdown.

"It looked like it was all over," said Burns. Strong safety Deron Cherry, going with Hancock, fell. But Mark Pineiro, appearing from nowhere, it seemed, streaked to where the ball was about to settle into Hancock's arms and knocked it to the turf, saving the day for dear old Rutgers.

FOOTBALL

THE JOE PATERNO SCHOOL OF FOOTBALL

By Paul Hendrickson

From The Washington Post
Copyright, ©, 1979, The Washington Post

The accent seems all wrong. It's full of hero sandwiches and screech-ing El trains. This is central Pennsylvania, gray-green and forested and whale-humped with mountains. The Nittany Lion once prowled here, not the Sharks and the Jets. So who is this Flatbush interloper with the coal-black hair and Coke-bottle glasses and comic, crooked grin?

Joe Paterno backs out of a low brick building at the far end of campus, where he has been closeted all this December morning with his assistants. He is still talking, still analyzing, still trying to find the shard of detail that might spell the margin between winning a national football championship on New Year's Day and losing one.

"Details," he sighs, climbing in the car, wrestling for his belt. "One more detail. Jeeze, you'd think we were playing the Dallas Cowboys."

Fifty-two-year-old Joe Paterno is the commander in chief of the Penn State football team. Which happens to be undefeated and ranked No. 1 in the country. Which happens to be going against the red swath of Paul Bear Bryant's Alabama, the No. 2 team, for the mythical national championship. In a hundred Pennsylvania mill towns these days, Joe Paterno is higher than God—or at least the governor. Which is what some people in the state once wanted him to run for.

He is headed toward lunch at the Nittany Lion Inn across campus. The inn is a great white colonial building gracing North Atherton Street, just across from the college golf course. Paterno often lunches here; it's an easy 60-yard toss from his office in creaky old Rec Hall.

The face and voice may say Brooklyn; the dress says Harvard Yard. Brown University, actually, which is where Joe Paterno played quarterback and got his bachelor's in English lit. That was in 1950. "He can't run and he can't pass," wrote the late Stanley Woodward of the spindly-legged, ragtag Paterno's play. "All he can do is think and win."

The thinker and winner is clad in a blue oxford button-down shirt, a striped tie, a rich woolen suit tinted blue. On his finger is a knuckle-sized ring from one of his team's bowl victories. Even on the field, Paterno is a classy dresser. He wears a shirt and tie, set off by white socks and cleats. He turns up the cuff of his pants and combs the sidelines coatless.

But not for this day. There is no game. There is not even a practice. This is the next-to-the-last day of classes before Christmas break, and Joe Paterno, who thinks of himself first as a teacher of young men, wants his boys to hit the books. The Sugar Bowl can wait—till tomorrow, when he'll work them plenty.

This is the coach who "recruits to commencement," who tells fevered alums, "Look, these kids aren't gladiators," who keeps insisting to anyone who'll listen that you can pursue athletic excellence without tunnel vision, who achieved fame as a kind of Aristotilian man's coach by turning down the million-dollar blandishments of the pros, the better to enjoy more Verdi, more discussions of Coleridge, more evenings with his family.

It's all part of Joe Paterno's Grand Experiment that winning doesn't have to be the only thing. Lombardi to the contrary. The talk has somehow gotten on to classical languages, in particular Latin and a Brooklyn Prep Jesuit named Father Birmingham. "Father Birmingham was the guy who got Bill Blatty to write *The Exorcist*. And me to read Virgil, I'd do 10 lines, he'd do 20. He kept after me. He knew I was going to a non-Catholic college, and I think he was trying to drum into me something about values. He thought of Virgil as a real Christian man."

Joe Paterno, who has spent the better part of the last 28 years drawing *X*s and *O*s on blackboards for 200-pound 19-year-olds, pauses here. Looks up, a smile glinting off the glasses. "You know, there's nothing like Latin to give a person an insight to what language is all about." He says this with airy nonchalance. Not smugness; the thought just came, that's all.

Nonchalance is the way in which Joe Paterno greets the world today. "Hey, hiya, Cap'n," he says to a mailman at the door to the inn, cuffing him affectionately. "Howareya? Been out to the Elks lately?"

"When are you going to sign that book, Joe?" scolds a matronly woman in the dining room.

"Well, when are ya going to bring it in, buddy?' he fires back, giving the lady a small hug, aware he has an audience. "I mean, if you weren't out running around every night . . ."

"Whatcha got here, chicken cacci-a-tor-e?" he says to the white-jacketed waiter at the buffet line, peering into a pot. "Got anything for a diet?" He sounds a little like a Brooklyn Rocky.

Outwardly, Joe Paterno's seas are calm.

This calm, this word-for-everybody, are bench marks of the Paterno style. "He comes right in here, sits down, waits his turn, just like any other guy," says a barber named Cal who has been cutting hair on South Allen Street for 20 years. "Joe's basically a reservist, though."

Says Bill Dulaney, journalism prof: "The students don't know the president of the university. The know the coach, Joe. I know my students bother him. They call him up on assignments. He talks to all of them."

Not that the Paterno style never lapses. He can be as shrill and vile as the next guy—when a play gets stupidly broken, when somebody shows up late for practice, when it looks as though his team isn't giving 120 percent. At half time during the season opener with Temple this year, when it wasn't going well, Paterno allegedly screamed in the locker room: "You're trying to wreck my reputation." Penn State won 10–7.

Says Jerry Sandusky, one of Paterno's most respected assistant coaches (who admits to some real ripsnorters with the boss): "He's an intense man, don't be naïve. There are extreme demands." Especially now, in the white heat of No. 1 fever.

"Could it be otherwise?" says Sandusky. How else could this be Paterno's eleventh bowl game in 13 years as a head coach? (He took over at Penn State in 1966.) How else could Penn State have been ranked in 10 of those years among the top teams in the country?

And how else could Joe Paterno have gotten to No. 4 on the all-time winning percentage list, trailing only Knute Rockne, Frank Leahy, and George Woodruff?

Says Mike Reid, former All-America tackle under Paterno, now a Cincinnati-based piano player and pop composer: "He is a master at diciphering what your abilities are and unmercifully making sure you don't cheat yourself." Reid says he once remembers Paterno telling a reporter that one of his returning players was "fat." He thinks it was purposeful. "All I know is I would have literally done anything to prevent him from calling me that. I wouldn't have eaten for a week."

Says Joe Rubin, retired professor of English, who has watched and admired Paterno since the coach was a skinny, unmarried assistant under the semilegendary Rip Engle: "It's the ego and psychology all mixed together. He works essentially on negative emotion."

Rubin says he remembers Paterno telling him awhile ago he has become a "folk hero"—and must live up to its demands. Paterno denies he has ever thought of himself in such terms. Even if that's what he is.

For years Rubin asked to play handball with Paterno. Singles always went better, he says. "When we played doubles, and Joe and I were on the same side, I never got much of a workout. He'd take the whole court." Afterward, says Rubin, Paterno would love talking literature. He was especially keen on Hawthorne. "That part of him's never been a myth."

Literature or law or even politics: What is essentially intriguing about the life of Joe Paterno is that the coaching profession was not inevitable. It seemed more chance than destiny. Puccini and Words-worth—not Red Grange and Doc Blanchard—were the names on Joe Paterno's lips in college.

But irony works its ways. At Brown, Joe called the signals; his brother George ran roughshod from fullback. Neither of the two Paternos was destined to make old Brownies forget Fritz Pollard or the Eleven Iron Men. But that was OK: Joe intended on law anyway.

When he graduated in 1950, Rip Engle, his coach and mentor, convinced Paterno to put off law school for a year and come with him to the boonies of Pennsylvania, where Engle had just been made head coach of a sometime football factory and land grant college. Penn State was 140 miles west of Philadelphia, 140 miles east of Pittsburgh. And three planets from Flatbush.

"Look, a guy gets a job. You don't know what you're getting into. But you go anyway and see what happens. Now, I admit there were a couple of times early when I really thought I'd blown it. Every time we'd lose a game, in fact, I'd start thinking about law school. And I hated the town, believe me, I hated the town."

He says this pushed back from his plate, coffee removed, the easier to make points with his circling, jabbing hands. Joe Paterno, broad-nosed, flat-jawed, looks like a club fighter—in mufti.

Nowadays, of course, Joe Paterno loves State College (which is the name of the town that encircles the University Park campus). The place is safe, clean, a healthy environment. The mountains ulti-mately found their pull, even on Brooklyn. His wife, Suzie (a Penn Stater whom he married in 1962, after 12 years in town as a bache-lor), likes it, too. As do the five kids. Their home, not pretentious, sits across from a small park, a brisk 25-minute hike from Beaver Stadium.

Joe Paterno so thrives on his job and his adopted town that some Pennsylvanians find it unthinkable he could ever leave and join the pros. God knows, he's had the offers. The Steelers, the Colts, the Raiders, the Eagles (along with Yale and Michigan)—all have come calling through the years.

Awhile ago the New England Patriots tried to buy him with a ridiculous $1.3 million. It nearly worked. Paterno said yes, went to bed, couldn't sleep, in the morning called back owner Billy Sullivan, and said no deal. He said he didn't want his kids just saying, "Dad, he was a good football coach, he won lots of games." He hoped for a little more than that. Damn the money.

Now the New York Giants want him. Dave Anderson writes about it in the *New York Times*. The Giants should make him an offer he can't refuse. Anderson says, "I'm not sure there is such an offer," says John Morris, Penn State sports information director.

Paterno says he's not interested, the Grand Experiment isn't over yet. His face is screwed in concentration. "You see, with the pro game, you're just zeroed into the one thing: the football game. There isn't room for . . . anything else."

He looks suddenly frustrated. Maybe he doesn't feel like naming these things. Instead, he says this: "The only way I can see that the pros might appeal would be, say, if you finally got tired of working with 19-year-olds. Or maybe sick of the recruiting. But, hell, you're bound to feel that once in awhile." He almost looks apologetic.

Joe Paterno will look you blue in the eye and say that today's televised tilt for the national championship is not very important. To him, "It's important to seniors and alumni and fans more than to me. If we get it, we'll have a big party and everybody will be happy . . . but we don't have to have it. What I'm trying to get across is this: Let's be as prepared as we possibly can. And if we win, we win; and if we lose, we lose. But either way, let's enjoy it."

He hunches forward—no, lurches forward. He wants this understood. "But even with that statement, paradoxically, I must tell you my pride is such that I want terribly—desperately—to win."

Flash of grin: "Although, I am reminded of Aquinas. Didn't he say, 'anticipation was the greater joy'?"

A moment later, coming back: "Goals, goals. Writers always ask me about my goals. Well, I really don't have any goals. That's part of my whole philosophy. I don't go into a season with specific goals. I get up in the morning, and there's something to be done. It might be mowing the lawn, it might be working out a defensive play. I just go about getting it done."

Early, as it usually happens. Says Joe Rubin: "I've seen him at 8 o'clock on a summer's day—this is June or July, mind you—heading toward his office. He's walking fast. He's absorbed in thought. That's the key to the guy: He works unbelievably hard."

People talk about the pressure, Joe Paterno says, "You want to know what the pressure is? It's not letting down all these guys across the state who are so vicariously identified with the Penn State program. It sounds crazy, but a football game can ennoble these guys, enrich their lives.

"It's like driving to Pittsburgh for the symphony, then coming home, and feeling high for the next three days. That's what's happening with our football program in this state. When it's right, when we win, when we've all pulled together, then it's almost . . . a work of art."

He leans back. "That's what the pressure's all about. Hell, I got guys who don't want to go to work on Monday because we've lost."

He is asked if he is mellower now. (A couple of years ago, Paterno's son fell from a trampoline and was seriously injured. Paterno missed a game; his friends say it changed him.) He says he despises the word *mellow*. "What I think has happened is that I've gotten a better feel for knowing how to get things done. I've learned how to back away from my intensity, handle things a little better softer maybe, with a little more kindness. I can be more sensitive to people's feelings now."

There have been enough who have despised him through the years. Don Abbey, a former Penn State fullback, once supposedly said: "He shouldn't be Coach of the Year. He should be Wop of the Year." Says Mike Reid, basically a Paterno admirer: "I have to think a large healthy portion of it was always for himself. Joe, above all, really had a sense of theater, the event. Sports as spectacle. He was right in there, letting the light shine."

Joe Paterno can flatten you with his honesty about himself. In 1976, the Nittany Lions went 7 and 5–which some people thought akin to heresy. Paterno thinks he knows what happened, "I lost control of the team and the season and myself. I did an awful lot of traveling. I got involved with making a lot of speeches—banquet speeches for IBM. I wanted to make some money. I went into the season tired. I never had the proper time to spend with the squad. I was arbitrary with the staff."

He doesn't breast-beat in this: just recited the facts.

One of Joe Paterno's secret assets is his recruiting strength. There are few better. When he is in those Chamokin parlors and Coaldale kitchens with Mom, he is just another nice Italian boy. They love him.

He has been known to stir the spaghetti with a wooden spoon while stirring the glories of Penn State football. No empty promises, though: There won't be cash under the table or cars from downtown merchants. You'll have to study. If you come, he says, you'll live in a dorm or a fraternity like everybody else. Penn State doesn't believe in pampered athletic dorms. By the end of the night, likely as not, he's got Mom and Pop and Junior in the cup of his hand.

Maybe sense of family, going back to Brooklyn, is the key to Joe Paterno. For 10 years in State College, before he was married, Paterno lived with Bets and Jim O'Hora. O'Hora, 31 years a defensive line coach for the Lions, is retired now. He and his wife figure they raised a couple of kids—and the young Joe Paterno.

"He couldn't be alone," says Mrs. O'Hora, who was pregnant with her third child when Paterno came to stay. "We had no furniture for him. We got a chest of drawers and a bed and a little orange crate from the A&P for his night stand. He was so happy."

He had 30 pairs of woolen socks, Mrs. O'Hora says. "One for each day. They always had holes in them. At the end of the month, he and

I would go down to the basement with the Woolite. He was just one of the family. He had his place out here in the living room. He'd take his shoes off and leave them there till morning. Our kids never bothered him in the least. He loved being around a family. On weekends, maybe, he'd go out to the Elks or the American Legion."

Finally, says Jim O'Hora, they kicked him out. He breaks up in memory. "It became apparent he'd never leave."

"Yeah," says Mrs. O'Hora, "and when he got his own apartment, it was right up the block. He kept coming over all the time."

But it all worked out: In less than a year, Paterno had met and wed Suzanne Pohland of Latrobe, Pennsylvania. Now there are five kids, oldest 15. She's great, says the coach of his wife. "You take her out, get a few drinks in her, and you can't shut her out. Course, I get a few bourbons in me, I'm ready to go too."

He is mugging comically, diddling with his tie. He sounds like somebody out of *Saturday Night Fever*.

Though Don Quixote isn't a bad thought, either. Don Quixote is one of Joe Paterno's heroes. A statue of him, gift of his class at Brooklyn Prep, stands on his stereo at home. "I don't know, as a kid the whole romance of competition thing . . . chasing windmills . . . that's all I wanted from life."

Joe Paterno has thought some about retirement, he says. "Lately, I've been giving it more thought. Say I want to get out in the next four, five, maybe six years. Well, you've got to be working on it now. I remember asking Darrell Royal before last season began how he knew it was time to get out. He said, 'Joe, what you want to do is leave some meat on the bones.' "

Part of that meat on the bone is that eastern football has proved itself as strong as football in any other section of the country. You don't have to be Texas or Oklahoma—or the Crimson Tide—to qualify for the national title. Joe Paterno has raised the standard. He's always been something of an eastern chauvinist. ("It's a major text to his constant sermon," says Joe Rubin.)

No, he says again, he's not interested in the professional ranks, and, yes, this is probably the last and only act. Like Carson on the *Tonight* show, Penn State may be as good as it gets for Joe Paterno.

He pauses. The lips come tight on that street-corner face. Head moves up and down a millimeter. "You know, my father was probably responsible for me and the way I turned out more than anybody. He was with Pershing, later went to law school at night for years. He used to say first, 'Did you have a good time?' and second, 'Who won?' He never lived to see me become head coach. Maybe he thought I'd never get over the wall—being an Italian Catholic from Brooklyn and all."

The cockeyed grin: "Course, what I like to do is fool people."

TABLE TENNIS

THE ARISTOCRAT OF HUSTLE

By Dave Hirshey

From the New York Sunday News Magazine
Copyright, ©, 1979, New York News Inc.
Reprinted by permission

The Fat Kid stepped off the bus triumphant. He was a little carsick and his pants were too short and he had to squint up West End Avenue through thick black-rimmed glasses, but a smirk crossed his face as he watched the bloated yellow school bus rumble off.

"So long, suckers," he said softly. He had humbled them all in Bunk 6 at Kezar Lake Camp, cut through the competition with such impudent ease that not even the redoubtable Herbie Schwartz had dared face him across the peeling Ping-Pong table.

Now as he dragged his dufflebag up to Ninety-sixth and Broadway, he could feel the thick red butterfly paddle his father had given him for his Bar Mitzvah ("Now that you are a man, my son, you can use sponge instead of sandpaper"). He pulled it out and hit a few imaginary smashes. Then the Fat Kid drew in his breath and stepped down into the dark basement beneath an old movie house. Awe descended, along with a shower of paint chips from the ceiling.

The Riverside Table Tennis Club. Enter here and find a chump.

This was not the Y, not your genteel basement rec room where secretaries pushed demure volleys at each other during lunch hour. The Fat Kid knew this was the place the players came, a subterranean inferno where only the best could stand the heat. Reputations rose and fell with each scorching smash. Losers slunk up the stairs and disappeared from the neighborhood; winners left at dawn, their pockets crammed with cash. And the most hardened bettors suddenly were overcome in the middle of a gut-wrenching match. Some fell to their knees on the cracked linoleum floor, others had to be pulled, quaking, from bathroom stalls.

The Fat Kid peered into the smoky room. Dangling 60-watt bulbs fought the gloom as little white spheres flew through the air at speeds the Fat Kid had never dreamed of. Tables dipped at precarious angles, propped by the stumps of broken paddles. People leaped, lunged, raced about, grunting in six languages. Korean masters dueled romance-language professors; pinstriped stock-brokers pulled off their shirts and wiped their faces on mono-grammed towels. In the corner, two gang members in leather jackets contested a point fiercely, a pile of chains and blades nestled in a sweat shirt beneath the table.

The Fat Kid sensed action. He craved it.

"Anybody want to lay three to two on a five spot?" yelled a skinny guy in a beret. He was holding a trash can lid. "I'm giving 18."

A murmur swept the room; the plickety plock stopped.

"Eighteen is a helluva spot with a garbage can," someone said. But nobody came forward.

"I'll take that bet," the Fat Kid heard himself saying. So what if the guy was three times his age. The Fat Kid thought. Hadn't he brought all the counselors to their knees at Kezar Lake? Who was this joker with the garbage can anyway?

The Fat Kid served first. He cradled the ball in his palm, tossed it in the air, and made a slashing motion with his paddle. The ball spun this way and that like a gryoscopic egg. He never did see the return, just heard the clunk of the garbage lid and the gasp of the gallery. 18–1. And so it went. 18–5, 18–11, 18–17, 18–21. Clunk. The Fat Kid slumped over the table, lighter by two weeks allowance.

"Who was that guy?" the Fat Kid muttered to no one in particular.

Sixteen years later, I found out.

Marty Reisman. Transcendent guru of Pong. Showman, actor, raconteur, author, gourmand. Marty Reisman. Money player, high-stakes con artist, backroom action guy. Play him for $100? You bet. Need a handicap? Take 15 points. Not enough? He'll play you with a shoe, a Coke bottle, his glasses, trash can lid. In the gospel according to Marty, you get them on the table at any cost. Toy with them, tease them with a couple of close ones. And then turn it on. A good hustler will kill you with confidence, with slow deliberate points, plucking wings off a fly.

"Putting the lock on," says Reisman, "describes the state of the art."

Like the time Marty put the lock on with the monkey. This is art: Reisman is at the table, in the middle of a big money match. In runs Betty the Monkey Lady. "Hey, Marty," she says, "I got to see the painter today. Can you take care of the monkey?" Betty's living with an organ-grinder and having an affair with the painter. Plunks the little ape on Reisman's shoulder and takes off. He can't quit so he decides to play with his right hand and hang on to the monkey with the other. More action. The monkey howls.

"I beat the guy easily," says Reisman, "although my shoes got a little wet."

Lest you think this is a circus, take a better look at the man. This is no glitzy hustler, no polyester cowboy who swats golf ball-sized truffles for some oil execs in a Houston hotel suite. Marty has credentials—17 national and international titles—and Marty has taste. Expensive taste: $100 custom shirts, 30-year-old wines, and the kind of women who get a rash from anything less than silk.

"Marty," says Reisman's long time exhibition partner Doug Cartland, "is the aristocrat of hustlers."

The overall impression is long and loose. The delicate, long-fingered hands of a pianist dangle from bony wrists cuffed with silk. Billowing sleeves suggest balletic grace and indeed, when he lands after leaping to parry an impossible shot, there isn't the slightest whisper from his custom suede sneakers. The ubiquitous beret never changes its angle; the man never breaks a sweat. His gaunt El Greco face looks as though it's never seen a moment's sun; the crease in his pants is as precise as his game. It has been 16 years since the Great Trash Can Hustle, but Reisman still has the same garden hose physique. Only the place looks different. Watching Marty shield his eyes like Dracula at dawn, I realize what it is.

Windows. The place has big picture windows, filtering sunlight into the room. You could no longer spend three days at Reisman's and think six hours had passed. And all those fluorescent lights shimmering above $150 Harvard Professional Tables. How was a guy to turkey his opponent into playing uphill anymore? More alarming was the clientele, the fresh-faced, nicely clothed people. People with children and coordinated jogging outfits. People drinking apple juice and munching granola bars between games. Then I knew the place had really gone to seed. It was handling family trade.

"Disgusting, isn't it?" asks Reisman. "The old place had a lot more panache." The old place on the north side of Ninety-sixth Street was torn down four years ago, but Marty simply packed up his blue and purple pimpled rubber Hock specials and headed across the street. Sent out the word that he was opening a new parlor.

"Within six months," he says smugly, "I had effectively closed down the two competing joints in town."

Since that fabled shootout, things at Reisman's have settled into its owner's natural pace. It opens soon after he rises at about 4 P.M., or whenever Reisman can pry an eye open long enough to toss someone the key. Early evening is slow. An elderly Chinese man curses softly in Mandarin at a malfunctioning black-and-white TV set while two Spanish kids overturn the coin-op soccer game to retrieve a ball. Someone punches the Coke machine. Nothing works well here but Marty, and he only gets rolling after 9 P.M., and a couple of stiff espressos.

Even then, his pace seems leisurely. That's part of the con. Take that huge pile of fluorescent lighting fixtures sitting against a side wall. The old place had odd lots like that, too—a gross of somebody's hot transistors, maybe 10 cartons of ballpoints. Judging by the dust, the lights have been here a long time, but like the best of hustlers, Reisman is a patient man. Some night, some sucker will come along who's opening a doughnut joint. Marty will work up a little action and he'll owe. But Marty will do him a favor, let him light up his doughnut joint with the whole lot for $500, cash. And hey, tellya what. Forget the C-note you just dropped on the table.

"Take a little, leave a little," is Reisman's philosophy, developed soon after he had taken the governor of the Philippines for $3,500 back in 1952. During a break for dried monkey meat, it was strongly suggested that the skinny American leave the governor's pride and well enough alone. Reisman promptly dropped a polite game and flew off to Taiwan and the next scam.

This and other tales are documented by the rogues' gallery of photographs that hang on the brick walls at Reisman's. They are all Marty Reisman, and he points to them often as if to verify his past. There is the serious table tennis champion in wire-rimmed glasses, posing with the trophy from the British Open; the cunning money player grinning like a mongoose from behind a banquet table with King Farouk; the steely-nerved smuggler posing innocently at a Buddhist temple in Hanoi; the grandiose exhibitionist leaping high above a table at Caesars Palace; the spellbinding raconteur holding Johnny Carson rapt. Reisman has carved a dozen lives for himself with a pimpled rubber racket and a rumrunner's wits. He has won and lost fortunes from here to Rangoon. Yet Reisman is still saving some picture hooks at the end of his wall.

"I'm just about to blossom," he says, sensing yet another Reisman Renaissance. This is a phenomenon that occurs every few years. It happens when the media, bored by Hollywood hustlers and commercial dream merchants, sniffs around to find the real American hero. Inevitably they discover Marty. First, they exhume him from beneath a mound of yellowed clippings showing him playing footsie with the Maharajah somebody or other. Then they dust off a few bright and trite lines and *voilà*—Mr. Original.

Last time it was China and Ping-Pong diplomacy. This time, it's Hollywood calling. Marty's book, *The Money Player*, is about to become a movie; Public Television is planning a documentary on his life; he's been asked to film a national beer commercial and play Vegas for a couple of thousand a pop.

"I'm a born again and again and again Jew," he says. "At least five or six times in the last decade."

Marty Reisman was born for the first time 49 years ago, just a double bounce from the *Jewish Daily Forward* down on East Broadway, son of a Russian émigré and bookmaking cabbie who ran policy numbers and lost half his taxi fleet in a single poker game. Marty watched; he listened to the night sounds of crap games in stairwells and domestic arguments with the light of dawn. His mother left; Marty ricocheted between parents and hotel rooms.

"Growing up with those insecurities," says Reisman, "I had a nervous breakdown before I was nine. I was so insecure I felt I was going to die, was obsessed with the thought that my heart might stop at any minute. It reached its culmination one day at school. I felt my eyelid flutter . . ."

And he awoke in Bellevue.

"It was a horror house," he says. "I wanted to get out so bad I learned to control myself in a month, then I outgrew this thing they called anxiety neurosis."

Not coincidentally, he began to play table tennis. It began with an inexplicable attraction to those little white balls that bounced onto the sidewalk from the table on the roof of a neighborhood settlement house. Marty became obsessed with them; scooped them up and hoarded them in a dresser drawer. When his father's girl friend discovered the cache she bought him a Ping-Pong paddle for his eleventh birthday. Pimpled rubber.

The skinny kid practiced at the settlement house until at 13 he was City Junior Champion and an accomplished parks hustler, skimming a week's beer money off players twice his age. At 14, the kid took his act uptown.

Lawrence's Broadway Table Tennis Club, a former Legs Diamond speakeasy that still bore the bullet holes of late-night raids, was the Runyonesque model for Reisman's own parlor. It was in Lawrence's that Marty got his degree in advanced hustling. The skinny kid became the Needle, and he could stick you bad. Reisman says it was the fear of going home busted that developed his kill shot, a devastating forehand smash clocked at 115 mph. The smash was his best offensive weapon, catching the ball low off the bounce and sending it back into an opponent's solar plexus like a heat-seeking missile. Later, the London press would call it the Atomic Blast.

The Needle had a legit side, too. Or at least he tried. All was going well at the national championships in 1945. Reisman had made it to the quarterfinals of the junior division when the pressure of the competition momentarily addled his street smarts. He took his customary $500 bet and handed it to a man who surely looked like the bookie he'd dealt with all week.

"S'matter? Can't handle the action?" Marty asked the red-faced man.

The president of the United States Table Tennis Association called the security guards who dumped the kid on the curb. Reisman was 15. A year later, Pong's Bad Boy came back to win the national junior title and earn a place on the three-man U.S. team that sailed for England. Along with his rackets, Reisman disembarked carrying several dozen pairs of nylons.

Like many of the top Pong junkies, Reisman took to smuggling and playing money matches to support his habit. The week Marty won the British Open in 1949, he also did a brisk trade in crystal and ballpoint pens. At 19, he felt he could hustle the whole plickety-plocking world. So when the offer came for an exhibition tour with the Harlem Globetrotters, Reisman and his partner Cartland jumped at it.

Running with the Globetrotters, the pair worked a trail of hustles and high jinks across three continents and 65 countries; living in cheap hotel rooms strung with socks and soup cans; beating the check at Maxim's; mayhem in Munich, two wacko Americaners playing five balls at once before 75,000 in a Berlin soccer stadium. They played "Mary Had a Little Lamb" by hitting balls at frying pans; snacked on preserved locusts between matches in Manila. In Thailand, they played through an earthquake ("I thought it was applause," says Reisman). Fifteen years older, Cartland was the straight man, a slow-talking southerner who Reisman claims has the first nickel he ever made. Marty was the guy who tried to sneak into the harem; the incorrigible partyer with an itch for action and near-fatal charm.

Those years were a high-stakes hobo's dream. Then without warning, Reisman's life changed at the 1952 World Championships in Bombay. His nemesis: two round pieces of sponge rubber glued to the paddle of Japan's demonic Hiriji Satoh.

"It was as if I were deprived of one of my senses," Reisman says of their match. "You're conditioned to react to the plickety plock and this sponge caused dead silence."

And deadlier spins. Reisman's Atomic Blast fizzled, impotent, off Satoh's sponge and Marty was humiliated. The consummate hustler had become the bewildered hustlee. For Reisman, the era of sponge descended like a silent shroud. He dedicated himself to revenge.

Smuggling and stroking their way to Tokyo, Reisman and Cartland worked to set up the Big Sting—a challenge match against Satoh and world doubles champion Nobi Hayashi. The backer: the Japanese promoter who was already marketing Reisman/Cartland dual signature Ping-Pong balls. They bit. So did Japan; there were 50,000 requests for tickets and a live national radio hookup. "We were playing for the highest stakes," says Reisman. "Pure ego."

And Marty was ready. There would be no rash of smashes this time, no blind offensive barrage that would allow Satoh to turn his power against him. Goddamn sponge. You could kill a 115-mph forehand with every ounce of your bodily strength and some little guy would stand back there, hold out a slab of foam rubber, and the ball would rebound back in your face. So Marty would have to wait, to push, push, push, until he found the opening and then go for the throat. It worked. Unaccustomed to taking the offensive, Satoh slammed and slammed, spun and spun, a desperate man rendered helpless by an opponent armed only with pimpled rubber and his indomitable hustler's spirit. *Sayonara*, Hiriji. The final scores were 21–9, 6–21, and 21–15 and when it was over the wildly cheering Japanese fans picked Reisman up on their shoulders and carried him around the theater.

When you're rolling a string of sevens, you keep throwing. Reisman and Cartland kept moving, flung themselves at every corner from Adelaide to Bali, cadging flights on military hops to play at U.S. bases, those great roosts of GI pigeons fattened on PX Pong tables. And not all the suckers wore dog tags. There was lunch with Prince Sihanouk, an audience with Pope Pius XII, a command performance for Egypt's King Farouk.

"You can't name a maharajah that I haven't played for," says Reisman.

And outside the palace gates, a little side action. Watches and perfumes crossed borders with impunity on the customs-free military flights; $500 watches nestled safely in the toes of Reisman's socks. For $1,000 a trip, he carried 20 pounds of gold bars from Hong Kong to Rangoon strapped to his bony frame in a custom-made vest. At 27, Reisman was at peak form, Errol Flynn with pimpled rubber, carving up the world.

"My whole life has been flirting with danger," Reisman says. "I'm not a guy to skirt through life hitting all the edges. I'm not into buffoonery like Bobby Riggs. There's an aura of chintziness and stealing about the hustler. But the money player—he's a gladiatorial hero, bare-chested to the enemy. It's like going out there in a hail of bullets. When I'm out there, the money is not as important as the excitement and drama. I'm a frustrated thespian. I need the attention, the recognition, and applause. When you're on before a crowd, the body and mind reach astonishing heights. You're constantly working, tightening all your forces, all your craftsmanship. It rises to a peak where you're eliminating all the imperfections in your game, a nirvana of concentration . . ."

Then sometimes, life intrudes. The light of dawn appears around the cracks of the door. For Marty Reisman, it was a woman.

She was beautiful and willful, the kind of dame who wouldn't answer Bogart's whistle. Yet she left a multimillionaire husband for an itinerant Ping-Pong player. There was marriage, and the pressure to provide. And there was a baby daughter.

"I was trying to make money in all directions," says Reisman. "Gambling, hustling, playing. Bought the Riverside Club and worked the joint 14 hours a day. No sleep, hardly eating. There were physical symptoms—blurred vision, forgetfulness. I was running myself into the ground."

Comes a big money match in Las Vegas. It could set them up for a year, keep the kid in booties. Reisman walks out to the table and suddenly, again that flutter of the eyelid.

"I felt a palpitation and it seemed an interminable time until I felt the next heartbeat. I screamed, 'Help me, save me. I'm dying.'" I clawed my way through a mob to get out of the arena."

And straight to a hospital. Once again, life had put the lock on Marty Reisman.

It was a year before he could pick up a paddle; soon after, his marriage was tabled for good. Serious national competition ended in 1960 when Reisman threw in the sponge he had used to defeat Bobby Gusikoff for the American title. Sponge had taken over, but it wasn't for him. "I refuse to prostitute my skills," he announces. "A sponge racket is like gravy covering up bad food." And he hated the silence. It was as though the steady plickety plock of pimpled rubber echoed the heartbeat he was straining to hear, confirmation of his existence.

"I'm not bitter, I guess I'm just a romantic," he says. "The players of yesteryear had a more romantic image. Maybe it was the primitive weapons, the pimpled rubber. It transmitted more of a struggle to the audience. Today, with sponge, the player's armed with a technological weapon. It's like soldiers who meet with submachine guns instead of two guys from the Wild West popping shots at each other."

So Reisman opted for the casual shootouts of the Wild West Side, ensconced himself below ground as a legendary star with orbiting weirdos—hustlers, physicists, pimps, and sociologists drawn by that compelling gravitational pull: ACTION.

It is these Riverside habitués who populate his life now; the maharajahs are in their declining years; his family broken. Reisman's daughter, Deborah, disappeared mysteriously two years ago at age 15, brainwashed, he believes, by religious cultists called the Oms. For nearly a year, Reisman worked with the police and the FBI trying to infiltrate the group, which he believes is in the business of black-marketing the babies its women produce. The last time Reisman saw Debbie, she could only hum.

"I think she'll be back unless she's dead," he says. "It remains as the only real sore point in my life."

Before he can get too morose, Marty begins pointing out the regulars in his place. He talks in caricatures rather than names: Freddie the Fence, Herbie the Nuclear Physicist, Betty the Monkey Lady, Louis the Commie, Tony the Arm. "I require constant intellectual stimulation," Marty says. Having quit school at 15, he sops up random knowledge like a desk blotter.

The result: a dizzying collage of the trivial and the sublime. He can quote you today's price on the London gold market, or a snippet of Proust. "It's all part of my gestalt," he explains.

"I've studied Marty for 20 years and he's always been a likable meatball," says Joe the 80-year-old archaeologist. "He likes to be around people who are authorities on all sorts of subjects. He'll pose as an expert on the Middle East if he's had a dish of couscous. Still, Marty's a likable meatball."

"Mahty."

Leaning out the steamed-up doorway of the Empire Szechuan Gourmet Restaurant on upper Broadway, a smiling Chinese woman draws Reisman and two visitors inside.

"Ah, Mahty." His waist is encircled by the arms of a smiling young girl.

"Mahty." Her sister is pulling out a chair, beckoning. Marty eats here often, frequently at 2 A.M. when the family has ushered out the last customer. Like a slender street cat, Marty slips in the door and takes his place at the table with the family, eating the "real Taiwanese stuff" that the chow mein trade won't touch. These people, too, are part of the polyglot collection of sweethearts and strays that make up Reisman's extended street family. Casually, they "do" for one another; a meal here, taxi fare there. And tonight, a Chinese cornucopia for the newspaper guy and his wife.

"Special for you only, Mahty," the waitress says as she sets a perfect golden flounder before him.

"Was Marty famous for his Ping-Pong in Taiwan?" I ask.

"Oh, yes. But much more for smuggling gold. Mahty was the best."

Uptown, Friday night. Nine o'clock. I spot Marty strolling along Broadway, cigaret dangling from his lips, head wagging like one of those rubber dogs you hang from a rear car window.

"Had a macrobiotic dinner tonight," he croaks. "Need espresso quickly." We duck into a Korean coffee shop.

"Espresso, straight, yes?" says the counterman, who knows.

"Make it a double," says Reisman. He slaps at an empty pocket and instantly, one of the Koreans is at his elbow with a pack of Tareyton longs.

"Caffeine and nicotine," sighs Reisman. "Now I'm ready."

Ten o'clock. Back at Marty's place, things are disappointingly dull. Some serious-looking law students; a few couples on a cheap date. Marty settles into a game of gin at $25 a hand. After nearly an hour, he is restless. He springs up and strides over to the center table.

Without a word, he holds up a Tareyton, a conductor commanding his orchestra's attention. All the action stops at surrounding tables and he starts to play the gallery.

"Ever see me break a cigarette? A startlingly audacious trick."

Dead silence as he sets the cigarette on the table edge and walks to the other side. He bounces the ball, swings, misses the cigarette by a foot.

"I know what you're thinking. I'm washed up. A failure."

Two more failed attempts. A fourth and he is visibly annoyed.

"Ashes to ashes," yells Joe the Archaeologist. "Dust to dust!"

Reisman smiles. "Three to two for five bucks?" he says softly. Dave the Writer bites. Reisman stares down the table, drops the ball, swings. The cigarette snaps cleanly in half.

Eleven-thirty. Back to the gin table. "Let's face it," Reisman says. "When I don't play, this place is Dullsville. What am I doing here every night?"

Herbie the Nuclear Physicist speaks up. "The Ping-Pong parlor is just an externalization of your soul," he tells Reisman. "Constant movement, constant turmoil. It's a womb to you. You could have moved this dump to a hundred better sites but you elect to stay in this environment. You can't leave because it's you."

Midnight. A disheveled, seedy-looking guy taps at the door and Marty gets up from his gin game to meet him. He reaches into his pocket, peels off a few bills, and comes back.

"Who was that?"

"Just a guy who's had a string of back luck. Needed $26 for a room."

Two-fifteen. Marty is engrossed in a friendly game of gin for $100 a hand with a gentleman from Yugoslavia who has a strange attachment to his briefcase, rubbing the clasp with one hand all the while he plays.

"Jewel thief," someone whispers. "Hot rocks."

The phone rings and Jerry the Semi-Retired Stockbroker picks up.

"It's for you Marty. Your girl friend."

Still holding his gin hand, Marty walks to the phone.

"No, the place is dead. I'm just sitting around talking to a reporter for the Daily News. These guys ask a lot of questions."

He hands Jerry an eight of clubs to discard, motions for him to pick up a queen of hearts.

"Cards? Nah. Figured I'd lay off after the last couple of nights. I know I promised you. Yes, I love you."

Marty throws the queen and draws again.

"Listen, baby, could you hold on for a second?" Marty cups his hand over the receiver and tosses his cards on the table.

"Gin," he says softly.

2:30. Enter two muscular black men in three-piece suits and fedoras. Marty introduces them around and explains that they're from Cameroon. The more sinister of the pair is a security man at the Red Apple Supermarket around the corner. A brown belt in karate, he is a sobering deterrent against shoplifting. However, he has found that 90 percent of the people he catches stealing steaks live in his building. Therefore, it is not wise to go home early. He waits at Marty's until 4 most nights, or until all the shoplifters have passed out on the stairs. Marty calls him the King of Voodoo and asks him to break the ceiling with his head for Dave the Writer here. He fails, explaining, "the leaves aren't right."

"Got to get some action going," cries Marty, jumping to his feet. "This place is dead. What do you say, Dave?"

"I'd love to see you play a money match," I reply, a match being best two out of three games. "I didn't say I'd love to *play* you a money match."

"C'mon. It'll make a good story. What's $5 to a major cartel like The News?"

"Five bucks?"

"Yeah, and I'll spot you 17."

"Seventeen if you play with your glasses."

"Eighteen sitting in a chair."

"Nineteen standing up," I demand.

"Nineteen! My God, that's an *impossible* spot. Nobody gives a 19-point spot. I have to play a perfect game. No margin of error." A sigh. "Okay. Nineteen points."

In the gospel according to Marty it says the easiest people to con are con men. Which is nice because I am trying to con Marty. I am no rank amateur. For one glorious week in 1971, I was actually a ranked amateur. No. 99 in the Pennsylvania State tournament. Only a cad would mention that there were 100 contestants.

During the five-minute warmup, I am careful to grip the racket like a meat cleaver, an old Reisman trick that fools no one. I cleverly hit my backhands off the table so that Marty can detect the soft underbelly of my game.

"Like the way you hit through that backhand," Marty says, flashing a private grin that suggests "kid's obviously got no forehand."

Turning to address the gallery of 15 insomniacs, he asks, "Anybody want a piece of this action?"

"I'll take the kid for five," says Herbie the Nuclear Physicist.

"Reisman hasn't played in weeks, he's out of shape. He's got his shoes on and he couldn't spot a monkey 19. Just relax, kid."

I take his advice and it's 19–12.

"Just keep it in play," I tell myself. "Wait till he makes a mistake or has espresso withdrawal." Nineteen–13, 19–14, Marty is bored and starts a yawn.

"Ever tell you about the time I issued that blanket challenge in Chicago? Said at a press conference I'd play anyone sitting down and give them 17 points."

Click, I've gotten lucky. A looping forehand nicks the edge and I have him 20–15. One to go.

"So anyway, the doorbell rings at noon and it's some smartass from the *Chicago Tribune*. Wants to know if the challenge still goes. Here I am, in bed, champagne bottles strewn around the room, a head like a tom-tom. I tell him OK and order breakfast. I figure if I beat him, I get a couple paragraphs, but if I lose . . ."

A second blessed accident, I chop back a return of serve and it clips the net, hangs for an agonizing second, and crawls over. Game, Dave the Writer.

"So I let this chump beat me," Reisman continues. "And he wrote a half a page. Sometimes," he says, peering over the net, "there's greater victory in losing."

I win the next game easily, 21–9, when Marty gets careless and hits two off the table. Herbie the Nuke Physicist rushes over and shakes my hand.

"Ten dollars with an 18-point spot," is all Marty will say.

Marty is all business now, driving a fusillade to my forehand, bam-bam-bam. I go down meekly, 21–19, the second game is more of the same, and the match is now even.

"How about a rubber for $20?"

"I think I've had enough, Marty."

"But we always play a rubber here." It isn't the statement that impresses me so much as the I'll-eat-your-kneecaps-for-breakfast look on the King of Voodoo. I agree.

Marty's working the crowd now, cruising the table, talking about everything and nothing. His plan is to slam and slam, driving me far enough back so he can drop a shot and tell an anecdote before I get to it. After 10 points, my body is soaked in sweat. My hands bleed, and a blister has developed on my left foot. I am near collapse. Marty is dancing.

"Remember the trash can," says an inner voice, and my resolve hardens. When Marty smashes, I race back six feet to return one, two, three slams. I keep giving him bizarre spins with my sponge until Marty pushes two backhands into the net. Twenty–15, mine. Marty runs off the next four points and Jerry the Semi-Retired

Stockbroker is at my side with Band-Aids and paper towels. I feel like the Bayonne Bleeder getting ready to go back in against Ali. I take my time, and the break in rhythm works.

For the first time in 35 minutes and five games, after over 100 points, Marty's concentration slips and he hits a shot to my backhand. Bang. Zoom. Twenty-one–19, Dave the Writer.

"I know what you're thinking," says Marty. "You're thinking I'm finished, washed up, over the hill. Can the aging champion recapture some of his former greatness and overcome yet another insurmountable obstacle? Ah, the drama and tension."

Marty is rolling. I serve and he whips off his glasses and returns the ball off the lens. He hits shots from behind his back, between his legs, nonchalantly flicks the ball back with the sole of his foot, and on game point shovels the ball at me with such heavy backspin that it hits on my side of the table and before I can get my racket on it, hops back across the net. The match is even. Again.

"I have to admit," says Marty, "I'm the most charismatic son of a bitch who ever stepped on a table."

Now it is down to one game and I silently congratulate myself on having fought the good fight. But what I don't realize is that Marty's concentration is eroding. After winning the first 14 points, he hits two consecutive shots to my backhand. Whap. Whap. Twenty–14. Marty serves from a kneeling position five feet behind the table, I drop the ball just over the net and am halfway into my victory leap when Reisman scoops it back. He wins the next four points and it is 20–18.

"Can you feel the tension in the air?" Marty asks. He rips a forehand drive deep in the left corner, I chop it back and the ball—can it be?—brushes the top of the net and falls dead. I have beaten Marty Reisman.

He peels off a crisp $20, and hands it over with a histrionic flourish. "For the Fresh Air Fund, I assume?"

"Yeah," I tell him. "I'll send a donation. And I'll sign it The Fat Kid."

GOLF

A PLACE FOR A SMILE AND A LAUGH

By Maury White

From the Des Moines Register
Copyright, ©, 1979, the Des Moines Register and Tribune Company

On an Easter Sunday when Jack Nicklaus became a born-again threat in the Masters golf tournament, Frank Urban (Fuzzy) Zoeller struck a blow for those who believe there is a place in golf for a smile and a laugh.

Possibly you saw the exciting finish on the second extra hole when the stocky 28-year-old from New Albany, Indiana, sank a putt that put an end to the legend that a rookie can't win the Masters and also relegated Ed Sneed and Tom Watson to the position of co-runners-up.

When this important putt, worth $50,000 for starters, dropped out of sight in the cup on the eleventh hole—where he had been very mediocre all three previous days—Zoeller flung his putter someplace close to Mars.

Hopefully, it either has, or will, come back out of orbit because I think I know where it may eventually wind up. But let me tell you about Fuzzy (who gets his nickname from his initials) and a conversation early in the week.

Zoeller is not a man easily awed. He came here with great respect for the tournament and course, but made it clear from the start that it didn't seem out of the realm of reason that a good golfer could win on his first try.

"Have you figured out what club you will give to Augusta National to put on display when you win?" asked an ink-stained ragamuffin who had talked with Zoeller a number of times at the Quad-Cities Open (where he won't be this year).

"Hell, I haven't even figured out what club I'm going to hit off the first tee," retorted Zoeller. "I have discovered one important thing about the course, though—those big pine trees don't move."

He's loose, all right. In addition to being one of the longest hitters on the tour, he's one of the great free-style conversationalists, who has a chance of becoming one of the heroes of the beer-drinking set, along with Arnie Palmer and Lee Trevino.

You knew, of course, that his very own mother loves to bug him at less-hallowed tournaments by wearing a T-shirt proclaiming she is a member of "FUZZY'S FANNY'S." Only broad-beamed people are eligible.

"God, I hope she doesn't wear it here," Fuzzy said the other day. But I don't think he really would have minded.

The 1979 Masters was something like your average professional basketball game. Sneed got out ahead, everything sort of cruised along until time was about ready to expire, and then all hell broke loose. Until it did, it was ho-hum.

Sneed had the title and let it get away. Tom Watson, who has won before, damn near did again. Zoeller, who really was just a figure on the fringe most of the day, came through at exactly the right times.

There has been a great deal of speculation during the last year or so that golf needs a new, colorful figure. Sports fans, there is a chance that we now have one, since Fuzzy is a genuine delight on and off the course.

He sings, whistles, smiles, admits that he almost feels guilty for taking money for something he'd do for nothing and if there was one thing to be regretted Sunday it was that his wife, Dianne, was back in New Albany.

She is pregnant. Oh, is she pregnant, like maybe two weeks away from delivering. Zoeller was talking about that Sunday morning, when he kept insisting that the tournament was still to be decided.

"Hell, I might fly her in and we could have the first child born on or near the sixteenth green," he quipped. "I've known her all my life. I insist she fell in love with me in kindergarten, but she won't agree to that."

No matter, they started dating in high school. Zoeller turned pro in 1975 and, for a while, did his very best to drink all the tour stops dry and accommodate as many beautiful galleryites as humanly possible.

His game has been better since he married and has given similar devotion to golf.

"I'm excited about becoming a father," he says. "A boy is going to be Beau Christopher and a girl will become Sonny Noel . . . no, I don't have any idea how you spell that. I like Hidy Ho, but she thought that was corny."

There are two kids in New Albany, Indiana, who must feel smarter than anyone this side of Yale or Harvard. Zoeller came to work Sunday morning bearing a blue Easter egg inscribed: FUZZY— 1979 MASTERS CHAMP.

"That's one great thing about being from a small town," he said, although 40,000 is somewhat larger than Aspinwall. "Everyone is close. Everyone is interested in you, and what you do."

The two youngsters had given the egg to a friend for delivering.

One of the nice things about Zoeller's first Masters was that his first round was played in company with Trevino, a guy who keeps everyone around in good humor. Another nice thing was a final 18 with Watson.

"Tom's easy to play with. He talks. He grinds, but he's good to play with," said Zoeller. And he was also full of praise for his newest friend and business associate, Jerry Beard, the Augusta National caddie who took him over.

Regular tour caddies are not allowed in this hallowed sanctuary, so a man must rely on new help.

"I feel like a blind man with a Seeing Eye dog, Jerry just led me around all week," insisted Zoeller. "I'm not sure how he got me, but he said he'd requested a young limber-back."

That's a fella who hits it out of sight—like Fuzzy.

That flying putter, by the way, had not been accounted for two hours after the round ended.

"I don't know what happened to it. I had more important things to do," said Zoeller. "That's my Betsy, but I got one in my car that's identical. I generally switch once a year just to prove to the club it's not indispensable."

Fuzzy showed up at the press conference in the green coat that is awarded to winners. Members must buy theirs. This one was merely on loan, though.

"Fits great. Fits great," said Zoeller. "Tapered just right. It belongs to Jack Nicklaus. I thought he was a little bigger than I am, but I guess he's not."

Funny thing, Nicklaus was fat when he won the first of his five Masters. The first one after he trimmed down, Jack showed up wearing the green coat that had belonged to the late Tom Dewey, who once ran for president.

Fuzzy was a delight on the platform, bantering and racing through a description of his round that never got any better than his capsule description at the start.

"It was a round of golf that started out slow and ended up real quick," he said. His humor is quick, often dry and you must pay close attention as he speaks rapidly.

There was a coin flip at the start of the playoff to determine the batting order and Fuzzy was last. Didn't bother him a bit.

"When your name is Zoeller, and so many things are done in alphabetical order, you expect to be last," he said. But the last was first after he rammed home that putt that sent the putter into orbit.

Later, much later, just before he finally got a chance to call Dianne and find out if he'd become a father because of the excitement, he grinned at the idea that he was the only golfer eligible for the "grand slam" but requested that no one expect him to start showing up at meets in tuxedos.

"Just because I win a golf tournament, why should I change?" he asked. No one was able to give a reason why he should. And I hope no one is ever able to convince him to quit laughing and smiling between shots.

HORSE RACING

THE GREAT REDEEMER'S COMPANIONS

By Jim Bolus

From The Louisville Times
Copyright, ©, 1979, The Louisville Times

Move over, Senecas Coin, Saigon Warrior, Rae Jet, and all you other awfully bad, awfully slow, and awfully awful horses whose owners had the audacity to run you in the Kentucky Derby.

Make room for Great Redeemer.

Unless Great Redeemer would unexpectedly make a complete turnabout, this creature has cracked the top 10. Make that the bottom 10.

Great Redeemer finished last in the Kentucky Derby on Saturday, 47½ lengths behind Spectacular Bid and 25 lengths behind the next-to-last horse, Lot o' Gold. After Lot o' Gold crossed the finish line, photographers on the track thought the race was over and began to move for the winner's circle. One person even made it all the way across the track before Great Redeemer finished the race.

Great Redeemer entered the Derby with an 0-for-6 record, having been beaten a total of 85 lengths. So now he's winless in seven starts, losing by 132¼ lengths, an average margin of 18.9 lengths.

As of right now, those numbers tell us all we need to know about Great Redeemer's ability. He now qualifies for membership to my list of worst horses ever to run in the Derby.

Just where Great Redeemer ranks is uncertain at this time, however. He should be allowed to complete his career before I can assign him a definite spot among these infamous horses. Just as history will tell us how good Spectacular Bid is, history will tell us how bad Great Redeemer is.

Going into this year's Derby, here were my rankings of the 10 worst starters of all time:

1. Senecas Coin (pulled up, 1949). Worst horse ever to run in the Derby, Senecas Coin was ridden by Jimmy Duff, who encountered a newsman in the paddock after the race and asked a reasonable

question: "Who win?" Duff certainly had no way of knowing. Senecas coin, after all, had been pulled up in the neighborhood of a quarter of a mile behind the victorious Ponder. His Derby race was no fluke, either. Senecas Coin started 53 times in his career. He lost 52.

2. Frank Bird (last in 1908). Nobody could agree on how far Frank Bird lost the Derby. The *Courier-Journal* said the horse was beaten "about a quarter of a mile," which was an exaggeration of sorts. One chart placed Bird 45 lengths behind the winner at the finish, another put the margin at about 29 lengths. One thing was certain: He wasn't close, which was the story of his life.

Frank Bird finished far back in six career starts, three of which resulted in last-place efforts. Those six races drew a total of 59 starters, all but six of whom finished ahead of Frank Bird.

3. Orlandwick (last in 1907). He did manage to win twice in 30 starts, but he showed his true class by being one of those who finished one race behind Frank Bird.

4. Pravus (last in 1923). Twenty career starts and never a winner. Wonder if he ever stopped to nibble on tin cans in the post parade?

5. Dick O'Hara (last in 1930). In 15 career starts, Dick O'Hara finished first one time and last on seven occasions.

Dick O'Hara was so badly outclassed in the Derby that even his owner, Chicagoan Pat Joyce, bet on another horse in the race.

One story had it that the only reason Joyce ran Dick O'Hara in the Derby was to win a bet that his horse would start.

According to another story, some Chicago con men printed up Derby lottery tickets with the names of three horses on each ticket. For a ticket holder to win, all three horses had to run in the Derby. The catch was that the name of Dick O'Hara, who had absolutely no business running in the Derby, appeared on every ticket.

Realizing that they had been taken, the purchasers of the tickets told Joyce of their plight, and he agreed to run his horse in the Derby to help them collect their prize money. Trouble was, the con men who organized the ticket scheme blew town. However, one of them was caught and prosecuted. He lost the case, but had no money. As a result, nobody collected a penny on the lottery.

6. Saigon Warrior (last in 1971). Even though he finished 72¼ lengths back, it's not true that they needed lanterns to find Saigon Warrior when he finally dragged himself home. Mike Barry says they were using flashlights.

7. Fourulla (next to last in 1971). Finished 14 lengths ahead of Saigon Warrior, but 58¼ lengths behind the winner, Canonero II. Flashlights for Fourulla, too.

8. Layson (third in 1905). How could a third-place finisher be so

bad? Easy. There were only three starters. Actually, Layson's career produced both good news and bad news. The good: He won three times. The bad: He lost 88.

9. Broadway Limited (also ran in 1930). Sold for $65,000 as a yearling, never won a race, never finished in the money, never earned a penny. Never should have run in the Derby.

10. Rae Jet (last in 1969). Rae Jet, who the chart said "Lost contact with the field," finished 42¼ lengths behind Majestic Prince.

Tommy Cosdon, who trained Rae Jet for the Derby, later said this horse had received more publicity than Frank Sinatra. Some of us wondered whether Rae Jet could outrun Sinatra.

BASEBALL

THE MEMPHIS RED SOX

By Kenneth Neill

From Memphis Magazine
Copyright, ©, 1979, Memphis Magazine, Towery Publishing Co., Inc.

Ezekial "Spike" Keyes is not a very big man. Today he doesn't weigh much more than the 136 pounds he weighed when he played for the Memphis Red Sox back in the 1940s. But seated at one end of his living-room couch in Clarksdale, he seems much larger. The room comes alive as he talks, waving his arms for emphasis.

Baseball is the subject of our conversation. Keyes was a pitcher, and a pretty fair one at that. "My fastball," he says proudly, "was just like a white streak of lightning." For several hours we talk about the players he pitched against and played beside. He has hundreds of stories. He remembers the time "Cool Papa" Bell scored from first base on a bunt. He describes the game in Philadelphia in which Josh Gibson held up on a curveball, only to change his mind at the last millisecond and hit a 500-foot home run with only one hand on his bat.

These memories mean a lot to Spike Keyes. But names like Bell and Gibson mean little to most Americans. Most have never heard of ball players like Willie Wells, Buck Leonard, Neil Robinson, and Verdell Mathis. Yet today these names might be household words, were it not for one thing: Like Spike Keyes, all of these players were black, and unlucky enough to have been born at a time when baseball was very much a white man's game.

One of baseball's first superstars when he played back in the 1880s and 1890s, Adrian "Cap" Anson is often considered the spiritual father of apartheid in American baseball. In 1887 Anson's Chicago White Stockings traveled to Newark; the scheduled pitcher for the Little Giants, their opponents, was one George Stovey, a black man. As Chicago's player-manager, Anson's response was swift: "If the nigger plays, we don't." Unwilling to buck the game's top drawing card, the Newark management backed down and played the game without the services of George Stovey.

What began with the pique of one racist soon hardened into national custom. Until 1947, not a single black American played major-league baseball, as a racial barrier more solid than the Berlin Wall was built around the national pastime. Of course, no such barrier existed, officially, but the power of white opinion was more than strong enough to compensate for the lack of legal sanctions. In classic pass-the-buck fashion, white players blamed the owners for the ban, while the owners blamed the commissioner, and the commissioner blamed the players. It was all a rather convenient way to circumvent the Fourteenth Amendment.

So what became of the Hank Aarons and Reggie Jacksons of the first half of this century? Well, they played very good baseball—not for the Yankees or the Dodgers, as they might have done if circumstances had been different, but for teams like the Homestead Greys, the Cleveland Buckeyes, and, yes, the Memphis Red Sox. These were the teams in the Negro National and American Leagues, which had their names but little else in common with their white counterparts.

Black baseball was a hand-to-mouth enterprise, for the owners, the players, and the fans. Operating on shoestring budgets, black teams spent much of their time barnstorming, playing as many as 250 games every season, moving from town to town across the country in battered old buses and eating out of grocery stores and the backs of the few restaurants that would serve them.

The Negro Leagues were never really well-organized. Teams were disbanded and reformed regularly, and few got any support from the white-controlled press. As a result there is little in the way of statistical information about the black players and their exploits. But one statistic makes up for many of these gaps: Today roughly 35 percent of all major-league players are black. In view of this, it seems reasonable to assume that many of the players in the old Negro Leagues could have made it to the top.

The first to get that opportunity, of course, was Jackie Robinson, a young, college-educated infielder for the Kansas City Monarchs who signed with the Brooklyn Dodgers in 1945 and went on to an illustrious major-league career that carried him into the Baseball Hall of Fame in 1962. Robinson's success was a victory for black America, and while older players like Spike Keyes never got the chance he did, they at least had the satisfaction of seeing the next generation of Negro League stars become bona fide major-leaguers. Players like Hank Aaron, Ernie Banks, and Roy Campanella took their first baseball steps in the uniforms of teams like the Indianapolis Clowns and Newark Eagles. And there were others. Spike Keyes remembers one Red Sox game in Memphis in 1949 when a young ball player for the Birmingham Black Barons named Willie

Mays made such a fantastic catch in center field that the bleacher fans passed a hat and gave him the proceeds in honor of the occasion.

Even earlier, a few black stars were lucky enough to get a chance to play against some of the best white players in unofficial exhibition games (which, incidentally, drew overflow crowds) against those few whites willing to play against them. In 1941 Spike Keyes went to California with the Satchel Paige All-Stars, who barnstormed that October against a white major-league all-star team put together by Cleveland Indian pitcher Bob Feller.

"This guy from the Cardinals, Johnny Mize, the one who could hit that ball so, he was out there with the white stars," Keyes recalls. "One day, he comes up to Satchel and said, 'Satchel, you beat us last night, who you gonna pitch tonight?' Satchel said, 'You see the kid sitting over there in that dugout,' pointing at me. 'We're gonna pitch him tonight.' Mize looked at me, laughed, and said, 'Satchel, with this 38-inch bat, I'll kill that kid over there.' So Satchel just said, 'Well, you'll get your chance tonight.'

"Oh, there was some throwin' that night. I threw that ball outa sight. I struck Johnny Mize out twice, and when we got to the dressing room, he came up to me and said, 'Just tell me this, boy. How is it you throw that ball overhand and make it rise?' And I said, 'That's my secret.' 'Well, there's one thing I do know,' says Mize. 'If you was white the Cardinals wouldn't turn you down for all the money in the world. Here, take this $20 and go buy yourself some chewing gum.' "

Tracing the origins of the Memphis Red Sox is rather like hunting Bigfoot: There are occasional tracks here and there but very little in the way of hard evidence. The team seems to have originated in the early twenties and underwent several changes of ownership until purchased by Dr. W. S. Martin, a successful black surgeon, in 1932.

The Martins were one of the more prominent black baseball families in America, W.S.'s brother owned and operated the Chicago American Giants, and while W.S. himself had only passing interest in the game, another brother, B.B., served as Red Sox general manager for over 20 years.

While none of the black clubs made money hand over fist, the Memphis Red Sox were one of the more solid Negro League franchises. The local club had one big advantage over most teams; it had its own ballpark, located at what is now the intersection of Crump and Danny Thomas. Martin Stadium was an unpretentious but functional facility which seated 3,000 until renovations in 1948 expanded seating capacity to around 8,000. When the Red Sox were in town, usually on weekends, most of these seats were filled, mainly by blacks, although there was a small section reserved for white spectators (Fire Department Chief Irby Klinck and businessman Abe Plough were among those who attended Red Sox games regularly). The team played most of its games on the road during the week, usually taking 60 percent of the gate receipts in towns like Greenville, Tupelo, Hot Springs, and El Dorado.

In fact, barnstorming and playing "on percentage" was so lucrative that for several years after the Martins purchased the club, the Red Sox were independent of any league affiliation and spent the summer traveling from Montana to Florida, playing against anyone and everyone who would play against them. In 1937, however, the Red Sox became charter members of the newly formed Negro American League, although since league games were played only on weekends, they continued to barnstorm during the week, slowly making their way from city to city.

On the field, the Red Sox had both good and lean years. As one of the top 10 black teams in the country, Memphis won most of its games against nonleague opponents. They won the Negro American League championship in 1938, although many Red Sox players today view the 1940 and 1941 teams as the strongest in the club's history.

After the color barrier was overcome in 1947, four Red Sox players made it into the big leagues: pitchers Dan Bankhead, Jehosie Heard, and Marshall Bridges, and first-baseman Bob Boyd. Boyd was by far the most successful, compiling a respectable .293 lifetime batting average during a nine-year career spent mainly with the Chicago White Sox and the Baltimore Orioles. But these players were just the tip of the iceberg. (The lucky few who were young enough to take advantage of the great, new opportunity.) As Bob Boyd says today from his home in Wichita, Kansas, "When I went from Memphis into the White Sox farm system, I felt like I was going backwards, playing for poorer teams. I knew that if I'd made it with the Red Sox I could make it in the majors."

Ironically, the breaking of the color line was a major setback for the Negro Leagues. Attendance fell off dramatically as the black community turned its attention to its "own" players in the now-integrated major leagues. The coming of television accelerated this decline. While the Negro American League struggled on in skeletal form until 1960, the Memphis Red Sox seem to have passed from the scene a little earlier, probably in 1958 or 1959; during the last few years of its existence, it was little more than a black semipro team. The final curtain was wrung down on this chapter of Memphis sports history in 1962, when old Martin Stadium was torn down. Today a truck terminal stands where Bob Boyd used to spray line drives and Spike Keyes used to throw his "white lightning" fastballs.

St. Petersburg, Florida, spring training headquarters for the New

York Mets, seemed the logical place to try to contact another Negro League star who made it to the majors. But Ron Hodges, team secretary, was not very encouraging: "Your chances of getting Willie are like getting a snowball in hell. Everyone's been annoying him lately." But my reference to the old black leagues rather than his recent election to the Hall of Fame seemed to cut considerable ice. In a minute or two Willie Mays was on the line, reminiscing amiably about his days as a Birmingham Black Baron.

"It was a great experience for me, really," says Mays, who played with the Black Barons from 1947 till 1949. "Actually I was still in high school, but I had a lot of guys taking care of me."

Willie doesn't remember much about his trips to Memphis: "I was so young that the other players wouldn't let me go many places." Nevertheless, he rattles off Red Sox names as if he had just played a doubleheader against the Memphis team last Sunday. He mentions people like Bob Boyd ("a very good hitter"), Frank "Groundhog" Thompson ("a little left hander with a chipped tooth"), Neil Robinson ("a big, strong power hitter"), Casey Jones ("a tall, skinny catcher with a fine arm"), and a dozen more. Some he has difficulty placing by position, but as he adds, "It was a different world from the majors. In those days, you played everywhere."

"Well, I'm glad he remembers me," says Casey Jones, shaking his head, when told of my conversation with Willie Mays. "I've got a scar on my knee that I'll carry with me to my grave, from a game in Martin Stadium when he came sliding into the plate."

It is a warm April evening at Verdell Mathis's house off South Parkway, and inside, five former Red Sox are gathered: Martin Carter, Jones, Frank Pearson, Joe Scott, and Mathis himself. While they gather only infrequently today, they spent hours, days, and months together on buses and baseball fields during the 1940s.

The conversation ranges far and wide. Everyone remembers Two Gun Pete, a black cop who would sit on the bench in Chicago just hoping for some altercation to break out on the field ("He whipped the black, the white, the blue, and the green," recalls Mathis). Then there was the time in Greenville when a less-than-punctilious umpire called a third strike on a Red Sox pitcher's pick-off throw to first base. Then in 1945 came the most tragic moment in the team's history, when star pitcher Porter Moss was shot and killed in a crap-game quarrel with a stranger on the train home from Cincinnati.

But by and large, life with the Red Sox seems to have been relatively happy. "We had a pretty good setup here," notes Marlin Carter, who played third base on the championship team of 1938. "The front office was straight. If you could get them to agree on something, that's what it would be. There were no paydays $50 short." He pauses and adds with a smile, "I've still got some teams that owe me money." (During the 1940s, Red Sox salaries averaged $300 a month, about a quarter of the white major-league average.)

Happy or not, theirs was a merry-go-round existence. "We traveled so long, you know," says former pitcher Frank Pearson, his voice still echoing the almost total fatigue of those days. It was not unusual for the Red Sox to leave Memphis after a Friday night game bound for a Sunday afternoon doubleheader in New York. "I can remember changing into our uniforms as the bus rolled over the Hudson," says first-baseman Joe Scott. Then there are the stories of 24-day road trips spent sleeping entirely on the bus. Casey Jones remembers the time the team arrived at St. Louis' Sportsman's Park for a game, just as the major-league Browns were leaving. "Zack Taylor, their manager, asked us where we were coming from, and we told him: Washington. He couldn't believe it: 'In that bus?' he said. But it was nothing to us; we just got out, ate some hot dogs, and played ball."

Inevitably, the conversation turns to the players themselves—the great ones, that is. As always, the first name out of the hat is that of the legendary Satchel Paige, probably the greatest pitcher that ever lived. I am reminded of a description given by another Red Sox player, second-baseman Jimmy Ford: "Brother, Satchel threw some fast balls. What he would do is throw one underhanded, the next one sidearm, and well, when he came overhand, I don't know, it was just too fast."

Paige, who helped the Cleveland Indians win the American League pennant as a 42- (or 52-, depending on whom you believe) year-old rookie in 1948, was as eccentric off the field as he was brilliant on it. "When Satchel felt like doing something he just went and did it," recalls Marlin Carter. "He could be traveling down the highway and see a good pond he'd like to fish. He'd tell the driver to stop the bus, and he'd just go out and go fishing, game or no game. He'd catch up with the team the next day, or maybe the next day."

Then there were the Red Sox stars, players like Ted "Double Duty" Radcliffe, so called because he was able to pitch and play behind the plate equally well. He was player-manager of the 1938 championship team. Larry Brown was another superb Red Sox catcher; he too went on to serve as manager in the late forties. Last but certainly not least was Neil Robinson, a slugging center fielder who could do it all. Robinson made the most appearances of any Red Sox player (eight) in the annual East-West All Star Game, the showcase of black baseball talent during the 1940s, when it drew 50,000 fans to Chicago's Comiskey Park each summer.

Larry Brown died in 1972; Radcliffe and Robinson now live in

Chicago and Cincinnati, respectively. But probably the best pitcher in the team's history was seated among us. Bob Boyd pays him the ultimate compliment: "Besides Satchel Paige, Verdell Mathis was the greatest pitcher I ever saw."

A product of Booker T. Washington High School, Mathis joined the Red Sox in 1940, and for the next five years he was dynamite. He started for the West in the 1944 and 1945 All-Star games and won both times. "Fastball, curveball, I had it all, without a doubt, from the beginning," he says almost clinically. "I just loved to play baseball."

Mathis's love of the game proved his undoing. Between pitching three of four games a week during the season and playing winter ball in Mexico or Venezuela, Mathis was probably pitching over a thousand innings a year. (Three hundred is considered maximum for a current major-leaguer.) By 1945 Mathis needed surgery to remove bone chips from his elbow. While he came back to pitch for four more seasons, he was never quite the same.

The Red Sox pitcher was but one of many black stars who narrowly missed out on the majors. Had the color barrier fallen in 1941 instead of 1947, the world would undoubtedly have heard a lot more about Verdell Mathis. But Mathis has few regrets. "I got to travel all over; anywhere I wanted to play I played, except in the major leagues." And traveling with the Satchel Paige All-Stars every October, Mathis did at least get the chance to barnstorm in California against some of the better major-leaguers. "You know, a lot of folks act surprised when I tell them I played against Stan Musial. Hell, yeah, I played against Stan Musial; what was that? Stan Musial wasn't any better than me, only he played a different position. I was a professional baseball player and so was he."

The session at Verdell Mathis's continues for several hours, but the time seems to pass in a flash. The stories go on into the night. Joe Scott talks about an umpire who needed to have his eyeballs scraped; Casey Jones about a team busdriver who had an uncanny knack for getting lost; Frank Pearson about a young Red Sox pitcher named Charley Pride who never quite made it on the mound but could sure sing nice tunes in the back of the bus as it rolled from town to town and state to state.

No doubt about it, one could have done much worse than to play baseball for the Memphis Red Sox. Joe Scott speaks for everyone: "It was just a picnic to play ball. It was such a great thing for us to have that experience."

GOLF

LUCKY OR GOOD?

By Gary Nuhn

From the Dayton Daily News
Copyright, ©, 1979, Dayton Daily News

Jerry Pate thought he could win it when he was five shots down with eight holes to play.

Gary Player thought he could win it even though he started the day nine shots down.

That's the way it is at the U.S. Open Golf Tournament. Whoever's in the lead feels like the first guy onto the beach at Normandy on D-day.

Hale Irwin was that man Sunday, three shots ahead when the final round began. That he survived while shooting a 4-over-par 75 (for a total of even-par 284) tells you something about the Open. You don't have to play perfect golf to win; you don't even have to play average golf. You have to be the man destined to win from the beginning—and Hale Irwin believes that above all else.

Last Wednesday, Irwin sat in the upstairs locker room at Inverness Club and talked about the difference between contending—as he had been doing consistently—and winning, which he hadn't done in 20 months. He said it was luck. "The guy who wins," he said, "is the guy who hits a tree and bounces back on the fairway."

So Sunday, he stood on the eighth tee with a four-shot lead and hit a miserable shot down the right edge of the fairway that began fading even farther right. It was not just headed for out-of-bounds, it was headed out of Toledo.

From the tee, all that could be seen were fans scattering behind the yellow gallery ropes and the ball disappearing into a clump of pine trees. A marshal took off his straw hat and flipped it high in the air. Everyone on the tee wondered why. It would soon be learned he had flipped his lid in disbelief at what he had seen.

Irwin shook his head and began walking. After he had walked about 100 yards and over a slight rise, he saw a ball in the right part of the fairway. He knew it wasn't playing companion Tom Weis-kopf's ball because Weiskopf had bullied one far beyond where this ball was.

It took only a couple more steps for Irwin to realize it was his ball, that he was the man who hit the tree and came back in the fairway. Hale Irwin had been talking about himself Wednesday. He was right, the man who hit the tree and bounced in the fairway would win the tournament. Only it would take more help from the fates, much more.

Two shots after the tree fairy's gift, fate caressed Irwin again. The eighth is a par five, so Irwin hit his second shot short and then hit a pitch over a trap that appeared headed for the wilds behind the green. Instead, it hit the pin, not a glancing blow, but as if hitting a wall, and bounced back eight feet away. "I might stand out there with 300 balls and not hit that pin," he said later.

You know without being told that he made the birdie putt. From a drive that looked like double-bogey; from a pitch that looked like bogey, Hale Irwin made birdie.

"I'd rather be lucky than good," he had said Wednesday. He didn't have to repeat it Sunday.

He probably won the tournament and the $50,000 there at the eighth, but he would have to hold onto it for 10 more holes and holding on in a U.S. Open is like riding a bull in a rodeo. Or, as Irwin said, "I just couldn't get to the barn fast enough."

The trouble was, Irwin was hitting the ball everywhere. From the fourth hole to the fifteenth, he didn't hit a fairway. "Never at any time did I feel like the lead I had was safe," he said, "because never at any time did I have a handle on what I was doing.

"I would say I started choking on the first tee. Everybody out there had to feel it. If you don't, I don't think you're human . . . or you're on something funny."

Still, leading by five on the thirteenth tee, he was loose. He drank a small cup of water and as he went to throw the cup away, a woman told him she was collecting the cups.

"Could I have yours?" she asked.

"I'll trade you mine for Jack Nicklaus's," Irwin said.

When he arrived at 17, he was still ahead by five. Safe? Hey, this is the U.S. Open. This is the one Bobby Jones gave away (in 1928) after leading by five; the one Arnold Palmer gave away (1966) after leading by seven; the one Sam Snead gave away (1939) with a triple-bogey on the last hole.

No lead is immune. Or, to paraphrase Yogi Berra, you're never in until you're in.

"As I stood on 17 tee, all I thought about was, 'Don't double-bogey,'" Irwin said.

He double-bogeyed.

Still, it wasn't close. Weiskopf, who had been hovering in second all day, was also choosing this moment to show U.S. Open backward mobility. He bogeyed 17 and left second place to two men who had already finished—Gary Player and Jerry Pate.

Irwin's lead was three. He could only lose if he pulled a Snead and triple-bogeyed. He gave it his best effort. His drive was in ankle-deep rough, his second was in a greenside trap.

The crowd swarmed down the eighteenth fairway behind the final twosome like people lining up for another Oklahoma land rush. Ahead, it was coast-to-coast humanity around the green. A perfect setting for a giant choke by this 34-year-old man with the wire-rim glasses, this man who looks so much like a bookkeeper.

The problem is, there is no release from tension in golf. In football, you hit somebody. In tennis, you are in constant motion. In golf, you store your tension. Irwin's storage tank was overflowing.

Minutes earlier, during his double-bogey at 17, Hale had blasted one out of the sand and completely over the seventeenth. If he did it again now at 18, a triple would be entirely possible. The eighteenth is not playable from the right of the green and that's where Irwin would go if he missed this sand shot.

He didn't. He lofted it softly six feet away. And now he had three putts to play with. He used two.

After picking his ball out of the cup, he staggered backward, feigning weak knees as Muhammad Ali used to do when he was hit but not hurt. Then he turned and smiled, his new braces glittering in the sun.

"Finishing like that is not my idea of championship golf," he said, "but it is two better than the next guy and that's all that counts. What's that commercial, 'Plop, plop, fizz, fizz, oh what a relief it is?' It is a relief.

"That probably was the hardest round of work—I can't call it golf—that I ever had."

The second-placers, Player and Pate, each shot better than Irwin Sunday. Player shot a gorgeous 68, Pate a yo-yo 72. But they had given Irwin too big a head start.

All three had been trying for their second Open titles. Player won in 1965, Irwin in 1974, Pate in 1976.

"The first one, I was more outwardly elated," Irwin said. "Now, I feel more pride than anything else. No, I'm not trying to prove anything to the world. I'm trying to prove something to me. All I can tell you is within myself, it's a very warm, very good feeling."

FOOTBALL

MOOD OVER MIAMI

By Ron Martz

From the St. Petersburg (Fla.) Times
Copyright, ©, 1979, Times Publishing Co.

Such a Super Bowl deal that Bob and Bunny Bickel had for you.

It would have been worth it to shlep on down to Miami Beach just to take advantage of it.

Such a deal.

For three days, Bob and Bunny Bickel offered three couples the run of their 83-foot yacht *Tulip II* and its three staterooms with private baths. The Bickels' chef would have served beef Wellington and Maine lobster on fine china, vintage wines in elegant stemware, and as much booze as the six could consume in three days.

But the bottom line was the inclusion of six tickets in the deal, six of the toughest tickets in sports, tickets to Super Bowl XIII.

The cost?

A mere $11,000.

Such a deal.

"It works out to be about $1,235 a day per couple, and that is really quite competitive," said Bunny.

Such a deal.

Give me your rich, your vibrant huddled masses America, yearning to breathe free, spending big, get sunburned and make fools of themselves at Super Bowl time, and South Florida will do a number on them.

This is the land of the fleece and the home of the economically depraved.

At the Orange Bowl today, neighborhood entrepreneurs will get up to $20 per car parking cars in driveways, on lawns, on porches and, if they can do it, on rooftops.

On Miami Beach this week a two scoop ice-cream cone went for a mere 95 cents.

A single cup of coffee cost 75 cents.

At press headquarters in the Americana Hotel in Bal Harbour, there was no price on the menu for lobster. But since you asked, it was $22. With no potato.

Holiday Inns in Miami offered a wonderful package for Super Bowl weekend: one room, four-night minimum, $100 per night.

The Metro Commission got into the spirit of things by passing a special ordinance to allow the early sale of liquor on Super Sunday. By a unanimous vote, the commission passed an "emergency measure" allowing bars and nightclubs, which normally aren't allowed to begin serving liquor on Sundays until 5 P.M., to open at 8 A.M. today.

"I'm incensed over this because it ruins the pleasure of the game when people are drunk," griped the Rev. Conrad Willard of the Central Baptist Church.

Sit down, Rev., there's money to be made.

"There are two things you need to be to live on Miami Beach," grumbled one writer, "old and rich, preferably in that order."

This is the land of opportunity. Everyone who comes here at Super Bowl time has the opportunity to be thoroughly conned and properly fleeced.

A note on the bulletin board in the hotel's press room, where several hundred of the 1,700 accredited media persons spewed out more than two million words on Super Bowl XIII, warns of numerous thefts in the Americana's hotel rooms.

One writer reported that his room had been burglarized and a $300 suit stolen.

But the report was quickly dismissed because nobody had ever heard of a sports writer who could afford a $300 suit.

Besides, most of the thefts were in broad daylight, as writers deftly heisted quotes from one another, quotes that they inserted into their stories which made it look as if they were working, thus justifying their existence in warm and sunny Miami Beach to their snowbound editors back home.

Super Bowl XIII is expected to dump more than $50 million into the economy of South Florida.

"This is the biggest single event a community can have," says Lester Freeman, executive director of the Greater Miami Chamber of Commerce.

But the weather here this week has been worth far more than $50 million to the local chambers of commerce. The warm winds and sunny skies which have inundated Miami this week are a far cry from the cold and rain which accompanied the last Miami Super Bowl, X, and last year's Dallas-Denver affair in New Orleans.

But unlike last year's overhyped orgy, when Dallas and Denver fans turned the French Quarter into a nightly, open-air party, Miami and surrounding communities have worn a mask of stoic indifference to the game.

What few cases of Super Bowl fever that have been reported have been quickly isolated and stamped out by massive doses of overpricing and numerous injections of security.

A scarcity of game tickets has also helped keep down enthusiasm.

Although more than 80,000 people are expected to jam themselves into the Orange Bowl today, becoming one of those 80,000 has been among the most difficult tasks in sports.

"This is the toughest Super Bowl ticket situation I've seen in a long time," said one National Football League official.

"If we had a million tickets we wouldn't have had enough. I don't know what it is, whether it's the site or the teams involved or what, but there are just no tickets to be had."

And that poses problems for some people, like Art and Al (no last names please), a couple of guys trying to make an honest buck selling Super Bowl tours. The tour sells for $850 and includes a ticket to the game.

But Art and Al never have game tickets when they sell the tours. They go to the game site and scrounge for every ticket they can get.

"You know what?" Art says as he works the lobby of the Marriott where the Steelers are staying.

"Every year we oversell. Every year we say, 'We don't oversell. We won't oversell.' But we oversell."

Art and Al sold 620 packages this year and by midweek had just over half their tickets. They were paying up to $110 each for a ticket whose face value is $30.

"We'll make it," says Al.

"We always do."

Such a deal that Art and Al have for you.

As has been the case in most of these season-ending extravaganzas, the game becomes secondary. And sometimes, it's not even that important.

What the players and celebrities do with their time is of week-long concern to those assembled here.

The star-gazing started earlier this week in a Fort Lauderdale emporium known as the Candy Store, a beach-front spot that features wet T-shirt contests.

A few of the Cowboys were in the place. Linebacker Thomas "Hollywood" Henderson was leading a parade of about 40 dancers around the floor in a "train dance" while several other members of the team were getting ready to judge, or assist in, the contest.

Then a couple of camera crews showed up and the Cowboys became very shy.

"Don't take my picture, man," said one player as he put his hand in front of the lens, "or my old lady back home will kill me and then I'll have to smash your body. Dig?"

The cameraman dug.

Later in the week, things began to pick up with the arrival of the celebs. At least they picked up for the celebs. The rest had been put to sleep listening to Pittsburgh coach Chuck Noll or hammered into indifference by the volume of words being churned out on the game and the sideshows which accompany it.

But the show goes on.

Don Rickles shows up. So do Melba Moore, Kenny Rogers, Michael Landon, Ethel Kennedy, Dean Martin, Andy Williams, et al. Some are there to help in the taping of an NBC special.

Lyle Alzado, who played in Super Bowl XII for Denver, is in Super Bowl XIII as a disco dancer. Alzado seems to be enjoying XIII as much as he did XII.

"The Super Bowl is now show business," says Alzado.

"Football has become secondary. That's the way it was when I played last year. That's why teams who go to the Super Bowl the first time get beat. They are overwhelmed."

The week's partygoing peaked Friday night with NFL commissioner Pete Rozell's intimate bash.

This year Rozelle rented the new, four-story, international terminal at the Miami International Airport to accommodate the 4,000 close friends he invited to the affair.

Getting people to the party may have been a greater logistical triumph than the D-day invasion of Normandy. The guests are bused or driven to the airport entrance three miles from the terminal. From there they are led in convoys across airport turnways to the terminal, where they are greeted by some of the 90 National Airlines stewardesses serving as hostesses to the party.

In addition to his 4,000 friends, Rozelle has invited six bands from various parts of the Caribbean, 4,000 dead lobsters, 1,000 pounds of baby back ribs, 500 pounds of lamb, 500 pounds of grouper, and enough booze to float the *Queen Mary*.

The cost is estimated at around $100,000.

There is nothing simple about the Super Bowl, no matter where it is held. It is bigger than any of us. It is bigger than all of us.

It plows along, scraping and gouging as it goes, making a few rich by allowing them to charge outrageous prices for ordinary things because the market will bear it.

And for the outrageous things, like a yacht with three staterooms and six tickets to the game, the price is almost beyond comprehension.

Such a deal Bob and Bunny Bickel had for you.

Such a deal.

BASEBALL

THE CIVIL-SERVICE GIANTS

By Allan B. Jacobs

From Harper's Magazine
Copyright, © , 1979, Harper's Magazine

The San Francisco Giants went civil service in 1980. The team—the players, the managers, the coaches, the bat boys, and the grounds keepers—all of them became civil-service employees of the city and county of San Francisco that year. It wasn't planned. It just happened.

After an unexpectedly good year in 1978, when the Giants actually finished third after leading for most of the season, the team fell to fifth place in 1979. Attendance, which had exploded to well over 1.5 million in 1978, sank to 1,500 to 3,000 on weekdays and 10,000 to 12,000 on weekends when the Dodgers were in town. So Bob Lurie sold the Giants near the end of the 1979 season to a Brazilian who had made it big selling Amazonian hardwoods in Georgia and was looking for his own tax shelter.

The new owner soon found out about major-league salaries, all those empty seats, and the other competition that was bidding for the fans' dollars in the Bay Area. He concluded that maybe he hadn't bought the best baseball franchise in the world, tax write-off or not, and began thinking and talking of moving the franchise, just as earlier owners had when fans stayed away from games. He felt sure he could break the Giants' lease arrangement for the use of Candlestick Park.

By now, few people paid much attention to that sort of posturing and threats to leave. Those antics made good press for a day or two, but it was well known that the Giants were locked into San Francisco for 20 years by virtue of an ironclad agreement they had signed with the city's Department of Parks and Recreation. Some long-forgotten lawyer in the city attorney's office had written a lease that bound the two parties together like Siamese twins.

Nevertheless, the city attorney always got a bit anxious when the

Giants threatened to leave. He asked a new, young assistant, Hadrian Ness, fresh from the University of San Francisco Law School, to check up on it: Could the Giants get out of the lease? The assignment had been given before and was considered good training by the old pros in the office. But Ness was eager to make his mark and took the job more seriously than his predecessors had. He also had no other assignments just then and wanted to be busy, lest some city councilman demand that his position be lopped off the payroll. City attorneys were about the only category of employees in San Francisco that didn't have civil-service protection, and that rankled Ness. After all, the rest of his USFLS classmates who went to work for the city (some 68 percent was the yearly average) were secure for life. Ness was pretty angry about that.

In his research, Ness made some interesting observations. He noticed that the lease was with the Department of Parks and Recreation, not with the city council or the mayor or the city. He recalled that the city charter said something about all Park-Rec employees having to be hired through the civil service. Ness also observed that the Giants' front office worked in space in Candlestick Park provided by Park-Rec. Some of the Giants' personnel were pretty chummy with the Park-Rec people. After all, they shared the same johns. On a few occasions (once when there had been a printers' strike in town, and once when someone had forgotten to reorder envelopes) the Giants had sent out letters on Park-Rec stationery. What are friends for? It was also a fact that Willie Mays's contract had once been sent with a letter that bore Park-Rec's seal. The head of Park-Rec had framed a photocopied facsimile, just for laughs, of course, and hung it on the wall behind his desk.

From these seemingly innocent observations and from one day seeing the Giants' grounds keepers digging up the pitcher's mound, raking the base paths, and cutting the infield grass—the kind of thing that the city's own gardeners did—Ness came to a startling conclusion: All of the team, including the players, were employees of the city and county of San Francisco, and should be treated as such!

Assuming Ness was right, that meant that, like all Park-Rec staff, the players would have to be hired by civil-service procedures. Among other things, they would have to pass exams, and any new players would have to live in the city. Fantastic! Ness's father, a union organizer/street cleaner working for the city at $18,000 a year, would be proud of him.

Ness went immediately to his boss to tell him the exciting news, but that august personage was out defending the city on a zoning case. So, while waiting, Ness had lunch with his newfound city-hall friend, reporter Russ Cone. He confided to Cone the significance of what he had found, knowing without having to ask that his friend would treat the matter confidentially.

The story that hit the afternoon paper was headlined CITY ATTORNEY SAYS GIANTS CIVIL SERVICE. The mayor was quoted on the evening news as responding, "Did the city attorney say that?" San Francisco, as any political-science student will tell you, has a weak-mayor form of government.

Governor Brown the Younger, reached at a San Francisco ashram, thought it was a good idea, but if this was just another ploy of San Francisco politicians to get state money in the post-Proposition 13 era, they had another guess coming. He said he hadn't been born yesterday, you know.

The commissioner of baseball said something to the effect that this was probably just another bit of nonsense coming out of San Francisco and needn't be taken seriously. He thought that San Francisco ought to start trying to solve its baseball problems instead of coming up with such tomfoolery.

Most observers thought that it was simply West Coast high jinks, that the idea was impossible and illegal on its face, and they had a good laugh.

Hadrian Ness didn't think it was funny. He took his severance pay and, with a small grant from the Civil Service Foundation, set up an office and brought the matter to court. Ness also managed to get an injunction against the Giants—or anyone else for that matter—using Candlestick Park until the case was settled. So a lot of people wanted the question resolved quickly. Anticipating appeals, the city and the Giants agreed to let the matter go directly to the California Supreme Court, where it was heard in late January of 1980.

The young grandson of one of the justices had just been traded by the Giants to a Cincinnati farm team in Tennessee. The justice didn't know where Tennessee was, was sure the boy had never been given a chance, felt the whole business of buying and trading players was like slavery, and thought he'd never see his favorite grandson again.

By a one-vote margin, the California Supreme Court agreed with lawyer Ness; the Giants had to be civil service.

San Francisco's ball team became the laughingstock of baseball in almost no time, well before the first pitch of the 1980 season. Baseball, like most other professional sports, was big business. Most fans knew that where the team played had almost nothing to do with the team itself. Place was incidental to the business/sport, a vestige of an older, more romantic time, when the owners also owned local breweries and the players might even live on the next street. In the modern era the players had almost never grown up in the cities where they played. They came from places like Cuba and Mexico. Only the bat boys lived in the home city.

It was an era of trades, options, release clauses, multiyear contracts, and making it while you could. Game times and places were determined more by the imagined needs of a preprogrammed national television audience than by local preference. Most people suspected that national and international TV ran sports anyway. It was clear that a local team, made up of local civil servants who came from and lived in San Francisco, could never compete in an international sport.

The players were dumbfounded. Civil service? Civil servants? They had only recently been given some freedom from the odious "reserve clause" that bound them for life to whichever team owned their contracts. They were making lots of money now that they were almost free to play for the highest bidder. Players knew that civil servants didn't make much money, no one called a civil servant could. So they quickly turned to their lawyers, agents, and contracts.

There was understandable confusion amid the fact and rumor that went the rounds. Old contracts would have to be honored, wouldn't they? Players could play out their options and then try to land with another team—but who would want them? Would there be pay cuts? The lawyers and the agents had a windfall of unexpected fees and commissions while looking after their players' interests. They felt secure in advising the latter to take it easy and see how things sorted themselves out. The season was about to start, and in all likelihood they would be secure for the year.

Player security was actually enhanced when Giants' manager Grubb tried to fire his third-base coach just before the season started. The coach had a drinking problem and was wobbly on the field three out of five days. He kept sending base runners home from second base on groundballs hit to the infield—the runners were always out by 40 feet. And Grubb had found out that the coach was having an affair with his wife. So Grubb fired the bounder, who promptly appealed to the Civil Service Commission.

Bernice D'Orsi, head of the civil service, advised her commissioners that drunkenness on the job, during games, had not been proved (Grubb wondered how you could prove that), that the coach sent the runners home on his best professional judgment and it was his judgment against the manager's (who, by sitting in the dugout, was farther from the actual scene of action), and that the wife-stealing business was personal, not professional and work-related. Grubb should certainly be able to make that simple distinction and not carry over a private relationship into the work environment. D'Orsi therefore recommended against the firing and was upheld unanimously by the commission. Grubb was dazed by the experience. He had always been able to fire coaches at will. It was one of his few pleasures. Worse yet, now that the business about his wife and the coach was out in the open, he would have to move out of his apartment. He had never had to do that before. He locked himself in the manager's office for three days and then looked for a new place to live.

Hearing the news, some oldtime players barely hanging on, as well as some rookies not quite out of the minor leagues but praying never to go back to the Fresnos of the world, were seen walking into the office of the civil-service union.

The season opened without incident. The mayor threw out the first pitch (to D'Orsi, for a little humor) and was booed by 4,000 paying fans. In his abbreviated speech he wondered if this might not be the dawn of a new baseball era, and was booed again. The game, against the Padres, started well. The Giants were hitting, mostly doubles. By the fourth inning, the third-base coach had sent three base runners to their doom at home plate; and then the roof caved in. The Giants lost, 12–1.

Team morale was none too good to begin with, and soon got a lot worse. Not many people came to the home games; most of them were silent when they did. Without kids clamoring for their autographs, players' fragile egos were hurt. No one asked for a city traffic engineer's autograph—why would they want a city baseball player's? San Franciscans backed winners, and it was clear that a civil-service team could not be a winner, so the fans stayed home and the players felt bad, and their playing suffered.

Road trips were worse. The team was laughed at in other cities. Players were asked over and over how it felt to be a civil servant. What would they do during the off-season, when all the other players got to stay home and fish and drink beer? Would they be street cleaners or, since they were part of the Department of Parks and Recreation, would they be playground leaders, or gardeners? The ball players didn't think that kind of question was too funny. They stayed in their hotel rooms, forgoing their usual lobby seats, where, in better times, they had been oohed and aahed over. Now, people stared and were more prone to point their fingers and snicker than to lionize. To top it all off, groupies who followed big sports teams stopped following the Giants. Civil servants, even if they were baseball players, didn't have much sex appeal.

In late May, in the eighth inning of a scoreless game in Philadelphia, Grubb went to the mound to replace Denny Sullivan, his rookie starting pitcher, who had just walked three Phillies on 12 straight bad pitches to load the bases. Sullivan refused to leave the game. He said he was doing fine and had a right to remain that was protected by civil service. It was a matter of professional opinion. Besides, this could be his first major-league victory. Grubb had told the kid to quit screwing around and to go take a shower. Sullivan refused. He was the pitcher, he had been designated the pitcher, and he had a right to pitch. They weren't even behind. Walks were as much a part of the game as strikeouts. They went into the records. It was like being fired without cause. He wanted a civil-service hearing.

Grubb went for Sullivan's throat. It took three Phillies to separate the two Giants, and the umpire threw them both out of the game. The story made national headlines. Here was the inevitable consequences of bureaucrats and lawyers meddling in places where they had no business. It made no difference to the baseball world that the Civil Service Commission later upheld Grubb's action on the grounds that a department head had the right to assign staff as he thought best to carry out the department's responsibilities. The commission did, however, censure Grubb for lack of physical restraint.

The baseball establishment came to the realization that the Giants were no laughing matter. By the All-Star break in early July, when the subject of the big-league meetings was what to do about the Giants, the team was already 25 games behind the leading Dodgers. Meetings of baseball moguls are seldom productive and this was no exception. There were indications that the Giants would be bankrupt by September, so baseball decided to wait until the season was over. In the meantime, the problem took care of itself. Well, almost.

As strange as it may seem, it was the totally bizarre circumstances of the Giants that began to have a positive effect on the team's fortunes. The first sign was when it became apparent that there was a hard knot of fans that showed up at most home games and sat together, isolated, out in the right-field stands. The 1,000 or so people were readily defined by all the vacant seats around them. They were, of course, civil servants. They took advantage of cheap tickets available to them as part of a promotion to stave off financial disaster and came every night. They soon found out that the afternoon rest-break that the union had won for them could be stretched into four or five innings on day games. They were a happy, funloving bunch who soon got to know and like each other and found Candlestick Park a good place to hold informal meetings to discuss working conditions and wages. They cheered on their union brothers in uniform, regardless of how the game was going or of how badly their heroes played. They were a positive crowd.

San Francisco's civil-service fans helped, but not enough to make any difference. The nature of San Franciscans made a difference. Remember, San Franciscans are the kind of people that voted for McGovern, legalizing pot, legalizing abortions, and the rights of homosexuals, and against Jarvis-Gann, the death penalty, and a lot of other things that later became important. To some of them, in July, the notion of their local team competing against the national and international impersonal institution that baseball had become gave the whole matter a David-and-Goliath character. There was no question but that the Giants were the Davids, and there was no question of which was the right side to be on, especially since the hometowners were getting beat up so badly. Fans could come out and joyfully cheer the Giants on and not be disappointed when they lost. More people, relaxed, came to the games to cheer (and laugh at) the underdog. It was nice to be seen there, like conspicuous consuming. Girls went alone or in pairs, and so did boys. Candlestick Park became a good place to meet other people, and maybe go home with them. It was an even better place to go once the management added white wine (served in little plastic goblets) and a remarkable mini-quiche to its choice of food. Still more people came.

The players felt they were being laughed at at first, but they joined in the good humor of it all and actually played better, losing less frequently.

Attendance jumped again when civil-service employees from around the Bay Area made the Giants their favorites and came from as far as Milpitas.

Civil servants from other major-league cities got the message. When the Giants were on the road they began to find themselves cheered on by whole sections of fans. These were local municipal employees coming to support the visitors. Hell, they were civil-service brothers all. It was possible to identify with the Giants, and they needed a hand. So the city employees of St. Louis came to cheer the Giants and boo the Cards. The Cards muttered about the fickle nature of their fans and went into a slump, losing four straight to the Giants.

Team morale went up. It skyrocketed when, in New York, some civil-service groupies showed up to give the boys support. Jocks were jocks after all, regardless of their civil status. The Giants took two of three from the Mets, and then murdered the Expos in three straight after someone translated the French banners, "*L'union fait la force—Vive les Giants.*"

Some young kids out in Walnut Creek were bugging their parents to move to San Francisco so that the kids could have a chance to make the Giants' civil-service regulated team. This was not lost on city politicians and city planners who for years had been looking for ways to stop the flight of middle-class families to the suburbs. Local baseball might just succeed where lousy schools had failed.

By the time the Giants returned from their road trip toward the end of July, they were a relaxed, winning bunch of guys. Morale was up, and they were playing over their heads. A 10- or 20-game fluke streak perhaps, but fun nonetheless.

As attendance rose, the team continued to play well. They were still 14 games out of first place by the end of July, a distinct improvement, but it was clear that they were too far behind to ever catch up.

In early August, two stars from the hated, league-leading Dodgers announced that they were playing out their options and would toil for whichever teams would pay them the most millions the next year. The two were already pocketing something in the vicinity of $700,000 a year—each. That made the Giants, with their civil-service aura, even more popular. (Management wasn't talking about how much three or four of its stars were making, or that 15 of the Giants were planning to do the same thing as the two ungrateful Dodgers.) The Dodgers went into a slump with the announcement of the impending defections, and they dropped nine straight, four to the Giants on a memorable weekend when 250,000 people squeezed through Candlestick's turnstiles to see the civil-service Giants.

By the end of August, they were only four games out of first place and were driving hard. Just then, Fidel Castro announced that he would love to come to the World Series if the Giants won. The idea of a public, socialist team was inspiring and could only help Cuban-U.S. relations. Even people from the Haight-Ashbury started coming to games after Fidel's announcement. The Giants took over first place on September 15, then won another three straight from Atlanta, and led the pack by three games on the twentieth.

San Francisco was a madhouse. There were only two weeks left in the season. Orders for World Series tickets were pouring in. Every hotel room was booked in anticipation. The papers and television were full of the Giants. No team had ever come from 25 games behind to win the pennant. And this was a civil-service team! Howard Cosell marveled over "the incredible vitality of this team and this town, the city by the Golden Gate."

In city hall, more than one observer commented that the workers there seemed to stand straighter and taller than usual. They were dressing better (fewer combinations of jackets and pants from different suits of slightly different colors) and seemed to have shine about them. The level of public service hadn't changed, but it was a more purposeful inefficiency. The mayor recalled that he had predicted a new era, and Governor Brown reminded everyone that the idea was his in the first place. Hadrian Ness was being wooed by the city attorney to take an important high-paying job, but was holding out for tenured status.

Manager Grubb was getting a divorce, but that didn't bother him since he had become a celebrity. He also had a wonderful, built-in scapegoat for the few times the Giants lost. He could publicly berate the performance of his third-base coach—"How can I manage when civil service makes me keep people like that?" No one could blame him if they failed on occasion. He had no control of the dolts. The team's success under such circumstances was due to his superior managing, the wonderful San Francisco fans, and a solid core of dedicated players.

On September 21, late in a game with Chicago that the Giants were leading by eight runs, the third-base coach had Billy Murphy, one of the dedicated ones, try to steal home for what would have been a superfluous score. Kretch, the Chicago pitcher, furious that the Giants would add insult to injury, threw his best pitch of the game, directly at Murphy. It broke Murphy's leg.

Murphy, the second baseman, was a steady but not outstanding member of the team. He just did his job, and a lot of people didn't even know his name. So it didn't seem to be a crucial loss—at least not until the new second baseman showed up the next day.

Gussie Johnson, sent by civil service to replace Murphy, was a big, strapping, fast, San Francisco-bred Chinese who had been batting .420 in the minors (albeit with the Golden Gate Park Dunes). The only trouble with Gussie was that he was left-handed.

Manager Grubb was livid. He screamed at D'Orsi that it was impossible to have a left-handed second baseman. A southpaw couldn't possibly make the pivot necessary on double plays. There had never been a left-handed second baseman in the history of baseball. Ask Cosell.

D'Orsi, as ever, was calm to the onslaught. She pointed out that Grubb was just using an old, old ploy of all the other department heads to undermine the civil-service merit system: They were always trying to create so-called specialist positions, geared to particular people, rather than general positions where many applicants could compete and get jobs by merit. Only recently, the city-planning director had been caught trying to create something called an urban-designer position, when it was clear that a city planner was a city planner. Just because the planner who passed first had a background in political economics (Marxism) was no reason that he couldn't design a park as well as the next planner. An infielder was an infielder, by God. None of this specialist second-baseman sub-category nonsense.

Besides, Gussie had competed in a well-advertised exam and had come in first. It made no difference to D'Orsi that Gussie had gotten such a high score by virtue of the extra points that came his way automatically as an armed-forces veteran. D'Orsi also let Grubb know that she had observed that there were no Chinese on the ball team. Was Grubb living testimony that the bureaucracy was bigoted, and was he looking for a civil-rights suit?

D'Orsi told Grubb that the civil-service union watched her every step. She was powerless, she couldn't set a precedent for the rest of the civil service. The union's attorneys would have the matter in the

courts for months, and in the meantime Grubb would have no
second basemen, not even a left-handed one. Anyway, if Gussie
didn't work out, then Grubb had the right to terminate him during
the first six months, if there was a good reason. Grubb perked up at
this, but only until he realized that two of the next three people on
the "infielder" list were over 45 (but under 60), part of a new, "Not
So Senior" minority group that was just emerging in San Francisco.
The third was known to be active in the women's movement. The
fourth person on the list might be a winner—he was young and
didn't know anything except how to play baseball—but he was much
too far down on the list to offer Grubb any hope.

Grubb wandered unevenly back to Candlestick Park. That afternoon Gussie had four hits and scored the Giants' two runs. In the
ninth inning, score tied 2–2, bases loaded, one out, the Cubs' batter
hit solidly to the Giants' shortstop, who threw to second base for one
out. Johnson's relay to first was not in time to catch the batter for a
double play, and a run, the winning run, scored from third. D'Orsi
heard the game in her office at city hall and was ecstatic about
Gussie's hitting.

The Giants were still two games ahead, and the next day Grubb
moved his right-handed third baseman to play second and tried
Gussie at third.

Grubb did fire Two-Fingered Brown, the backup catcher that civil
service sent. Brown had a rifle arm but no control of where the ball
went when he threw it. That characteristic hadn't been screened out
in the civil-service exam, which was three-quarters written (and
tested the player's knowledge of baseball) and one-quarter actually
playing in the field. Brown, a reader, had done magnificently on the
written exam (100 percent), so it didn't matter that he only got a
score of 40 on the playing part of the exam. His combined score of
85 was more than enough to pass, and with the 15 extra points he got
for being handicapped, he came out on top.

Brown had a mania for trying to pick runners off at first base,
having done that once successfully in the Little League 10 years
earlier. In a game against Houston, not two days after the Gussie
Johnson incident, Brown tried to pick a runner off at first. The
throw, like a shot, hit pitcher Montefusco on the kneecap and that
was all for Montefusco for the season and for the Giants that day.

It wasn't all for Two-Fingered Brown, though. Grubb fired him,
and his firing was upheld (this being Brown's probationary period,
when department heads had absolute discretionary rights). But, as a
gesture of kindness and humanity (Brown had two wives and three
kids to support), the Civil Service Commission directed that his
name be returned to the bottom of the civil-service "catchers" list, so
that he might have a chance with some other "department." D'Orsi

didn't point out to them that no other city department used catchers, two-fingered ones least of all. As luck would have it, no one else was on the list at that time (the others who had passed the exam had since moved out of town), so the bottom of the list was the same as the top of the list and Brown was back with the Giants, duly certified, the next day.

The Giants' lead was down to one game. The season was drawing to a close.

There are people in San Francisco who will tell you that the season ended the next day, when a new outfielder showed up—in a wheel-chair. Most people close to the situation will tell you that never really happened—it was at best a prank pulled by the visiting Dodgers.

It is certain, however, that Manager Grubb had a nervous break-down the next day. Whether it was the Two-Fingered Brown inci-dent, or the Gussie Johnson affair, or the third-base coach's affair with his wife, or just his hatred of D'Orsi, or one of a thousand other reasons is hard to say. Trained people—civil-service psychologists at San Francisco General Hospital—are searching for an answer now.

Some observers will tell you that San Franciscans live in their own world. They will tell you that there was a World Series in 1980, just as in other years, and that to hear people talk around city hall, the civil-service Giants were in it—or could have been.

For some people in San Francisco, it is still September, October and the World Series are just around the corner, and the Giants may damned well make it. All they need is a good, left-handed first baseman and there's a terrific, can't-miss prospect just waiting to win it all for the Giants. He was second on the civil-service list. The new manager, an expert from Berkeley's School of Public Policy, is in the process of firing the right-handed first baseman the civil service sent, but that could take a while because the case is being appealed.

Some city-hall watchers will tell you that time does not stand still, that it is Monday of the last week of the season and they, the Civil Service Commission, will be meeting this very afternoon to decide the issue. It's on their agenda. They will tell you that there is great expectation in the Giants' offices and dressing rooms in Candlestick Park. The Giants are only one game behind and a pennant is still in sight.

A civil-service clerk, on the staff of the Civil Service Commission, will tell you, just as he told his wife five minutes ago during his break, that a lawyer for the civil-service union, representing the right-handed first baseman, has requested a postponement, and that such requests are almost always honored. Maybe they will decide the matter next week. Maybe the season won't end.

WORLD SERIES GAME VI

THE CANDY MAN DELIVERS

By Lou Chapman

From the Milwaukee Sentinel
Copyright, ©, 1979, Milwaukee Sentinel

The Pittsburgh Pirates had a feeling in their bones they could do it. And put the word *bones* in capital letters.

Bones is the nickname of Kent Tekulve, who saved a 4–0 victory for the Pirates in short relief Tuesday night and evened the Series at 3–3.

The team calls him that because at 6-feet-2, 158 pounds, Tekulve looks like a guy who has been in traction too long. When he turns sideways on the mound, it's a wonder he doesn't disappear.

To the Baltimore Orioles, Tekulve looked like the Jolly Green Giant as he struck out four and gave up a harmless single after coming in the seventh for starter John Candelaria.

The loss was particularly painful to the Orioles, who had hoped to wrap up the Series before 53,759 of the home faithful. But it was probably most painful to Candelaria, who ached all night but managed to put down the Orioles on six hits through six shutout innings.

The Candy Man, as he is called by The Family, pitched just one inning in September and struggled through a late-season muscle tear in his left side. It bothered him again this night but not until the sixth inning.

"Candy thought he felt a twinge when he was warming up for the sixth, but when I went to talk to him, he said he was all right," said Pirate manager Chuck Tanner. "I was concerned about it all the way. I was going to get him, but he pitched through it. In my opinion, he's one of the greatest money pitchers in the game."

Slumped on a stool after the game, Candelaria could hardly move. He admitted his side bothered him, but not enough to make him leave early.

"If you were in the pain I'm in right now, well, let's just say I'm happy we're going seven games," said Candelaria, 14–9 during the regular season. "At the end, I couldn't twist my body. I knew I had to get out and not try to be a hero, not try to win it by myself. It means too much."

Candelaria struck out only two but did not walk a batter and did not allow two base runners in any inning except the first.

Candelaria was the loser last Friday, 8–4, at Three Rivers Stadium, allowing eight hits and six runs in three innings. He refused to blame his injury for that showing, however.

"I was fine physically then," Candelaria said. "I just got the ball up and I got my tail kicked. Maybe I shouldn't have gone out after the [67-minute] rain delay, but when I warmed up again, I felt strong."

The 6–7 left hander admitted being down mentally after Friday but obviously felt even worse with his team trailing, three games to one, after Saturday's loss.

"I was down because we were down, but I felt I had let the team down Friday night," said Candelaria. "But this was a big one for us, and I feel like I helped redeem myself. I knew I couldn't afford to give up much against a guy like [Oriole starter Jim] Palmer."

And Tekulve, knowing the pain Candelaria was in, could not give up for the sake of his teammate, even though he had the great baseball mind of Oriole manager Earl Weaver working against him.

The slinky pitcher with the submarine delivery had the tin can tied to him Saturday when Weaver unloaded four left-handed hitters in a big six-run eighth inning.

This time, the little manager spaced out his left handers, and Tekulve orbited in space higher than the Birds.

The Candelaria-Tekulve one-two punch made it the fourth combined shutout in the Series. Luis Tiant, who was then with the Boston Red Sox, turned in the last Series shutout. He beat the Cincinnati Reds, 6–0, in 1975.

"They [the Orioles] have hit the ball hard, but we've been lucky enough to get an out in key situations," Tekulve said. "Tonight was a good example. They had men on base a couple of times and hit the ball hard at our infielders, but we got double plays. We have been able to hold them down a little bit in the last couple of games but that doesn't mean anything when we go out there tomorrow."

Palmer, the loser, drives a white Mercedes with "ACE" on the license plates. But this time, the Pirates trumped the Birds' ace by tacking together two-run innings in the seventh and eighth.

"I told you we were gonna win it in seven, I told you when were down 3–1," said the third baseman Bill Madlock, who made several excellent defensive plays. "We do everything the hard way. You saw that by watching us all season. It was the same thing tonight. We had the opportunity to do some things in the first inning. We had Omar [Moreno] and Tim [Foli] on second and the guys you want coming up—Dave Parker, Willie Stargell, and John Milner—but we didn't do it.

"Still, we kept battling."

The Orioles have prided themselves on smart defensive execution throughout the first five games. But this time they had a couple of defensive lapses and cost Palmer the game.

Oh, Rich Dauer and Benny Ayala weren't charged with errors, but they didn't make the plays when they had to.

Dauer's failure showed up flagrantly in the seventh after Moreno delivered a one-out single to right, and Foli beat out a hit behind second as Palmer got his glove on the ball but couldn't contain it.

Parker then singled past Dauer, who later claimed that "the ball knuckled on me." The hit scored Moreno and advanced Foli to third. Stargell then brought home some more bacon with a sacrifice fly to Ayala in deep left, scoring Foli.

Weaver was asked later whether he thought Dauer should have stopped the ball. The manager diplomatically replied, "It was a tough play. It was sinking."

Weaver was then asked if he thought Palmer blew the double play on Foli's hit.

"First of all, Palmer pitched real good," Weaver said. "And the third baseman and the first baseman were guarding the lines. The ball just tipped off Palmer's glove, and it slowed the ball down.

"But we should have gotten runs earlier. It's too bad. Palmer pitched excellent."

Ayala made an error in judgment in the eighth after Ed Ott's one-out single to right, Phil Garner then drove one toward left, and Ayala, who was on first, came in on the ball as it later bounced over the left-field fence for a ground-rule double.

Ott had to stop at third and scored on Bill Robinson's sacrifice fly to Ayala. Moreno then singled to center, scoring Garner. Moreno had been known as Omar the Out Maker in this series and redeemed himself slightly with his RBI.

The speedy center fielder had left 15 teammates stranded on the bases.

So now the Pirates have the job of unpacking. They had their luggage piled on trucks, which would have taken them to the airport for the long flight home had they lost.

However, they were optimistic enough to reserve their hotel rooms for another day and catcher Steve Nicosia keynoted their feelings before the players' pregame introductions.

"C'mon, guys, we need this one," he said. And the team responded.

"Man, it's five-card stud showdown now," Parker shrieked in the clubhouse afterward.

"Keep doing it, Bucs—gotta keep doing it—gotta do it one more time," added second-baseman Phil Garner as the Pirates broke into rhythmic clapping, whistling, and high school type cheering in which they spelled out P-I-R-A-T-E-S.

Stargell and Garner both stressed that the only way Pittsburgh can win the series is by playing the way they have the past two games, rather than the way they did through the first four games.

"We just feel if we can keep playing tonight and like we did in that last game in Pittsburgh, well, we'll take our chances," said, Stargell. "It took us a while to get there tonight, but we knew something was going to break."

Parker put it this way: "I know the Orioles gotta be thinking.

"We're an explosive ball club and we've been playing some kind of defense . . . the attitude of this ball club is always positive—I don't think you should be in competitive athletics if you're not positive.

"We've been fighting back all year and this is right where we want to be now, to come back from being down three games to one, that just makes it even more dramatic," he said.

And because of the high-pitched enthusiasm flowing through the team right now, Madlock and many teammates said they liked their chances of taking game number seven, in which Pirates right-hander Jim Bibby will start against left-hander Scott McGregor.

"We felt after we beat Mike Flanagan in Sunday's game we beat their best and we don't think anyone else can beat us," Madlock. "We never play good when we're ahead but when it's even we figure it's our ball game."

Only three clubs have come back from a 3–1 deficit to win. The New York Yankees of 1958 were one of them, and it should be vividly recalled in Milwaukee. The then Milwaukee Braves had a 3–1 edge in that classic.

Weaver and his Birds are not worried about Wednesday's game.

"I'm going to pitch the same as before—the same as any other game," McGregor said.

WORLD SERIES WRAP-UP

STARGELL AND WEAVER: THEY SET THE SERIES FLOW

By Thomas Boswell

From The Washington Post
Copyright, ©, 1979, The Washington Post

Willie Stargell's Pirates and Earl Weaver's Orioles can take their rest now, lie down for an aeon or, at least, a long warm winter of content.

Every Buccaneer and Bird should buy a golden easy chair with his Series share, for they were very good and deserve a happy hibernation.

The teams which just stretched baseball's season down to the last vivid innings of a seventh World Series game are not so much reflections of their towns as they are extensions of their leaders.

Those who try to chew this October feast by mixing Iron City beer with Chesapeake crab cakes will get only indigestion. The cities—Pittsburgh and Baltimore—are not at issue here. The men—Stargell and Weaver—are.

The whole flow and feeling of this classic emanated from these two central characters—the brainy, excitable Weaver with his chain-smoking strategy and the stoic, brawny Stargell with his phlegmatic, wine-sipping dignity.

Weaver, his tactical battle plan drawn for weeks, almost won in a blitz before the Pirates knew what hit them. But for a half-dozen tantalizing "ifs" in the second game, the Orioles might well have swept. Don't laugh. The Pirates didn't.

The Orioles attacked like rabid gamblers—scoring five runs in the first inning of the first game—throwing conventional strategy out the window, disdaining the bunt and the "take" sign, and finally building a six-run, eighth-inning comeback around a wave of pinch hitters to take a 3–1 lead in games.

The little Napoleonic manager's tactic was simple: Win fast, before they can figure us out, before they understand our hidden strengths and our equally concealed weaknesses.

That's why Mike Flanagan pitched the fifth game in Pittsburgh, going for the kill instead of letting the majors' leading winner get extra rest for a return to Baltimore. The first rule of the blitz is to forget the supply lines.

The Pirates were on their knees—reduced to left-hander Jim Rooker as a starting pitcher.

Other champions might have waited, head bowed, for the ax, especially when one final blow fell—the death of Manager Chuck Tanner's 70-year-old mother on Sunday morning.

If the Orioles mirror Weaver's manic intensity and alertness—a team of superstitious students who analyze the game, yet fear black cats—then the Pirates are the opposite.

Stargell, naturally, sets the mood. He is the quintessential patient slugger—the stolid man who is willing to ignore the aggravation of striking out more than any player in history for the sake of these 471 times when his syrupy slash of a swing has sent the ball out of the yard.

On the next-to-last day of the regular season, Stargell made a nationally televised error to lose an extra-inning game that might have ruined the Pirate season. His reaction was to yawn, play cards with the clubhouse man, and say, "I screwed up. I've done it before and I'll do it again."

The next day he hit a home run.

No team in baseball is so placid under pressure as the Bucs. The reason is Stargell.

Figuratively, the Pirates rub the stomach of their baseball for a sense of peace. Within The Family—a notion which is entirely Stargell's creation—the aging 230-pound first baseman has mastered the role of "Pops."

Like an actor who seemed miscast in the flashy parts of his youth, Stargell has been reborn to play the guru. He knows it, loves it, and wouldn't cast aside the persona for the world.

"What goes around, comes around," the Pirate says. Which means, the wheel of fate turns.

So, in the sixth inning of the fifth game, with Baltimore ahead, 1–0, and Flanagan cruising along with a three-hitter and six strikeouts, the wheel turned, the karma changed.

Flanagan walked Tim Foli—a lead-off man who chokes the bat a foot. The Pirates stirred like Frankenstein when the first lightning jolt hits him.

A single, a bunt, and Stargell was at the plate.

Moments later, the Oriole center fielder was by the warning track, catching Stargell's long sacrifice fly.

The game was tied, 1–1, and the Birds' spell broken.

Weaver gambled once more, pitching to two-time batting champion Bill Madlock, instead of walking him to get to Rookie Steve Nicosia, who hit .063 for the Series.

The percentages blew up in Weaver's face—you can only buck them so long. Madlock singled, the Pirates led, 2–1, and the big Baltimore crap-out had begun.

Flanagan had lost and Rooker had not—the 23-game winner trumped by the four-game winner.

When the Orioles feel a chill, it is always the bats that freeze first.

Few clubs are as prone to profound team slumps as the Orioles, or admit to being so totally bewildered by them. The Birds' normal remedy—the only one Weaver has any faith in—is old-fashioned witchcraft.

Their drought—two runs in the last 28 Series innings, compared to those five runs in the first inning of the first game—had reached such a desperate point that Weaver refused to take the lineup card to home plate before the final game.

Instead, he gave it to his good-luck charm coach, Frank Robinson, who handed it to the umpire left-handed behind his back. When your trump card for the seventh game is the triple-reverse whammy, you're in a World Serious of trouble.

One deep, dark Oriole secret—the mere suggestion of which brings a glare of betrayal to Weaver's eyes—is that a diet of slow southpaw curveballs is often a harbinger of The Slump.

Weaver feels about left-handed junkballers the way the pharaoh felt about locusts. Sure, often the O's light up a lefty like a pinball wizard. But when they don't there's a snowballing effect—a shudder through the team—like the five consecutive games in August when left handers held them to a .114 team average.

When the syndrome strikes, the Orioles assume the fetal position, close their eyes, and try to ignore the horrid thing until it goes away of its own accord.

The Birds thought they had frightened away their private ghoul—like flashing a crucifix at Dracula—when they kayoed John Candelaria in the third game. Maybe Tanner had not noticed how pathetic they looked against Rooker in long relief in the opener.

But the Bucs, who apparently scouted the O's backward and didn't know that southpaws were the best way to incorporate Kiko Garcia and Bennie Ayala into the Bird defense, finally had to do the right thing as a last resort.

Rooker was the bogeyman in the fifth game who got the Three Rivers Stadium crowd back to boogieing to Sister Sledge. Candelaria did the same for six shutout innings in the next game, and who should get the final win but lefty Grant Jackson?

Even including the O's' five-run inning off the Candy Man after a 67-minute rain delay in the third game, the ERA of the Pirate left handers was 2.47.

If Stargell's quiet, lumbering calm was the perfect remedy for the

Pirates' 3–1 deficit dilemma, then Weaver's frenetic superabun-
dance of nervous energy was left without an outlet as his team slid.

For one thing, it's tough to be feisty and combative when you've
got such a rotten head cold that you have to carry a towel to blow
your schnoz and wipe your eyes.

Also, one of Weaver's pet tricks was denied him. In time of crisis,
he invariably draws pressure to himself to take if off his players,
whether the method be a tirade at umpires (his favorite), a protest, a
strange lineup shake-up, or any sort of curious behavior he can
dream up.

It is absolute baseball doctrine not to argue—not to say one tiny
word—against an umpire during a Series. In 76 classics only two
managers have been ejected, and one of those was Billy Martin.

And Weaver obeyed the precedent—never turning his cap
around and going beak to beak, never playing ring around the
maypole.

Without Weaver as a lightning rod to draw the flashes of media
and television attention to himself, the Oriole players had an unusual experience.

When things went wrong, suddenly they were the ones getting
grilled by 500 reporters. The torture left at least three Orioles as stiff
as if they had visited the electric chair.

In the first three AL playoff games, Al Bumbry reached base eight
times. The O's' offense purred. Then, he helped end game three
with a disastrous game-losing muff of a liner.

The Bee was stung by megamedia overkill. Thereafter, he was 3
for 24 (.125) and stole zero bases.

DeCinces, after making two errors in one inning in the Series
opener, got the same harsh, "Well, Doug, how does it feel to fall on
your face in front of 70 million people?"

DeCinces didn't get a hit in the next four games and had a
terminal case of the fielding jitters. He finally found himself with
four hits and what might have been a Series-turning defensive gem
in the last two games.

Then it was Eddie Murray's turn. He hit .417 in the playoffs, then
started the Series by reaching base in seven of his first eight at-bats.
He was going to be October's child.

However, he closed the game two show with a debatable cutoff
grab, and suddenly he was on the couch of the nation's sports
psychiatrists. From that moment on, Murrray was 0 for 21.

Perhaps the correlation is accidental. But it's dramatic.

Just as dramatic was the way that Weaver's game strategy, so
tactically sound for the 162-game haul, seemed slightly out of sync
with the realities of short-term Series play.

Weaver is a roll-the-dice, leave-the-players-alone manager who breaks out in hives when he sees other managers bedeviling their players with constant sacrifice bunts and "take" signs.

If the stone were rolled away from the baseball crypt and Weaver were allowed inside to read the sacred hieroglyphics, he is certain that they would say, "A walk, a bloop, and a three-run homer is the secret of baseball."

"If you play for one run, you lose by one run," says Weaver, the king of the baseball big-bang theorists.

In the three games that Baltimore won, the O's erupted for explosions of three, five, five, and six runs. In their other 58 innings, Baltimore generated just seven runs.

Traditionally, run-scoring is lower in the Series, and home run hitting, in particular, is down. The reason is simple. Cold October air, chilly hitters, enormous pressure, and a warm, constantly active hurler create all the conditions for a dead-ball-style game.

Weaver has taken four teams to the Series in 11 years. Once, the home run bats came through—in 1970 when the Birds hit 10 four-baggers off a weak Cincinnati staff in five games.

But three times Weaver has taken his big-inning style of ball to the Series and been shut down.

In 1969, his O's hit .146 with three homers in five games and lost to the Miracle Mets despite a 2.72 Baltimore ERA.

In 1971, Baltimore hit .205 in a seven-game loss to Pittsburgh with just five homers. The Bucs won despite modest runs total of two, two, three, three, four, four, and five.

Now, in 1979, the Birds hit .232 with just four homers in seven games from a club that had 181 homers in a 159-game regular season.

Once again, Baltimore's starting pitching was superb with six excellent efforts out of seven.

But, in the final three defeats, that big inning never came. Meanwhile, the O's' Big Three—Flanagan, Jim Palmer, and Scott McGregor—never had the aid of those little one-run innings that keep a hurler from thinking that boxes of dynamite are buried under the mound.

In a seven-game Series, the O's never deviated from 1927 Yankees-style station-to-station baseball. Baltimore had one sacrifice bunt, one attempt for a bunt hit, no hit and runs, and only two steal attempts.

The O's' attack was either thunder or stagnation. Ironically, all four of Baltimore's big innings, worth 19 of their 26 runs, were opened up not by their own hitting but by Pittsburgh errors or blatant misplays.

Weaver's tactical style has given him the third-best regular-season winning percentage in history—which probably is an accurate reflection of his spectacularly high status in the game. However, post-season play remains his Achilles' heel—the place where his record is solid, but could be better.

While the Orioles tried to pull, swinging for the fences, the Pirates amassed the second-highest team average in Series history (.323) by spraying the ball to all fields. Stargell took care of the limited Buc power—all three Pirate homers.

In fact, the eight regulars in the Pirates' normal starting lineup—the one they used most frequently all year—had a combined .372 mark.

The lowest average among those Pirate regulars was .333.

In the end, this Series was the pleasantest sort of anomaly—an event without losers, an affair that revealed the worth of several lesser-known characters.

Even the Orioles, once they have time to reflect, will have a hard time castigating themselves. Even those who are probably berating themselves most cruelly now will take a kinder view of their performance if they view the whole postseason as one great test.

For those 11 October games, Ken Singleton hit .364, Kiko Garcia .355, and Rick Dempsey .323. Those two deep end-of-Series slumpers—Murray and DeCinces—each produced 11 runs in 11 games, which is excellent. Only Bumbry (.189) and Gary Roenicke (.143)—who were probably the two biggest team-transforming surprises of the season—really suffered.

When this Series is recalled, it will not be the great swaths of boredom that flash to mind—the rain and snow delays, the procrastinating to accommodate TV, not the longest night game in Series history (3:18) and not the longest day game (3:48).

Rather, it will be the marvelous indeterminancy of this Series. Neither of the teams was clearly better. As late as the bottom of the eighth inning of the final game —with Murray at bat and the bases full in a 2–1 game—there was no way to know who would win, who should win, or why they would do it.

Only in retrospect is there a visible shape—a shadowy one at that. These Birds 'n Bucs were not all-time great teams—except perhaps in toughness and heart.

A case could be made that each of the first six games was not so much won as lost. Every vital rally, every turning point was an equal mixture of heroism and defensive frustration.

It is impossible to imagine the Oakland A's of 1972–74, or the Cincinnati Reds of 1975–76, or the New York Yankees of the past two years beating themselves under pressure so frequently as these foes managed.

These were teams of vivid personality, not clubs with fully formed, forged-in-the-fire baseball characters.

Despite their swagger and bulk, their high jinks and professed brotherhood, the Pirates made enough fundamental gaffes to have lost in a rapid four or five games.

By the final three games, the Orioles had shown how a team that has no Hall of Fame everyday players can go into its shell, each man hoping someone else will shoulder the load—a few players even looking like they couldn't wait for the last out to arrive so that they eyes of millions would leave them alone.

Amid this Series of bright personalities, unpredictable successes and failures, two famous and totally developed baseball characters stood above the rest—those of Stargell and Weaver—each dominating the mood and performance of his team.

This October stage suited Stargell best, because, finally, he was able to take matters into his own strong hands.

Weaver was left only with proxies. By the end, even his left-handed, behind-the-back lineup-card whammy had failed him. He could only wipe his eyes and watch.

FOOTBALL

THUNDERING FATTIES

By Vic Ziegel

From New York Magazine
Copyright, ©, 1979, News Group Publications, Inc.

The cabdriver had a question. And a story.

"Do you know this Howard Cosell? A woman friend of mine met him the other night at a party, the Miami Dolphins reunion. This is a very influential woman, knowed her a long time. She got no reason to lie to me. Said she took her 14-year-old boy to the party and this Cosell was there. Kid asked him, 'Mr. Cosell, who do you think is gonna win the Super Bowl, Dallas or Pittsburgh?' According to the woman—now this is hearsay, I guess, but she's an influential woman—according to her, Cosell told the kid, 'Son, who gives a shit?' "

There was, to be sure, a great deal of hearsay during Super Bowl week. Then again, the driver did have an honest back-of-the-neck.

The listener meant to check the story with Cosell, congratulate him on stepping so accurately into America's most expensive sports spectacle. But what if Cosell denied having said it? ("An out-and-out fabrication. A canard and a falsehood and I can prove it. And how much money did you make last year?")

Cosell, the ABC sportscaster, was in Miami to tape NBC's Super-Bowl Saturday Night. Fortunately, he is able to rent out to other networks. The Super Bowl would have been just another afternoon of thundering fatties if not for the presence of blue-chippers like Howard, O. J. Simpson, the Jamaica Military Band ("It has played as far afield as Trinidad, at the opening of the Federal Parliament of the West Indies, now defunct"), Thomas "Hollywood" Henderson, Joe "Can Man" Graham, Art "Harpo" Metrano, Sandy Bain (the party planner who saved the NFL from putting two chicken dishes on the Caribbean buffet), Bill Pescado, assorted cabdrivers, Tiny and Joey (white parrots), the sad little guy at the bar, the Connecticut radio man, stone crabs, and, in the skin-tight pink-and-purple velour pantsuit, waiting for a customer, Super Bowl or no Super Bowl, Laverne ("I tried 'Shirley' for a couple weeks, but I think I'm more the 'Laverne' type").

Miami, just before the Super Bowl, was a city of parties surrounded by water. And anything else you might add to a drink.

"I'm so happy," Bill Pescado doesn't realize he's shouting. "Look!" the bartender is pouring him a Stolichnaya. Nobody ever handed a Stolichnaya to Bill Pescado without something in return.

When Pescado actually works, he helps a friend answer the telephone. The friend is a bookmaker. Pescado doesn't bet on football. Doesn't much like the game. He's at NBC's party in the grand ballroom of the Omni Hotel because somebody had an extra ticket. "The Super Bowl? I don't need it. I live on a houseboat. When it's Super Bowl time the big party boats come down and shake up the water. But this"—he points to the buffet tables that run the length of one wall—"this could make me a born-again fan. I've got drink at my fingertips, food at my touch, and music to my ears."

The band is playing a Glenn Miller medley as Pescado lindies to the NBC buffet. His beard and beret give the servers something to think about.

"What's that?" Pescado asks.

"Veal," he's told.

"What kind of veal?"

"Excellent veal."

"And that?"

"That's chicken. Average chicken." A few minutes later he's surveying the cheese tray. "That's blue cheese," he says. "And this is Brie, right?" He jabs toward a wedge of Port Salut. "What's that?"

The server is glad to help. "That's cheese too."

For NBC, the Super Bowl played for three hours, 31 minutes. At $190,000 for each 30-second commercial, that's, hmmm, a sweet piece of change.

"It's not a tough sell," says Bert Zeldon, NBC's vice-president for sports sales. "For the companies who want to be associated with this event it doesn't matter what the cost is. If the price scares some people away they might go for the pre- or postgame price."

And for the first time, at the bargain rate of $130,000 for 30 seconds, you can advertise during the sudden-death period. "We tried it at the World Series on extra innings," Zeldin says, "and it worked once. It's really a super buy for the Super Bowl because obviously people are going to watch the sudden death."

What's that? you say. What if there is no sudden death? What happens then? Well, friend, there's always 1981, and NBC Sports Sales is already taking orders for that game. (The other guys have it next year.) "We're asking $225,000 for 30 seconds," Zeldin admits. "A few people wanted to make the long-term commitment, and when we told them the price they didn't flinch."

The NBC party was the night after the National Football League party, when the NFL feeds everybody it knows. About 4,000 this year. The site, the four floors of the National Airlines terminal. At the top of the escalator a hostess is waiting with a kebab of chicken, cherries, and kumquats. This morsel is interrupted by a screech. Of course, riding their bicycles across a high wire strung between two indoor trees are Tina and Joey, the madcap white parrots.

Since it is clearly silly time, there is nothing to do but search out their agent. How many of these parrots can ride the high wire? "Only Tina and Joey." Is it easier for a boy parrot or a girl parrot? "Only when it comes to laying eggs."

He hands me a business card. The people from the Turks and Caicos islands give out huge shells. A man is rolling cigars. His lovely assistant is giving them all away. I stop at a bar and spot a sad little guy.

"I can't believe it," he is saying, staring at the floor. "It's gone."

The bartender looks concerned, "Where was it?"

"Right here." The little guy points to the floor. "Jesus, this is unbelievable, I had it a second ago. Oh, Jesus."

My question: What did you lose?

"My seashell," he says. "It was one of the real heavy ones."

Paul Zimmerman, the *New York Post*'s sports columnist, strolls by. "The New Orleans party last year was better. After it was over we went to see a stripper who put champagne glasses on her boobs and drank out of them. 'It ain't sexy,' she said, 'but it is different.' "

Since it is best for them not to hear such conversation, the players are not invited to these affairs.

The Steelers are confined to a hotel near the Miami airport; Dallas, in a softer setting in Fort Lauderdale. And each morning, as regularly as nausea, the sports writers are bused into each camp to meet the players and eat breakfast. (Definition of a veteran sports writer: He holds off on breakfast until the visit to Lauderdale. The Cowboys put out an ambitious spread—quiche, cream-of-chicken crepes, popovers. The one category that belonged to the Steelers was their impressive collection of single-serving cold-cereal boxes.)

The coach steps to a microphone, usually when the strawberries are being spooned, and waits for questions. Pittsburgh's Chuck Noll is great fun at these sessions, because he's more likely to go berserk. And he looks more like a football coach than Dallas's stony-faced Tom Landry. Without his television suit and fedora, Landry, at 54, resembles a trim school custodian.

"Chuck, if you could tell TV viewers what one thing to look for as an indicator to the final score, what would that be?"

"If I were to tell TV viewers what I think would be an indicator, I'd probably be misleading them the way they usually are."

"Can you get away with more in the Super Bowl than you can in the regular season?"

"I don't think I like that question. I think it presupposes something."

"Chuck, would you talk about your respect and admiration for Art Rooney after working 10 years for him?" "Chuck, would you say something about Lynn Swann's season?" "Why doesn't the halfback call the signals instead of the quarterback?" "Chuck, can you teach a quarterback to survive out there or is that a crap shoot?"

"I don't think I understand the question."

The star of the Dallas press conference is Thomas "Hollywood" Henderson, the quipping linebacker. You can call him "Thomas" and you can call him "Hollywood" and you can call him "56," but don't call him . . .

"Thomas, why don't you want people to call you Tom?"

"I got a niece named Monique and I don't want her to grow up calling me 'Uncle Tom.' "

"Thomas, do you talk as much on the field?"

"Depends. Say, I'm playing against somebody who's not too good-looking. I'll say, 'Hey, man, I'll bet if I follow you home somebody ugly answers the door.' "

A latecomer asks Henderson to repeat his appraisals of Pittsburgh quarterback Terry Bradshaw ("He couldn't spell 'cat' if you spotted him the c-a-") and tight end Randy Grossman ("He only plays when everybody else is dead").

"Thomas, aren't you tired of saying the same things over and over?"

He smiles. Leans forward, brushing a microphone cord dangling near his ear like a bellpull. The other microphones lean with him. "Hey, man, I've seen the day I couldn't be in the Langston, Oklahoma, *Gazette* and now I'm on page one of the *New York Times.*"

Thomas has a long Seder table to himself, the only defensive player to be so honored. The other Cowboys are at small square tables covered in Dallas-blue cloth. Each table has the players' names and numbers on place cards. (A first-time observer would think it was visitor's day at a model prison.) There is an overwhelming temptation to approach each and every player on both teams and ask this one question: What would you consider a small quantity of cocaine?

Hollywood is next seen at the taping of O.J.'s Super Bowl extravaganza. Where he's introduced to Cosell's wife as "the poor little black kid from Texas I made into a big star." The introduction was made by Mr. Cosell.

Singer Melba Moore posed for a photograph with O.J., who dropped an arm around her shoulder. "Melba, you and I could be tough," Art "Harpo" Metrano is watching all this, grinning. "My credit on this show is creative consultant, head writer, and starring in. I made the Juice what he is tonight." Ted Knight is another guest. "I wouldn't have done this show if it wasn't for O.J."

"It's A.J.," says Harpo.

"Right," says Knight. "A.J."

Happily, there's a cabdriver who wants to take me away. "Do you want to know what I find disturbing about the Super Bowl?" he asks. No, not really. "It's local government's persistence in telling us about the alleged spin-off of business from an event of this magnitude. I find it isn't true. The average cab isn't making additional sums of money. You see, when you have the Omni Hotel, which is a mega-structure in itself, containing, as it does, various shops, restaurants . . ."

I know Joe "Can Man" Graham thought Super Bowl XIII was a wonderful game. Can Man collects and sells empty beer cans to whoever buys empty beer cans. An hour before Pittsburgh's 35–31 success Can Man estimated he had $50 in secondhand aluminum. He gave Pittsburgh fans much of the credit. Their uniform seemed to be funny hat, Ban-Lon shirt, zipper jacket, beer. There's no way of knowing how many vinyl-covered living rooms they deserted for the trip to Miami.

The seat cushions were $5, Big Smokey frankfurters $1.35, souvenir half-time record albums $6.50, caramel crunch to benefit the Miami youth center $3 a box, and I found one reasonable man selling a game ticket for $40 (well below scalpers' minimum) "because that's what I paid for it. My wife decided the last minute she didn't feel like going. She got her father coming in tomorrow and he always gets drunk. Come on, Mac, it's a good seat." Sure it is. "Look, it's on the 45. Gimme 40 bucks and it's yours. I wouldn't kid you . . . I'll be sitting next to you."

The people who tell me this was the greatest of all Super Bowls deliver that opinion with a certain amount of relief. It's understandable. Earlier Super Bowls, on a scale of 1 to X, produced a series of zzzz's.

At the end of the day I kept thinking about my companion on the bus ride to the Orange Bowl. He was a young radio man from Connecticut, delighted to be "the only broadcaster here from New England besides the guy from BZ in Boston." He said he was responsible for the morning show and then the noon news. The rest of the time was spent writing commercials or showing grade-school kids around the station. I got the feeling there were more kids than commercials.

"Sometimes they'll ask really intelligent questions," he said. "I try to be as helpful as I can be. A tour of a radio station could change their lives forever. In 20 years, they could be down here covering the Super Bowl, that's really something, isn't it?"

"Sure is," I squeezed his shoulder. "How do you live with the guilt?"

BASKETBALL

THE FAT LADY IS SILENCED

By Art Spander

From the San Francisco Chronicle
Copyright, ©, 1979, Chronicle Publishing Co.

The Fat Lady has been silenced. The opera is over. For the Washington Bullets, the NBA championship series was a tragedy in five parts.

The Seattle SuperSonics turned the Bullets' slogan of last year—"The opera isn't over until the Fat Lady sings"—into meaningless words last night. And in the process the Sonics turned themselves into the NBA champions.

Trailing by nine points late in the third quarter, the Sonics came back with—what else?—great defense and backcourt scoring to defeat Washington, 97–93, and take the best-of-seven finals, four games to one. The four wins were in succession.

For a while, as 19,035 Capital Centre fans shouted their last hurrahs, Washington seemed determined to extend the playoffs one more game even without starting guards Kevin Grevey and Tom Henderson, both of whom had gone out earlier with injuries. The Bullets were rolling. They led, 69–60, with only 1 minute, 32 seconds left in the third quarter.

But then came pro basketball's version of the Crash of 1979. The Bullets collapsed. They didn't score for the next 4 minutes, 48 seconds. By that time, Seattle's Freddy Brown had hit several times from downtown, Dennis Johnson had hit from everywhere, and the Sonics were in front, 72–69. Even the loyalest of the Bullets' fans sensed the end was near. Sonic veteran Paul Silas was certain of it.

"It was all over," said Silas. "You could see it in the Bullets' eyes. I knew we had it won."

They did—thanks to great shooting down the stretch by Johnson and the other half of the Sonics' Gold Dust twins, Gus Williams. Washington showed its character by coming back itself, narrowing an eight-point, fourth-quarter deficit to two points. But Seattle showed its one-two punch, Gus and D.J., who fired in jump shots under pressure.

When the final buzzer sounded, the ecstatic Sonics ran to a locker room as full of irony as it was of sweat and splashing champagne (cheap Charmat bulk-processed stuff from New York, by the way).

A year ago, in the decisive seventh game of the championship series between the Bullets and the Sonics in Seattle, D.J. and Gus had failed—and the Bullets' Fat Lady was hitting high C. D.J. that night was 0 for 14 from the field, a fact Bullets coach Dick Motta brought up in a press conference two days ago, trying to psych out Johnson. And that night a year ago Gus fouled out.

But last night Williams—as was the case in the previous four games of this series—was the leading Seattle scorer, getting 23. And Johnson not only ended up with 21 points, five assists, and a blocked shot, but also with the series' Most Valuable Player award, chosen by *Sport Magazine*.

"I'm glad I got the award," said Johnson, the third-year guard from Pepperdine who plays defense like Van Cliburn plays the piano—marvelously. "It could have gone to anyone on this team."

That statement was not false modesty. The Sonics got contributions from everyone—last night and during the whole series. When they needed a rebound, Jack Sikma or Paul Silas or Lon Shelton was there to get it. When they needed a basket, Sikma or Williams or Brown or either of the Johnsons, John or Dennis, was there to get it.

Defense they always got—as befits the team that leads the league in that statistical category.

In four of the five games, the Bullets failed to score 100 points. Last night, after Washington had scored eight straight to go in front, 63–55, with 5:37 to play in the third quarter, the Sonics held them to 11 points in the next 12 minutes, 37 seconds.

"It was only a matter of time until we played our game," said Silas. He was on the Boston NBA champions of 1974–76. But he said, "This championship means more than the others. Boston was supposed to win. We weren't."

John Johnson, who had a series-high 35 assists after six last night, echoed Silas.

"People never believed in us," said Johnson. "But we knocked off each team one by one and now there's only one left. Us."

The Bullets, as Washington center Wes Unseld pointed out, finished second. For the third time since 1971, they lost four straight games. They had been swept, 4–0, by Milwaukee in the 1971 championship and 4–0 by the Warriors in the 1975 championship.

This loss was probably preordained. Center Mitch Kupchak, a key in the Bullets' victory last year, never got out of street clothes because of a back injury. The Bullets' guards never got out of trouble. And then last night Grevey pulled a hamstring three minutes into the game and Henderson sprained a foot one minute into the second half.

"I was pleased the way my team was determined to hold off the inevitable," said Motta.

The Sonics are a 12-year-old team formed before the 1968–69 season. And now they're on top.

"Sheee...," sighed Dennis Johnson. "An NBA championship. I've got something every other basketball player wants for a lifetime, and I got it in three years."

GOLF

THE GOOSE SLAYER

By Dave Kindred

From The Washington Post
Copyright, ©, 1979, The Washington Post

As to why a doctor killed a goose at Congressional Country Club, we shall soon discover by jury trial.

The doctor has retained the Watergate lawyer of John Dean, who, if not a cooked goose, was at least a canary singing White House secrets. Though witnesses say the doctor attacked the goose in retribution when it honked during his putt at the seventeenth green, the doctor insists it was not goosicide but euthanasia: His approach shot, he said, wounded the fowl and so he ended its suffering by applying his putter to its head.

This could be a landmark case in golf because it promises an answer to the question of whether a golfer is bound by the laws of rational society, although hundreds of years' experience has demonstrated that the game is temporary insanity practiced in a pasture.

Who among us has not wrestled with the devil over the result of a four-foot putt for all the marbles? Now we see a doctor in the dock over a contretemps with a goose, and we must kiss our putter thanks, for each knows that there but for the grace of God . . .

The great Bobby Jones once explained why he threw clubs in anger, "It's gone forever, an irrevocable crime, that stroke," he said of a foozle. "And when you feel a fool, and a bad golfer to boot, what can you do except to throw the club away?"

So who is to know what the sainted Jones would have done had a kibitzing goose rent the stillness at the moment he drew back Calamity Jane on a four-footer to win the Open?

Ky Laffoon, an Indian who played the PGA tour in the 1930s, punished his clubs for misbehavior. He held his putter's head in a lake and screamed, "Drown, you SOB, drown!" He also lashed the incompetent instrument to the bumper of his car and drove on down the road, sparks flying as the poor thing scraped the pavement at 50 mph.

Laffoon saw enemies everywhere, even under the velvet turf. At 5:30 every afternoon, he took his handgun on patrol of that day's course in pursuit of gophers that he believed he could hear tunneling at the most important times in his matches. We dare not ask what Laffoon might have done to a loudmouthed goose.

Whatever ill happens in golf, the player has no one to blame but himself. This is, of course, the sure route to the funny farm. "The fraility of the human mind is shown in utter nudity," said author Arnold Haultain in 1908, "not hidden under cover of agility or excitement or concerted action . . . and so these exposed men make excuses to cover their failings . . . the nature and number of which must assuredly move the laughter of the gods."

"The least thing upset him on the links," P. G. Wodehouse wrote of one of his golf-story heroes. "He missed short putts because of the butterflies in the adjoining meadows."

In his playboy days, Raymond Floyd withdrew from the Masters because (he said) he sprained his back brushing his teeth. George Archer's ball once came to rest dead behind a tree and he asked help from an official, looking at the ground as he said, "Those are burrowing animals and I can get relief from burrowing animals' holes."

To which the official said, "George, those are red ants. Play."

A fish leaped into the air, breaking the lake's surface, as Tommy Bolt moved into a tee shot at the eighteenth hole of the 1960 U.S. Open. "Always throw clubs ahead of you," Bolt had said. "That way you don't have to waste energy going back to pick them up." This time Bolt used no energy at all because, after jerking his tee shot into the lake, he promptly hurled his driver after it, presumably aiming to spear the offending fish. Like Laffoon's putter, Bolt's driver drowned. Would a yakkity goose be safe near this man?

"It is a game proverbially provocative of reprehensible expletives," Haultain said of golf.

Damned right.

When Walter Hagen advised us to smell the flowers, he didn't mean the (reprehensible expletive deleted) azalea in the right rough and though Jones wrote that we all are "dogged victims of inexorable fate," I will start you two up on the front nine if Bobby did not use plainer adjectives of greater pungency whenever he launched a club.

If, as the prosecution will try to prove, the doctor at Congressional was put off his stroke by the honking of that goose and so killed it, a jury of the doctor's peers—which is to say men afflicted by golf—will need to know much more than is now public knowledge.

Was the putt on the fateful seventeenth green for a birdie? How long a putt was it? Sidehill? Did the doctor have to hurry his round in

order to pick up his wife's cleaning? Did the Nassau ride on the putt?
Was it inside the leather and yet no one spoke up except the goose?

Anyway, in his summing up, John Dean's Watergate lawyer might
tell the jurors about Lefty Stackhouse, who toured the pro circuit in
Ky Laffoon's days. Lefty drove a Model T—until one reprehensible-
expletive-of-a-day when he shot 80-something and exacted retribution from his Model T.

Lefty shattered the windshield, ripped off the door, slashed the
seats and then, opening the hood, went after the engine. Served it
right for having delivered him to the golf course.

FOOTBALL

ENGULFED BY THE TIDE

By Tracy Dodds

From The Milwaukee Journal
Copyright, ©, 1979, The Milwaukee Journal

Atop a mountain of struggling, straining bodies, Alabama line-backer and a Penn State tailback met face-to-face.

They had a head-on collision at the peak of a mass of humanity that grew out of the goal line on the football field inside the Super-dome here Monday.

At stake was the 1979 Sugar Bowl title and perhaps the national collegiate football championship. It was a monumental classic.

It was a standoff, dead even. Both football players stopped cold upon impact.

That, however, was a victory for the Alabama linebacker. And it saved a 14–7 victory for his Crimson Tide. It also made Alabama the leading candidate for the nation's No. 1 ranking.

Quite a big play, but it also gave that heroic linebacker a headache.

The linebacker, Barry Krauss, a 6-foot-3, 238 pound All-America, whom the Buffalo Bills are seriously considering making the No. 1 pick in the pro football draft, was knocked unconscious when he crashed into the tailback, Mike Guman.

His helmet cracked open from the impact, and the face mask broke off.

"And now, I have a headache," said Krauss, who was heading out of the locker room with his Most Valuable Player trophy under his arm. "That was just one of the hardest hits I ever had. I just met him head-to-head. He was coming pretty hard, and so was I."

And so it went throughout the New Year's Day battle between No. 1 ranked Penn State and No. 2 ranked Alabama.

Krauss may have saved the day by turning the ball back to Ala-bama with 6 minutes 39 seconds left, but his was not the only big play of the game.

As Penn State Coach Joe Paterno said, "It was a game with a lot of bang-bang plays, and most of them went Alabama's way. That is to Alabama's credit."

And Alabama was willing to accept the credit. It was a suspense-filled, hard-fought game, and when it finally belonged to the Crimson Tide, Coach Bear Bryant and his team thought that they deserved a big reward.

"I think we deserve to be ranked No. 1," said Alabama quarterback Jeff Rutledge. "But we thought that last year, too, so we're not going to get too excited too soon.

"That's why you didn't see too many of us jumping up and down and hollering. We know they might give the national title to someone else like they did last year."

Alabama lost to only one team this season—Southern California. And because USC beat Michigan in the Rose Bowl, 17–10, and because USC also lost only one game this season, USC is making a claim to the national title. As is Oklahoma, which was impressive in its 31–24 victory over Nebraska in the Orange Bowl.

"There will be arguments over it, I'm sure," Rutledge said. "But I think we're a lot better team than USC. We've improved greatly since we lost that game to them early in the season.

"They were rated third or fourth when we lost to them, and then they turned around and got beat by a team that wasn't even rated.

"I think the Penn State defense is No. 1 in the country, the way they were rated, and I think we won a big ball game by beating Penn State."

Well said.

And although Alabama was in control most of the day, the game hung in the balance until the very end, threatening to turn at any moment on one of those bang-bang plays.

After Alabama had stopped Penn State on the goal line, preserving its 14–7 lead, it seemed that Penn State's top-ranked defense had answered the call and held the Crimson Tide without a first down deep in their own territory.

Alabama had to punt. Woody Umphrey, who had helped to give Alabama great field position all afternoon, kicked his only bad punt of the game—a 12-yarder from the Alabama 8, out of bounds at the Alabama 20.

New life for the Nittany Lions?

No, it was not to be. A 15-yard penalty against Penn State for having 12 men on the field gave Alabama a first down at the Alabama 23-yard line. The penalty was 15 yards, instead of the normal 5, because all 12 players participated in the play. The penalty is 5 yards if a player is trying to get off the field when the play begins.

Alabama moved only to its own 35 on the possession, but by the time Penn State got the ball again, only 2:42 remained.

And afterward, Paterno and the Penn State team were not revealing the name of the extra player who forgot to run off the field.

"The kid just didn't come out," said Paterno, whose team won the 1969 Orange Bowl when Kansas had 12 men on the field, giving Penn State a second shot at the winning touchdown. "We won one that way one time in a bowl game, and now we blew one the same way. That's the first time we've had 12 men on the field in probably five years."

In the final two minutes, Penn State quarterback Chuck Fusina, an All-America who finished second in the Heisman Trophy voting, was unable to pull the game out with his series of desperation passes.

"Their linebackers made some excellent plays," Fusina said, "I don't think they blitzed as much against other teams. But they just seemed to be at the right place at the right time in their defensive coverages today."

So, Alabama got the ball back at the end of the game—a couple of times.

With 12 seconds left, Fusina put up a last-hope pass that was intercepted by defensive back Mike Clements and returned 42 yards to the Penn State 9.

Certainly, with two seconds on the clock, Alabama could have kicked a field goal and improved the score.

"Some of my coaches wanted to kick a field goal," Bryant said. "I just wanted to get the clock over."

And once the final seconds had been run off, Bryant and his team could celebrate the fact that they were able to overcome Penn State's No. 1 ranked defense.

Tony Nathan, who gained 127 yards, was largely responsible for Alabama's ground game, which ran up 80 yards in the first quarter against a Penn State defense that gave up an average of just 54 all season.

"They have a good, good defense," Nathan said. "There wasn't anything easy about that ball game. I got a lot of hits. Some said we dominated early. I don't know about dominated, but I know it was a tough game."

So how did Alabama manage to roll over that Penn State defense?

"We knew we had to outquick 'em," Nathan said. "With those two tackles, there was no way in the world we would try to throw 'em around."

Those two tackles, All-Americas Bruce Clark and Matt Millen, were solid and impressive, but big plays and heroes were the name of this game.

Rich Milot of Penn State was the first hero of the game, when he saved a touchdown with 2:33 to play in the first half.

Rutledge, who was under pressure from Clark, threw what would have been a scoring pass to fullback Steve Whitman. But Whitman tipped it and Milot intercepted it and returned it 55 yards to the Alabama 37.

That should have been good for a field goal, at least, but on third and 10 from the 37, Alabama tackle Byron Braggs caught Fusina for a loss of 15 that saved a score the other way.

With 1:11 left before half time, Alabama started passing. Penn State helped out by calling two time-outs in succession, and the Crimson Tide scored with eight seconds left in the half on a 30-yard pass from Rutledge to split end Bruce Bolton.

"We had planned to run out the clock," Bryant said. "We were in our victory offense."

But the time was there, so Alabama used it, and led at the half 7–0.

However, in the third quarter, Penn State came back with an interception, which led to the Nittany Lions' only touchdown.

Rutledge threw a pass to split end Tim Clark, who seemed to be open. But Penn State safety Pete Harris, the brother of Franco Harris of the Pittsburgh Steelers, went flying between Clark and the football and picked it off, demonstrating how and why he led the nation in interceptions.

Five plays later, including a 25-yard pass to Guman, Fusina passed 17 yards to Ken Fitzkee for a Penn State touchdown with 4:25 left in the third quarter.

Fusina aimed for a spot at the back of the end zone, and Fitzkee raced in, looked over his right shoulder, and pulled the ball in.

But Alabama came back when Lou Ikner returned a Penn State punt 62 yards. Ikner would have had a touchdown were it not for Matt Bradley, a freshman who just plays on the special teams.

"Their punter overkicked his coverage," Ikner said. "So I just took a look at where everybody was and took off. The play was designed to go right, but I went left where I could get one-on-one with their kicker. I thought I might make it all the way. I almost did."

Instead, he was stopped at the 11-yard-line, and Rutledge and halfback Major Ogilvie finished the job. Ogilvie took a pitch and ran eight yards up the left sideline for the eventual winning touchdown with 21 seconds left in the third period.

From there on, it was defensive heroics. Another touchdown was saved when Alabama defensive back Don McNeal intercepted a pass intended for flanker Bob Bassett in the end zone. Bassett, McNeal, and Jim Bob Harris all collapsed in a heap in the end zone, but McNeal came up with the football.

But then Alabama made a mistake on offense that could have cost the Crimson Tide the game. Still in their own territory, with a third and five at the 25, a pitch from Rutledge to Nathan was fumbled away and picked up by defensive end Joe Lally.

"I checked off at the line of scrimmage, " Rutledge said. "But we couldn't hear for all the crowd noise. I knew I was going to pitch it, but Tony didn't. You can't play what you can't hear."

And that should have been the biggest break of the game for the Nittany Lions. That gave them the ball on the Alabama 19. An 11-yard gain put them on the 8 with a first down.

Four tries. Four times they come up short. The first was a gain of two. The second was a gain of five on a pass to Fitzkee, but McNeal again saved the day by covering his man deep and then coming back out of the end zone to meet Fitzkee and drive him back at the one-yard line.

On the third try, Rich Wingo stopped fullback Matt Suhey, and that set up Krauss' meeting with Guman.

"I think that we could have beaten any team in America today," Bryant said. "And I'd like to think that today will count."

TENNIS

THE REUNION

By Bud Collins

From The Boston Globe
Copyright, ©, 1979, Bud Collins
Courtesy The Boston Globe

The court was green. It had never been green before, not on the television screen through which Jana Navratilova had visited this place called Wimbledon so many times. Seated beside a grass tennis court for the first time in her 46 years, she was startled by the richness in color and texture of this plot within the Center Court stadium, but it was a day of such vivid hues and tones for Jana Navratilova—a coming-in from the gray of Czechoslovakia—that she would always remember it, a gorgeous painting hanging in the gallery of her mind.

Now, as the elusive sun turned full attention on the venerable playpen, two sturdy young women in white appeared from behind a forest green wall. They marched together toward the net, then turned and curtsied to the Royal Box, specifically to the Duchess of Kent. This dated homage to royalty might seem offensive to the folks back in Czechoslovakia, but the Wimbledon custom was only amusing to those who witnessed it because the Queen of Aces, reigning champion Martina Navratilova, was bowing to a mere duchess.

Nevertheless, if you were close enough, you would have noticed that Jana Navratilova was crying behind her gold-rimmed spectacles while she joined 15,000 others in applause for her daughter. "You see," she said later, "I was not thrilled by Martina's defection because I thought it meant I might never see her again. But we—my husband and I—had told her if she ever had to do it—to go without telling us. It is a little easier that way for everybody."

They were seeing each other again, the mother and her daughter, the defector, after nearly four years apart. Their reunion was taking place without the public's knowledge. Few other than Martina's closest friend Sandra Haynie, former U.S. Women's golf champion, knew the tall, auburn-haired woman in a gray checked pantsuit seated beside Haynie was the mother who had become a distant voice on the phone. Martina won the loneliness of nonperson status for herself as far as her motherland was concerned. When she walked out of Revnice, a small town not far from Prague, for the last time in August of 1975, she "knew I wouldn't come back. There was a secret police report saying I was planning to defect. It wasn't true, but when they believe it is true they will make it impossible for you to leave."

Two weeks later came her stunning declaration of defection during the U.S. Open at Forest Hills. At 18 Martina was going it alone in America. The government would not permit her parents to visit her, and phone calls and letters were their only connection. When she toppled Chris Evert for the Wimbledon title a year ago, Martina said, "I don't know whether I should cry or scream or laugh. I feel very happy that I won, and at the same time I'm very sad that I can't share this with my family."

Now she was sharing with one of them. "I'm so happy I can't express it," Martina said. "I was so nervous Monday night when I went to the airport to pick my mother up. I learned Friday she'd be coming, that the government had finally OK'd it. I didn't tell anybody because we'd been clobbered by reporters. We wanted it for ourselves. When she came out of customs we just stood there.

"We couldn't say anything. Then we were crying and talking, and we haven't stopped."

They had to stop momentarily for a tennis match, which seemed incidental. Tanya Harford, a 20-year-old South African, was the designated first-round stiff for the champion, but Tanya refused to show the respectful degree of rigor mortis. Harford agreed it was a marvelous sentimental journey to Wimbledon for Jana Navratilova, but she wasn't aware of it during the match—"and even if I had been I still would have been trying to beat Martina."

Harford, a sprightly kid with unruly rust-colored hair and a wicked forehand volley, started off as the witch of Center Court. "No, I didn't like the first set," said Mama. "I could just see the headlines," recalled Martina of her early difficulties: "CHAMPION BEATEN IN FIRST ROUND, DISTRACTED BY MOTHER."

But Martina began cudgeling the balls with her own wicked left hand, and round one of visit and tournament had a happy 4–6, 6–2, 6–1 ending. At 2–2 in the second set, the scoreboard lights went out—the first such power failure here since the board was electrified more than 30 years ago—and so did Harford, while Navratilova turned up her own voltage for a nine-game run.

It was the determined run of the missing parent, Miroslav Navratilova, through Czechoslovakian bureaucracy that sprang his wife on a two-week visa. Martina hopes to settle the entire family, including younger sister Jana, with her in Dallas if this is an indication that the government may at last display some heart.

"I sent an invitation to my family to attend the tournament," said Martina, "but they couldn't get that approved. Then the All England Club [proprietor of the Wimbledon Championships] sent an official invitation, and my father took it to Prague, to government offices, and eventually to the secretary of the prime minister. The prime minister, Dr. Rubomir Strougal, is a tennis fan. I know he was a fan of mine before I left. He OK'd the visa. If my father hadn't decided to go right to him it would have taken months the way things work."

For an instant the oppression of the Navratilova family lifted, along with Martina's morale. "This gives me a lovely nudge toward another championship. Naturally I want to win it for my mother."

Twelve months ago the family drove to Pilsen to catch the telecast over the German border. Czechoslovakian TV didn't take the show since Martina was in a starring role. They watched the familiar girl on the familiar drab court. But yesterday the court was as green as Jana Navratilova's new hopes for her family—perhaps freedom?

Her English was uncertain, but she had a fine translator in Martina. There was nothing uncertain about her joy. The smiles were warm, the brown eyes animated, taking it all in. She nodded as Martina said, "The championship was the greatest day of my career, but this is the greatest day of my life."

"My girl," said Jana, "is prettier, and," she laughed, "skinnier."

But what did Mama bring for the champion? Of course, cookies. Home-baked just before the flight to the green court.

GENERAL

WHINES AND WHIMPERS

By Pete Axthelm

From Newsweek

I have been listening futilely in recent weeks for the sound of that celebrated modern phenomenon, the tennis boom. As two talented kids won the singles championships of the U.S. Open, it should have been a good time for songs of the young at heart—accompanied by the resonant rhythm section one expects of a sport in a state of boom. Instead, the Open courts rang mostly with shouting and cursing and whining. And when it ended, one question lingered. Is this the way big-time tennis will begin its decline? Not with a boom but with a chorus of whimpering?

Tennis is still flourishing at its clay and asphalt roots, where millions enjoy the game at clubs and public courts. But at the pro level, the game is headed for trouble. One easy way is to blame the fans. As the sport has grown, it has attracted some new and occasionally rowdy spectators, who have never been steeped in the tradition of watching in silent appreciation and expressing displeasure with soft, respectful whistles. But such unschooled newcomers also happen to buy the tickets that have made modern stars into millionaires, so perhaps they deserve a little understanding. If the fans lack dignity and decorum, they may be reflecting the spirit of players who lost those qualities at about the time they huddled under their first tax shelters.

The modern tennis hero, we learned at the Open, expects to practice his art in silent, near-perfect surroundings. But if things go wrong, he does not suffer in similar silence. The tournament at Flushing Meadow, New York, should have been billed as the U.S. Excuse. Again and again players complained that the courts were too hard, the lights too glaring, the planes overhead as noisy and distracting as some fans. Losers numbed us with a litany of groin pulls and back spasms; hardly anyone seemed to hold a head high and admit to losing on merit. In an era when many great athletes shake off pain and shun alibis, tennis gave us a championship in which the most quoted figure was the official doctor, who doled out excuses like a principal sending sick children home from school.

Tennis fans have no reason to question the validity of all the ailments and distractions at the Open. They do have cause to recall past champions like Rod Laver, Ken Rosewall, or Arthur Ashe, who kept their pains and problems to themselves—win or lose.

Bjorn Borg has already carved out his place in history. But last week the greatest player of our time was also a distressing symbol of this era. From the start of the tournament, Borg and his coach and racket-carrier Lennart Bergelin complained about the night matches that help to make the Open so lucrative. Borg has long compiled a large part of his fortune in indoor matches under lights on the U.S. tennis tour. But in the Open, which he has never won, he wanted special pampering—day matches only. He was refused, and eventually lost to Roscoe Tanner at night. Bergelin was quick to blame the lights, and even hinted that Bjorn might not return to the Open if it retained its night scheduling. If the supposedly indomitable Swedish champ can't have things his own way, he might just stay home and sulk.

John McEnroe, the new champion, does most of his pouting on the courts. In private, this devastating athlete can be a nice enough kid; in fact, his supporters spent a good part of this Open explaining how poor John was misunderstood. But when he steps to the service line, with his perpetually put-upon expression and his insistence that every line call and crowd reaction go his way, his public posture is all too easy to understand. Call it spoiled. When his act was pitted against the obscene clowning of Ilie Nastase, it produced one of the low moments of tennis history.

The details have been endlessly debated by now. When McEnroe stalled, Nastase mimicked him and outdid him. Umpire Frank Hammond tried to penalize Nastase, but the crowd roared so long that the match was held up. Hammond was removed, and McEnroe finally won. I do not blame Hammond, whose decision was technically correct, or tournament director Bill Talbert, who removed the umpire in the interest of crowd control. But during the delay, while the players waited insolently, I thought of other sports. We think nothing, for example, of putting some teen-ager on a foul line while thousands of basketball fans wave banners and scream in his face—and we expect him to make that crucial foul shot. But when a few rallies over the net could have silenced an unruly crowd, two tournament-hardened tennis stars couldn't bring themselves to play because of the noise.

There were some welcome exceptions to the Open nonsense.

Tracy Austin, the new women's champ, is one prodigy who has been developed but not spoiled by her family and coaches; her fellow teen-ager Pam Shriver is another delightful hope for the future. And the dethroned champion, Chris Evert Lloyd, maintained her stature as one of the classiest leaders in any sport. The Austin-Evert Lloyd final was a dull and grinding base-line battle, and a disappointment to Chris. But in lieu of excuses, Chris had only praise for Tracy. Later, Chris set a small personal record that I will cherish as long as any of her victories over the years. Of all the 224 sportsmen and women in the Open singles, Evert Lloyd was the only one to stop by and thank the embattled Bill Talbert for taking the trouble to run the tournament for all of them.

While tennis waits for its other 223 stars to learn something from Chris or from history, I think the sport's best friend may turn out to be the National Basketball Association. While the Open was going on, the NBA's Indiana Pacers signed a 135-pound woman for an unsuccessful tryout. With this single inspired stroke, basketball momentarily prevented tennis from retiring the trophy for being the most ridiculous sport we've got.

BASKETBALL

CAGING THE BIRD

By Jim Cohen

From The Milwaukee Journal
Copyright, ©, 1979, The Milwaukee Journal

The organized ecstasy was barely muffled by the steel door of Michigan State's locker room.

There was spelling. Loud and sharp spelling. More and more emotional with the recitation of each important letter.

P, the Spartans yelled. O, they yelled. T-E-N-T-I-A-L.

Potential.

As they had after every game during this long and draining season, they spelled that key word aloud, allowing the reverberations to filter into their souls.

But the significance of the word was altogether different here Monday night, after they had defeated Indiana State for the National Collegiate Athletic Association basketball title 75–64.

For the first time, it was not a goal, but an accomplishment.

For the first time, the Michigan State Spartans, preseason choices of many as the best college basketball team in the country, but midseason disappointments to all, had finally reached their potential.

In the last college basketball game of the 1978–79 season, they accomplished what they had set out to do several months earlier.

They won the NCAA tournament, and with it the general recognition of being the best in the country.

And they won it with such force that nobody should feel offended that Michigan State, with a 26–6 record, has the third worst record of any team to win the NCAA title. Because, like the 1958 Kentucky team, which had a 23–6 record, and the 1977 Marquette team, 25–7, the Spartans were certainly worthy champions.

In a final game that had every reason to be close and exciting, the Spartans dominated the No. 1-ranked and 33–0 Indiana State Sycamores so clearly that the game was neither particularly close nor particularly exciting.

From the start of the game, when Michigan State's Earvin Johnson took charge, the Spartan's victory was awesome in its simplicity.

It was against an excellent Indiana State team, and in its own way, it was probably even more impressive than any of the four lopsided victories that put the Spartans into the final.

Because this time the Spartans had to do something that no other team had done against the undefeated Sycamores. They had to stop the incomparable Larry Bird.

And not only did they stop the best college player in the country, they came close to humiliating him. They found his weaknesses, exposed them, and worked them for all they could get.

It was a shattering night for Bird. Afterward in the Michigan State locker room, while the big stars of the game were talking to most of the media workers in the interview room, center Jay Vincent of Michigan State talked to a couple of reporters about Bird.

"I could tell he was very frustrated out there," Vincent said. "I've never seen his shooting so far off, and I think it was because he was frustrated. I was really surprised. He was panicking. He was talking to himself. 'I gotta get the ball. I gotta get the ball.' But he didn't get it, and he was mad.

"He kept telling his guards, 'Gimme the ball. Gimme the ball.' He was mad. He was cussing them out. Finally, when he got the ball, he had to go 30 or 35 feet out to get it. And when he shot those air balls, he really seemed down."

The superbly talented Bird did not play nearly up to his standards Monday night, forcing shots, throwing up air balls, and getting burned on defense with unusual frequency.

He had 19 points and 13 rebounds, but he made only 7 of 21 shots from the floor, committed 6 of his team's 10 turnovers, and was personally victimized as Michigan State built an early lead that it never lost.

Michigan State, utilizing its quickness and shielding its weaknesses, earned most of the credit for Bird's unimpressive showing. It would have taken Bird's greatest game ever to combat Michigan State's constantly moving offense.

Bird was flustered all night by Michigan State's zone, which managed to double-team Bird without being burned by the other Indiana State players. He had difficulty getting the ball, and when he got it, he had difficulty doing anything with it.

"The key to our zone is having quick players," said coach Jud Heathcote of Michigan State. "It couldn't work with slow players, because they have to be able to guard a man and an area at the same time. But we had great quickness, anticipation, and adjustment.

"We usually had one and a half or two men guarding Bird. If he was facing the basket, we had one man on him as tight as he could get. If he put the ball on the floor, our off guard would double-team him. If he went to the key, our middle man would double-team him."

Said Johnson, who had 24 points, 7 rebounds, and 5 assists and was voted the tournament's most outstanding player, partly because of his defense, "With two men on Bird and three men in the passing lanes, he couldn't do anything. We made him give up the ball quickly, and when he shot, he had to use a higher arc against our tall guys."

Vincent added another interesting piece of analysis.

"Bird's the best shooter I've ever seen," he said. "But we noticed in their semifinal game against De Paul that if you put a hand in his face, he wouldn't shoot. That worked for us."

Bird also was burned on defense, as coach Bill Hodges surprised most observers by having him guard dangerous Gregory Kelser at the start of the game. Michigan State built an 18–10 lead, and Kelser accounted for 12 of those points with 4 assists and 4 points.

"I was very surprised that Bird guarded me at the start," Kelser said. "Usually, he guards the weaker offensive forward. But I was glad to see it. I knew he wasn't quick enough for me, and I could do some things on him. I was able to get by him and pass off."

Indiana State's baseline defense was poor all night, as Michigan State frequently had open men underneath who made easy baskets. That was as big a reason as any for Michigan State's 60.5 percent shooting from the floor, compared to Indiana State's 45.7 percent.

The Sycamores, showing the pressure that goes along with playing in the NCAA championship game, also were hurt by poor free-throw shooting. They made just 10 of 22 attempts and missed the first shot in a bonus situation several times.

Except for a brief period midway through the second half, when Indiana State narrowed the margin to six points, 52–46, Michigan State was always in control. Even with a few players in foul trouble, the Spartans applied constant pressure with their zone defense and hit the boards hard.

Clearly, they proved to be the better team Monday night, and in a season that has lacked a dominating team, the Spartans deserve the national championship as much as anyone.

They climbed up the hard way, through the rigors of a Big Ten schedule. But in the last half of the season, they were as good as anyone, losing only at Wisconsin in the conference finale.

The sentimentalists were with Indiana State, the upstart team from Terre Haute that, with a final 33–1 record, still does not receive enough credit from some observers.

But the traditionalists were with Michigan State, and the Spartans' victory was a boost for the college basketball establishment and the concept of being toughened and tested by playing a difficult regular-season schedule.

This NCAA final, however, may be remembered most, not for the teams involved, but for the two superstars. Bird and Johnson are two dynamic players, and it might have been merely by chance that Johnson was the better of the two on this memorable night.

FOOTBALL

WOODY IS ALIVE AND IN EXILE IN COLUMBUS

By Bob Greene

From The Chicago Tribune
Copyright, ©, 1979, Bob Greene

Darkness had just given way to dawn. The visitor waited on the sidewalk outside the hotel. Across Columbus's Third Street, the sign on the Ohio State Federal Savings and Loan Building flashed that it was 35 degrees.

A gray pickup truck pulled to a stop. The visitor walked around to the passenger side and climbed inside.

"Thanks for picking me up, coach," the visitor said.

"Well, that's all right," said Woody Hayes. "I'm glad to have the company."

Hayes was behind the wheel of the truck. It has been almost a year since his career as head football coach at Ohio State University was brought to an end when he slugged a Clemson University player during the Gator Bowl. Hayes is a national catchphrase; the words *Woody Hayes* bring nods and knowing smiles whenever they are mentioned. Now there is a new football era in Columbus; a new coach, Earle Bruce, has an undefeated team, and Woody Hayes's 28-year reign is past tense.

Now the new coach is preparing his team for the season's climactic game with Michigan, and that is the talk all around Columbus; but Woody Hayes still lives. He gets up every morning at his house at 1711 Cardiff Road, and he goes through the day. He is 66 years old; behind the wheel of his truck he wore a dark blue business suit and a brown felt hat pulled down hard over his white hair.

"We're going to Westerville, Ohio," Hayes said. "I'm supposed to talk to some high school students. It's . . . what do you call it? When you tell them what they're supposed to do in life?"

"Careers Day?" the visitor said.

"Right," Hayes said. "Careers Day. I'm supposed to tell them about the coaching profession."

A woman in a station wagon backed out of a parking space, causing Hayes to stop. In the front seat the woman's son, a teen-ager, dozed, his head resting on his chest.

"Look at that kid," Hayes said. "Now there you have a drug victim."

"Oh, come on, coach," the visitor said. "That kid's not on drugs."

"Well, he's either a drug victim or a lazy son of a bitch," Hayes said. "Yessir. Lazy. I know about these things. Too many people like that out there today."

Hayes headed onto Int. Hwy. 71, on his way to Westerville. He talked nonstop; he seemed happy to have a listener. His subjects shifted quickly from international politics to literature to history to women's rights, sometimes with no interconnective phrases. It was cold in the truck, but he did not turn the heater on. He talked all the way to Westerville.

"Now where is this place?" he said to himself as he drove down Main Street. "It's Westerville North High School, but we're heading south. Doesn't make any sense. I don't know why they build these schools so far out in the country. The kids can't walk, and it makes them soft. Wastes gasoline. People don't . . . people don't think."

He found the high school and pulled into the parking lot. He left the truck next to the students' cars; on the way into the school he passed a man, perhaps a teacher, who did not say hello. "Good morning," Hayes said.

When the man had passed from earshot, Hayes said, "They don't even say hello. That stupid . . . He didn't even say hello. People are so unfriendly these days. Back in Newcomerstown when I was growing up, everyone said hello to everyone. Things have changed. People act stupid."

The speech was in the high school gymnasium. There were several hundred students present; when Hayes talked about coaching, it was in the present tense ("On our team we tell our players . . . When we're getting ready for a game . . ."). Suddenly, though, for some reason not readily apparent, Hayes shifted his talk to United States intervention in Japan following World War II. He was shouting, combative, and he stepped from the microphone, as if it were not loud enough for him. He approached the students in the bleachers, and he bellowed:

"Do you know who that man was? No, you don't want to say his name because you think he was too much of a chauvinist! Well that man's name was . . . Five-Star General Douglas MacArthur!"

The students sat in silence, bewildered. Hayes seemed to realize something, and returned to the microphone, where he quickly finished up his talk about coaching.

In the truck on the way back to Columbus, he talked about his pain for the first time. He said that after having Ohio State football be his whole life, he could not bring himself to attend a game this year. Most Saturdays, he said, he spent in a cabin he had built down in Noble County.

"Sometimes I listen to the games on the radio," he said. "But I can't go.

"You know, the worst thing in the world is feeling sorry for yourself. Self-pity will kill you. I can't have it.

"You can't dwell on what used to be. You can't bring it back. The football . . . I've got to separate myself from it."

For a few minutes Hayes and the visitor rode in silence. Then Hayes cleared his throat, as if to cut off the thoughts that had filled the truck, and he said:

"Do you know what president of the United States I feel the least use for?"

"Who's that, coach?" the visitor said.

"Woodrow Wilson," Hayes said.

"Why's that?" the visitor said.

"Come on, you know," Hayes said.

"No, I don't," the visitor said.

"Because Wilson wasn't a man's man," Hayes said. "Yessir, he wasn't a man's man."

And on he drove, a legend in exile, heading down I-71 in pursuit of the rest of his life.

RUNNING

CRAIG VIRGIN: A HEARTLAND SAGA

By William Barry Furlong

From The Runner
Copyright, ©, 1979, The Runner

Dawn thoughts are bleak thoughts. At least for Craig Virgin. "I don't look at the scenery in the morning," he said. "I just try to get the body going." It is Sunday morning, quiet except for the call of birds. He is in his running suit, and he is wearing spectacles; sleep lingers in the corners of his eyes. "I couldn't get my contact lenses in this morning," he said.

Virgin's morning loop on the farm roads near his home in central Illinois is four miles; his afternoon loop is usually 13 to 17 miles. He does not indulge in the scenery until later, and then he does not seem to indulge in it so much as experience it viscerally. The part of the country is the heartland of the nation—the center of population for the United States is literally only 11 miles south of Craig Virgin's home. But this particular landscape is not the vast horizon-stretching prairie. It is a tumbled, upthrust land with tangled woods, small fields, and back roads still broken by winter's frost. It is spring in the Mississippi River basin, and in west central Illinois the colors of spring are browns and blacks with a texture of dampness or wetness—they are the colors of mud. But it is the character—not the color—of the land that has meaning and impact on Craig. There is an air of expectation in the heartland, a belief that personal goals can be attained. It is where a person can feel he can achieve success, because he is an individual. "I'm not quite sure I'd ever be completely happy away from here," Craig said.

Craig Virgin is 23 now, hard-muscled, whippet-lean at 5-feet-10 and 140 pounds, and celebrated even in those enclaves of the country where individualism is not often noticed or applauded. "10,000 MARK FALLS," headlined the *Washington Post*, "CRAIG VIRGIN RUNS 27.39.4 IN AAU." Virgin has been running for nine years now and has been breaking records almost from the start. Seven years ago he lowered the national high school two-mile mark to 8:41 (since lowered to 8:36.3), four years ago he won the NCAA cross-country title, three years ago he made the U.S. Olympic Team, and in 1979, he became "an overnight sensation." He went into a marathon for the first time last January and set an American record for a first-timer (2:14.40) and then he ran a 10-mile minimarathon in New York City and, in record time, beat Bill Rodgers by a minute. "I often thought what would happen if I could match him on the down-hills"—where Rodger's reputation is unassailed—"and then put it to him on the uphills," Craig said.

Suddenly, Craig Virgin found himself—without a coach to guide him, without a public relations machine to support him—on the way to becoming one of the nation's most acclaimed hopes for the 1980 Olympics, in both the 10,000 meters and the marathon.

In one sense, Craig Virgin fulfills the American Dream: He is young. He is purposeful. He is intelligent. He is articulate. He is unafraid of hard work. He is at home in the most worldly and most earthy of situations. Yet he is not in awe of himself; his 13-year-old brother—who is not in awe of him, either—often bosses him around. He is good-looking without appearing to know it. He has a dazzling smile ("thanks to $1,000 worth of orthodontics work," said his mother, Lorna). He has fined-boned, clean-chiseled features, and his tumbling russet-colored hair somehow never seems to get mussed. He likes, in the American tradition, to drive very fast—he has a souped-up Fiat X19 that he urges at frightening speeds up the back roads of his homeland; "I've gotten it up to 110, but I don't want to go faster because I'm afraid the heads might blow," he confessed. Also in the American tradition, he does not like to accept a discipline—not even from cops or coaches—not generated from within, though he does not flinch from the hardest discipline dictated by his inner self. He runs up to 117 miles a week in training, has run this week three major long-distance races in four days (winning all), and also has run three "Pick-up" races, two 10,000 meters, and a one-mile, in eight hours to celebrate an Olympic fund-raising in his home town.

His town is Lebanon, Illinois, population 3,564. It is about 21 miles east of Saint Louis, and it goes back about 150 years as a settlement. The trip into history is not a distant one: Lebanon still has covered sidewalks—just like out of the old Western movies—with roof poles whose paint is dried and flaking and whose bottoms are held up by quickly implanted cement hooves, cast and hardened some time in the past when the main street began to settle. It is both farm and a college town (McKensee is located here), but for most of its life it was content to be pretty much of nothing more than a cross in the road. "It was a stagecoach stop in the last century," said Craig Virgin.

Craig Virgin did his early running along the dusty roads and neatly edged lanes of Lebanon. He still does. "Over there," he said, indicating a park on the outskirts of town, "is where I started my first real cross-country race." Virgin was 14 at the time and had barely done any running; he was up against one of the genuinely fine young runners of central Illinois. Craig beat his opponent in this first cross-country effort. "Because," Virgin claimed, "he stopped to go to the bathroom. I passed him, and he never had a chance to catch up." Virgin seemed neither amused nor gratified by the incident. He simply accepts it. But from this, he did learn to keep his kidneys tame, or empty, whatever it took to win. In the heartland, you know the functions and the demands of the body, and Craig Virgin happens to know them better than most.

The farm that he grew up on—and where he still lives—is three miles north of the town's main intersection. "We grow wheat and corn, and keep 33 acres in permanent pastureland," he said. The land, pushed around thousands of years ago by the thick lip of a glacier, is so gnarled and broken that farms are small (by plains standards) and hard to work. Vernon Virgin—more fair skinned, sunburned, and compact than his son—has 834 tillable acres here, pastureland for cattle; but he owns only 175 of them. The rest he plants, crops, and works for relatives and friends.

The family lives in a sturdy red brick house on the top of a high hill. "It's got to be over 100 years old," said Craig. "You don't think we'd build a house like this, do you?" He points out the way tight, crowded rooms were built inside the house, and how wings and floors were clearly burned off over the years. Down the hill to the south are several low, sleek warehouses and an office building. That is where Vernon Virgin runs an additional business that sells special equipment for the raising of livestock. This side business is fast-growing, with multimillion-dollar customers. For years Vernon ran it from his living room for extra income. He started it in one of those many years when the farm economy was in desperate shape and "I needed money to pay for Craig's medical bills," he said quietly.

Craig had congenital kidney trouble. It struck Craig first when he was in kindergarten and continued as an acute problem until he was in junior high. He went through years of constant medication and treatment, and surgery several times. For a while, he had to route his urine into a catheter strapped to his leg during long periods in which the doctors were trying to relieve the stress on his kidneys. Then he was told by his doctors that he would have to give up his ailing right kidney just when his left kidney seemed stricken by the same disease. The doctor told his parents that "they didn't think he would live until he finished school." Yet Craig survived and came to triumph in long-distance racing with, as he sometimes says, "only one and a half kidneys functioning." And with only a few pronounced obsessions about maintaining his health.

Because of his kidney problem, Virgin could not play contact sports. But he did go out for basketball which, in the Midwest, is still considered more a finesse than a combat sport. He had only two problems: "I had no coordination, and I couldn't shoot," he said. But he hustled hard on defense "and so I didn't get cut." His coach, Richard Neal, noticed one very significant thing: Every time the team ran laps, Craig Virgin ended up very far in front, and without complaint. On a hunch, he suggested that Craig come out for cross-country. "The first day I went out," he said of the days when he was 13 to 14 years old, "I beat the best of the varsity. And lapped most of them." The victory was a revelation to him: "For the first time, I realized that one guy could beat another guy with more talent because he was gutsier."

His high school running was improvisational. Lebanon High had no track in those days, so Craig did his workouts on the road in and around town. "For intervals, we ran on the baseball field," he said. There were almost as many meets as practices—"sometimes we'd have three meets a week, on Tuesday, Thursday, and Saturday." Virgin would compete in anything that wasn't a short sprint—the quarter-mile. He was not terribly fast—"my best in the quarter-mile was 52:8. I couldn't always beat a good quarter-miler."

Virgin was better in the middle distances. At age 15 in 1971, he became the first sophomore to run below nine minutes for two miles, with a 8:57.4. Two years later *Track & Field News* named him the nation's outstanding runner of the year. That spring of 1973, Virgin ran one mile in 4:05.5, two miles in 8:41, and 5,000 meters in 13:52.8 (defeating the Russian Juniors in the Soviet Union). He was much sought-after by colleges all over the country. He visited many of them and finally chose the one closest to home—the University of Illinois, located in Champaign, only a few hours' drive from Lebanon.

At Illinois, he became the "most valuable freshman," but without the requisite speed for great miling. Virgin showed real promise in the longer events. In his sophomore year, he ran six miles in 27:48.8. The next season he won the NCAA cross-country title, and in June 1976, Virgin set a collegiate record for 10,000 meters when he placed second to Frank Shorter in the U.S. Olympic Trials. Virgin's time was 27:59.4.

On the night before the race in Montreal, he suffered severe abdominal pains. Virgin believes it was either food poisoning or a viral infection of some kind—through vomiting and other elimination, he lost a great deal of weight and water. He refused medication; he did not want to risk having drugs found in his body if he was screened after the race. He was very weak and dehydrated, but he went out and ran the race. Virgin finished sixth in the second heat. The experience merely sharpened his appetite for running in future Olympics.

After graduating from the University of Illinois in 1977, Virgin tried for a while to go the modern route of big-time sports promotion: He became the first "name" runner to join the Athletics West Club in Eugene, Oregon. The membership gave him a coach, Harry Johnson; a team that provided a supportive structure; and a certain promotional thrust—which whether we approve of it or not is very much needed in all phases of modern sports. But all of this was alien to the experience and needs of Craig Virgin. He was accustomed to an atmosphere which produced and cherished people of great individual strength. Even his high school and college coaches, Gary Wieneke at the University of Illinois for one, recognized this and developed a flexible way of training Craig Virgin. They recognized that the "loneliness of the long-distance runner" is a loneliness of mind and spirit, not just one of his physical being. Virgin is often not a fit subject for group-think. "There are a lot of athletes, very good athletes, who just want to show up and have somebody tell them what to do, so they don't have to think. They just go out and do what they're told."

This was not one of Craig Virgin's inclinations. He likes making decisions; just turning himself over to a coach and being even slightly submissive is frustrating to him. "Doing that just takes some of the satisfaction out of it," he said. Still, he devoted a full year of conscientious effort to the Athletic West Club, and he did, as a matter of fact, turn in his then best times in the 5,000- and 10,000-meter runs. But then his vague sense of dissatisfaction became an active one. Not only did he feel that he was not in control of his training but that he was not even consulted, or considered, on where and when and how he might run in competition. Further, he found that he could not explore aspects of running that, increasingly, tantalized him. This was a track club where performers concentrated on track, not on side "hobbies" such as road-running. In time, Craig Virgin began to wonder whether or not to accept being some coach's version of himself, or to try to be himself. He didn't simply want to take from coaches; he wanted to give back to them in performance, in help, and he wanted to give something of his true self.

"He was very bright," said Harry Feldt, one of his high school coaches. "He was helpful not only in figuring out what he had to do but in helping us teach some of the younger runners." But gradually, Craig found that this reciprocity wasn't possible at Athletics West, that there could be no exchange because the atmosphere was, he felt, overly disciplined, even "autocratic." He began to yearn not just for the environs of home but for the values of individualism it encouraged. "It didn't make sense—if you trained there for the 1980 and 1984 Olympics, that would have been six years in that atmosphere," he said. "I wouldn't have had anything left of here [referring to his home] by that time."

So he returned to the heartland. He left Athletics West late in the summer of 1978. "It was over a long time before I left it," he said. He was, after all, choosing to leave the protective cocoon that so many young athletes so desperately desire. He was going out on his own. The costs—inflicted even by the protector—quickly became apparent. Coach Johnson was quoted in a Eugene newspaper saying, "I don't believe Craig can be effective in any group situation except his family. He doesn't really want a coach, he just wants somebody around to pat him on the back. I still say he's the most talented distance running prospect in the country. But his 13:25 [for 5,000 meters] and his 27:57 [for 10,000 meters] aren't that great, except in this country." Johnson was also quoted as saying that he saw no value in adding road-racing to a track regimen: "I don't think a guy can do both and be world class." Finally, another runner in Athletics West, Doug Brown, appeared to strike out at the very quality of Craig Virgin's that is his greatest strength, his individualism: "He's a fish out of water working with a group," Brown said, "and he refused to accept coaching. I think everyone else conceded the fact that they were going to be coached when they came here."

Virgin was shaken by the publication of these put-downs. "They really got to me for about two weeks," he said. But he would not reply in kind. "I have no desire to slander Athletics West, Harry Johnson, or Eugene," he told John Conrad of the Eugene *Register-Guard*. "I'm grateful to the people . . . in Eugene who were so good to me." In time, he came to understand that the put-down is the way organizations seek to protect themselves against the strength of the individual; it is what they do to warn other individuals to stay in line. "Then I was sure I had made the right decision," said Craig. Indeed he had: Within nine months he'd cut (through his own coaching, his own program of development) 17 seconds off his time for the 10,000 meters and come within one second of the Olympic record (27:38.4 by Finland's Lasse Viren in 1972).

Virgin's success did not happen by accident. It was the product of mental as well as physical labor, and of the discipline of planning and self-analysis. As soon as he got home, Craig sat down at a typewriter ("I can think pretty well at a typewriter") and painstakingly filled 10 large notebook-sized sheets of paper with reflections about his goals, needs, and a program for his first year at home. He set goals in each of three areas of running—track, cross-country ("win the AAU championship"), and road-racing. He wrote out "some philosophies my training program must reflect" ("a solid plan with distinct direction, yet retaining the flexibility to react to injuries or illnesses, stale plateaus in training, environmental conditions"). And he laid out a specific training program, allowing for "competitive weeks" (85–90 miles) and "noncompetitive weeks" (100–110 miles). With considerable sophistication, he built into this a schedule that would emphasize one of the three aspects of running at various times of the year ("March-April, road-racing and light track training, starting to make the transition to faster, shorter races of 10 miles and under"). He wrote out specifically how he would have to improve his running ("faster times and a confident, more competitive kick . . . improve on my ability to handle and implement surges") and what times he expected to achieve through that improvement ("attempt my first marathon, strive to break 2:15. Mile: 3:59.0 The 10,000 meters: 27:35"). He picked out what races he would enter and where. In Europe, he thought he would get much tougher competition in cross-country and long-distance track.

He analyzed what he would need: For coaching insights, he felt he could go to Gary Wieneke at Illinois. For training facilities that would provide cover against harsh midwestern winters, he selected five possible sites, including those at Champaign-Urbana, Illinois, and Boulder, Colorado. Additionally, all he would need from weight-training to medical care, he wrote out in simple personal terms: "I feel the need to talk with some authorities to put together a good, quick and effective stretching and flexibility program."

Then Virgin went on to list exactly what resources he had in his home area to meet the needs of his program. He identified 21 places and ways he could get the workouts he had mapped out ("1×3-mile loop, rolling hills; 1×7-mile loop, all roads, severe rolling hills; one 18-hole golf course in Lebanon, five-mile total, first nine holes short and hilly, second nine holes long and rolling; one Tartan track at Florissant Valley Community College, 35-minute drive"). And finally, he measured closely the resources he had in his own home that would help him in the program ("weight-training: I have in my possession a rusted barbell with 110 pounds of weight. Also I own a set of 10-pound dumbbells. I plan on purchasing a bench-press sit-up board").

By the time Virgin was finished, he had a program so detailed the it might have rivaled a plan to re-create the universe. He put it into effect precisely as scheduled: Just after dawn on October 1, 1978. " . . . A.M.—ran four miles easy, recovering"—he noted in a log of the event—"from a party the night before. P.M.—ran seven miles at a brisk pace, felt good." The opportunities in his home area proved better than expected. The high school had built a cinder track since he'd graduated (and later was to upgrade it with a more modern surface) so that he had a nearby flat oval to use for track. The roads—back roads that have neither name nor number—turned out to have a certain limber quality that he had not encountered elsewhere. The chat—the tiny ground-up gravel that is usually kicked by the wheels of cars and truck to the side of the road—was particularly useful when the road itself was broken up and pocked with holes caused by the deep winter frosts, "It give you about 14 inches on the side in which to run," Craig notes. The winter snows did not prove to be as much of a problem as he'd expected, though the snowfall in the Midwest was exceptionally heavy last winter. Furthermore, the impact of man on nature provided certain advantages that nobody could have anticipated—i.e., telephone poles that became distance markers no snow could ever obscure. And finally, the glacial upthrust of aeons ago gave the land a configuration that Craig Virgin came dearly to love: "I love the challenge of going uphill," Craig said, "because it gives you the chance to test yourself—your physical strength, your mental strength—when you are terribly tired."

Most of all, being in home country gave Virgin a chance to work out his preoccupations—some might say his obsessions—with people who know and understand him. He's had so many problems with his health in the past that he's become very sensitive to how his body feels, functions, and reacts under the stress of his long-distance running. "I give a lot of attention to keeping this car in perfect tune," he said one night careening down a back road at 75 mph in his Fiat X19. "Why shouldn't I put as much effort in keeping this machine"— he indicates his own body—"in perfect tune?"

Because he lives in his home country, he can consult specialists he knows and trusts—and who know him—in every phase of medicine having to do with the machinery of running. As it happens, he has a cousin, Dr. James L. Rehberger of Highland, Illinois, who is a chiropractor involved in sports medicine, and who is very familiar with the problems of Craig and the Virgin family. "The Virgin side of the family has always had a particular problem with the neck structure," Dr. Rehberger informs me. "When he [Craig] gets fatigued, you can see his head starting to flap back . . ." Over the years, Rehberger has helped relieve Craig's long-term problems of body-and-bone structure. Virgin drives up to see Dr. Rehberger every week or so, particularly when he feels something somewhere going wrong. ("I had sciatic pain on my left side . . . I could tell something was wrong because I wasn't getting full power out of both legs . . ."). The idea is not simply to keep the body machine in perfect tune but to remove certain poisonous concerns from the mind. "The big danger in a long race," says Craig Virgin, is "mental panic. That you can't possibly take all this pain. You've got to keep your mind open. I'm convinced that the body is capable of a lot more than the mind will accept."

While doing all this, Craig Virgin logged his performance and reaction in every workout and every race. It is in his nature—a meticulous nature that demands not only that he "do" but that he understand the "doing." Thus, his brief record of the USTFF cross-country race in Madison, Wisconsin, on October 21, 1978. ". . . Could not shake Lacy [Steve Lacy of Wisconsin] . . . I felt Lacy getting stronger in front of the crowd. Began to rationalize the defeat to myself. Suddenly I felt him start to weaken and I threw in one more tempo change and got a gap on him. I ran the fifth mile uphill and into the wind. Fought for a 50-yard lead. Thought the top of the hill would never come . . . Finished the 10,000-meter course in 29:42.7 to Lacy's 29:53.0. I was very grateful to win.

"Began to tighten up immediately. Jogged down two miles. My body had a reaction for six more hours . . ."

Then on January 14, 1979, Craig recorded this about running the marathon, "My first marathon. 2:08:51 for 25 mi. in the marathon, 2:14:40 total. Fastest first-time marathon for American." Virgin told me that he had picked San Diego because he wanted to run his first marathon in the December-February period—that was part of his carefully laid-out plan—which, in turn, dictated that it would be in a sunny warm-weather environment in the South or West. He did not quite anticipate that the marathon would start when his body system—his metabolic cycle—might be down. "Got up at 5:30 in the morning," the record continues. "Consumed 10 fructose tablets with three glasses of water . . . 7 A.M. start . . . Bit off 25th-26th mile in 4:46 . . . Sprint like crazy over last 200 meters. So excited that I ran a victory lap in the stadium . . ."

Then the next-day report, January 15, 1979: "This is the worst I ever felt after a race. Took me 20 minutes to go two miles. I could just barely get one foot in front of the other . . . Went to Tijuana, Mexico. Got sick. Now my whole body aches . . ."

The way that the whole physical and psychological cycle comes together, in workouts and in racing, is reflected in this week-long segment of three races in four days:

Monday, April 23: A.M.: Ran four miles @ moderate pace (26–27 minutes). P.M.: Ran one mile warmup @ Florissant Valley Community College. Ran 12×200 with 200 m. jog between each. Averaged 29 for all of them. Ran a low 27 for my last one. Ran hard but did not strain. Warmed down three miles easy over a hilly course. Felt good about my last hard workout of the week. However I am tired and my legs are going dead. I just hope they can recover in two–three days.

Tuesday, April 24: A.M.: None. Rested. P.M.: Ran four miles. Did light weight workout.

Wednesday, April 25: A.M.: None. Rested. P.M.: Ran five miles on soft golf course. My legs are still a little tired.

Thursday, April 26: A.M.: ran two miles easy. Flew to Philadelphia for Penn Relays. P.M.: Warmed up one mile. Weather atrocious!!! Despite little warmup and weather, I went the 10,000 meters in 27:59.0. A good time for the first race of the year on the track. Had to fight a bad back the whole race. Warmed down easy for three miles.

Friday, April 27: A.M.: Spent three hours in the psychotherapy room trying to get some relief for my aching back and sore legs. P.M.: Ran four miles @ moderate pace. Drove to New York.

Saturday, April 28: A.M.: Slept in. Got up and took a hot bath for my legs and back. Got ready for the Trevira Twosome Ten-Mile race in Central Park. Warmed up an easy mile and stretched well. Got into a head-to-head battle w/Bill Rogers [sic]. I won by 1:04 with a tremendous time of 46:32.7 for ten miles, a new American record for the distance. Ellison Goodall, my partner, also won. Hence we made a clean sweep of the team victory. I warmed down an easy two miles. After much partying and a lot of press conferences, I caught the next flight to Saint Louis, still in my sweats. Have to get some rest before the race in Saint Louis. I'm really happy with these two races in three days.

Sunday, April 29: A.M.: Got up at 6 to run my third race in four days. Thank goodness it is something I needed—a low-key race in Saint Louis. Warmed up two miles easy. Won the Famous Barr Gateway Arch 10,000-meter run in 30:28. Went out and tried to cruise comfortably at sub-5:00 pace as if it were a marathon. My legs and feet are a little shock-sore. I'm grateful to get through this test in good health. Warmed down two easy miles. P.M.: none. Rested and went to the lake with Cindy. [FYI: his girl friend.]

Monday, April 30: A.M.: I feel a little tired but good otherwise. Ran four miles @ easy pace. P.M.: Ran four miles @ moderate pace. P.M.: Ran 11 miles over hilly terrain. Felt good. Ran 6×100 strides. Did weight workout and flexibility workout, especially for lower back.

Conspicuously missing from the diary is the struggle to solve one of the subtlest problems facing the runner who wants to establish himself as his own man: how to get the money to do it. People who work in organizations get salaries, expense accounts, medical insurance, dental insurance, pension plans, workmen's compensation, social security, and scores of other benefits they never think of— until they don't have them. Even athletic clubs provide such benefits: They offer expenses for travel, they often find jobs for their members.

But with runners such as Craig, there is an extra dimension: The cost is not only in money but in time, and in the peculiar way they wear against each other. Virgin must not only have the money for equipment and travel—some of which comes from promoters—but he must have the time to make all the contacts necessary for getting into the races that he thinks vital for his development. Consider just one phase of his program: getting into tough European competition. "There are some days when I phone Europe two or three or four times," he said. And those days go on and on. In other circumstances, the club would make those calls—taking the time and spending the money—and then would come up with his travel expenses in getting to Europe to face the competition. The maddening little hooker: The time that Craig Virgin—or any individual—spends in paper work and administration takes time from working in a job that might pay his expenses. For the athletes who belong to it, the organization not only handles the paper work and travel costs but frees the athlete to put time into a paying job . . . that it has gotten for him.

The way that Craig Virgin met all of these demands was by scrambling. Literally. His father gave him a job on the farm and some of his duties involved scrambling around, helping to herd the cattle. "It's not easy as you think to beat a cow. When they want to run, they can really go," Craig explained. He paused to consider the problem in its fullest and most dramatic dimension. "I've put a lot of effort into researching this," he continued in mock seriousness, "and I want you to know that I've found out something very important about cattle: They can go fast but they can't go far. I can't outrun 'em but I can outlast 'em." His father also gave him a job in the equipment business. One with maximum flexibility. For Vernon Virgin was himself a runner—slowed, then stopped by injury—and he knows that there is something within Craig that makes Craig feel about running the way his father feels about farming, that no matter how hard and lonely and at times agonizing it is, there's nothing else he'd rather do.

TENNIS

THE NET BREAKS

By Gene Quinn

From the Philadelphia Daily News
Copyright, ©, 1979, Philadelphia Daily News

Pay out $563,600 in prize money and you'd think someone could fork over a few bucks for a new net.

Here was Roscoe Tanner, minding his own business, cranking up one of those 140 mph serves against Bjorn Borg. It was only deuce in match game against a player who's making the world forget about ordinary mortals like Tilden and Budge and Laver.

Tanner tosses the ball into the air and cuts loose with one of those left-handed buzz-saw offerings that could have carved a new eye in Hurricane David. It falls short into the net. But wait, the net is sagging, a cord has snapped! Tanner's up 2–1 in sets and 5–3 on his serve and Borg's bid for the Grand Slam is hanging by one of his blond hairs . . . and the net breaks.

This remarkable story about a No. 4 seed's attempt to reach the semifinals by stopping Bjorn Borg's 31-match winning streak took a heart-wrenching turn for the worse before it got better. After National Tennis Center workers used seven minutes to replace the net, after Tanner had scored with a big serve to reach match point, the roof appeared to cave in.

Borg hit a big, fat moonball right at Tanner, who was standing at the net. He cocked, fired, and smacked an overhead that had match written all over it . . . right into the stands. Deuce. Borg won the next point, and the next, taking the game to make it 5–4. Borg held serve at 5–all, Tanner—concentration returning—held, and Borg held again to bring on a tie breaker at 6–all.

This time Tanner was back in the groove. The serve was there, the tough shots at the net were there, too. He served a monster to Borg, who flailed a backhand wide and the match was Tanner's, 6–2, 4–6, 6–2, 7–6, (7–2).

This was a rematch of the Wimbledon final, which Borg won, 6–7, 6–1, 3–6, 6–3, 6–4. That triumph, along with Borg's French Open, is one half of the Grand Slam. The U.S. and Australian Opens are the other half. But the Swede created a monster on the green carpet of South London earlier this summer. Tanner, bolstered by the confidence he found by going five sets with Borg, has been pointing toward the fast Deco Turf II surface here. Bjorn Rune Borg just happened to get in the way.

"It [Wimbledon final] has been a factor in my play overall," said Tanner, his bushy perm and sweaty face glistening in the lights of the interview room. "When you go five sets in a final like Wimbledon, it's important to your confidence."

The Australian tennis writers who were banking on Borg winning the Slam Down Under this fall were making airline reservations back home with Tanner serving for the match in the fourth set. When the net snapped, a line of sagging Aussie jowls snapped to attention. You'd have thought someone put something in their pipe tobacco. The buzz on press row was that Tanner couldn't overcome such a distraction. Surely it would be double fault, double fault . . . all the way to the showers.

"When I broke serve at 5–4," said Borg, "I came back into the match. I think it [the delay] bothered him more than me. He was serving for the match and was juiced up."

"My first thought I won't tell you," said Tanner of blowing the crucial overhead. "It's unprintable. My second thought was, 'It's deuce, let's get it back.'

"When it was 5–all, I was thinking, 'Maybe I can break this game.' It was not time to panic. I was up, 2–1, in sets. I knew with a tie breaker coming up it was no time to panic."

Tanner won the first and third sets with a hard first serve, a well-placed second, touch volleys at the net, great groundstrokes, and even a couple of lobs. Ever since the strong-armed guy came down from Lookout Mountain, Tennessee, they've said he had a one-dimensional game. But no more. He has worked with Dennis Ralston, honed his game. It was evident at the U.S. Pro Indoor in Philly last winter when he beat John McEnroe in the quarters before falling in the semis to Jimmy Connors, whom Tanner could meet in the final here Sunday.

"Bjorn didn't serve quite as well or volley quite as well as he did at Wimbledon," said Tanner. "I had a lot of lucky points and a lot of unlucky points—like the overhead at match point."

Amazingly, Borg made good at 73 percent of his first serves to Tanner's 49 percent. But Tanner made only 24 unforced errors to Borg's 37. Even the Ice Man can't win when he's hacking the ball into the net.

"I don't think I served as well as I did at Wimbledon," said Borg, his face the same stone bust he displays when he wins. "I had too many errors because he was putting so much pressure on me."

Any thoughts about the Grand Slam—which hasn't been won since Rod Laver did it in 1969—going down the tubes?

"I didn't think about the Grand Slam," he said. "I was trying to win this tournament—the U.S. Open. If you think about those things it puts too much pressure on you."

Borg likes Tanner's chances against anyone remaining in the draw. Tanner will meet the winner of today's Vitas Gerulaitis-John Kriek quarterfinal. Jimmy Connors, who beat Pat Dupre, 6–2, 6–1, yesterday, faces either John McEnroe or Eddie Dibbs.

Tanner was asked about a possible letdown in Saturday's semis after such a tiring, emotional victory last night.

"I have two days to rest," he said.

"Hey, this is the U.S. Open . . . not the Chattanooga Open."

Maybe they can tell that to the guy who buys the nets.

GENERAL

HE BRINGS LIGHT INTO THE WORLD

By Ron Rapoport

From the Chicago Sun-Times
Copyright, ©, 1979, Chicago Sun-Times

I think it was in Toledo that I first really missed him.

There was this crazy business about planting a tree in the middle of a golf couse because a couple of the pros had figured out a way to cheat and the people who run the U.S. Open were going nuts and we were all having a wonderful time writing it.

We were laughing and nudging each other every time we thought of a good line—sports writers do a lot of that when they are at a big event together—but when my story was finished I realized there was one thing I wanted to do then and I could not do it.

I wanted to get up and walk over to where Jim Murray was sitting and peek over his shoulder and see how he was handling it. But he wasn't there. The one writer in the country for whom this story was made in heaven was sitting at home trying to deal with the fact that he is nearly blind.

To say that Jim Murray is the world's finest sports writer is roughly equivalent to calling King Kong a large monkey. The statement is not inaccurate, but it hardly does the situation any justice. In the sense that he took a fairly limited form, bent it totally out of shape for his own purposes, and left it almost unrecognizable, he is the only true genius who ever played this game.

Those who aspired to write sports could read the great stylists—Red Smith, Jimmy Cannon—and tell themselves that on their best days, when the idea was sensational, the material was dynamite, and the words were flowing, they could begin to approach them. These masters were by and large doing what a lot of other people were doing; they were merely doing it ten times better.

But with Murray, this charade was over early. He did nothing less than reinvent the sports column and you simply had to surrender yourself to his uniqueness. Though he has been writing for the *Los*

Angeles Times for 20 years, he has produced no imitators—no successful ones, anyway—and it has become clear that when he is gone there will be no one to take his place.

Despite the fact he stands alone, however, Murray is probably the most influential sports writer of our time. When somebody asked me how I was handling the U.S. Open's hastily planted tree, I had come to the end of my three or four one-liners (Murray would have thought of 100 and written 50) and I said I was doing my Jim Murray imitation.

When I asked somebody what he had written on the first day of the tournament, he said he had done a Murray on Toledo. Which is to say, he had made fun of the place. This is a Murray on Florida: "Florida is a body of land surrounded on three sides by sharks and on the fourth by Alabama and Georgia, if you think of that as any better. The alligator is the only true native and he's an improvement on some who came later."

Murray is, you see, funny. Laugh-out-loud, hold-your-sides, don't-eat-breakfast-while-you're-reading-him funny. It is a gift that has made the call for his services come from 131 papers even if it has not always endeared him to the objects of his affection. After he called the Indianapolis 500 the run for the lilies and America's only sanctioned 33-man suicide pact, his credentials for that race often would be mislaid mysteriously. When he teased a Russian track team competing in a dual meet with the United States, it took an official apology from the publisher of his paper on the floor of the Los Angeles Coliseum to keep the event from being canceled.

Murray's record of sustained comic brilliance sometimes obscures the fact that he can work the other side of the street just as well. When Robert Kennedy was murdered, it was Murray who best expressed the rage people felt. When the Hall of Fame announced it was establishing a separate wing for players from the Negro leagues, it was Murray who screamed they were segregating the place and got baseball to beat a quick retreat. When he hastily and unthinkingly wrote a line that some people thought was anti-Semitic, his subsequent apology began, "Some of my best friends are Jews," and I'll be damned if he didn't even pull that risky gamble off.

But it is his comic sense that earns him the bulk of his living and not even three eye operations that failed to restore a detached retina and three weeks during which he had to lie facedown even while he ate have robbed him of that. In his first column after the final unsuccessful surgery, the fourth sentence was, "You might say that Old Blue Eye is back." He went on to explain that it was his good eye, the left one, that failed him; he never could see much out of the other eye, which is blurred by cataracts. Today, he says, he can see the big *E* at the top of the chart but not much else.

Well, this is beginning to sound like an obituary and that is the last thing I intend. Murray is still writing, although on a reduced schedule and with the help of a clerk his paper has assigned to read to him and drive him places and take his dictation. (It is impossible to describe to people who do not write a lot how hard it is to dictate copy rather than to type or write it, to see it on the page as it is taking form, to change it as you go.)

There is still the possibility of an operation on his right eye, although he is understandably wary of it because if it fails, even the few rays of light that do penetrate could be lost. He could be totally blind.

I only know that if they ever start thinking of writing my obituary and send somebody by to ask me what my greatest thrills were in this business I will say something like this:

I will say I once saw Nolan Ryan pitch a no-hitter in which he struck out 17 batters. I will say that I once walked in from the backstretch of Churchill Downs with Seattle Slew. I will say that I once sat in a small dark room on a Pennsylvania mountaintop for an entire afternoon listening to a Muhammad Ali monologue. I will say that I once saw the game in which UCLA set an all-time college basketball consecutive winning streak. I will say that I once went for a ride on a yacht that won two America's Cups.

And I will say that I once wrote headlines for Jim Murray.

GOLF

SAM SNEAD: HE JUST KEEPS ROLLIN' ALONG

By Nick Seitz

From Golf Digest
Copyright, © , 1979, Golf Digest, Inc.

The setting is a lavishly catered suburban dinner party the week of the Westchester Classic, given by the world's most sociable golf magazine. Sam Snead—the story of the year, the game's answer to Old Ironsides, the center of attention this night—has repaired to the game room halfway through the obligatory cocktail hour, his second and last light gin and tonic in hand, there to engage Lon Hinkle, the well-known explorer, at the checkers table.

Approximately three minutes and 10 moves later, the game is over and Hinkle, having been obliterated, is shaking his head in wonder at Snead's devastatingly canny play.

During dinner Hinkle says, "That checkers match showed what makes Sam so great. He loves to play games, loves to plot strategy three moves ahead. He has the enthusiasm of a youngster."

I don't know about you, but for me the most memorable moments of the 1979 season were provided by an enthusiastic young Samuel Jackson Snead, age 67 going on 27. His heroics in the Ed McMahon Quad Cities Open and the PGA Championship, in particular, are indelible highlights not only of the year but of the decade . . . of the century.

In the second round of the Quad Cities in July he became the first man in the history of the PGA Tour to shoot his age—then in the last round he shot better than his age with an astonishing 66, walking so briskly his young playing partner Mark Mike (Mike Mark? Mark Mork?) had trouble keeping up.

"I've admired him all my life," Mike says. "In Georgia, where I come from, he's a legend—but then I guess he's a legend everywhere golf is played. I got so involved in watching him shoot his 66 I neglected my own round, and shot 77. He birdied the first hole, a par 5, and that got him going. He hit his iron shots right at the flag all day, and on the eleventh hole he sank about a 40-foot putt. He shot 31 on the back side, and on the last hole he drove the ball over 300 yards, he was so pumped up. He was obviously pleased with the way he was playing, but he never said anything about shooting his age. We talked about fishing a lot, and he helped me with my swing. He has a tremendous shoulder turn, especially for a man his age, and he told me to be sure and turn the left shoulder under the chin on the backswing."

Frank Bear played with Snead the first two days at the Quad Cities and is still marveling at his age-equaling 67. "He holed it from across the green five times," says Beard. "Sam has a self-imposed reputation as a poor putter, but I've played with him a hundred times over the years and never seen him have a bad putting round. He's always been a good lag putter, and when I play with him he makes the short ones, too, with that sidesaddle style."

Beard was paired with Snead earlier in the year for two rounds at the Jackie Gleason tournament, but Snead did not strike the ball well, and Beard wondered if he finally had come to the end of the trail.

"He didn't look good at all, and I was upset," Beard recalls. "Here was this lifelong idol of mine, this man who has won more tournaments than anybody else, playing very badly, collapsing on his shots. Then it sank in on me that Sam was soon going to be 67 years old, and at that age a man has a right to play badly. How many 67-year-olds do you know who are even physically active, let alone competing successfully against the best golfers in the world?

"I didn't see Sam again until the Quad Cities, and I couldn't believe the difference in his game. He was considerably longer with all his clubs, and he was really playing. That's a difficult course, and the day he shot 67 was blistering hot, but Sam just chugged along and put together a tremendous round.

"He's a terrific playing companion, if you let him know early on that you appreciate who he is. You defer to him in little ways— asking him about the 1942 PGA Championship which he won, having him check your swing, never stepping on his story lines. You don't make it overt, but you let him know that you know he's Sam Snead, and he'll open up to you.

"He was enjoying himself immensely at the Quad Cities, but then Sam's the only man I know who actually enjoys every round of golf he plays, whether it's in a tournament or just a casual game with friends at home. He keeps score in every practice round and treats it as if it's the only 18 holes he's ever going to play. Afterward he reviews every single shot he hit, and he goes over his round again that night in bed.

"I don't think any of us realized what he'd done when he shot that

67, because you don't think of Sam as being that old. I missed the cut and went home, and the next day I picked up the paper and read about Sam shooting his age, and I thought, 'By gawd, that's right, he did!' "

Two days later, after he shot 66, Snead was brought to the press room and seemed generally unimpressed by the history he'd made, perhaps because he's shot his age somewhere or other every year since he turned 60 ("It gets easier every year," he clucks). Tom Place, the tour press director, remembers that Snead interrupted his own hole-by-hole recitation several times to indulge his fondness for telling semirisqué jokes in his best mountaineer's cat-that-swallowed-the-mouse voice, one featuring a young woman of questionable repute who married a nice young golfer and soon confessed she had been a hooker, to which he replied, "That's all right, honey, we'll just move that left hand a little more on top of the club."

Toward the end of the interview session, Sam said he had "wanted to get a charge up because the PGA Championship's comin' up in two weeks and I almost won there at Oakland Hills in 1972." That comment presaged Sam's stealing of the show, nationally televised, at the PGA.

The eighteenth hole at Oakland Hills is arguably the toughest on a long, tough course, a 459-yard uphill par 4 with a rolling, heavily bunkered green. All Sam did was birdie it three times in four days!

"And what people don't realize," points out New Jersey club professional Harry Dee, who used to tour with Sam, "is that those three scores actually were eagles. The hole normally plays as a par 5."

Behind the scenes at the PGA, in the locker room and on the practice green, Snead was boggling the minds of some of the young pros by kicking the top of a seven-foot doorway on a dare and plucking the ball out of the cup without bending his knees. An amazingly resilient and robust physical specimen for any age, he exercises regularly to maintain his flexibility and strength.

"I use a stretching device to tone up my arm muscles," he says. "With my left hand in the middle of my chest, I'll pull the thing with my right hand, then I'll change over and pull it with my left hand, and I get to where I can do that 100 times in the morning and again in the evening before I go to bed. As you get older you can't do so many sit-ups and exercises like that, so you have to find other ways to keep as much of your elasticity and muscle condition as you can.

"You have to be able to make a good turn on your backswing to play well and get much distance, and when I was in my prime nobody turned more than I did. Now I have a little leg and back trouble, and I'm thicker around the middle, and I don't turn as much as I should and that causes me to hit some off-color shots. I'm fortunate I had such a big swing to start with. Most average players I see don't turn enough, for whatever reason. Lots of times I'll play with a weekend golfer and I won't say a thing to him all the way around except 'Turn!' and pretty soon he'll start hittin' it 15 yards farther."

Snead, whose weight has climbed from 185 bull-like pounds to 200 in recent years, much to his disgust, is peculiarly dexterous, loose-jointed, and long-armed. He can rotate a full drinking glass all the way around the outside of one hand, using only the fingers of that hand, without spilling a drop. And he can put his head down between his legs so far his elbows touch the floor. (Though Sam's arms are unusually long, his clubs are an inch longer than standard.)

Given his exceptional body and the fact he has played golf virtually every day for the past 50-plus years, it is easy to explain Snead's longevity in physical terms. He was a born athlete; someone once said that watching him hit practice balls is like watching a fish practice swimming. After all these years he's still the country boy from the West Virginia hills just doing what comes naturally, without having to worry about it or work at it. Right?

"That's all malarkey," Snead bristles, his steely gray eyes catching fire. "I've worked as hard at this game and thought about it as much as anybody else. Bein' self-taught I had to develop different keys I could relate back to when I needed to make a correction. I've hit a million and a half golf balls in my time, and I've had a plan in mind for every one of 'em."

Nowadays people who know Sam well and have played golf with him for a long time talk more about his underrated mental abilities than his physical gifts, and they make a convincing case. Snead's fellow members of the Golf Digest Professional Teaching Panel have a respect for his golfing mind that borders on awe.

Says Bob Toski, affectionately known to Snead as "Mouse," "Sam doesn't attack the ball the way he used to, but he knows how to play with all 14 clubs in the bag, which is something the average golfer and particularly the senior player can learn from. He's also very innovative and deserves a tremendous amount of credit for learning to putt in a different manner late in life so he could prolong his career. I think there will come a day when many, many golfers will putt sidesaddle the way Sam's putting. It took a lot of courage for him to change putting styles like that when everyone else thought it looked funny."

Says Peter Kostis, "Most older players are so concerned with losing distance that they lose sight of how to manage themselves and the course. The thing that impresses me so much about Sam is the way he places his shots and plays within himself. He knows when to play safe and when to go for it."

At this point I told Peter of a conversation I had about Sam with George Burns, the bright young tour pro from Long Island. George was playing with Sam not long ago and hit his second shot on a long par 5 into the water trying to reach the green. Sam told George then that he had revised his strategy and never goes for the green in two unless he can reach it with an iron—and he was scoring half a shot lower on the par 5s as a result. Snead, George emphasized, keeps close tract of how he plays different types of holes and shots, and is adaptable enought to adjust his game based on what he learns: "Takin' inventory," Sam calls it.

This reminded Toski of a story he heard from tour player Tom Kite about a practice round Kite played with Sam and Bobby Cole at Augusta National. Sam, who has never enjoyed parting company with a dollar, was losing a bet to Cole. At the par-5 thirteenth, Sam suggested to Cole that he cut the corner on the dogleg. "When I was your age, son," Sam drawled, "I used to just hit it over those trees and have me a middle iron to the green."

Cole tried it and hit a splendid shot that climbed and soared—and hit the top of a tree and dropped into the creek. How, he asked, had Sam ever managed to bring off that shot?

"Son," Sam said, "when I was your age, those trees were only this high."

Says another of our teachers, Jim Flick, "Sam has very, very keen powers of observation and retention. I've heard him say that when he was playing the tour full time he could identify every player merely by looking at the shoes in front of the lockers. His memory of shots he's hit down through the years is fantastic. If you ask him about his playoff with Ben Hogan in the 1954 Masters, he'll tell you which greens they missed and how many putts they took to get down and how long the putts were."

Adds Dr. Cary Middlecoff, a close friend of Snead since the two played the tour together in the 1940s and 1950s, "People always talk about Sam's great talent, and he has great talent, but in the last 25 years he's developed a remarkable ability to correct his swing in the middle of a round. If he starts duck-hooking, you can bet that in two or three holes he'll have it stopped. Hogan once said that golf is a game of constant correction, and it is, and Sam's mental alertness and preparation are crucial to his lasting so long so well."

The perceptive Middlecoff can talk about Snead all night if the company, the surroundings, and the refreshments are right, and he nearly did one evening after dinner at our Pro Panel instruction meetings at Innisbrook in Florida. "He's 40 yards shorter now—he's in the middle echelon on tour off the tee—but he hits more fairways and greens than he did before. He doesn't talk technique a lot, but he damned well knows it and knows how to teach it.

"I just wish I had half his enthusiasm," marveled Middlecoff. "You know, winning on that new senior tour wouldn't mean anything to me, but Sam's all excited about it. He'll be like a kid with his first set of new clubs out there."

Snead, apprised of Middlecoff's remarks, beamed and said, "I like competition. I play just as hard for $5 as I do for $50,000. Most folks don't understand that, but I think that's the way you have to be. I have to play for a little money to get my interest up, but I don't care how little. I don't think anybody will even try to play as long as I've played. I'm gonna play in my fortieth Masters in the spring—1980 will mark my sixth decade on the tour—and that'll be enough tour golf for me. But I'll play the senior tournaments and maybe one or two others, and I'll enjoy it. What the hell, I can only fish and hunt so much. I just love to play golf."

WOMEN'S BASKETBALL

NOW PLAYERS SMELL NICER TO BUTCH

By Jeff Prugh

From The Sporting News
Copyright, ©, 1979, The Sporting News Publishing Co.

They are basketball's "Bad News Bears."

As collegians, some of the players were four-year letter women. Now, as professionals, they are coached by a man who spews four-letter words.

"Paula! Dammit all!" he roars from the bench. "Hey, Cindy and Wanda! What the hell are you doin'? . . . Turn around! Face the ball! How many times do I have to tell ya?"

And then Bill (Butch) van Breda Kolff stomps and shrieks, fusses and cusses, flails his arms, crumples a plastic water cup in his hand, and flings it disgustedly to the floor.

Such is life in the Women's Professional Basketball League, where van Breda Kolff—coach of the first-year New Orleans Pride—is a born-again baiter of referees and verbal butt-kicker of players.

It all is like watching old flashbacks of van Breda Kolff in the NBA, back when he coached men with the same bombast and Pattonesque authority during stops with the Los Angeles Lakers, Detroit Pistons, Phoenix Suns, and New Orleans Jazz.

Well, almost.

"The difference here," van Breda Kolff is fond of saying, "is that the players smell so much nicer and you see hair-rollers in the locker room."

Otherwise, it was the same old Butch one recent evening when 8,452 fans—a record crowd for the league, now in its second year—watched his team lose its regular-season debut to the New York Stars, 120–114, in the Louisiana Superdome.

Van Breda Kolff, a tall, blustery man with a voice as deep as the furrows in his face, is 56, going on 80.

When he became coach of the New Orleans (now Utah) Jazz five years ago, he awoke one morning, looked into the mirror, and said to himself, "Dammit, you're 51 and you're still running around with those 21-year-old basketball players."

He still was doing it a year ago, but in obscurity as athletic director and head basketball coach at the University of New Orleans, after having been fired by the Jazz (who have moved to Salt Lake City this season).

Then came a fateful visit by van Breda Kolff to a local bar one night earlier this year. There, Steven Brown, vice-president and general manager of the newly formed Pride, introduced himself to van Breda Kolff and asked if he would like to coach the new women's team.

Van Breda Kolff laughed. But weeks later, he changed his mind and resigned at UNO, where he had disliked having to shuffle administrative paper work, anyway.

Now, even though he is back in full-time coaching, it is almost like starting over again. He is teaching players who still are learning the nuances of setting up the offense, beating the 24-second clock, breaking the full-court press, and shutting off rival fast breaks in a league where they earn between $6,000 and $20,000 a year.

"I used to yell at my players in the NBA because they had so much ability and didn't hustle or work hard," van Breda Kolff said. "Here, I yell at the women for making the same mistakes over and over. They work harder than the men. It's just that they don't see the entire court as well. The women coaches they had in college taught them fundamentals—such as passing and the changeover dribble— but they don't know the finer points of playing in this league."

On opening night here, someone gave van Breda Kolff two cigars to light up a victory. Red Auerbach style. But it was van Breda Kolff who did a slow burn.

Again and again, he sprang from his chair, stalking the sidelines, wincing at every missed basket by the home team and bellowing orders to his players.

"Move, Sybil! You can beat her!" he exhorted. "Jeezus! Get away from her, Swilley! . . . She always goes to her right! Make her dribble left, will ya? . . . Oh, God, will you listen to me?"

A few feet away, a craggy-faced man at the press table sat with his wife and whispered to a visitor: "Butch wouldn't care if he was in a seminary."

And unlike his NBA years, when some players answered van Breda Kolff's bark by unleashing their own scathing words to his face, the Pride players generally take it all in stride, except for one or two who every now and then glower in disgust at their new coach.

As Brown remarked, "I really think that Butch likes this level of coaching better than anywhere he's been [including Princeton during the Bill Bradley era]. He's very protective of the girls."

During the first game, a New Orleans player was knocked violently to the floor in a collision with an opponent. Van Breda Kolff threw himself onto the floor in a mock reenactment of the play, hoping that the official would whistle a foul. No whistle blew. But van Breda Kolff blew his top. "You're an idiot!" he screamed at the official.

Later, when van Breda Kolff harangued the officials again, he was slapped with a technical foul, just like the old days. He muttered a couple of six-letter words.

"Tell 'em, Butch!" a male spectator shouted from the front row. "Yeah," another yelled, "give 'em hell, Butch!"

To be sure, it was theater of the absurd. It upstaged home-grown country singer Doug Kershaw, the "Ragin' Cajun," who sang the national anthem too fast for the concert band's accompaniment, and the San Diego chicken mascot, which danced at midcourt, flaunting a brassiere

Earlier, a Catholic priest, the Reverend Peter Rogers, delivered the invocation, which he ended by saying, "We pray that we will score points, many points, Lord, with You and our game of life. Amen. Go Pride!"

The crowd cheered, but was moaning at game's end.

Van Breda Kolff's team played a crisp-passing, screening, and pattern game to mount a 65–50 lead over the taller, faster, more experienced New York team early in the second half. But then the New Orleans players ran out of stamina, sloppily threw the ball away, and lost their lead forever during the fourth quarter.

And van Breda Kolff lost his cool.

"Move the ball, dammit!" he shouted repeatedly.

Now tiny beads of sweat formed on van Breda Kolff's brow. He leaped out of his chair and brushed a hand through his shaggy, graying hair. Then he slumped into his courtside seat and gazed at the scoreboard, which showed New York leading, 102–95, with eight minutes left.

Suddenly the public-address announcer told the crowd: "If the Pride scores 105 points tonight, drop by your local Popeye's Fried Chicken and recive a free leg!"

The crowd perked up. So did the home team, which made a last-gasp run at the Stars, but fell short. "Chicken-bleep referees! They're like the NBA," van Breda Kolff grumbled during a time out. "Thanks a lot for this game, ref!" he yelled with sarcasm.

When it was over, several reporters gathered outside the Pride's locker room, which was guarded by a uniformed New Orleans policeman and policewoman. "This is gonna be kicks," a local male reporter with a tape recorder said. "I can't wait."

But this was not to be a night when male reporters would be

interviewing women athletes as they emerged from the showers. Such an event was not to be—yet, at least.

The policewoman escorted the press to an adjoining, empty locker room, "I wonder," one male reporter said to another, "who's doing to be the first guy to file a lawsuit demanding admission to a women's locker room?"

Next door, van Breda Kolff talked privately to his players, who sat in their sweaty uniforms. Five minutes later, van Breda Kolff emerged to field questions from reporters before allowing them into the women's locker room to interview the players, who still were in uniform.

After the game, a New Orleans defeat, Cindy Williams (5-4), a playmaking guard from Southeastern Louisiana, was being treated for a broken big toenail.

Van Breda Kolff reentered the room and asked the reporters to leave. "Hurry up!" he said. "The girls have to get dressed. It's time to get out of here!"

The reporters soon departed, leaving behind the players and two souvenirs of their coach's stormy baptism into women's basketball.

On a table where Cindy Williams mopped the blood from her painful toenail were two cellophane-wrapped cigars that Butch van Breda Kolff had to save for a happier night.

BOXING

PALOOKAVILLE, U.S.A.

By Pete Bonventre

From Newsweek

Ever hear of Leroy Jones? He's a heavyweight fighter from Denver, Colorado, and he has an undefeated record. The names of his opponents, however, read like the passenger list of a one-way train to Palookaville. But among the heavyweight contenders, Jones is rated No. 3 by the World Boxing Council, No. 4 by the World Boxing Association, and No. 6 by *Ring* magazine. Something's wrong here.

The heavyweight division is now filled with retreads, ham-'n'-eggers and no-names, and nobody is more concerned about the situation than the people who make money on championship fights. "It takes two to tango," says matchmaker Gil Clancy of New York's Madison Square Garden. "The champ has to fight someone the public thinks has a chance to win—or else he doesn't sell tickets."

John Tate recently earned the WBA version of the heavyweight title by winning a unanimous decision over Gerrie Coetzee in South Africa. The other champ is Larry Holmes, who wears the WBC crown. Two different governing bodies recognizing two different champions is an absurdity. But most boxing fans really don't mind enduring a split championship if the champions are matched against opponents who can fight. Yet where are they?

Perhaps the biggest reason for the lack of heavyweight talent is Muhammad Ali. For two decades, he overwhelmed the division with his ability, personality, and popularity. Ali victimized even the fiercest fighters—such as Sonny Liston, Joe Frazier, and George Foreman—and his will to reign as champion prompted one trainer to theorize about his "mystical" quality in the ring. "Muhammad dominated the scene for so long, and there was no room for anybody else," says Angelo Dundee, who trained Ali. "The big guys started going into football and basketball instead of the gyms. What future did they have in boxing? How could they beat the great Ali?"

Ali often boasted that boxing would die when he retired. Ironically, the sport as a whole is prospering. Ali's huge shadow tended to obscure the lighter divisions, but now that he's going, boxing fans are once again beginning to appreciate the sweet science of the little guys. The welterweight division, for example, is a promoter's dream. It contains two strong champions—the WBA's Pipino Cuevas and the WBC's Wilifredo Benitez—and a string of genuine contenders, including former lightweight champion Roberto Duran, Thomas Hearns, and Sugar Ray Leonard, who draw record-breaking crowds and impressive TV ratings. Rarely have two more exciting champions than featherweight Danny Lopez and junior lightweight Alexis Arguello ruled their divisions. And look for Marvelous Marvin Hagler to beat Vito Antuofermo and bring new luster to the middleweight division with his ferocious hooks.

There aren't any Haglers on the heavyweight horizon. Ken Norton recently retired. Earnie Shavers underwent eye surgery three weeks ago and may never fight again. Ron Lyle is too old, and Jimmy Young too fat. Other rated heavyweights are either punching bags like Scott LeDoux and Alfredo Evangelista of Spain or easily forgettable pugs like Italy's Lorenzo Zanon and somebody named Dominigo D'Ella from Argentina. Two South African fighters, Coetzee and Kallie Knoetze, are rated by the WBA but not by the WBC because of their country's apartheid policies.

"When Norton retired, I had to slip somebody into the No. 10 spot," says *Ring* editor Bert Sugar. "I put in Leon Spinks. I had no choice. I had to put in somebody, so Leon got to be No. 10 with a total of eight pro victories. His best effort of the year was going down three times in the first round against Coetzee."

Into this vacuum has stepped 28-year-old Ed (Too Tall) Jones. The former All-Pro defensive end is 6-feet-9 and 248 pounds, and he makes his pro debut this week in New Mexico. Jones is being paid $45,000—the largest first-fight purse in the history of the sport. "Everybody's laughing about Too Tall," said Dundee. "Well, I ain't laughing. The division is wide open, and anybody with talent can come up and dictate things. They'll come, but it'll take time."

Mike Dokes, Greg Page, Randy Cobb, and Gerry Cooney are a few of the young fighters who have a future shot at making a name. But until then, the only championship bout with any credibility is a match between Holmes and Tate. If they fought today, the smart money would favor Holmes. He's a classy boxer, and his long, wicked left jab stings like a bee. But on the basis of his last two fights, his legs are questionable. The 24-year-old Tate has improved dramatically since winning the bronze medal in Montreal. He is a punishing body puncher, and his stamina is remarkable for a 240-pounder. But he is still vulnerable to a jab and a sneaky right counter, and needs at least another year of fighting to polish his footwork. "Larry is the real champion," says Richie Giachetti, Holmes's trainer. "But I won't knock Tate. I can't afford to. We're rapidly running out of opponents."

Tate will probably meet Holmes next October, when the networks are squared off in a new fall season and willing to pay a small fortune for a ratings boost. Tate is tied to Bob Arum, and Holmes to Don King. These two promoters are more colorful than their fighters. Arum graduated from Harvard Law School, and King is an ex-con who used to run numbers in Cleveland. Their bitter rivalry is often more compelling than their promotions, but both men have talked about an uneasy truce for a Holmes-Tate match. Arum, who once remarked that Holmes "has the courage of a mouse," said that he would gladly stage a winner-take-all bout. "That just doubles the profits," he said.

"Arum isn't the kind of person I want around me," says King. "But for a one-shot deal, under the right conditions, I'll work with him. I'll do it for Larry. I want to unify the title." And sell a lot of tickets, too.

GENERAL

DAD DOESN'T KNOW BEST

By Leigh Montville

From The Boston Globe
Copyright, ©, 1979, The Boston Globe
Reprinted courtesy of The Boston Globe

I always thought that sports should be the easiest part. I was wrong again.

The little boy is seven. The little girl is four. Nothing about being a father is easy.

I dress the boy in little pajamas based on the Green Bay Packers' uniform with a No. 12 on the front and I wonder if I am pushing. I dress the girl in pink pajamas with a frog on the front and I wonder if I should be pushing. Should they both be wearing numbers? Frogs? What?

I bought the boy a baseball glove on his sixth birthday and he put it away in a closet. He has touched it maybe a half-dozen times. Was I pushing? Was he too young? Will I buy the girl a glove on her sixth birthday? Or will I give her the boy's glove as a hand-me-down? What?

The boy came home from school one day with baseball cards. I secretly was happy. I built a dollhouse for the girl. The boy liked it better than she did. He plays with it often. I secretly wish he would go back to the baseball cards. I know that I am wrong. Does it show?

I don't let either of them watch the killer shows on television, but on a random Saturday afternoon I will watch a prizefight from Las Vegas or somewhere. They will watch with me. "Why are those two men hitting each other?" they will ask. I will tell them it is just a game. What am I saying?

I find I will explain anything they want to know about sports. I will describe Kansas City as well as the Royals if I am asked. I will tell them how to figure out an earned run average when I know my listeners don't even know what third base it. Why am I so patient about sports and not some other things? Am I selling? Am I directing? Pushing?

I am terrified of becoming "The Little League Father." I don't want to be one of those guys who talks all the time about "my boy" and argues all the time with the coach and the umpires and everyone available. I don't want to be one of those driving fathers, making my son or daughter shoot 100 foul shots before dinner. I play catch, once in a while, with my kids in the street, and somehow feel embarrassed when some other adult sees me.

I took my kids ice-skating during the winter. They would fall down and sometimes cry and want to go home. I told them they should get back up and try again, that nothing in this life was easy, that the pain wasn't bad enough to cry. I heard myself talking and wondered if Vince Lombardi somehow wasn't standing beside me. But should I have brought them home? What?

We went to the ball park, Fenway, for a spring afternoon. They spent two innings in the seats, three at the concession stands, and then they wanted to go home. I was the only one in the family who was disappointed. Why was I disappointed?

What do I do about lessons? Leagues? The time is coming. I see older kids being driven all over the place in big station wagons to play baseball or learn hockey or gymnastics or something. Is that what you are supposed to do? Do you sign up your kids and tell them, "Go, you'll like it"? Or do you just wait until they say they want to go. I'm waiting—I'm no pusher of leagues and schools and full-fledged uniforms and the rest—but am I right?

I worry about handing out sex roles. Why shouldn't the girl be given the same opportunities to play sports as the boy? She should. I know she should. At the same time, I watch the kids playing on the street and I somehow watch the little girls as little girls, I am wrong. Does it show?

What is the value of sports? I am not even sure of that. I once read a letter to the editor in *The New York Times* from a middle-aged guy who said he had followed sports all of his life and was sorry that he had. Did we realize how many hours he had wasted just looking at standings and box scores, memorizing trivia that did nothing but soften his brain cells? Did we know how many other things he could have done with all of that time? I didn't have an answer for him then—except that maybe he would have used that time for watching *Ramar of the Jungle* reruns instead of curing cancer. I don't have any answer for him now.

I suppose that my whole thought is that I want my kids to be "happy" and somehow "happy" always has been associated with sports for me. I know that doesn't necessarily mean "happy" for them, but I sometimes can't help myself. My idea is that I will just leave sports on the front steps, available, ready to be taken if either the boy or the girl or both want it. My problem is that I keep peeking around the corner to see if they have made a move yet.

Am I pushing? Am I not pushing enough?

I had hoped that these questions and others would be answered on this Father's Day by the gift of some sort of omniscient manual that would tell me everything I should do as a father and exactly how I should do it.

I received a necktie.

BOWLING

"WE DON'T THROW GUTTER BALLS HERE"

By Franklin Ashley

From Sport Magazine
Copyright, ©, 1979, Franklin Ashley

The best I ever rolled, or shot, or whatever you call it, was 100. Bowling was never a serious thing. It was less than a sport and barely a game, something played by drunks with one free arm, by matrons with empty afternoons, by college kids without enough money for a real night out. It was a game televised when football wasn't on. Its sound was as musical as the rhythm of an Akron assembly line.

I had never bowled at all except as a baby-sitting chore in Easly, South Carolina. I had used it as a diversion for my six-year-old brother-in-law, who liked hitting things and biting me. Not even the limited physical exertion of bowling attracted a nonathlete like me.

Then one day in March of 1978 I stepped up to the line in the practice round of the $100,000 Bowling Proprietors Association of America (BPAA) U.S. Open in Greensboro, North Carolina, a legal illegal entry. The lights and the cameras flashed at my back. My teal-blue Adidas shirt was heavy with sweat. Nothing to it, I thought, as I prepared to throw a few balls. The first one shivered down the gutter and made a sound like it had struck a large empty drum. "Hey!" came a voice from the next lane. A slim figure in a magenta shirt glided over to me. In an archetypal New Jersey accent, he explained the problem. "Listen, buddy, this is the U.S. Open. We don't throw gutter balls here."

I thanked him and tried to get the proper approach. I also tried to look slim and magenta loving. I swung my arm, the ball sailed down the lane . . . and into the gutter again. Whooma. Whooma. Loud laughter behind me. I was in big trouble.

"Hold it," came a New York voice. "Keep your thumb toward your body."

I turned and saw one of bowling's slickest second-line stars, Johnny Petraglia, slipping on rose-tinted glasses as he approached me. Petraglia's hair shone like spun mahogany and his body consisted of more frame than flesh, nearly touching 6 feet but weighing less than 150 pounds.

A Staten Islander in his thirties, Petraglia's first recorded earnings as a pro, $300, came in 1965, and these days he was a $40,000-a-year man with his own Brunswick signature ball. Moustached and heavy-lidded, he magnetized the autograph-seeking children of Greensboro. Like most of the pros in this practice round, he had started on Lane 40 and worked his way to my end, trying out each lane. But I had stayed on Lane One the whole time to stay out of the way.

"Keep your thumb inside," Petraglia repeated. I nodded and slung the ball again. Five pins fell.

A noncommittal "Yeah," from Petraglia, who then said, "mind if I throw a couple?" The pins went up like Nagasaki. When Johnny finished he whispered, "Who are you, anyhow?" I said I was doing a story for *Sport* and mumbled that my average was only 100, but not always.

John shook his head, his complexion glowing blue-white in the fluorescent light. "Man, why did they send somebody like you?" Then he stepped off the lane before I could tell him more. Only three lanes away was Mark Roth, who had won a smidgen less than $100,000 the year before. Bowling's other superstar, Earl Anthony, who had topped the $100,000 total twice, was not at this tournament. But many of the second-line stars were here, the men who annually average between $20,000 and $30,000 in winnings on the Professional Bowlers Association tour.

By various Byzantine convolutions the BPAA had slipped me into this tournament. The 239 other entrants were either regulars on the pro tour or had pummeled and slammed their way through BPAA state tournaments to qualify for this $100,000 competition. Embarrassed at my performance, I grabbed my ball and eased out the side door. I wanted a beer real bad.

The bowlers stayed at the Rodeway Inn. Once inside, I could have been in Des Moines or Seattle or Salinas or Dallas. The same tan rugs, the same Formica tabletops, the same scrambled eggs, the same red candles in fishnet holders in the bar, the same Emmylou Harris songs.

And beer. Tables of beer, pitchers of beer, wet circles of beer, signs for beer.

"Pass me by, if you're only passin' through," the song began as another quarter fell in the crack of silence. I saw myself in the mirror. Me and 50 of the bowlers who were staying here. All following the PBA rules that require that they be beardless, their hair above the collar. There were no women customers or groupies in the Rodeway Bar. Only sad men on a Sunday night. Bowling, I decide, is not the kind of sport that's made for fighting or loving. The appeal is the chance to win money and the outside hope of an hour on ABC-TV. There is no grassy playing field, no fresh air, no balletic leaping, no graceful pirouetting, no one-on-one physical confrontation. The bowler's gallery—though standing-room-only during tournament play—looks like a Little League bleacher, and the players wear only half a uniform, a bowling shirt and street pants.

I looked at the men around me, and the air turned heavy. "Hey, bartender," I called, "gimme a Bud."

Then I heard it. A mumble about "some guy down here screwing up the tournament." Two boys in Ban-Lon shirts were growling and grumbling.

"No, No, No," Blue Ban-Lon barked to Green Ban-Lon. "*Sport* magazine, not *Sports Illustrated*. They sent him to do a George Plimpton kind of act. You know, bowl with the pros?"

"Yeah, but Plimpton never played in the real thing," Green said. "It was all exhibitions. Not the real thing."

Blue took a swig from his glass. "Looks like they could of at least sent the real Plimpton. Instead, we got a phony Plimpton trying to do the real thing."

"It's gonna throw everybody's game off," Green said. "I'll bet he doesn't even know what double-jumping is."

He was right about that. Double-jumping was sure to cause me further embarrassment. In pro bowling, a pair of lanes must be open on each side of your own pair of lanes before you can make your approach. But there is no clue in the system that tells you it is your turn. The day before, I had asked Dick Battista, a lefty with a heart transplant, about double-jumping.

Battista, a red-faced native of Astoria in Queens, New York, and a former Johnny Carson propman, is constantly hustling the fact that he is the only 50-year-old athlete in the world with a 19-year-old heart inside him.

"Dick," I had asked, "how do you know when it's time to bowl?"

"Hey!" Battista yelled. "I got nothing to lose in talking to you. I got a heart could go out on me any minute. Make a hell of a story. You know what I mean? But listen, if you feel like it's your time to bowl, you step up there and bowl! Don't take any crap off anybody. Just bowl."

Still uncertain, I asked, "What if they . . . ah . . . say it's their turn?"

Battista's red face purpled. "Look! It ain't their turn! You know what I'm saying? When you decide it's your turn to bowl, you bowl. You know what I mean?"

I didn't understand, but now in the Rodeway Bar I was shaken loose from memory by Blue Ban-Lon's next line: "If I find that guy—it's gonna be him and me. Him and me! What's he look like?

Hunh? Anybody seen him?" He looked around the room. "Let's find him!" The Ban-Lon brothers rose.

I was able to make it to the elevator because just outside the men's room they mistook the fatty reporter from the Charlotte *Observer* for me. As the doors hissed shut I heard someone say, "Damn! This ain't the guy."

In my room among the clutter of empty aluminum cans and candy bar wrappers, I looked at the tournament roster. There were three squads which would rotate throughout the tournament. I would be bowling with squad "C," along with Don Johnson, George Pappas, and Mark Roth, all with averages well above 200. I could see the paper shake in my hands as I sought out my "partners." The first name I spotted was "Jay Tartaglia" from Port Chester, New York. Maybe he would tell me whether or not I should leave in the indigo night. I could slink back to my home in Columbia, change my phone number, and get a mailbox downtown.

I found Tartaglia in his room not 20 paces from mine. He had black hair and a fat nose and was in his mid-twenties. He looked like one of those guys in *Saturday Night Fever* who yells, "Hey Tony! You ain't mad, are you?" Jay could not have weighed over 150 pounds. His roommate, Todd Strebel, also in our squad, was even smaller, about 5-feet-9, 125 pounds. In 1977, Strebel had won $5,375 on the pro tour. Tartaglia was not even listed in the program.

I explained my problem to the pair, suggesting I was a somewhat better writer than bowler. But I still thought that with a few tips, I might be able to glom enough bowling technique to avoid complete humiliation.

"How much did you say you bowl?" Strebel asked incredulously.

"A hundred. A hundred, but not always."

"No kidding?" Strebel said.

"No kidding."

Tartaglia smiled, his heavy eyebrows jerking up. "Hey. Hey, I got it. Maybe you could tell everybody you were in an accident. And . . . and it damaged your—" He pointed at me.

"Your brain!" Strebel added. "You had brain damage."

Tartaglia fell back on the bed laughing. "Yeah, people'll feel sorry for you and sorta help you."

When I asked for quick pointers, Strebel snorted, "Everybody hits the pockets here. There ain't any tricks. You gotta come in here knowing how to do it. Then you work on shading your game."

"You'll probably set a world's record," Tartaglia said. "The furthest in the red of anybody."

I felt by heart vibrating. To be in the "red" meant the bowler was under 200 pins per game. A pro's score is computed on a card and projected on an overhead screen. If he's really cooking the score will be in black, but if he is rolling a mere 187, he would receive 13 big fat RED numerals. Tartaglia speculated that I would probably end up with 850 to 900 in the red and I would be remembered forever for it—a sort of "Wrong-Way Corrigan" of bowling.

I thanked both of them for their merciless candor and went back to my room to practice my approach. It was quite peculiar. I took five steps forward, then stopped dead like a spooked racehorse. I then let the ball go from a stationary position. From there the ball could easily spin into its natural path—the gutter.

I felt the cool surface of my ball, a black 16-pounder. It had been given to me by Dan Toma, the owner of Star Lanes bowling center in Columbia. Despite my 225-pound size, I had been more comfortable with a 10-pounder. But Toma insisted I take the 16-pound cannonball, the maximum weight allowed. It was a little like rolling an Oldsmobile, but I finally had become proficient enough to avoid splitting my thumb as I released the ball.

I went over my approach again and again without improvement, finally stumbling over to the bed. I lay down with my ball on the next pillow. Maybe looking at it could do something.

The phone call came near 2:30 A.M. as I lay there fully clothed and semiconscious.

"Frank," the voice whispered. "This is John. John Petraglia. Me and some of the boys wanna come down and talk to you."

I dumped the ball onto the rug and in less than two minutes heard the knock. I wished I had had some heat to wrap in a towel, maybe a Walther PPK.

"The boys" soon settled in my room. Slumping into a black vinyl chair was Everett Schofield, district manager of Brunswick, a fiftyish man carrying a drink in his right hand. The tallest of the five visitors was the orange-haired Dave Davis, like Petraglia a veteran left-hander who regularly wins some $40,000 a year on the tour. Standing next to Davis was Petraglia, who was staring at his feet.

Pacing the room, his eyes all pupils and fire, was George Pappas, the chairman of the tournament committee. Pappas, known as the "Mouth of the South" and one of the few top players to come out of Dixie, has earned slightly more than Petraglia and Davis over the last three years.

Sitting on the arm of another chair was Leroy Harrelson, the PR man representing Brunswick. Harrelson had cottony gray hair, a pink face, and looked like he'd just been cleaned and pressed.

"Guess you know why we're here," Petraglia croaked.

I waited.

"I'll take it," Pappas cut in. He tried to smile. "The point is, Frank, everybody saw you bowl today."

"Yeah," I said. "I'm not too much of a bowler——"

"Yeah," Davis said, "that's why we're here."

Pappas held up his hand. "Look, we represent—we just met with 30 or 40 guys downstairs and everybody says it. If you bowl—we're walking out. We're not gonna have a tournament."

The PR man waved his fingers and said, "Franklin is listening."

Then Pappas's mouth twitched. "Frank, you just can't do it. With you up there it's a damn farce."

Everett burped and shouted, "Franh!" slurring the *k* into an *h*. "Goddamn it, Franh, I cain't let you bowl. I just cain't let you goddamn bowl."

"He's got a right to bowl," Petraglia said.

"I cain't let him do it, and that's that," Everett said.

Pappas scowled. "Everett, he's gotta right to bowl. The BPAA put him in. They're the ones at fault."

"Franklin understands this, fellows," the PR man said.

"I cain't let him goddamn bowl," Everett said.

"Everett, lemme handle it!" Pappas yelled.

Davis said, "He's got a right to bowl."

Petraglia squatted down by the bed. "Look! Look, Frank, we think bowling deserves a story . . . but if you step in there, it cheapens the whole thing."

"Franklin hears you," PR announced. "He hears you."

"I almost punched out one of those bowlers downstairs, Franh!" Everett screamed. "Giving me some crap about you. None of his business. He's just a damn bowler. I'm not gonna take anything off him——"

"Hold it, Everett," Pappas snapped, then said to me: "The point is, you wouldn't compete against Arnold Palmer in the Masters or Staubach in the Super Bowl."

"That isn't my story. I might, though, if I got the chance."

Finally PR stood up. "Fellows, Franklin is a southern gentleman. He teaches at the University of South Carolina. He's a gentleman."

"Frank," Petraglia said, "bowling needs the story." His voice was gentle. "We want it. But a lot of the guys spent time, money, blood, and a lot more to get here."

"Yeah," Davis said. "They're on the line for money."

"And they're afraid," Petraglia went on, "that you could affect their game if you stayed in."

"Frank," Pappas said. "I've never seen the bowlers so united about one thing: you not bowling."

I was furious and exuberant. I sat back on the bed and said, "I'm really pissed off that you guys came down here to my room at 2:30 in the morning like genteel wizards of the KKK and put the heat on. But"—I tried to look noble—"but I don't wanna hurt the tournament and cause everybody to walk out so"—I gave them a couple of seconds—"you can count me out." To be honest, I was relieved.

Everett, who had been practically catatonic, jerked up and said, "You're a great American, Frank. A damn great American."

When the group shuffled out the door, Petraglia turned and shook my hand. "I want you to know," he said softly, "this is one of the most embarrassing moments of my life—and thanks."

I nodded and shut the door. They were right, of course. Bowling is a very serious business to professionals. What I had never seen before were the faces of those who gave so much of their lives to bowling, to the 40 one-inch strips of pine and maple, the cacophonous harmony of falling pins, the lonely nights on the road with the watered beer and country music. I understood some of their rage, their frustration at the exposure and wealth that flows to players of football, basketball, baseball, golf, tennis et al.

Half on the edge of sleep I yanked my memory back to yesterday morning's practice session. Larry Lichstein was in the backroom examining bowling balls to make certain they conformed to PBA standards of weight and material. An aging bowler with a head as shiny as his ball stepped up to the table.

Lichstein weighed his ball and said, "You got too much side weight with this one."

The bowler frowned and retrieved his ball. "Aw, Larry, I don't care. I probably won't cash anyway." He ambled out of the room.

Larry turned to me and raised an eyebrow. "That's a hell of an attitude, isn't it? But you can't blame him." He rubbed his hands together. "There are only about 50 of these guys who are worth a damn and only two of them make big money." He picked up a new sphere. "It's a downer for bowlers, you know. The Chicago Cubs pay Dave Kingman $225,000 to bat .220. Roth, our best player, only made a hundred grand last year. Hell, Kingman couldn't carry Roth's bowling bag."

During practice that week Roth rarely failed to strike. He regularly fell into what is called "dead stroke," a sense of knowing that every ball he rolled would scatter 10 pins. His concentration, timing, and execution were precise, as could be expected from the 1977 PBA Bowler of the Year. Despite Roth's skills, though, the fact remained that few people outside the sport know him. That reminded me of something else Larry Lichstein had said about the current status of bowling: "Face it, Frank. There's champagne, there's liquor, and there's beer. We're beer. And that may be all we'll ever be."

Now fully awake, I lay back wishing I had a Bud. I was glad I was out of the tournament and that the bowlers were competing as they should. In my separation from them, I suddenly felt close to all those bowlers.

TENNIS

CAN A GOOD MALE CLUB PLAYER BEAT A WOMAN PRO? GUESS!

By David Wiltse

From Tennis Magazine
Copyright, ©, 1979, Tennis Magazine

A while ago, several friends and I were watching the final of a women's pro tournament on television when one of them, let's call him Charlie, said with some disdain: "I could beat her." I don't remember who the woman players were, but it hardly matters. They were obviously two of the top female professionals in the world.

Now Charlie was, and still is, an average club player. It was amazing enough that he thought he could beat a woman pro. But what was more astounding to me was that most of the men were agreeing with him; that is, they agreed to the extent that they all thought they could beat her, too.

There were a number of women present at the time and, whether from courtesy or intimidation or actual belief, they all seemed to agree with the assumption that the average man is better than a top woman professional.

Something was seriously amiss here, I felt. Didn't anyone remember the Bobby Riggs versus Billie Jean King match? Did any of these guys seriously think they could beat Riggs, who couldn't beat King?

"Charlie," I said gently. "You can't beat me, and I know I can't beat her."

Just how, I wondered aloud, was Charlie going to stay on the same court with her when he never in his life had sustained a rally longer than five strokes per point. He pointed to the television screen. "Look at that!" he exclaimed with the tennis player's equivalent of moral outrage. "She's looping the ball! Looping it! I'm bigger, stronger, faster, I'd outrun her, outhit her, then come to the net and eat her alive." I didn't bother to point out that Charlie comes to the net an average of three times per set.

However, since everyone was clearly in agreement with him, I began to think maybe I was wrong. Maybe male physical strength would translate automatically, regardless of skill, into tennis dominance. Maybe I was just displaying chauvinism in reverse.

So I decided to put the matter to a test. Beth Norton, a world-class pro whose home is near mine in Connecticut, happened to be taking a sabbatical from the tour for a few months. I phoned her and proposed a serious match. She graciously agreed.

Norton was the national girls' 18-and-under champion in 1975. She turned professional soon after that and has been playing the women's circuit sporadically since then due to a rash of injuries. Even so, she managed at one point to rank No. 20 in the world on the women player's computer. And she stood at No. 29 last spring when she left the tour temporarily to develop a two-handed backhand under the guidance of her brother and coach, Tim, who is himself an active satellite player.

Beth Norton was perfect for my purposes for a number of reasons. First, she is one of the best players in the world, with victories over Rosie Casals and Kerry Reid to her credit. Second, she is small—5-feet-3 and weighs 115 pounds. I'm eight inches taller and outweigh her by 60 pounds. With Betty Stove or Pam Shriver or Martina Navratilova, there might be some questions as to whether I was actually stronger. But Norton is no bigger than my wife and I know I can outplay my wife.

I'm not only stronger and bigger, with a wider reach, than Norton; so is virtually every man I know. If masculine strength had anything to do with it, clearly I was superior.

A word about my own game before we get to Norton's. I'm an A-level club player, standing at 5.5 on the National Tennis Rating Program scale (which rates players from 1.0 for beginners to 7.0 for experts). And in the past six months, I've had a good deal of tournament experience. I've played against some with high sectional rankings and even one former international star.

You will note that I said I have played against them, not that I have beaten them. The point is that although I am not greatly skilled myself, I have recently become accustomed to facing real pace and depth and deception. I had some basis for comparison by which to judge Norton's game. And I have upon occasion, the shots with which to test another player.

Norton and I played our match on Har-Tru at the Four Seasons Tennis Club in Wilton, Connecticut. It was a beautiful, warm day, virtually windless. I can't claim weather, sun, wind, fatigue, or tension as an excuse. The court was in excellent condition and I felt fine.

Before the match, I tried to assess my "advantages." I was bigger, but so what? The thing about tennis is that even though it is a one-on-one competition, you take turns hitting the ball. If my size theoretically gave me an advantage at the net, it had nothing to do with her size. If Stan Smith is at the net, is it any easier for a tall player to pass him than a short player? For a Peter Fleming to pass him rather than a Harold Solomon? I think not, because Smith's size is an absolute advantage, not a relative one.

I am certainly stronger than Norton, but it wasn't a weightlifting contest. Strength in tennis has meaning only as it translates to hitting the ball, and power in tennis comes from racket-head speed, weight transfer, and taking the ball on the rise. Brute strength is the least important factor. If you doubt that, watch Sue Barker cream a forehand sometime.

I may not be faster than Norton, but we would be running separate races, and once I got to a ball, I still had to do something with it.

But I did have one real advantage. I was going to make the rules. What I wanted was to have Norton play her best, to try as hard as she would on the tour, and let me assess her strokes and cunning so I could report to Charlie in terms he would understand.

What I did not want was for her to give me the courtesy games or take it easy or feel sorry for me. I wanted her, as much as possible, to be under some sort of pressure.

I started off by giving myself a one-point lead in every game; that is, I started each game with the score 15-love in my favor.

If one point wasn't enough, I retained the right to up my ante at any time. I felt like a gambler playing with marked cards—not entirely ethical, but secure.

It was a false sense of security. I learned something very quickly in the match. A better player is not only better because of what he or she can do to you (huge serves, blistering cross-courts, cannonading topspin) but also because of what he or she refuses to allow you to do. If you are used to hitting a forehand approach shot deep to the backhand corner and coming in for a put-away, as I am, and instead you are met with a screamer that is either out of reach or on top of you so fast you haven't even changed to a volley grip yet—then you've got problems, my friend.

That, in essence, was the nature of our match. Norton's ground strokes were deep, hard, and well-angled. She seldom hit them with such pace or angle that I couldn't return them. But there was such a great consistency that it took its toll like a series of kidney punches. No single one of them hurt too much, but before I knew it I was bleeding internally.

The steady depth and pace of her groundstrokes kept me pinned back and thoroughly defanged my aggression. I agreed in principle with Charlie's battle plan of whanging a hard one and coming to the net; but he forgot to say just how he was going to belt a forcing shot from behind his baseline. What I whanged instead with greater frequency as the match progressed were short balls. I might as well have tossed her my racket.

The short balls were gone. Period. Not with astounding force, but with an absolute certainty. If I ran left, she went right; if I went right, she went left. If I feinted left, then stayed right, she went left. If I stood in the center, I had a good vantage point for admiring the topspin ball as it landed in one corner or the other and leapt away.

Despairing of hurting her with my normal groundstrokes, I resorted to looping moonballs to her backhand and barreling to the net. I had a certain amount of success with this tactic early in the match when Norton was not yet confident in her newly reconstructed two-handed backhand. But as the match went on, the stroke became as well oiled as the rest of her game and the moonball had no more success than anything else.

The few times I attempted a passing shot, I had to hit a very, very good ball, or it was all over. Her volley was sharp and sure, and she seldom gave me a second shot at it.

The one area where her size proved a disadvantage was covering the lob. She was forced to chase down several lobs that I think a person my size might have handled with a leaping smash. The difficulty in developing this disadvantage into any kind of strategy was to lure her up to the net without taking a ball down my throat. Drop shots didn't do it; she was on them like a cat on a mouse. The only shot that worked was the one that took us both by surprise, the wood shot. Unfortunately, although I hit it with fair frequency, I can't do it when I want to. So much for the lob as a weapon.

Another of my aborted strategies was to attack her serve. Her serve attacked me, instead. It didn't seem right for someone that small to be hitting serves that hard. They weren't bullets, exactly, they weren't aces, but they were all hit deep, hard, and with kick. I very early decided my best tactic with her first serve was to just return it and try for depth.

Her second serve had more kick on it, if less pace. I attacked a few and paid the price.

Which left me with my serve. I have a good serve; it is the one weapon that keeps me in matches with superior players. It is a much better serve than Charlie's in all respects. Unfortunately, it was not a better serve than Norton was used to seeing.

I served well and consistently, and just as well and just as consistently, she hit the returns back deep and firm. When I ventured to the net behind my serve, she put a few into my navel, then took pity on me and whipped the rest past me.

After the match Norton complimented me on my play and said that I had served well. "You have a nice serve," she said. "A couple of girls on the tour have serves like that."

Ah ha! "Who?" I asked eagerly, figuring she's say Navratilova or Shriver or Virigina Wade.

She thought for a moment. "Oh, Kate Latham's second serve is a lot like that," she said.

Kate Latham? Kate Latham's second serve? That, Charlie, is the kind of competition she's used to.

Oh, I know, you want to hear the score. Well, in the first set when I did my best and had one point advantage, we played fairly even. After the first set, I dropped the advantage—fool that I am—and played her straight. She was also loosened up by then and she starting hitting out. It was a most unfortunate combination for me.

Let's just say she beat me. No, let's say she beat me very badly. I'm not about to tell you the score. I don't want to have to live with Charlie saying: "I could do better than that!" No, you couldn't, Charlie. She's much too good.

BASEBALL

THE BOYS OF WINTER

By Hugh Mulligan

From The Associated Press
Copyright, ©, 1979, The Associated Press

It's a shame no Sparky Lyle, Jim Bouton, or other baseball Boswell was hunched over a typewriter or a tape recorder invoking the muse when semipro baseball was the weekend rage throughout the land.

Now there would have been a subject for classic biography.

Passion, poverty, violence (sometimes on the part of the umpires), exotic backgrounds (Union City, New Jersey, the Bushwick section of Brooklyn, York, Pennsylvania), suspense, romance, characters galore: semipro baseball had it all.

The subplots were far more interesting than whether George Steinbrenner fired his secretary for bringing back chopped liver instead of tuna on rye. In those days teams didn't have secretaries; most of them didn't have owners. And who could afford a tuna fish sandwich?

Certainly not Mighty Casey, who probably got all of 10 bucks for the game in which he struck out in the bottom of the ninth with the bases loaded and left Mudville for dead at the end of that 4–2 all time thriller.

Still this was five bucks more than Harvard man Ernest Lawrence Thayer got from the *San Francisco Examiner* for penning the classic comic poem that has become the national anthem of our national pastime.

Anybody who yelled "Play me or trade me" back in those days could find himself in a vacant lot back of a mill in Lowell, Massachusetts, without a bus ticket or even the offer of a ride home.

Only the classy teams like the House of David and the Detroit Clowns had their own bus. The House of David wore full-length beards and slaughtered the innocents with their flying spikes to show their biblical background. Solomon-like, they also traveled with their own umpire, who sometimes rented his Hassidic dark garments to don ordinary pinstripes and catch the second game of the doubleheader.

His name was "Big Red," after his fiery beard rather than his squat stature. I once saw him lift the mask of a catcher who had questioned a balk call, deck the doubter with a hammy fist that still contained his whisk broom, then bellow, "play ball" to resume the entertainment before threatening rains forced the management to refund the patrons' half dollars. This was the price of a bleacher seat and even at Sunday doubleheaders you didn't get it back if the opening game went beyond the bottom of the fourth.

I broke into semipro ball at the age of 11 as a hot dog and soda salesman with the old Long Island City Springfields, affectionately known as "The Springies," toward the end of the Great Depression. Franks went for a dime apiece then, as did the sodas, and free admission was our only commission, despite the skills involved. You had to balance a tray of steaming hot dogs without spilling the mustard on some guy's straw boater, lug an icebox full of pop bottles on your back, retrieve the empties from under the bleachers, and expertly flip coins into the top of the stands when some big spender impressed his girl by breaking a buck.

The first game I ever worked, the Detroit Clowns came to town. They were a white team baseball equivalent of the Harlem Globetrotters, fine players who could yuk it up with monster-sized gloves, exploding cigars for the ump, running out a bunt on a tricycle, and staging a triple steal that included making off with the bases and the water bucket.

Long before Bill Veeck brought him to the majors, I saw Satchel Paige pitch for the Jersey Black Giants. He was getting long in the tooth then, but his famous hesitation pitch hung in the air like the Goodyear blimp. At times he would fake a fastball, the catcher would slam his mitt, and the umpire would bawl, "steeerike." If the batter doubted a pitch had been thrown, Old Satch would assume a look of outraged innocence, shake himself all over in a frantic search until the missing ball rolled out the cuff of his baggy pants.

Pete Grey, the one-armed outfielder who also made it to the majors, came to town one day with a team from Ohio (Sandusky?) that, if I remember rightly, featured a one-legged first baseman and a pitcher who could throw two balls with each hand almost simultaneously. "Strikes one and two, balls one and two," the umpire would soberly announce.

There was an all-girls team from somewhere in Colorado and a Florida outfit that played on donkeyback. There were fine serious teams too, like the Lancaster (Pennsylvania) Red Roses, the Danbury (Connecticut) Invincibles, the Glendale (Long Island) Farmers, the Homestead (Pennsylvania) Greys, and the Rhode Island Reds. The

Bushwicks were so successful they had their own stadium in Brooklyn and played on Saturday afternoons as the East Orange, New Jersey, home team, just reversing their shirts to display their alternate identity.

Some of the semipros were young talent on the way up, like Hank Greenberg with the Bay Parkways. Most, however, were old pros, journeymen players who had served their time in the minors, maybe even made it to Triple-A and a stint in the majors. These were the boys of winter, playing out their days because they loved the game even more than we did. Even the great Grover Alexander ended his days with The House of David. I think Babe Herman, who used to let triples ricochet off his head when not blasting homers for the Dodgers, wound up his career as a semipro idol. I seem to remember him both hitting and causing a homer at Bushwick park.

TV spelled the doom of semipro ball, and the game hasn't been the same since. At least nobody writes poems about it anymore. Just nasty books.

FOOTBALL

BEAR BRYANT CLAIMS HE'S SLIPPING

By Hubert Mizell

From the St. Petersburg (Fla.) Times
Copyright, ©, 1979, Times Publishing Co.

Age alters the image.

Twenty years ago, Bear Bryant was already a Paul Bunyanesque legend. A fierce, whip-crackin' and butt-kickin' football coach who was said to conduct University of Alabama practices with all the salt and compassion of a Parris Island drill instructor.

Was Paul W. Bryant ever really that tough? Probably. Depends on whom you ask. But, the contemporary Alabama Bear is so different. So drastically mellowed. More grandfather than dictator.

"Winning isn't as important to me as it used to be," said the Bear, "but it sure beats hell out of losing." If Bryant is around long enough for Alabama to win 31 more games, he will pass Amos Alonzo Stagg as the winningest college football coach in history.

"It might surprise you, but that [record] means little to me," Bryant said in that syrupy bass voice. "It embarrasses me to talk about it. Makes it sound like I won all them games by myself. Heck, I've had more help than any man alive."

Bryant has a rare level of security in such a volatile and uncertain profession as coaching. You wouldn't fire the Bear of Alabama any more than you'd fire the queen of England. He will retire when he's ready, or he will die in the coaching saddle with that houndstooth hat shading the well-traveled face.

"I'm not afraid of dying," he said at a philosophical moment. "I hope to be a better Christian by then. I talk to some of my kids [players] about it, but I can't say I really feel born-again. I don't know if you can always feel those things. But I do talk to The Man. I get down on my knees every day . . . well, I don't really get down on my knees. I'm too old."

He was 66 on September 11.

Bear can put himself down without fears of puncturing his image. He can rationalize his importance to the Crimson Tide program. He can mumble about having slipped as a football mind. It matters little. As long as 'Bama wins the way it has in the Bryant era, there will be no doubting the magic of having him patrol the sidelines.

"I used to be a good coach," he said, stabbing a fork into his poached eggs on a recent morning. "I've just gotten lazy. Football has kinda passed me by, but I still know something about winning. My assistants do all the coaching. I can't keep up with the changes . . . motion this way, motion that way."

He began to indicate that the added labor of serving as athletic director might be cutting into his coaching time. "People are always needing answers," he said. Then, on short reflection, Bryant went on to say, "Well, truthfully I don't do much as athletic director, either. I guess I really have gotten lazy.

"One thing I do always do is make substitutions. I don't want any of my coaches criticized for sending the wrong player into a football game. If it's messed up, it's me that did it."

If and when Bryant retires, he vows to "leave Alabama with a strong program." He says he wants the best possible person hired as replacement. That is contrary to what some other coaching legends have done. They have recommended hiring men of lesser skills. Some bumbler who will have 4–7 and 5–6 seasons and make the old coach look even better.

In 33 seasons as a head coach, Bryant has a record of 284–77–16 (.775 percentage). An average of 8.6 wins a year. In 22 seasons at Alabama, he is 193–38–8 (.824). Stagg died in 1965 at the age of 102. He needed 54 seasons at Springfield (Massachusetts) College, the University of Chicago, and College of Pacific to win his 314 games.

Stagg coached when college crowds and media communications weren't what they are now. His notoriety was extensive, but by all measures there is no coach with the fame level of Paul Bryant, an old boy from Arkansas who seems to be John Wayne with a whistle.

Bear seldom loses, but when he does there is a pattern to his postgame speech. He takes all the blame. He slams himself for "a dumb game plan." Bear says he called the wrong play at a crucial moment. This is the same fellow who a day earlier would say, "I don't do the coaching anymore."

His shoulders are wide as all of Alabama.

Bryant was at the College Football Hall of Fame in Mason, Ohio, on an NCAA promotion tour. He strolled the edifice with Penn State Coach Joe Paterno, the man he defeated in last January's Sugar Bowl to win a fifth national championship.

"We came to a beautiful mural showing Don Hutson catching a pass," Paterno said. "I said to Coach Bryant, 'Hey Bear, isn't that you in the background?' It was. Bryant and Hutson were All-America teammates that season at Alabama. I asked Bear if his uniform number had been retired."

Bryant's number isn't. It can't be.

"Except for Hutson and Dixie Walker, we all switched jersey numbers every game," he said. "That way, we kept everybody guessing. The most important thing was that switching the players' numbers was the only way they could sell programs."

At nearly every stop, Bryant is asked how long he plans to coach. "As long as I don't embarrass the university, I'll keep on," he said. "It may sound corny, but I most of all want every player I work with to become a better person. There's a lot of education that won't come out of books, but it can be taught on the football field. Lessons that last for a lifetime in a tough world."

Bryant sat for a while with Jones Ramsay, veteran University of Texas sports information director. Ramsay was publicity man at Texas A&M in 1956 when Bear's last Aggie bunch won the Southwest Conference championship the season before he went home to coach at Alabama.

"We just had a reunion of that A&M team," Bryant told Ramsay. "They gave me this," he said, showing a heavy and diamond-decorated ring. "It means so much to me, to see how good all those boys have done with their lives. I'm wearing this ring instead of all the national champion rings I have from Alabama."

Bryant's safe-deposit box is heavy at the bank in Tuscaloosa, nearly as weighted as his monetary holdings. He has lost track of the rings, but estimates "at least 40 watches" in the cache of athletic rewards.

"I had been wearing a good watch, a Rolex," he said, "but I found out it was worth $4,500 and I put it in my lock box. I've also got a pocket watch they gave me as an outstanding player at Alabama 45 years ago. But I'm wearing this old thing we got for playing Sugar Bowl."

Bryant spoke fondly of his upcoming Alabama team. "People outside of Alabama think we'll win," he said, "but people inside Alabama are not very excited. But I'm excited. Our team thinks it can win and I think so, too."

Losing is a rare subject in this life.

BASEBALL

FAREWELL TO CATFISH HUNTER

By Joe Soucheray

From the Minneapolis Tribune
Copyright, ©, 1979, Minneapolis Tribune

Jim Hunter has his son, Todd, along with him on the current
Yankee road trip that began in Kansas City last Monday and con-
cludes in Texas on Wednesday. It's a long but relatively safe journey
as opposed to swings through the double-bolt lock towns of Detroit,
Cleveland, and Chicago.

Todd Hunter is 10, chunky and round-faced like his father, and
even their pleasant drawl is so similar as to be distinguished only by
the difference in octave. Jim Hunter came out of the country at 19
and now, in his last summer in a major-league baseball uniform, he is
showing his only son those baseball towns that might include glimps-
es of what country is left.

"When I first signed with the Yankees," Jim Hunter said, "a man
wanted to give me an apartment rent-free right downtown, in Man-
hattan. He said it was worth $2,000 a month and I checked it over,
saw that it was big enough for my family. But it was 20 floors up. I
told the guy to forget it, I didn't care if it was $100,000 a month. I'd
go crazy in a place like that."

Hunter made the comments early the other afternoon when he
and his son were the only Yankees in the clubhouse at Metropolitan
Stadium. Hunter can't stand hotels so he comes to the ball park
early. His son has a uniform that he wears to play made-up games in
the clubhouse and Hunter was wearing his long underwear against
the chill of the day. A man wanted to see him one last time, before
Hunter retires this year at the age of 33 to his peanut and soybean
farm in Hertford, North Carolina, before his flowing hair and
flowing motions are gone for good.

Hunter might never start another game. The Yankee front office
called him in before the start of this road trip and advised him that,
considering the investment in Ken Clay and Jim Beattie, they would
have to be looked at long and hard down the stretch. Didn't bother

Hunter much except that he would love to help the Yankees down the stretch. He has won 224 games, with Kansas City, Oakland, and New York, and in 1976 he became only the fourth pitcher in this century to record 200 wins before his thirty-first birthday. Do not forget, either, his five World Series wins during three straight championship years in Oakland, or his perfect game in 1968 against the Twins, or his remarkable capacity for humanity. "The sun," Jim Hunter once said when things were not going well for him on the Yankees, "don't shine on the same dog's ass every day."

But this is the last year of Hunter's five-year contract with the Yankees—a contract that made him a household word, signed as it was, on New Year's Eve 1974, but never spoiled him—and, true to his word, he will not return. He has had enough. His son is 10, his daughter is 6, and there is another child due this fall, and James Hunter has had enough baseball. He will go home to the farm. The accumulation of even more Hall of Fame statistics are as meaningless to him as the spent shells from his shotgun. Besides, a man came looking for the memories.

"My best memory was the first time I won my twentieth game in a season," Hunter was saying. "It was 1971. Oakland got into Kansas City at 1 A.M. the night before I'm scheduled to pitch. I wanted to go hunting. Me and Paul Lindblad and Dick Green decided not even to go to bed, so we could go hunting at 4 in the morning. Sal Bando came up to me and said, 'You've got a chance to win 20, get some sleep.' Naw, didn't need it. We all went hunting and got back to the hotel about 3 in the afternoon. Took a shower and went to the park. Won my twentieth."

"How did you get the name Catfish?" The name is not familiar and Hunter has often said that back home in Hertford everybody calls him Jim.

"Before I even met Charlie Finley," Hunter said, "he called me on the phone and asked me if I had a nickname. I said no. He asked what my interests were. I told him hunting and fishing. He says, "Well, you ran away from home when you was six years old. Your parent looked for you all day and when they found you you had just pulled in two catfish and were about to pull in the third."

It never happened, of course. Hunter was the youngest of eight children and Abbott Hunter, who died last month, was too busy to look for lost children. He farmed, other people's land mostly, and worked in the logging woods. He never wanted his children to become farmers or work in the logging woods where you could get your foot mashed or your hands jammed between trees. Until this year Abbott Hunter often visited his famous son in New York.

"And he wouldn't ever go to bed in New York," Jim Hunter said. "He was afraid to."

It was Hunter's farm—despite his father's message, Hunter and his brother Ray own a 110-acre working farm not a half mile from where they were raised—that ultimately caused him to seek release from Finley in 1974. Before the public knew of Hunter's novel free agentry, he and Finley spoke over the phone. Finley asked what it would take to keep Hunter. Hunter told his boss that not only would he stay, but he would play for the previous year's salary, if only Finley would buy back the 400 acres Hunter was forced to sell to repay a loan from Finley that enabled Hunter to buy the farm. It would have cost Finley $400,000. He declined.

"So I moved," Hunter said. "Bought a place in New Jersey that had a yard. It's already sold. The first thing I'm going to do when I get home is take Ray fishing. He's been working all year without even one day off. When I was a kid I always hoped Hertford would grow into a big town, now I hope they keep it small."

The Yankees will miss Hunter, just as surely as the fans will miss watching him when he is right. Roy White will miss Hunter's humor and character. Bucky Dent will miss the same. Graig Nettles, who fights for comedian honors himself, will miss his ride to the ballpark. Lou Piniella will miss "the dignity, the composure, and the class."

"What is class?" Hunter was asked.

"Coming from the country and all," Hunter said. "I'd guess it's being too dumb to be scared of anything. To give 100 percent. Not 110 or 115 percent like some guys say. There ain't but 100 percent to give."

FOOTBALL

THE FINAL GUN FOR WILKINSON

By Skip Bayless

From The Dallas Morning News
Copyright, ©, 1979, The Dallas Morning News

He appeared at a time when heroes were in vogue. World War II had just ended. From sea to bloody sea, we had defended our life, our liberty. One nation under God, we had conquered.

There was a heaven. There were heroes.

Sleep well, Uncle Sam, for MacArthur and Patton and Eisenhower were guarding your shores. They had inherited Jefferson's mind, Washington's courage, Lincoln's strength. They were indestructible.

With each telling, their war tales grew taller. Audie Murphy and young Jack Kennedy walked larger and larger than life. Who wanted to hear the real stories? Our heroes gave us hope.

With guns quiet, we looked for new ones. We found them on the football field.

The year was 1946. He had spent the last four serving his country. From 1934 to 1936, he had played both guard and quarterback at Minnesota. The Golden Gophers had won two national championships. He was tall and slim and strong and blond. This Charles Wilkinson had the look of a hero.

He had been gifted with a strategic mind. He was a leader of men. One day, he wanted to get into politics. But in 1946, he wanted to be the best darn football coach ever.

Jim Tatum, Oklahoma's head coach, noticed young Wilkinson was different, special. In 1946, he hired Wilkinson as an assistant. In 1947, when Tatum took the Maryland job, Charles (Bud) Wilkinson, age 31, replaced him.

In 1947, Billy Bidwill was a ball boy for his daddy's team, the Cardinals.

The first Wilkinson team was 7–2–1, the second 10–1, the third 11–0. Young Wilkinson began exploiting this formation called the split T, a rough version of which he'd learned during the war at Iowa Pre-Flight School. He took a raw-as-crude halfback named Billy Vessels and made a Heisman Trophy winner out of him.

Through the fifties, Bud Wilkinson grew college football heroes like wheat. Up they sprang: Jerry Tubbs, Tommy McDonald, Darrell Royal, Eddie Crowder, Jim Owens, Jack Mitchell, Max Boydston, Tom Catlin. With his teams, Wilkinson's reputation spread from sea to shining sea. Hero worship was focused on the heartland.

But his legend really began to grow in 1953. In '53, Billy Bidwill was a young executive with his daddy's team, the Cardinals.

In 1953, Wilkinson's Sooners began winning, and they didn't stop for 47 games. The Streak, they shook their heads and called it. The Streak, probably, will never be bettered.

The Streak immortalized Bud Wilkinson. He was enshrined in the American psyche. He represented stability and ingenuity. He was clean of speech and habit. He was the strong, silent type, humble in victory, stoic in defeat. The Bud Wilkinsons had made America the invincible lady she was. Bud Wilkinson was a winner.

He would finish with a 145–29–4 record. The longer he coached, the whiter that thatch of hair got. There was something comforting about watching Ol' Bud. At once, he seemed so old and wise, so young and determined. Oklahomans were proud of Will Rogers. But they worshiped Bud Wilkinson.

Then, in 1963, it was over. Wilkinson had endured 3–6–1 and 5–5 seasons. Some had whispered he'd won 47 straight only because so many young studs wanted to play at Oklahoma. Some had said Wilkinson didn't do as much coaching as his assistants did.

But the red bloods wouldn't listen. Ol' Bud had showed 'em, finishing up with 8–3 and 8–2 seasons. Ol' Bud was and always would be a hero.

But where do heroes go for the winter? Are they given a rocker in the Hall of Fame, where they preserve their glow, their legend? Bud Wilkinson ran for the U.S. Senate in 1964. Bud Wilkinson lost. To Oklahomans, Ol' Bud was a football coach, not a politician. Let him do some TV football commentary. Let him serve honorarily in the Kennedy, Johnson, and Nixon administrations. That's where Ol' Bud belonged.

In 1972, William V. Bidwill became chief executive officer of the St. Louis football Cardinals.

But down deep, Wilkinson didn't want to be a hero. He wanted to be a football coach. In 1978, when Bill Bidwill gave him the opportunity, Ol' Bud couldn't help himself.

As a wide-eyed youth, Bidwill had followed him in awe. Bidwill was convinced: Bud Wilkinson merely could stand on the sidelines and the Cardinals would win a Super Bowl.

At age 62, Bud Wilkinson, immortal, became a rookie pro football coach. The irreverent chortled. The worshipers worried.

Many insiders considered Bidwill little more than a buffoon. He had inherited a team, but not the sense to run it. The fear was, with Bidwill making the important decisions, Wilkinson could coach legendarily and lose. But how could you tell Ol' Bud that?

And, too, football and its players had changed. Big money was the name of this game. Heroes were an endangered species. These guys didn't want to hear about 47 in a row, but about six figures.

The year was 1978. It was painful, watching Bud Wilkinson stand stoically through another streak—eight straight losses. Though the Cardinals rallied, winning six, losing two the second half, Ol' Bud's glow had dimmed.

Wilkinson's Saint Louis team was 3–10 this season. The truth hurt; Bud Wilkinson could not be a legend after his time.

Wednesday, Billy Bidwill fired Bud Wilkinson. Bidwill had ordered him to go with the future—Steve Pisarkiewicz. Wilkinson stuck steadfastly by the past—veteran quarterback Jim Hart.

Bidwill said he just "made a mistake" when he hired Wilkinson. That's all, just a little mistake. Who wants a 3–10 coach?

Where have all the heroes gone?

BASEBALL

AS CLEAN AS FARRAH'S TEETH

By Hal Lebovitz

From The Cleveland Plain Dealer
Copyright, ©, 1979, The Plain Dealer

Scene. Office of William Bergerwine, president of a new hotel and gambling casino, Bally-Hi, going up in Atlantic City. Bergerwine is seated at his desk. Willie (Hey-Hey) Ways, former major-league baseball player, now in the Hall of Fame, enters.

BERGERWINE: Come in, Willie. Have a seat. Great to see you.

WILLIE: Nice place you're gonna have here. When are you going to open?

BERGERWINE: End of November, I hope. That's what I wanted to talk to you about.

WILLIE: Hey, I don't know anything about gambling. I mean nothing.

BERGERWINE: I know, I checked you out. That's why I want you.

WILLIE: Huh? What you want me to do?

BERGERWINE: Public relations. Play golf with some of the guests. Make appearances for us at civic functions in Atlantic City. Make appearances in other cities for us. We'll book you 10 days out of every month. The rest of the time is yours.

WILLIE: For how long and how much?

BERGERWINE: We are offering you a 10-year deal at $100,000 a year. Also, we'll pay all your expenses and there'll be a suite in our hotel for you and your family.

WILLIE: Wow. Bet you think I'll lose it back to you at the tables.

BERGERWINE: That's another thing. In the contract it says you can't set foot into the casino. I want to keep it clean from baseball. Which reminds me, are you still working for the New York Mets?

WILLIE: Yeah. I have two more years to go on my contract. I get $50,000 a year, but I don't have to do much. Just show up in spring training, take a little batting practice now and then. Appear at some Old-Timers games. I also work for Colgate and for the Ogden Corporation. Make appearances for them, too.

BERGERWINE: You'd have to quit the Mets, Willie. We don't want anybody working baseball to be associated with us. Don't want to be contaminated.

WILLIE: What do you mean?

BERGERWINE: Well, we run a clean operation. We're checked by the Securities and Exchange Commission. Our stock is listed on the New York Stock Exchange. New Jersey and Nevada have special commissions constantly checking us out. We can't afford to have anybody working in baseball and for us at the same time.

WILLIE: What's wrong with being associated with baseball?

BERGERWINE: Well, there's stealing in baseball, isn't there?

WILLIE: Heh-heh-heh. You mean base-stealing? You're some kidder, Mr. Bergerwine.

BERGERWINE: Yeah, that was a joke, But you have a lot of club owners who own racehorses, some who have pieces of racetracks, some who were involved in strange deals in becoming rich. At least one who has pleaded guilty to breaking the law. Everybody connected with us has to be cleaner than Farrah Fawcett's teeth.

WILLIE: Won't the commissioner of baseball get mad when I tell him I've got to quit the Mets?

BERGERWINE: Sure he will. But let him clean his own house and then it will be OK for you to stay in baseball, too.

WILLIE: This is going to get into the papers, that you're asking me to get out of baseball.

BERGERWINE: It's about time somebody blew the whistle on all the double-talk in baseball. Ball players go to the racetrack all the time. You know and I know some of the biggest stars in the game who lose bundles there. There's card-playing in the clubhouse. Gamblers come to the ball park. They talk to players and umpires. They allow things in baseball that would cause us to have our license revoked.

WILLIE: But it's the great American game. I love it.

BERGERWINE: I love it, too. It's the phony double standard and the hypocrisy we don't want to be part of. We're an open, above-board gambling operation. No coverup. What you see is what you get. I told Frank Sinatra the other day, if he wants to perform in our casino he can't sing the national anthem at the World Series.

WILLIE: Oh, thet'll be a slap at baseball. Can I still play in Old-Timers games?

BERGERWINE: Oh sure. That's like a high school reunion. You can go to them, too.

WILLIE: Can I still work for Colgate?

BERGERWINE: Of course. They're clean. They make soap.

FOOTBALL

THE GHOST OF THE GIPPER

By Loel Schrader

From the Long Beach Independent, Press-Telegram
Copyright, ©, 1979, Long Beach Independent, Press-Telegram

"Has anybody talked to the ghost of the Gipper lately?" I asked.

"What?" replied Roger Valdiserri, assistant athletic director at Notre Dame, a pained expression creasing his face.

"The ghost of the Gipper—has anyone talked to him lately?"

Valdiserri's eyes rolled in their sockets.

"Gosh, I don't know. I can't keep track of all these legends around here."

I wouldn't be put off.

"Where's Cartier Field?" I asked.

"Go out the front door and make two rights. You'll see it."

"I'm going to see if I can find him there."

"Be my guest."

Cartier Field is where the Fighting Irish played their football games before Notre Dame Stadium was constructed in 1930.

But I leaned against the canvas and yelled: "Geooorrge. Oh, Geooorrge, George Gipp, are you here?"

A security guard drove up.

"Looking for someone?" he inquired.

"The ghost of the Gipper," I said.

He laughed. "Why are you looking for him here?"

"I thought he might still be hanging around Cartier Field?"

"Well, this is the new Cartier Field. The old one was right over there where the new library stands, the one with the Touchdown Jesus mosaic."

He put a hand on my shoulder, "Besides, mister, I hear his ghost hangs around Washington Hall. It's just past the old field house."

"Why Washington Hall?"

"Well, the way I hear it, he was sleeping off a hangover on the steps of Washington Hall on a cold November morning in 1920, and he caught an infection that eventually led to his death a month later. Besides, they used to have a pool table in there."

"George Gipp, a three-time All-America, the one and only Gipper, the guy they're always winning one for, drank and played pool?"

"Yes, and he smoked and gambled a great deal."

"I can hardly believe that."

He revved the motor of his car, said, "Take your choice," and sped off.

I headed toward Washington Hall. Surely there had to be a mistake.

On the way, I passed the old field house, where Knute Rockne used to take the Gipper and other players for practice on cold days.

A girl was working on ceramics inside the field house.

"Have you talked to the ghost of the Gipper?"

"Who?"

"The ghost of the Gipper. You've heard of the Gipper, haven't you?"

"Noooo. Oh, wait a minute. Is he one of those football players?"

Whew! One of those players? He was *the* player.

I turned away and left. Serves the school right for letting girls enroll.

A hundred yards away, I found a building with "1881" stamped in stone on it.

Two students were sprawled on the front steps. They looked at me inquiringly as I surveyed the building for a name.

"Are you looking for something?" one of them asked.

"The ghost of the Gipper. Have you heard of the Gipper?"

He winked at his buddy. "Sure, I've heard of him, but I haven't heard from him, or his ghost."

"What building is this?" I asked.

"Washington Hall."

"Thanks." At least I'd found it.

Students were entering a two-tiered lecture hall as I went into the building. I waited until the doors to the lecture hall were closed.

Then I called out: "Geoooorrge, Geoooorge Gipp. Are you here?"

Moments later, two students came out of the lecture hall, a quizzical look on their faces.

"Were you the one making that noise?" they asked.

"I was calling for the ghost of the Gipper," I replied.

They grinned. The short one said: "If we hear from him, we'll let you know. Why don't you leave your business card?"

"Go to hell."

They left and I resumed my search. I moderated the volume of my call. "George Gipp, are you there?"

I heard a noise at the bottom of the stairwell, so I scurried down there. "Is that you, George?"

"Holy Toledo," said a voice, "am I ever hung over."

"Is that you, Gipp?"

"Yeah, what do you want?"

"I want to know all sorts of things about you. Like, did you really ask Rock to win one for you someday? You know, when the going got tough and the odds were against Notre Dame, to win one for the Gipper?"

"Where did you hear that?"

"Rock said it. He told his team before the 1928 Army game that you asked him that. And they went out and won one for you."

I heard a laugh. "Did Rock really say that?"

"Sure."

"That old con man, he'd do anything to win a football game."

"Then you didn't tell him that on your deathbed?"

"Are you kidding?"

"How about the story that he discovered you when you kicked a football back over the fence from the baseball field?"

"Naw. Somebody slipped me 150 bucks—that was a lot of money in those days—and told me to come down here and play football for Rockne."

"Are you sure you're the ghost of the Gipper?"

"Dang right. Get me a pool table and I'll prove it."

"How about a football?"

"I'd rather play pool."

I was becoming disillusioned.

"How do you think the game with Southern Cal will come out?"

"Who's Southern Cal?"

"You've never played them."

"Say, mister, I really need a little rest. I wonder if you'd excuse me while I sleep this thing off."

"Sure, Gipper. Before I leave, is there anything I can do for you?"

"Yeah, ask the boys to win one for me."

"OK, I'll tell the Irish you want them to win one for the Gipper."

"By the way, could I borrow a sawbuck from you?"

"Yes, but what do you need it for?"

"I want to get something down on the game."

GENERAL

SPORTS BEAT? DON'T FORGET TO DUCK

By Murray Olderman

From Newspaper Enterprise Association
Copyright, ©, 1979, Newspaper Enterprise Association, Inc.

In Boston, a pro football player shoves an elbow into a writer's eye and they wind up on the floor throwing punches at each other. In San Francisco, a baseball pitcher threatens to hit a writer over the head with a chair.

Steve Carlton, an ace pitcher with the Philadelphia Phillies, hasn't talked to writers in several years. Neither has George Hendrick, an outfielder with the Saint Louis Cardinals. And the spirit is catching.

When Chicago Cubs outfielder Dave Kingman doesn't like what's written about him, he says, "I ain't gonna talk no more." Same with Jack Clark, the Giants' outfield star, and countless others.

In recent years, the relationship between athletes and the press, always tenuous, has become, in a word, terrible.

Last December, I saw Gene Upshaw, who fancies himself as the spokesman of the Raiders and has political aspirations beyond football, confront an Oakland columnist on the team plane and berate him in four- and nine-letter words in an ugly and uncomfortable scene merely because the columnist had written some opinions of the poor performance of the team.

When the glowering guy delivering it is 6-feet-5 and weighs 265 pounds, the physical threat behind such an attack is implicit. Personally, I experienced the same thing from Reggie Jackson during the World Series five years ago.

Normally, the tribulations of the press in covering sports shouldn't concern readers. Yet the schism between the two is so pronounced that it affects the news reaching the public and in some cases creates it. There never has been a more antagonistic feeling on covering sports.

Why this deterioration?

Today pro football players seem conditioned to regard approaches for interviews as a nuisance and sometimes they're downright rude in rebuffing them. Baseball players are even worse. And the attitudes carry over into virtually every sport. Jimmy Connors in tennis is a pain for a writer trying to do his job.

The reason is that the athlete and the writer are no longer members of the same economic class. They used to be, to put it simplistically, working stiffs together.

That was before the free-agent revolution that created instant millionaires among athletes. A decade or two ago, the average ball player and the established writer were making the same kind of money, sharing common problems and life-styles. They were peers.

But now a "beat" man covering a club and making a salary of $25,000 annually is dealing with a player often making $350,000 and more a year. He's also dealing with sensitive and frequently arrogant psyches.

So when he writes something critical, the athlete snorts: "How can that punk who's not making one-tenth of what I make write that kind of garbage about me? I don't have to take it."

Of course, there is nothing new about writers tangling with athletes. In the 1950s, Earl Lawson, a Cincinnati baseball writer, once slugged it out with Johnny Temple of the Reds. Even playboy Bo Belinsky attacked an older writer, Braven Dyer, 15 years ago. But they were isolated instances. What's different today is the climate. A longtime observer such as Leonard Koppett traces the chronic conflict that exists now to the Nixon-Agnew attack on the press in the late 1960s and early 1970s, which alienated the reader from the journalist.

A sports corporation (i.e., team) is insensitive to the needs of the writer because its owner's interest has shifted from newspapers, once the sole avenue of getting to the public, to television exposure—where the bucks are. TVs top executive echelon isn't oriented to journalism but to show business, whose hype is to make the performer look good. Even when there's a Howard Cosell, the athlete doesn't threaten to bash him in the nose; he threatens to sue, if he dares.

There has also been increased management of the press, which started with NFL Commissioner Pete Rozelle and his minions. The expansion and professionalization of the public-relations man in sports created barriers behind which the athlete could hide comfortably. Clubs now arrange interviews. The iconoclastic sports writer looking for something different is discouraged.

It must also be said that the attitudes of sports writers have changed, too. Not all of them exercise probity in their quest for interesting copy. Yet they have become more probing and more pungent in their observations of the sports scene. There aren't too many sycophants among the modern breed.

Personally, I think that's progress. But don't forget to duck.

FOR THE RECORD
CHAMPIONS OF 1979

ARCHERY
World Champions
FREESTYLE
Men—Darrell Pace.
Women—Jin Ho Ki.
National Field Archery Assn.
BAREBOW
Men—Roger Arnold.
Women—Gloria Shelley.
FREESTYLE
Open—Richard Johnson.
Women's Open—Lonna Carter.

AUTO RACING
World—Jody Scheckter.
U.S. Grand Prix—Gilles Villeneuve.
USAC—A.J. Foyt.
USAC Stock—A.J. Foyt.
Indy 500—Rick Mears.
Daytona 500—Richard Petty.
NASCAR—Richard Petty.
24 Hours of Le Mans—Klaus Ludwig and Bill and Don Whittington.
IMSA Camel—Peter Gregg.

BADMINTON
World Champions
Singles—Liem Swie King.
Women's Singles—Lene Kappen.
Doubles—Tjun-Tjun and Wahjudi.
Women's Doubles—Verawaty, Wigoeno.

BASEBALL
World Series—Pittsburgh Pirates.
American League—East: Baltimore; West: California; playoff: Baltimore.
National League—East: Pittsburgh; West: Cincinnati; playoff: Pittsburgh.
All-Star game—National League, 7–6.
Most Valuable Player, AL—Don Baylor, California.
Most Valuable Players, NL—Keith Hernandez, St. Louis and Willie Stargell, Pittsburgh.
Leading Batter, AL—Fred Lynn, Boston.
Leading Batter, NL—Keith Hernandez, Saint Louis.
Cy Young Pitching, AL—Mike Flanagan, Baltimore.
Cy Young Pitching, NL—Bruce Sutter, Chicago.
AL Rookies—Alfredo Griffin, Toronto and John Castino, Minnesota.
NL Rookie—Rick Sutcliffe, Los Angeles.
NCAA—Division I, Fullerton State; Division II, Valdosta State; Division III, Glassboro State.

BASKETBALL
NBA—Seattle SuperSonics.

NBA Most Valuable Player—Moses Malone, Houston.

Scoring—George Gervin, San Antonio.

NCAA Div. I—Michigan State; Div. II—North Alabama; Div. III—North Park, Ill.

College Player of the Year—Larry Bird, Indiana State.

NAIA—Drury

AIAW—Old Dominion.

NIT—Indiana.

Junior College—Three Rivers CC.

Women's J.C.—Northern Oklahoma.

AAU Men—Christian Youth Center.

AAU women—Anna's Bananas.

BIATHLON

World 20 km.—Klaus Seibert.

U.S. 10 km.—Lyle Nelson.

U.S. 20 km.—Ken Alligood.

BILLIARDS
World Champions

3-Cushion—Raymond Ceulemans.

Pocket—Mike Segal.

Women's Pocket—Jean Balukas.

BOBSLEDDING
World Champions

2-Man—Erich Schaerer-Josef Benz.

4-Man—West Germany.

BOWLING
PBA Tour

Leading Money Winner—Mark Roth.

ABC Champions

Singles—Ed Bird.

Doubles—Nelson Burton Jr.,-Neil Burton.

All-Events—Nelson Burton, Jr.

Women's IBC

Singles—Betty Morris.

Doubles—Mary Ann Deptula-Geri Beattie.

All-Events—Betty Morris.

Queens—Donna Adamek.

National Duckpin Congress

Singles—Dave Moody.

Women's Singles—Doris Holshouser.

Doubles—Wayne Wolthouse-Gary Hamilton.

Women's Doubles—Brenda Willig-Elaine Green.

BPAA

Open—Joe Berardi.

Women's Open—Diana Silva.

BOXING
Professional Champions

Heavyweight—John Tate, recognized by World Boxing Association; Larry Holmes, recognized by World Boxing Council.

Light Heavyweight—Marvin Johnson, WBA; Matthew Saad Muhammad, WBC.

Middleweight—Vito Antuofermo.

Junior Middleweight—Ayud Kalule, Uganda, WBA; Maurice Hope, WBC.

Welterweight—Jose (Pepino) Cuevas, WBA; Sugar Ray Leonard, WBC.

Junior Welterweight—Antonio Cervantes, WBA; Sang-Hyun Kim, WBC.

Lightweight—Ernesto Espana, WBA; Jim Watt, WBC.

Junior Lightweight—Samuel Serrano, WBA; Alexis Arguello, WBC.

Featherweight—Eusebio Perdoza, WBA; Danny Lopez, WBC.

Junior Featherweight—Ricardo Cardona, WBA; Wilfredo Gomez, WBC.

Bantamweight—Jorge Lujan, WBA; Guadalupe Pintor, WBC.

Flyweight—Betulio Gonzalez, WBA; Chan-Hee Park, WBC.

Junior Flyweight—Yoko Gushiken, WBA; Sing-Jun Kim, WBC.

CANOEING
Flatwater
KAYAK

500 Meters—Terry White.

Women's 500—Linda Dragan.
1,000—Terry White.
Women's 5000—Ann Turner.
10,000—Brent Turner.

CANOE
500 Meters—Roland Muhlen.
1,000—Roland Muhlen.
10,000—Kurt Doberstein.

COURT TENNIS
U.S. Open—Barry Toates.
U.S. Amateur—Ralph Howe.

CROQUET
Singles—Archie Pack.
Doubles—Pack-Jack Osborn.

CROSS COUNTRY
World Champions
Men—John Treacy.
Women—Grete Waitz.
United States Champions
AAU—Alberto Salazar.
AAU Women—Margaret Groos.
NCAA Div. I—Henry Rono, Washington State.
NCAA Div. II—Jim Schankel, Cal. Poly, San Luis Obispo.
NCAA Div. III—Steve Hunt, Boston State.
NAIA—Sam Montoya, Adams State.
AIAW—Julie Shea, North Carolina State.
Junior College—Pedro Flores, New Mexico.
Junior College Women—Maria Tilman, Phoenix (Ariz.) College.

CYCLING
World Champions
TRACK RACING
Sprint—Lutz Hesslich.
Women's Sprint—Galina Zareva.
Pursuit—Mikolai Makarov.
Point Race—Jiry Slama.
Time Trials—Lothar Thoms.
Pro Sprint—Koichi Nakano.
ROAD RACING
Men—Gianni Giacomini.

Women—Petra de Bruin.
Pro—Jan Raas.
Tour de France—Bernard Hinault.
United States Champions
ROAD RACING
Senior—Steve Wood.
Senior Women—Connie Carpenter.
TRACK RACING
Sprint—Leigh Barczewski.
Women's Sprint—Sue Novara.
Pursuit—Dave Grylls.
Women's Pursuit—Connie Carpenter.
TIME TRIALS
Men—Andrew Weaver.
Women—Beth Heiden.

DOG SHOWS
Best-in-Show Winners
Westminster (New York)—Ch. Oak Tree's Irishtocrat, Irish Water Spaniel, Anne E. Snelling.
International (Chicago)—Ch. Lou-Gins Kiss Me Kate, standard Poodle, Terri Meyers and Jack and Paulann Phelan.
Santa Barbara—Ch. Thrumpton's Lord Brady, Norwich Terrier, Ruth Cooper.

FENCING
World Champions
Foil—Aleksandr Romankov.
Epée—Philippe Riboud.
Saber—Vladimir Lazlymov.
Women's Foil—Cornelia Hanisch.
United States Champions
Foil—Michael Marx.
Epée—Tim Glass.
Saber—Peter Westerbrook.
Women's Foil—Jana Angelakis.
National College Champions
Foil—Andy Bonk.
Epée—Carlo Songini.
Saber—Yuri Rabinovich.
Women's Foil—Joy Ellingson.
Women's Team—San Jose State.

FOOTBALL
College
Eastern (Lambert Trophy)—Pittsburgh.

Eastern (Lambert Cup)—Carnegie-Mellon.
Eastern (Lambert Bowl)—Delaware.
Heisman Trophy—Charles White, USC.
NCAA Div. II—Delaware.
NCAA Div. III—Ithaca.
Atlantic Coast Conference—North Carolina State.
Big Eight—Oklahoma.
Big Ten—Ohio State.
Ivy League—Yale.
Mid-American—Central Michigan.
Missouri Valley—West Texas State.
Ohio Valley—Murray State.
Pacific 10—Southern Cal.
Pacific Coast AA—San Jose State.
Southeastern—Alabama.
Southern—Tenn., Chattanooga.
Southland—McNeese State.
Southwest—(Tie) Houston, Arkansas.
Southwestern—(Tie) Grambling, Alcorn State.
Western Athletic—Brigham Young.
Yankee—Massachusetts.

Professional
NATIONAL FOOTBALL LEAGUE
NFC—Los Angeles Rams.
Super Bowl—Pittsburgh Steelers.
CANADIAN FOOTBALL LEAGUE
Grey Cup—Edmonton Eskimos.
Player of the Year—David Green, Montreal Alouettes.

GOLF
Men
U.S. Open—Hale Irwin.
U.S. Amateur—Mark O'Meara.
Masters—Fuzzy Zoeller.
PGA—David Graham.
British Open—Severiano Ballesteros.
Tournament Players Championship—Lanny Wadkins.
World Series—Lon Hinkle.
Tournament of Champions—Tom Watson.
Vardon Trophy—Tom Watson.
Leading Money Winner—Tom Watson.
PGA Player of the Year—Tom Watson.

Canadian Open—Lee Travino.
U.S. Public Links—Dennis Walsh.
USGA Senior—Bill Campbell.
USGA Junior—Jack Larkin.
NCAA Div. I—David Edwards; Div. II—Tom Gleaton; Div. III—Mike Bender.
NAIA—Sam Houston State.
Women
U.S. Open—Jerilyn Britz.
U.S. Amateur—Carolyn Hill.
Ladies PGA—Donna C. Young.
Leading Money Winner—Nancy Lopez.
Player of the Year—Nancy Lopez.
USGA Senior—Alice Dye.
USGA Junior—Penny Hammel.
USGA Public Links—Lori Castillo.
AIAW—Kyle O'Brien.

GYMNASTICS
World Championship
MEN
All-Round—Alexandre Ditiatin.
Floor Excercise—Kurt Thomas.
Rings—Alexandre Ditiatin.
Vault—Alexandre Ditiatin.
Horse—Zoltan Magyar.
High Bar—Kurt Thomas.
Parallel Bars—Bart Conner.
WOMEN
All-Round—Nelli Kim.
Floor Exercise—Maria Filatova.
Balance Beam—Nadia Comaneci.
Bars—Tie-Yanhong Ma, Maxi Gnauck.
Vault—Tie-Dumitria Turner, Melita Ruhn, Nelli Kim, Steffi Kraker.
Team—Rumania.
All-Round
AAU Elite—Peter Korman.
AAU Women's Elite—Jackie Cassello.
NCAA Div. I—Nebraska.
AIAW—Cal. State, Fullerton.
NCAA Div. II—Illinois-Chicago Circle.
NAIA—Centenary.
USGF—Men, Bart Conner, Women, Leslie Pyfer.

HANDBALL
U.S. Handball Assn.
FOUR-WALL
Singles—Naty Alvarado.
Doubles—Stuffy Singer-Marty Decatur.
Masters Singles—Jim McKee.
Masters Doubles—Ron Earl-Marty Goffstein.

HARNESS RACING
U.S.T.A. Awards
Horse of the Year—Niatross.
Pacer of the Year—Niatross.
Trotter of the Year—Chiloa Hanover.
Aged Trotter—Doublemint.
Aged Trotting Mare—Doublemint.
Aged Pacer—Try Scotch.
Aged Pacing Mare—Try Scotch.
3-Year-Old Trotting Colt—Noble Hustle.
3-Year-Old Pacing Colt—Hot Hitter.
3-Year-Old Trotting Filly—Classical Way.
3-Year-Old Pacing Filly—Roses Are Red.
2-Year-Old Trotting Colt—Noble Hustle.
2-Year-Old Pacing Colt—Niatross.
2-Year-Old Trotting Filly—Cranford.
2-Year-Old Pacing Filly—Misty Misty.
Leading Race Winners
TROTTING
Hambletonian—Legend Hanover.
Yonkers Trot—Chiola Hanover.
Kentucky Futurity—Classical Way.
Roosevelt International—Doublemint.
PACING
Little Brown Jug—Hot Hitter.
Cane—Happy Motoring.
Messenger—Hot Hitter.
Driscoll—Dream Maker.

HOCKEY
National Hockey League
Stanley Cup—Montreal Canadiens.
Leading Scorer—Bryan Trottier, Islanders.

Most Valuable Player—Bryan Trottier.
Leading Goalie—Ken Dryden.
World Hockey Association
Avco Cup—Winnipeg Jets.
Regular Season—Edmonton Oilers.
Most Valuable Player—Dave Dryden, Edmonton.
Leading Scorer—Real Cloutier, Quebec.
Leading Goalie—Dave Dryden.
Amateur
World—Soviet Union.
NCAA—Minnesota.
NCAA Division II—Lowell.
ECAC Div. I—New Hampshire; Div. II Eastern Conference—Lowell; Western Conference—Middlebury.
Western Collegiate—North Dakota.
Central Collegiate—Bowling Green.
NAIA—Bemidji State.

HORSE RACING
Eclipse Award Champions
Horse of Year—Affirmed.
Older Horse—Affirmed.
Older Filly or Mare—Waya.
3-Year-Old Colt—Spectacular Bid.
3-Year-Old Filly—Davona Dale.
2-Year-Old Colt—Rockhill Native.
2-Year-Old Filly—Smart Angle.
Sprinter—Star de Naskra.
Grass Horse—Bowl Game.
Steeplechaser—Martie's Anger.
Owner—Harbor View Farms.
Breeder—Claiborne Farm.
Trainer—Laz Barrera.
Jockey—Lafitt Pincay.
Apprentice Jockey—Cash Asmussen.
Leading Race Winners
Kentucky Derby—Spectacular Bid.
Preakness Stakes—Spectacular Bid.
Belmont Stakes—Coastal.
Brooklyn—The Liberal Member.
Champagne—Joanie's Chief.
Coaching Club American Oaks—Davona Dale.
Flamingo—Spectacular Bid.
Florida Derby—Spectacular Bid.

Jockey Club Gold Cup—Affirmed.
Marlboro Cup—Spectacular Bid.
Metropolitan—State Dinner.
Suburban—State Dinner.
Travers—General Assembly.
Turf Classic—Bowl Game.
Wood Memorial—Instrument Landing.
Woodward—Affirmed.
Epsom Derby—Troy.

HORSE SHOWS
World Cup
Jumping—Hugo Simon.
American Horse Shows Assn.
Hunter Seat—Mark Leone.
Saddle Seat—Gihley Tway.
Stock Seat—Laurie Richards.

ICE SKATING
Figure
WORLD CHAMPIONS
Men—Vladimir Kovalev.
Women—Linda Fratianne.
Pairs—Tai Babalonia-Randy Gardner.
Dance—Natalia Linichuk-Gennadi Karponosov.
U.S CHAMPIONS
Men—Charles Tickner.
Women—Linda Fratianne.
Pairs—Tai Babalonia-Randy Gardner.
Dance—Stacy Smith-John Summers.
Speed
WORLD CHAMPIONS
Men—Eric Heiden.
Women—Beth Heiden.
Sprint—Eric Heiden.
Women's Sprint—Leah Poulos.
U.S. CHAMPIONS
Outdoors—Erik Henriksen.
Women's Outdoors—Gretchen Byrne.
Indoor—Bill Lanigan.
Women's Indoor—Patti Lyman.

JUDO
AAU National Champions
132 lbs.—Keith Naksone.

143 lbs.—James Martin.
156 lbs.—Steve Sack.
172 lbs.—Brett Baron.
189 lbs.—Leo White.
209 lbs.—Miguel Tudela.
Over 209 lbs.—Dewey Mitchell.
Open—Shawn Gibbons.

KARATE
Kata—Albert Pena.
Women's Kata—Vicki Johnson.
Kumite—Tokay Hill.
Women's Kumite—Vicki Johnson.

LACROSSE
NCAA Division I—Johns Hopkins.
NCAA Division II—Roanoke.
Women—Penn State.

LUGE
World Champions
Men—Guenther Dettlef.
Women—Melitta Sollman.
AAU National Champions
Men—Frank Massley.
Women—Donna Burke.
Doubles—Gary Schmeusser.
North American Champions
Men—Mark Jensen.
Women—Nadeau Danielle.

MODERN PENTATHLON
United States Champion
Men—Greg Lesey.
Women—Gina Swift.

MOTORBOATING
Unlimited Hydroplane
Season Series—Bill Muncey.
Gold Cup—Bill Muncey.
Offshore Racing
U.S.—Betty Cook.
South American—Billy Martin.

PADDLE TENNIS
U.S. Singles—Robbie Rippner.
Doubles—Sol Hauptman-Jeff Fleitner.

U.S. Women's Doubles—Annabel Rogan-Nena Perez.

PARACHUTING
United States Champions
MEN
Overall—Cliff Jones.
Accuracy—Rick Kuhns.
Style—Chuck Schmutz.
WOMEN
Overall—Cheryl Stearns.
Accuracy—Cheryl Stearns.

PLATFORM TENNIS
United States Champions
Doubles—Clark Graebner-Doug Russell.
Women's Doubles—Yvonne Hackenberg.

POLO
United States Champions
Open—Retama, San Antonio.
Gold Cup (18-22 Goals)—Retama.
College (Indoor)—California-Davis.
Cup of the Americas—Argentina.

RACQUETBALL
United States Champions
Open—Marty Hogan.
Women's Open—Karin Walton.
Pro—Marty Hogan.
Women's Pro—Karin Walton.

RACQUETS
United States Champions
Open—William Surtees.

RODEO
U.S. All-Round—Tom Ferguson

ROLLER SKATING
World Champions
Men—Michael Butske.
Women—Petra Schneider.
Dance—Fleurette Arseneault-Dan Littel.

Pairs—Karen Mejia-Ray Chappatta.
United States Champions
Singles—Michael Glatz.
Women's Singles—Moana Pitcher.
International Singles—Lex Kane.
Women's International Singles—Joanne Young.
Pairs—Tina Kneisley-Paul Price.
Dance—Fleurette Arsenault-Dan Littel.

ROWING
World Champions
MEN
Single Sculls—Pertti Karppinen.
Double Sculls—Alf and Frank Hansen.
Pairs—Bernd and Jorg Landvoigt.
Pairs with Coxswain—Gerd Uebler, Juergen Pfeiffer.
Fours—East Germany.
Fours With Coxswain—East Germany.
Eights—East Germany.
WOMEN
Single Sculls—Sanda Toma.
Double Sculls—Cornelia Linse-Heidi Westphal.
Quadruple Sculls—East Germany.
Pairs—East Germany.
Fours—East Germany.
Eights—Soviet Union.
United States Champions
Men—Greg Stone.
Women—Louis Novey.
IRA—Brown.

SHOOTING
National Skeet Shooting Assn. Champions
Men—Todd Bender.
Women—Marina Pakis.
Grand American Trapshooting Champions
Men—Dean Shanahan.
Women—Debbie Moore.

SKIING
World Cup Champions
Men—Peter Leuscher.
Women—Annemarie Proell.

World Alpine Champions
MEN
Downhill— Peter Mueller.
Slalom— Ingemar Stenmark.
Giant Slalom— Ingemar Stenmark.
Combined— Andreas Wenzel.
WOMEN
Downhill— Annemarie Proell.
Slalom— Regina Sacki.
Giant Slalom— Christa Kinshofer.
Combined— Annemarie Proell.
World Nordic Champions
MEN'S CROSS-COUNTRY
Overall— Oddvar Braa.
WOMEN'S CROSS-COUNTRY
Overall— Galina Kulakova.
Nations Cup Team
Soviet Union.
Collegiate
NCAA— Colorado.
AIAW— Middlebury.

SOCCER
United States Champions
North American League— Vancouver White Caps.
American Soccer League— Sacramento.
Challenge Cup— Brooklyn Dodgers.
Amateur— Data Graphic, Atlanta.
Junior— Imo's Pizza, St. Louis.
Collegiate Champions
NCAA Division I— Southern Illinois-Edwardsville.
NCAA Division II— Alabama A. & M.
NCAA Division III— Babson.
NAIA— Quincy.

SOFTBALL
United States Champions
MEN
Fast Pitch— Clark and Sons, East Providence, R.I.
Slow Pitch— Nelson Manufacturing, Oklahoma City.
WOMEN
Fast Pitch— Leslie Fay, Wilkes Barre, Pa.
Slow Pitch— Miami, Fla. Dots.
Collegiate— Texas Woman's University.

SQUASH RACQUETS
U.S. Squash Racquets Assn.
Singles— Mario Sanchez.
Singles 35's— Tom Poor.
Singles 40's— Raul Sanchez.
Singles 50's— Henri Salaun.
Collegiate— Ned Edwards, Pennsylvania.
U.S. Women's Squash Racquets Assn.
Singles— Heather McKay.
Senior Singles— Goldie Edwards.
Collegiate— Gail Ramsey, Penn State.

SQUASH TENNIS
U.S. Open— Pedro Bacallao.

SWIMMING
U.S. Long-Course Champions
MEN
100-M. Free— Ambrose Gaines.
200 Free— Rowdy Gaines.
400 Free— Brian Goodell.
1,500 Free— Brian Goodell.
100 Back— Bob Jackson.
200 Back— Steve Barnicoat.
100 Breast— Bill Barrett.
200 Breast— John Simons.
100 Butterfly— Grant Ostlund.
200 Butterfly— Steve Gregg.
200 Ind. Medley— Jesse Vassallo.
400 Ind. Medley— Jesse Vassallo.
400 Freestyle Relay— Florida AC.
400 Medley Realy— Longhorn AC.
800 Freestyle Relay— Florida AC.
WOMEN
100-M. Free— Cynthia Woodhead.
200 Free— Cynthia Woodhead.
400 Free— Cynthia Woodhead.
800 Free— Kim Linehan.
1,500 Free— Kim Linehan.
100 Back— Linda Jezek.
200 Back— Linda Jezek.
100 Breast— Torry Blazey.
200 Breast— Tracy Caulkins.
100 Butterfly— Mary Meagher.
200 Butterfly— Mary Meagher.
200 Ind. Medley— Tracy Caulkins.
400 Ind. Medley— Tracy Caulkins.
400 Freestyle Relay— Pleasant Hill (Calif.) AC.
400 Medley Relay— Longhorn AC.

800 Freestyle Relay—Mission Viejo, Calif.

National Collegiate Champions
MEN
50-Yd. Free—Ambrose Gaines, Auburn.
100 Free—Andy Coan, Tennessee.
200 Free—Andy Coan.
500 Free—Brian Goodell, UCLA.
1,650 Free—Brian Goodell.
100 Back—Carlos Berrocal, Alabama.
200 Back—Peter Rocca, California.
100 Breast—Graham Smith, California.
200 Breast—Graham Smith.
100 Butterfly—Par Arvidsson, California.
200 Butterfly—Par Arvidsson.
200 Ind. Medley—Graham Smith.
400 Ind. Medley—Brian Goodell.
400 Freestyle Relay—Tennessee.
400 Medley Relay—California.
800 Freestyle Relay—Florida.
1-M Dive—Gregg Louganis.
3-M Dive—Matthew Chelich.
Team—California.
NAIA—Simon Fraser.

WOMEN
50-Yd. Free—Sue Hinderaker, USC.
100 Free—Gail Amundrud, Arizona State.
200 Free—Gail Amundrud.
500 Free—Jo Clark, Stanford.
1,650 Free—Jo Clark.
50 Back—Linda Jezek, Stanford.
100 Back—Linda Jezek.
200 Back—Linda Jezek.
50 Breast—Allison, Arizona State.
100 Breast—Renee Laravie, Florida.
200 Breast—Debbie Rudd, Southern Cal.
50 Butterfly—Joan Pennington, Texas.
100 Butterfly—Joan Pennington.
200 Butterfly—Dianne Johannigman, Houston.
100 Ind. Medley—Joan Pennington.
200 Ind. Medley—Joan Pennington.
400 Ind. Medley—Diane Girard, Texas.
400 Freestyle Relay—Arizona State.
400 Medley Relay—Stanford.

800 Freestyle Relay—Florida.
1-M Dive—Janet Thorburn, SMU.
3-M Dive—Janet Thorburn.
Team—Florida.
AIAW—Nevada, Reno.

National Collegiate Champions
MEN'S DIVING
1-M Dive—Greg Louganis, Miami.
3-Dive—Matthew Chelich, Michigan.
Team—California.

WOMEN'S DIVING
1-M Dive—Janet Thorburn.
3-Dive—Janet Thorburn.
Team—Florida.

SYNCHRONIZED SWIMMING
World Champions
Solo—Helen Vanderburg.
Duet—Vanderburg-Kelly Kryszka.
Team—United States.

TABLE TENNIS
United States Champions
Singles—Mylan Orlowski.
Women's Singles—Kayo Kawahigashi.

TEAM HANDBALL
United States Champions
Open—West Coast Club.
Women's Open—Northeastern Club.
Collegiate—U.S. Military Academy.

TENNIS
International Team Champions
Davis Cup (Men)—United States.
Federation Cup (Women)—United States.
Wightman Cup (Women)—United States.

United States Open Champions
Singles—John McEnroe.
Women's Singles—Tracy Austin.
Doubles—John McEnroe-Peter Fleming.
Women's Doubles—Betty Stove-Wendy Turnbull.
Mixed Doubles—Greer Stevens-Bob Hewitt.

Other United States Champions

Clay Court—Jimmy Connors.

Women's Clay Court—Chris Evert Lloyd.

Junior—Scott Davis.

Junior Women—Mary Lou Piatek.

NCAA—Div. I, Kevin Curren, Texas; Div. II, Arjun Fernando, Southern Illinois-Edwardsville; Div. III, Mark Tappan, Redlands.

NAIA—Garry Seymour, S.W. Texas State.

AIAW—Kathy Jordan, Stanford.

Junior College—Mike Brunnberg, Miami, Fla.

Junior College Women—Karen Gulley, Schreiner (Tex.) College.

Foreign Opens

Wimbledon Men—Bjorn Borg.

Wimbledon Women—Martina Navratilova.

Australian Men—Guillermo Vilas.

Australian Women—Chris O'Neill.

French Men—Bjorn Borg.

French Women—Chris Evert Lloyd.

Professional Champions

Leading Money Winner—Bjorn Borg.

Women—Martina Navratilova.

TRACK AND FIELD
U.S. Men's Outdoor

100 M.—James Sanford.

200—Dwayne Evans.

400—Willie Smith.

800—James Robinson.

1,500—Steve Scott.

3,000—Henry Marsh.

5,000—Matt Centrowitz.

10,000—Craig Virgin.

5-Km. Walk—Dan O'Connor.

20 Walk—Neal Pyke.

50 Walk—Marco Evoniuk.

110 Hurdles—Renaldo Nehemiah.

400 Hurdles—Edwin Moses.

High Jump—Franklin Jacobs.

Pole Vault—Mike Tully.

Long Jump—Larry Myricks.

Triple Jump—Ron Livers.

Shot-Put—Dave Laut.

Discus—Mac Wilkins.

Javelin—Duncan Atwood.

Hammer—Scott Neilson.

U.S. Women's Outdoor Champions

100 M.—Evelyn Ashford.

200—Evelyn Ashford.

400—Patricia Jackson.

800—Essie Kelley.

1,500—Francie Larrieu.

3,000—Francie Larrieu.

10,000—Mary Shea.

5,000 Walk—Sue Brodock.

10,000 Walk—Sue Brodock.

100 Hurdles—Deby LaPlante.

400 Hurdles—Edna Brown.

400 M. Relay—Tennessee State.

1,600 Relay—Prairie View.

3,200 Relay—Oral Roberts.

Sprint Medley Relay—Prairie View.

High Jump—Debbie Brill.

Long Jump—Kathy McMillan.

Shot-Put—Maren Seidler.

Discus—Lynn Winbigler.

Javelin—Kate Schmidt.

NCAA Outdoor Champions
DIVISION I

100 M.—Jerome Deal, Texas-El Paso.

200—Greg Foster, UCLA.

400—Kasheef Hassan, Oregon State.

800—Don Paige, Villanova.

1,500—Don Paige.

3,000—Henry Rono, Washington State.

5,000—Syndey Maree, Villanova.

10,000—Suleiman Nyambui, Texas-El Paso.

110 Hurdles—Renaldo Nehemiah, Maryland.

400 Hurdles—James Walker, Auburn.

400 Relay—Southern Cal.

1,600 Relay—Louisiana State.

High Jump—Nat Page, Missouri.

Pole Vault—Paul Pilla, Arkansas State.

Long Jump—Larry Myricks, Mississippi College.

Triple Jump—Nate Cooper, Villanova.

Shot-Put—David Laut, UCLA.

Discus—Bradley Cooper, Florida State.

Javelin—Tom Sinclair, Washington.

Hammer—Scott Neilson, Washington.

Team—Texas-El Paso.

Other Champions
AAU Decathlon—Bob Coffman.
AAU Women's Pentathlon—Jane Frederick.
Boston Marathon—Bill Rodgers, Joan Benoit.
New York City Marathon—Bill Rodgers, Grete Waitz.

VOLLEYBALL
United States Champions
USVBA Open—Nautilus Pacific.
USVBA Women's Open—Fireside Mavericks.
AAU—Vessel's Quartermaster.
AAU Women—Fireside Mavericks.
NCAA—UCLA.
NAIA—Graceland.
AIAW—Hawaii.
Pro—Tucson Sky.

WATER POLO
World—Hungary.
AAU Outdoor—Newport, Calif.
AAU Women's Outdoor—Seal Beach, Calif.
AAU Indoor—Pepperdine.
AAU Women's Indoor—Long Beach, Calif.
NCAA—U.C., Santa Barbara.

WEIGHTLIFTING
World Champions
114 lb.—Kanybek Osmonaliev.
123—Anton Kodjabashv.
132—Merek Seweryn.
148—Yanko Rusez.
165—Roberto Urrutia.
181—Uri Vardanian.
198—Gennadi Bessonov.
220—Pavel Sirchin.
242—Sergei Arakelov.
Super Heavy—Sultan Rachmanov.

AAU National Champions
114 lb.—Jon Chappell.
123—Pat Omari.
132—Phil Sanderson.
148—Dave Jones.
165—Dave Reigle.
181—Tom Hirtz.
198—Jim Curry.
220—Kurt Setterberg.
242—Mark Cameron.
Super Heavy—Tom Stock.

WRESTLING
World Freestyle Champions
105—Sergei Kornelaev.
114—Yuji Takada.
125—Hideaki Tomiyama.
136—Vladimir Yurmin.
149—Mikhail Charachura.
163—Lee Kemp.
180—Iftvan Kovaacs.
198—Khasan Ortcuev.
220—Illia Mate.
Over 220—Salman Chasimikov.
NCAA Champions
118—Gene Mills, Syracuse.
126—Dan Lewis, Iowa.
134—Darryl Burley, Lehigh.
142—Dan Hicks, Oregon State.
150—Bruce Kinseth, Iowa.
158—Kelly Ward, Iowa State.
167—Mark Churella, Michigan.
177—Mark Lieberman, Lehigh.
190—Eric Wais, Oklahoma State.
Heavy—Fred Bohna, UCLA.
Team—Iowa.

YACHTING
U.S. Yacht Racing Union
Mallory Cup (Men)—Glenn Darden.
Adams Trophy (Women)—Allison Jolly.
Sears (Junior)—Bill Lynne Jr.

WHO'S WHO IN BEST SPORTS STORIES—1980

WRITERS IN BEST SPORTS STORIES—1980

MAURY ALLEN (One for the Books), tied for this year's best feature story award, is a sports reporter for the *New York Post*. He began his career with the *Seymour* (Ind.) *Times* after Army service, joined the *Levittown* (Pa.) *Times*, and then worked for *Sports Illustrated*. In 1962 he joined his present paper. He is the author of *Where Have You Gone, Joe DiMaggio?* published in 1975. In addition, he is the author of nine other sports books and has merited many appearances in *Best Sports Stories*. He won a first place in the coverage competition that this book offers in 1975.

FRANKLIN ASHLEY ("We Don't Throw Gutter Balls Here") teaches in the College of General Studies at the University of South Carolina in Columbia and is a senior editor of *Sandlapper Magazine*. He is also an author of a book of poetry, *Hard Shadows*, and has written for *Harper's, New Times, People,* the *New Republic,* and *Paris Review*. This is his first appearance in *Best Sports Stories*.

PETER AXTHELM (Whines and Whimpers) joined *Newsweek* in 1968 as sports editor and has covered the sports beat extensively. In 1970 he became a general editor of *Newsweek* and he has written over 30 cover stories. Honors include an Eclipse Award from the Thoroughbred Racing Association, Page One Awards from the Newspaper Guild, a National Headliners Award for consistently outstanding columns, and a Schick Award for professional football writing. He has contributed to most of the better magazines, such as *Esquire, Harper's,* and *Sport*. His writing has also included many books on sports, a work on literary criticism, and the definitive book on basketball, *The Inner City*. He graduated from Yale in 1965, worked for the *New York Herald Tribune,* later for *Sports Illustrated,* and then went to *Newsweek*. He has appeared in *Best Sports Stories* frequently.

SKIP BAYLESS (The Final Gun for Wilkinson), who earned broad recognition for investigative sports reporting with the *Los Angeles Times*, is the new lead sports columnist for the *Dallas Morning News* and is making his freshman appearance in *Best Sports Stories*. Although only 26, Bayless has covered major events in virtually every sport for the *Miami Herald* and *Los Angeles Times,* including the Super Bowl, the World Series, NBA basketball, the Ali-Spinks heavyweight championship fight, and two horse-racing Triple

Crowns. He won the Eclipse Award last year for the nation's best horse-racing coverage. An all-star student and athlete in high school in Oklahoma City, Bayless attended Vanderbilt University on a Grantland Rice Scholarship and graduated *cum laude* in English and history.

PHIL BERGER (Boxing's His Business) has been a free-lance writer for 13 years. He is a former associate editor of *Sport Magazine* and has been published in *Playboy* (from which a story on Leon Spinks shared the Best Magazine award a year ago), *Penthouse, New York, TV Guide,* and *The Village Voice,* among others. He is the author of many books, including *The New York Knickerbockers' Championship Season* and *The Last Laugh: The World of Stand-up Comics.* This is his second appearance in *Best Sports Stories.*

JIM BOLUS (The Great Redeemer's Companions) is a sports writer for the *Louisville Times,* where this story appeared. He has won four national writing awards. With colleague Billy Reed, he also won the National Headliners Award and the Sigma Delta Chi Distinguished Service Award. Other awards have been presented to him by the Ocala-Marion Chamber of Commerce, the Florida Chamber of Commerce, and the Florida Breeder's Association, the last for his feature story about Florida Breeds that have run in the Kentucky Derby. He has also written considerably for magazines. This is his second appearance in *Best Sports Stories.*

PETER BONVENTRE (Palookaville, U.S.A.) has been a general editor of *Newsweek* since 1976. He has covered such varied events as the Olympic tragedy in Munich, Bobby Fischer's chess playoff in Iceland, and the Ali-Frazier fight in Manila. He joined *Newsweek* in 1969 and two years later became the associate editor of his department. His fine work has been selected four times for *Best Sports Stories.* Previously, he worked as an assistant sports editor at the *New York Times.* He is a graduate of the University of Pennsylvania, where he majored in journalism.

THOMAS BOSWELL (Stargell and Weaver: They Set the Series Flow) won the 1978 news-coverage award in *Best Sports Stories* with his story on Reggie Jackson's exploits in the World Series that year. He is the only roving national baseball writer on any paper, covering the game for the *Washington Post* from coast to coast and from sandlot to World Series. At other times, the 1969 Amherst College graduate writes features and columns on almost every sport. He has appeared in *Best Sports Stories* for the last four years running and has won National Associated Press Awards in both the news and column categories.

LOU CHAPMAN (The Candy Man Delivers) has been with the *Milwaukee Sentinel* for more than 26 years. He has covered four major-league sports teams—the baseball Braves and Brewers and the pro basketball Hawks and Bucks. He is a graduate of Marquette University and won six writing awards from the old Hearst organization. He contributed to the *Saturday Evening Post* and the *American Weekly* and is presently a correspondent for *The*

Sporting News. He also authored a paperback book on the Milwaukee Braves. He has twice been named Wisconsin Sports Writer of the Year, and he has appeared in *Best Sports Stories* on a number of occasions.

JIM COHEN (Caging the Bird) is making his freshman appearance in this collection of sports stories. At present he is the assistant sports editor of the *Milwaukee Journal.* He has been there for five years and has covered college sports and pro basketball. He is a 1972 graduate of the University of Wisconsin. He has also worked for the *Boston Globe* and the *Springfield* (Mass.) *Union.*

BUD COLLINS (The Reunion) is one of America's best-known tennis writers and television broadcasters and one of the most respected reporters of all sports. He is a columnist for the *Boston Globe*, has received warm critical acclaim for his books on Rod Laver and Evonne Goolagong, and has been a regular contributor to *World Tennis Magazine.* He has made many appearances in the *Best Sports Stories* anthologies.

BILL CONLIN (Roberto Clemente's Ghost Prowls), winner of this year's best news-coverage award, has covered major-league baseball for the last 14 seasons for the *Philadelphia Daily News.* Before that he worked five years for the *Philadelphia Bulletin*, covering basketball, football, and various college sports. He is an avid tennis player, surfer, and small boat sailor. He shared the 1965 news-coverage award with Robert Lypsyte and has appeared in *Best Sports Stories* on four additional occasions.

TRACY DODDS (Engulfed by the Tide), at 27, has been working as a sports writer for the *Milwaukee Journal* for six years since her graduation from Indiana University in January 1974. She covers Big Ten football and boxing as her primary beats, but she also does extensive coverage of auto racing. This story is her second in the *Best Sports Stories* series.

WILLIAM BARRY FURLONG (Craig Virgin: A Heartland Saga) is a one-time sports columnist and magazine writer who has carved out a new career as a management consultant to business and universities. (His specialty: a particular application of matrix management.) He has been, in the past, a Washington correspondent and author of books on sports, medicine, and classical music. He has worked as a ghostwriter for figures in sports, science (for example, he was ghostwriter for the astronauts), business, and government. His fine writing has merited a number of appearances in *Best Sports Stories.*

JOE GERGEN (The "Old Lady" Bows Out) has covered virtually every form of sports activity during his 12 years at *Newsday*, the last five as sports columnist. But he admits he wasn't prepared for cricket, which he encountered on last summer's journey to the shrines of Wimbledon and Henley and to the granddaddy of golf tournaments, the British Open. Nothing really seemed to happen, but the field was beautiful, the players were elegantly dressed, and he soon fell asleep in the sun. Good show. He is a graduate of Boston College who labored five years at United Press International before joining *Newsday*. He won the National Headliners Award for sports writing in 1971. This marks his seventh appearance in *Best Sports Stories*.

BOB GREENE (Woody Is Alive and in Exile in Columbus) is a syndicated columnist for the *Chicago Tribune*. This is his first appearance in *Best Sports Stories*. His reports and commentary appear in more than 120 newspapers throughout the United States, and he is the author of five books, including a compendium of the best of Bob Greene, which appeared in 1976. He is also a recipient of the National Headliners Award for excellence in column writing.

PAUL HENDRICKSON (The Joe Paterno School of Football) is an ofttime contributor to the *Best Sports Stories* anthologies. At 35, he is a staff writer for the *Washington Post*, specializing in profiles. He previously worked at the *Detroit Free Press* and the *National Observer*.

DAVID HIRSHEY (The Aristrocrat of Hustle) has worked at the *New York Daily News* for the past nine years and is now a columnist and associate editor of the *Sunday News Magazine*. He is a contributing editor to *Sport* magazine and has written for *New York* magazine and *Sports Illustrated*. He has co-authored two books, including *The Education of an American Soccer Player*, selected by the *Boston Globe* as "the best sports book of 1978." He is best known for his humorous profiles of the eccentrics in sports. This is his fifth appearance in *Best Sports Stories*.

ALLAN B. JACOBS (The Civil-Service Giants) is making his first appearance in this sports anthology with this tongue-in-cheek vision of what it would be like if a pro baseball club came under civil service. His talents are varied and range from short-story writing to photography, which has earned him a number of major exhibitions. His main vocation is city planning, and his work has been utilized by the cities of Cleveland, Pittsburgh, Calcutta, and San Francisco, where he has directed the planning department for the last eight years. He is Chairman of the City Planning Department at the University of California and is the author of an important book in that field, *Making City Planning Work*.

ROGER KAHN (Past Their Prime), winner of the 1980 magazine award, has won three previous magazine awards in this sports anthology: the first in 1960, the second in 1969, and the third in 1970 with "Willie Mays, Yesterday and Today," a fine analysis of Willie Mays as both player and person. He began his newspaper career as a copyboy, then became a sports reporter with the late *New York Herald Tribune*, went to *Newsweek* as sports editor, and then to the *Saturday Evening Post* before settling down as a regular sports columnist with *Esquire*. He is a graduate of NYU, free-lances a great deal, and has authored many books, one of which, *The Boys of Summer*, became a best seller. He teaches creative writing in the summer session at the University of Rochester.

DAVE KINDRED (The Goose Slayer), a *Washington Post* sports columnist, is a five-time winner of the Kentucky Sports Writer of the Year Award and also won the 1971 National Headliners Award for general interest columns. He was sports editor of the *Louisville Times* and then of the *Louisville Courier-Journal* before joining the *Post* staff. He is the author of two books on basketball in Kentucky. A native of Atlanta, Illinois, he is a graduate of Illinois Wesleyan. This is his sixth inclusion in *Best Sports Stories.*

TONY KORNHEISER (Body and Soul) celebrated his tenth year in the news-paper business by spending the first half of 1979 at the *New York Times* and the second half at the *Washington Post.* He is no longer a full-time sports writer, but tries to keep his fastball sharp by writing sports once a month. In 1978 he won the *Best Sports Stories* feature competition with a profile of Reggie Jackson. His work has also appeared in such magazines as *Esquire, New York, Rolling Stone, New Times,* and *Cosmopolitan.* In 1977 he won the Associated Press Sports Editors competition for best sports feature story of the year. He and his wife, Karril, live in Washington, D.C. This is his eighth straight appearance in *Best Sports Stories.*

HAL LEBOVITZ (As Clean as Farrah's Teeth) is a graduate of Western Reserve University who started his career as a high school chemistry teacher but then became a sports writer because of his avid interest in athletics. He began writing for the *Cleveland News* and then went to the *Cleveland Plain Dealer,* of which he is now the sports editor. His popular column, "Ask Hal," has earned him numerous writing honors. He is a past president of the Cleveland chapter of the Baseball Writers Association of America and is a regular contributor to *The Sporting News* and the Gannett News Service. His work has been included in *Best Sports Stories* many times.

GEORGE LEONARD (Now They Know Where Rutgers Is) is one of the fine writers of sports in the South. He is in his thirty-eighth year at the *Nashville Banner,* which he joined in 1936 after his graduation from the University of Alabama. In 1964 he won first prize in the news category of *Best Sports Stories* with his article "The Forgotten Man." With Fred Russel he co-authored the book *Big Bowl Baseball.* He is a former president of the Southern Baseball League, has four sons, coached Little League football, and has appeared in this sports collection on four separate occasions.

RON MARTZ (Mood Over Miami) is a general assignment reporter and columnist for the *St. Petersburg Times,* where this story appeared. He covered the Tampa Bay Bucaneers for their first three years. He formerly was assistant sports editor of the *Cocoa* (Fla.) *Today* and wire editor of the *Fort Pierce* (Fla.) *News-Tribune.* At age 32 he says his most noteworthy accomplishment was to marry Cindy, his wife, and produce twin sons, Christopher and Colin. This is his first appearance in *Best Sports Stories.*

HUBERT MIZELL (Bear Bryant Claims He's Slipping) is 40 and sports editor of the *St. Petersburg* (Fla.) *Times.* He was formerly a feature sports writer for the

Associated Press in Miami and New York and has covered almost all of the world's great sports events, including the Olympic Games. He has been a frequent contributor to *Best Sports Stories* and has also done work for *Golf Digest.* He began his newspaper career at age 17 on the *Florida Times-Union* in Jacksonville.

LEIGH MONTVILLE (Dad Doesn't Know Best) has been a sports columnist for the *Boston Globe* for six years. Prior to that he covered the misfortunes, he says, of the New England Patriots football team. He also worked for the *New Haven Journal-Courier.* This is his second appearance in *Best Sports Stories.*

HUGH MULLIGAN (The Boys of Winter), columnist and far-roving reporter for The Associated Press, has covered cricket at Lord's, camel racing in Abu Dhabi, the pope at a Galway racetrack (where His Holiness said mass), and wars in Vietnam, the Middle East, Ulster, Biafra, and Angola. All in all, Mulligan's assignments have taken him to 110 countries, plus a visit to the North Pole in a Navy blimp. In the past year he has filed by-line stories from Transylvania, Tahiti, and Tibet. When neither thither nor yon, he resides in Ridgefield, Connecticut, catching up on his column, "Mulligan's Stew," which appears in more than 500 newspapers. This is his first appearance in *Best Sports Stories.*

KENNETH NEILL (The Memphis Red Sox) is associate editor of *Memphis* magazine. Born in Boston in 1948, he attended Yale University (B.A.) and Trinity College, Dublin (M.Ed.). He is the author of several high school-level textbooks in modern world history. His most recent work, *The Irish People: An Illustrated History* (1979), is a Book-of-the-Month Club Alternate selection. This marks his first appearance in *Best Sports Stories.*

DAVE NEWHOUSE (The Old Yankees), who tied for the best feature-story award, is a sports columnist for the *Oakland Tribune,* where he has worked for 16 years. During that time, he has won several awards for his sports writing. He was a pro football writer for 10 years before becoming a columnist last year. Besides co-authoring a book on the Rose Bowl, he has written for *Sports Illustrated, The Sporting News,* and numerous other publications. He is 41, a native of Menlo Park, California, and lives with his wife and two sons in Oakland.

GARY NUHN (Lucky or Good?) is making his first appearance in *Best Sports Stories.* He has won first places in national writing contests each of the last four years, twice in golf and twice in college basketball. He has also won first places in Ohio AP and UPI contests. A native of Geneva, New York, he graduated from Ohio State University in 1966, spent two years at the *Middletown* (Ohio) *Journal* and has been at the *Dayton Daily News* for the past 11 years.

MURRAY OLDERMAN (Sports Beat? Don't Forget to Duck) has appeared frequently in *Best Sports Stories.* He is a contributing editor of the Newspaper

Enterprise Association and his columns and cartoons are syndicated in 700 newspapers. He has degrees from Missouri, Stanford, and Northwestern and is the author of seven books on sports. He is a recipient of the Dick McCann Award for outstanding writing on professional football, and he has done 12 murals for the Pro Football Hall of Fame. A native New Yorker, he is now stationed in San Francisco.

EDWIN POPE (Nothing Left but Heart), sports editor of the *Miami Herald*, won the 1979 National Headliner's Award for consistently outstanding sports columns in 1960 and 1979. He is only the second columnist who has won the award twice, Jim Murray being the other. Pope was the nation's youngest sports editor when he took a job with the *Athens* (Ga.) *Banner-Herald* at age 15 in 1943. A graduate of the University of Georgia in 1948, he wrote for United Press International and the *Atlanta Constitution* and was executive sports editor of the *Atlanta Journal* before joining the *Miami Herald* in 1956. He has been represented in *Best Sports Stories* more than a dozen times.

JEFF PRUGH (Now Players Smell Nicer to Butch) is Atlanta Bureau Chief of the *Los Angeles Times* and travels throughout the South, writing about politics, civil rights, and slice-of-life stories. For 13 years after his graduation from the University of Missouri, he was a *Times* sports writer, reporting on college football and basketball, major-league baseball and tennis. He also became one of the first American sports writers to visit Castro's Cuba when he reported on the Olympic volleyball trials in 1971. He is the co-author with Dwight Chapin of *The Wizard of Westwood*, a biography of UCLA's retired basketball coach, John Wooden. This is his fourth appearance in *Best Sports Stories*.

GENE QUINN (The Net Breaks) is making his debut in the *Best Sports Stories* anthologies. He is night sports editor of the *Philadelphia Daily News* and writes a weekly TV sports column as well as covering tennis—which means the U.S. Open and the U.S. Pro Indoor in Philadelphia. Twenty-six years old, he has been with the *News* for three years. He is a former runner-up in the Pennsylvania Newspaper Publishers Association writing contest. He modestly proclaims that he is a terrible weekend tennis player.

RON RAPOPORT (He Brings Light into the World) is a sports columnist for the *Chicago Sun-Times*, where this feature appeared. He formerly worked for the *Los Angeles Times* and the Associated Press. He is the author of three books on sports subjects and numerous magazine articles. This is his first appearance in *Best Sports Stories*

JOE RESNICK (Howe: History on Skates) works for the Associated Press in New York but wrote this story, which appeared in the *Kansas City Star*, on a free-lance basis. He was graduated in 1976 with a major in mass communication from Emerson College in Boston, a year after becoming articles editor for *Action Sports Hockey Magazine*. His last two years have been with The

Associated Press, writing features; among his assignments was the 1977 Stanley Cup final. His free-lance work has appeared in the *Boston Globe* and *The Sporting News* as well as the *Kansas City Star*. This is his first appearance in *Best Sports Stories*.

LOEL SCHRADER (The Ghost of the Gipper) has been a sports writer and columnist for 38 years, all in the Knight-Ritter chain. At the *Long Beach* (Cal.) *Independent Press-Telegram*, where this story appeared, he has covered college football, professional baseball, college basketball, and college hockey. He is a bachelor of philosophy with a major in journalism and is also a J.D. from Western State University and its College of Law. This is his third appearance in *Best Sports Stories*

NICK SEITZ (Sam Snead: He Just Keeps Rollin' Along) probes into golfers' lives and his findings are interesting and helpful. He majored at the University of Oklahoma in philosophy, a discipline interested in "cause and effect sequences," which probably led to his concern with the techniques of the game. His major contribution to the game, besides being the editor of *Golf Digest*, is his analysis of the bewildered golf pro who suddenly finds he can hack it no longer and resigns himself to the fact that he must now become a country club pro. It is then "Dr. Seitz" steps in for consultation and restores athletes like Miller, Beard, and Weismiller to the tube. Lately he got a hole-in-one, but it was disallowed. He doesn't say why.

JIM SMITH (In Pursuit of Loftier Goals) has worked for *Newsday*, in which this story appeared, since 1966. He is presently covering the New York Giants and for the last few years has also covered local college sports and the Cosmos soccer team. Before that, he was a news reporter for two years and served in the Army for three. He is 31 years old and lives in Northport, New York. This is his first appearance in *Best Sports Stories*.

JOE SOUCHERAY (Farewell to Catfish Hunter) has been the featured sports columnist of the *Minneapolis Tribune* since 1976. He is 30 and joined the *Tribune* in 1973 after two years with a firm that published magazines for a number of the nation's airlines. During his four years at the College of St. Thomas in St. Paul, Minnesota, Soucheray was a member of a successful rock group—a group that went on to record two albums after Soucheray abandoned professional drumming for a career in journalism. Soucheray has appeared on three previous occasions in *Best Sports Stories*.

ART SPANDER (The Fat Lady Is Silenced) worked for the *San Francisco Chronicle* (where this story appeared), and then became the lead columnist on the *San Francisco Examiner* in September 1979, filling a position that had been empty since the death of Wells Twombly two and a half years earlier. After graduation from UCLA he worked at the Los Angeles UPI and later at the *Santa Monica Evening Outlook*. In 1970 he won the coverage prize in *Best Sports Stories*, and his work has merited many other inclusions. He contributes to various sports magazines and co-authored with Mark Mulvoy the book, *Golf: The Passion and the Challenge*. Spander also writes a monthly wine column for *San Francisco Magazine*.

MAURY WHITE (A Place for a Smile and a Laugh) has been with the *Des Moines Register* since 1946 and for a good part of that time he has been writing sports columns. A graduate of Drake, and a three-time letterman in both football and baseball, he has been fortunate enough to sit in on some of the high points in national sports. He is a past president of the Football Writers Association, a 1966 *Sports Illustrated* Silver Anniversary honors winner, and the 1977 recipient of the Jake Wade Award for distinguished sports writing from the College Sports Information Directors of America. He has merited many appearances in this anthology.

DAVID WILTSE (Can a Good Male Club Player Beat a Woman Pro? Guess!) writes for the stage, films, and television as well as an occasional piece on sports. He was awarded the 1972 Drama Desk Award as Most Promising Playwright for his Lincoln Center Production of *Suggs*. He has been a contributing editor of *Tennis Magazine* since 1978. Mr. Wiltse lives in Weston, Connecticut, with his wife and two daughters.

VIC ZIEGEL (Thundering Fatties) has just been named a contributing editor at *New York* magazine, where he is writing a new sports column. From 1962 to 1977 he worked for the *New York Post* as a sportswriter and columnist. He co-authored the 1978 Macmillan best-seller, *The Non-Runners Book* and the CBS television series *Ball Four*. He has written for many of the finer periodicals and newspapers, including *Sport, Look, The Village Voice*, the *New York Times*, and the *Washington Post*. He has merited many appearances in this sports anthology.

PHOTOGRAPHERS IN
BEST SPORTS STORIES—1980

MIKE ADASKAVEG (A Chip Off the Old Block), 27, is a 1976 graduate of Central Connecticut State College in New Britain, with a B.A. in psychology. He has been employed by the *Journal Inquirer* (Manchester, Conn.) as a photojournalist and auto racing columnist since January 1977. While attending college, Adaskaveg worked for the *Southington* (Conn.) *News* as a sports reporter; the *Plainfield* (Conn.) *Canal Line Times* as sports editor, and the *Meriden* (Conn.) *Record and Journal* as a photographer and schoolboy sports reporter. He held this position at the *Record and Journal* prior to being hired at the *Journal Inquirer*. Adaskaveg's investigative reporting on deaths in local auto racing accidents won numerous awards in 1978, including awards from both AP and UPI.

JOHN E. BIEVER (Insurance Sign in the Right Place) is one of the fine young photographers in the northern area of our country. He has been a staff photographer at the *Milwaukee Journal-Sentinel* for five years and in 1974 was a co-winner as Wisconsin News Photographer of the Year. He is a 1973 graduate of the University of Wisconsin (Milwaukee), where he received his B.A. in business administration.

JOSEPH CANNATA, Jr. (Fierce Foursome Frustrated by Fair Catch) is making his third appearance in *Best Sports Stories*. He has been a staff photographer of the *Hartford Courant* for six years and is the treasurer of the Connecticut News Photographers Association. He resides in New Britain, Connecticut.

DAN DRY (Backing into 6-Feet-4) works for the *Louisville Courier-Journal*. He majored in journalism at Ohio University in Athens, Ohio, and as a senior won the Ohio Associated Press photography prize and also the William Randolph Hearst National College Photojournalism Award. In addition, he merited the Best Portfolio for the Atlanta Southern Seminar on Photojournalism. This is his second appearance in this sports anthology.

STEPHEN D. DUNN (Eye Popper) was born in New England, graduated from Eastern State College, and started in the photography field in 1974 for a small Connecticut weekly. He then went over to a daily in *Manchester*, Connecticut, for five years. At present he is a staff photographer for the *Hartford Courant*. In 1976, 1977, and 1978 he placed in the annual Connecticut News Photographers' Photo Competition. This is his second appearance in *Best Sports Stories*.

ROBERT EMERSON (A Rocket's Racket Retired) attended the University of Rhode Island and got his newspaper start with two small papers in the same state. He was named New England Photographer of the Year by The New England Press Association while working for these two papers. In 1974 he went to the *Providence Journal* and in 1976 was named Photographer of the Year by the NPPA, Region 1. In 1978 he became president of the Rhode Island NPPA, serving in that capacity until taking his present position on the staff of the *Miami News* in 1979. This marks his second appearance in this anthology.

MELISSA FARLOW (Swan Dive into Coach's Arms) won first place in the 1979 *Best Sports Stories* with an action photo shot which was her first entry. She was graduated from Indiana University with a B.A. in journalism in 1974 and has been a staff photographer with the *Louisville Courier-Journal* and *Louisville Times* since then. Her work has won awards twice in the National Press Photographers' Pictures of the Year Contest and in the Southern Atlanta and Indiana Photographers' Contest.

RIC FELD (Action at Two After One) is making his first appearance in *Best Sports Stories*. He was born in Brooklyn, New York, and was graduated from the Staten Island, New York, Newhouse School of Public Communications, and received his B.S. in journalism from Syracuse University in 1972. He worked in the northern Virginia area before coming to his present paper, the *Orlando Sentinel Star*, where he is the assistant newsphoto chief. He has received a number of awards, both regional and state.

JACK GAKING (A Dog-Gone Ball) is making his second appearance in *Best Sports Stories*. He has been a staff photographer for the *Roanoke Times & World-News* for the past 23 years, making him one of the more accomplished veteran lensmen on the East Coast. He has won a number of photo awards in the state of Virginia and was named State Photographer of the Year on two occasions.

JUDY GRIESEDIECK (Our Cups Are Being Run Over) is making her first appearance in this annual sports anthology. Originally from Saint Louis, Missouri, she now works for the *Hartford Courant*. She was graduated from Pitzer College in Claremont, California, lived in Washington, D.C., and snapped shots for the Washington Diplomats. She has free-lanced for the *New York Times*, Associated Press, *Soccer America* and several dailies in Virginia.

PETE HOHN ("A Thing of Beauty Is a Joy Forever"—Keats) is making his seventh appearance in a row in the photo competition of this sports anthology. He has been a photojournalist for the past 27 years, and 25 of them has been with one paper, the *Minneapolis Tribune*. His humorous photo of Patty Berg won the Best Feature category in 1976. He has been awarded many citations for his fine camera work on both national and regional levels.

RICHARD LEE (Jaw Breaker) is currently a staff photographer of the *New York Post*. His fine touch has been revealed a number of times in this sports anthology. Previously he was on the staff of the *Long Island Press* and was a regular contributor to the *New York Times* and to many of the nation's finer magazines. Honors for his work have been bestowed upon him by the New York Press Photographers' Association, New York State Associated Press contest, and the Press Photographers' Association of Long Island.

BUZZ MAGNUSON (No Triple, Just Three Pieces of Wood) has been a photographer for 25 years for the *St. Paul Dispatch*. This would classify him as one of the fine lensmen of the middle United States. His assignments have included every news category: features, sports, fashions, and spot news. He grew up in a photo-oriented household: his father shot pix for the AP and his older brother does work for other newspapers in the area. Buzz Magnuson served with the Army in Korea as a photographer and went to photo school in New Jersey. This is his fifth appearance in *Best Sports Stories*.

FRED MATTHES (Hooked on Soccer) is a staff photographer at the *San Jose Mercury-News*. His excellent workmanship is attested to by his many awards. They include a first place from the Pro Football Hall of Fame with a feature photo displayed permanently at the hall, and a later, second place photo also featured at the same hall. He garnered a winner from the California Newspaper's Association, 13 various annual awards from the Forest Lawn Press sponsored by the California Press Photographers' Association, first place in the AP sports photo contest in 1978; first place, Western Region, in the Mark Twain contest, and best shot award for 1978 from the San Francisco Press Club. His work has appeared every year in this collection from 1973 to 1980.

WILLIAM MEYER (Petty Larceny) is a 28-year-old staff photographer for the *Milwaukee Journal*. With this entry he has become a seven-time contributor to this sports collection. He attended the University of Wisconsin (Milwaukee), competed in field sports and won college division All-America honors for the discus in 1970.

CHARLES R. PUGH, JR. (Quarterback Socked and Sacked) has been a three-time winner in *Best Sports Stories* photo competition. His two early prizes were in the action category and the last one, in 1978, was in the feature class. He began his distinguished photographic career with the *Johnson City* (Tenn.) *Press-Chronicle* and at present is with the *Atlanta Journal-Constitution*.

JAMES A. RACKWITZ (Cowboy Roundups—Horses, No!, Tigers, Yes!!) was born in Saint Louis and started out as a copyboy for the *St. Louis Post-Dispatch*. From 1950 to 1954 he served in the U.S. Navy as a tail-gunner/photographer with air squadrons operating out of Hawaii during the Korean conflict. After his discharge he joined Acme Pictures and later UPI Newspictures. After four years with the wire service he joined the photo staff of the *St. Louis Post-Dispatch*, which he will have served 21 years next April.

ELI REED (Goalie Grounded, Scorer Celebrates) came to the *Detroit News* in 1978 after a number of years as a graduate student in photography. He studied at the James VanDerZee Institute Photographic Workshop in 1973 and received a grant at the International Center of Photography. He has worked on *Zygote Magazine* as a photographer and illustrator for the Floating Foundation of Photography, as instructor of photography at Somerset Community College, and at the *Middletown* (N.Y.) *Times Herald-Record*. This is his first appearance in *Best Sports Stories*.

DAVID L. RYAN (Reins, Reins, Don't Go Away) is a *cum laude* graduate of Boston College. He started photography at the age of 10 with his dad, who was a news staff cameraman with the Boston papers. In 1968 he went to work for the *Boston Globe* sports desk doing research on athletes. He was assigned to industrial photography from 1972 to 1974, and then as a spare photographer covering all types of subjects. In 1976 he became the youngest winner of the News Photographer of the Year Award for New England. Shortly afterward he became a staff photographer on his paper. This marks his first appearance in *Best Sports Stories*.

ART SEITZ (It's Called the Laid-Back Forehand) obtained a B.S. in advertising from the University of Florida and an educational doctorate at Florida Atlantic University. He went to work for the *Palm Beach* (Fla.) *Post* and then became a free-lance photographer. His early tennis shots soon gave him a national reputation. He also has merited three selections in *Who's Who in American Universities*. His work has been featured by *Tennis Magazine*, *Time*, *Sports Illustrated*, *Newsweek*, *Signature*, *World Tennis*, *Life*, and *Playgirl*. His corporate clients include American Express, Pepsi Cola, Avis, and Avon. His camera work has ranged from the top of Golden Gate Bridge to two hours with Jimmy Carter and family in Plains, Georgia. This is his first appearance in *Best Sports Stories*.

JOHN A. STANO (Please Don't Let It Be a Mirage) is a 1979 graduate of Wayne State University in Detroit. He majored in journalism and minored in photography. Presently he is a free-lance photographer and shoots for the Detroit Pistons, Detroit Convention Bureau, and the *Monthly Detroit* magazine. This is his first appearance in *Best Sports Stories*.

WARREN L. TAYLOR (The "OHS" on the Uniform Says It All) was born in Ames, Iowa, and attended Drake University, where he received a B.A. degree in journalism. After graduation in 1970 he did Army duty in Frankfort, Germany, and then returned home to become a staff photographer for the *Des Moines Register and Tribune*. This is his first appearance in this anthology of sports stories, and he made it as a winner.

THE YEAR'S BEST SPORTS PHOTOS

BEST ACTION PHOTO

THE "OHS" ON THE UNIFORM SAYS IT ALL, by Warren Taylor, *Des Moines Register and Tribune*. Rose Curran, left fielder for the Ottuma, Iowa, High School's girls', softball team, smashes into left-field fence but hangs onto ball for an out. The action occurred in the semi-final of the Iowa State Girls' Softball Tournament. Opponent in the game was Ankeny, which went on to win championship. Copyright, ©, 1979, *Des Moines Register and Tribune Co.*

BEST FEATURE PHOTO

JAW BREAKER, by Richard Lee, *New York Post*. This is a shot that may remind you that you have a date with the dentist. The man sitting astride the shark, a 14-footer, is Captain Tom Cashman. This white shark was caught off East Moriches, Long Island, after a day-long struggle. Copyright, ©, 1979, New York Post Corp.

OUR CUPS ARE BEING RUN OVER, by Judy Griesedieck, *Hartford Courant*. Runners grab quick cups of water as they pass the halfway point in third annual "Run, Walk or Jog for the Health Of It," five-mile road race at Veterans' Memorial Park in East Hartford, Connecticut. Copyright, ©, 1979, Judith T. Griesedieck.

IT'S CALLED THE LAID-BACK FOREHAND, by Art Seitz, *Tennis Magazine*. The creator of this unusual shot is Jimmy Connors. Experts agree it is not an easy shot. If you try it, however, the key is to keep one foot firmly planted on the ground while you peer over your chest. Be sure to draw in your navel while you plan where you want to return the approaching smash. One other thing: don't be surprised if after the shot you experience a sudden letdown. Try your best not to shout an obscenity at the judge. Copyright, ©, 1979, *Tennis Magazine*.

REINS, REINS, DON'T GO AWAY, by David L. Ryan, *The Boston Globe*. Amy Shoemaker hangs desperately to the reins of the horse as she is thrown off after attempting a jump at the Hamilton-Winham horse trials. She was spun to safety because of the horse's momentum and got right back on again to continue the event. Copyright, ©, 1979, *The Boston Globe*.

NO TRIPLE, JUST THREE PIECES OF WOOD, by Buzz Magnuson, *St. Paul Dispatch*. Rod Carew, California's league-leading-batter, may not be the splendid splinterer that Ted Williams was, but in this shot he splinters his bat and still gets enough wood on the ball to bloop in two runners and cap a four-hit performance to lead his team to an 11–6 rout of the Twins. Copyright, ©, 1979, *St. Paul Dispatch/Pioneer Press*.

HOOKED ON SOCCER, by Fred Matthes, *San Jose Mercury-News.* In a high-school soccer game, San Jose's Primo Jauregui and Leigh High School's Pat Ridley accidentally hooked their arms as they went for a head ball, and Mr. Matthes, the photographer, came away with this unusual picture. Copyright, ©, 1979, *San Jose Mercury-News.*

BACKING INTO 6-FEET-4, by Dan Dry, *Courier-Journal* (Louisville, Ky.). This picture was snapped at a Kentucky State high-school track meet. The young high jumper gave it all he had as he tried to clear the bar. If you want to see a king-sized effort, hold the picture upside down. Copyright, ©, *Louisville Courier-Journal* and *Louisville Times*.

A CHIP OFF THE OLD BLOCK, by Mike Adaskaveg, *The Manchester* (Conn.) *Journal Inquirer*, catches hockey player Gordie Howe and his son Mark hard at work for their team, the Hartford (Conn.) Whalers. Daddy Howe, in the left picture, playing in his thirty-second professional season, is tying up a Los Angeles' Kingsman. His son Mark is throwing a king-sized check in the lower photo at another Kingsman, Barry Gibbs. Both are employed by the Whalers and were instrumental in winning this game 6–3.

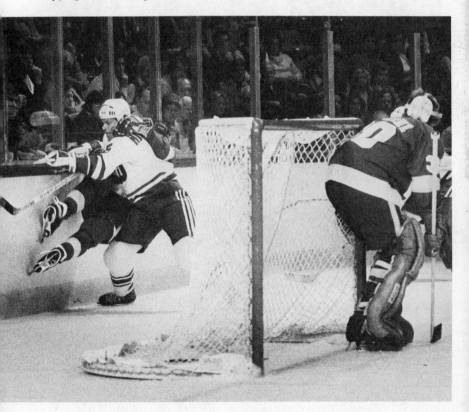

EYE POPPER, by Stephen D. Dunn, *Hartford* (Conn.) *Courant*. As umpire
Leon Shedroff gets set to call Middletown's Kyle Zupan out at third base, his
astonishment is accompanied by eyeball protrusion that rivals the action.
The event occurred at an American Legion baseball tournament in Middletown, Connecticut. Copyright, ©, 1979, *Hartford Courant*.

A ROCKET'S RACKET RETIRED, by Robert Emerson, *The Miami News*. "The Rocket" Laver throws his racket up in a gesture of disgust after missing an easy shot in the "Legends of Tennis Tournament" held in North Miami. Laver was playing Roy Emerson at the time of this action. Copyright, ©, 1979, the *Miami News*.

INSURANCE SIGN IN THE RIGHT PLACE, by John E. Biever, *The Milwaukee Journal*. It appears as though these two Milwaukee Schlitz pro softball players might just need the protection the insurance sign posted on the outfield wall behind them offers. The action occurred at a game between the Schlitz and Minnesota Norsemen teams at Joecks Field, Lannon, Wisconsin. Copyright, ©, 1979, *The Milwaukee Journal*.

A DOG-GONE BALL, by Jack Gaking, *Roanoke Times & World-News*. There was this championship game in Salem, Virginia, and this big dog ran out of his seat and snagged the ball. It was retrieved and the crook was firmly ejected and not allowed to return to his box. The team from Salem won, but the thief missed the ensuing excitement. Copyright, ©, 1979, *Roanoke Times & World-News*.

"A THING OF BEAUTY IS A JOY FOREVER"—KEATS, by Pete Hohn, *Minneapolis Tribune*. Hohn, the photographer, has an uncanny eye, and knew how to get something special from his camera. He positioned himself above gymnast Theresa Schneider and grabbed this beauty of a shot. The 17-year-old was preparing herself for a national championship. Copyright, ©, 1979, *Minneapolis Tribune*.

ACTION AT TWO AFTER ONE, by Ric Feld, *Orlando Sentinel-Star*. Brother Bobbie Allison (center) holds the foot of driver Cale Yarborough (right) as sibling Donnie Allison (left) uses his helmet as a truncheon to belabor their common enemy and racetrack opponent. This donnybrook arose when Donnie Allison, who was leading the Daytona 500, collided with Yarborough and ended his chances of winning. Copyright, ©, 1979, *Orlando Sentinel-Star*.

SWAN DIVE INTO COACH'S ARMS, by Melissa Farlow, the *Courier-Journal* (Louisville, Ky.). This exulting player has just thrown in the two-pointer that clinched the championship for his team. He executed this swan dive from the point close to where he scored the basket. His coach was waiting to greet him with open arms. The game was between Eastern and Morehead University. Copyright, ©, 1979, *Louisville Courier-Journal* and *Louisville Times.*

FIERCE FOURSOME FRUSTRATED BY FAIR CATCH, by Joseph Cannata, Jr., *Hartford* (Conn.) *Courant*. With this foursome of Wesleyan players barreling in on Trinity's Nick Bordiere, he coolly negotiates the most difficult catch of the rainy afternoon. He had called for a fair catch but slipped in the mud and fell over backward. As he lay there, the ball fell close to him and he grabbed it. Copyright, ©, 1979, *Hartford Courant*.

PLEASE DON'T LET IT BE A MIRAGE, by John Stano, *Detroit News*. As James Stano grasped frantically at what he thought might be succor, it proved to be the real thing, a popsickle! Stano gulped down three of them and knocked off one marathon, all in the time of 4:08:51. Action took place at Royal Oak, Michigan. Copyright, ©, 1979, *Detroit News*.

GOALIE GROUNDED, SCORER CELEBRATES, by Eli Reed, *Detroit News.* Goalie of the Tea team, John Feely, on ground, is bewailing his fate probably because his teammate Juan Cano (far left) has made too belated an arrival to be of any help. The happy player is Brian Tinnion of the Express soccer team, who with extended arms is giving a triumphant salute to himself and to the ball he has just kicked for a score. Copyright, © 1979, *Detroit News.*

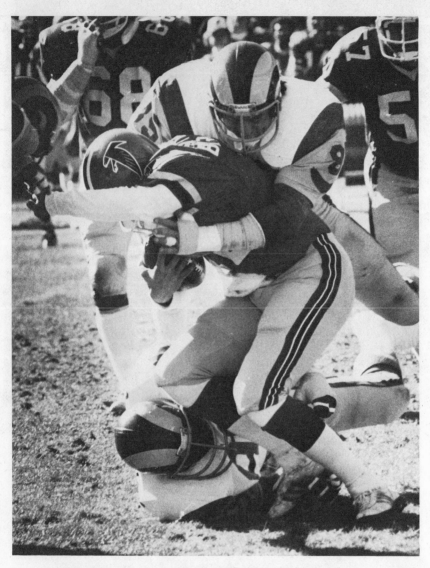

QUARTERBACK SOCKED AND SACKED, by Charles R. Pugh, Jr., *Atlanta Journal-Constitution*. Steve Barkowski of the Atlanta Falcons is being harassed by Los Angeles' Jack Youngblood, whose arms are lovingly embracing Barkowski just before slamming him to the ground. This would make the fourth sack and a miserable afternoon for the Falcon quarterback. Where Barkowski could eventually hide became more important than the game itself. Copyright, ©, 1979, *Atlanta Journal-Constitution*.

PETTY LARCENY, by William Meyer, *The Milwaukee Journal*. Larry Petty of the University of Wisconsin makes like a ballerina as the ball is shaken loose by an Indiana player, Landon Turner (32). Copyright, ©, 1979, *The Milwaukee Journal*.

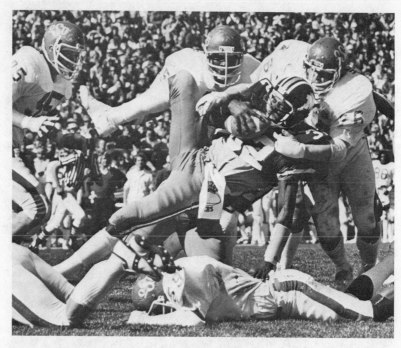

COWBOY ROUNDUPS—HORSES NO!, TIGERS, YES!! by Jim Rack-
witz, *St. Louis Post-Dispatch*. Missouri tailback James Wilder gets a rude
welcome from a gang of Oklahoma tacklers after gaining a yard in game at
Columbia, Missouri. The Cowboys who defanged Tiger Wilder are Steve
Henzler (76); Dean Prater (95); and Ricky Young (59). Oklahoma won in
upset, 14–13. Copyright, ©, 1979, *St. Louis Post-Dispatch*.